KT-558-797

The Island of the
Day Before

UMBERTO ECO

The Island of the Day Before

Translated from the Italian
by William Weaver

SECKER & WARBURG
London

First published in Great Britain in 1995
by Martin Secker & Warburg Limited,
an imprint of Reed International Books Limited,
Michelin House, 81 Fulham Road, London SW3 6RB
and Auckland, Melbourne, Singapore and Toronto

Copyright © 1994 by R.C.S. Libri & Grandi Opere SpA-Milano
English translation © 1995 by Harcourt Brace & Company

Published by arrangement with Harcourt Brace & Company

This is a translation of L'ISOLA DEL GIORNO PRIMA

The author has asserted his moral rights

A CIP catalogue record for this book
is available from the British Library

ISBN 0 436 20270 0

Printed and bound in Great Britain by
Clays Ltd, St. Ives plc

Is the Pacifique Sea my home?

—John Donne,
"Hymne to God my God"

Stolto! a cui parlo? Misero! Che tento?
Racconto il dolor mio
a l'insensata riva
a la mutola selce, al sordo vento . . .
Ahi, ch'altro non risponde
che il mormorar del'onde!

—Giovan Battista Marino,
"Eco," *La Lira*, xix

Table of Contents

The Island of the
Day Before

CHAPTER I

Daphne

I take pride withal in my humiliation, and as I am to this privilege condemned, almost I find joy in an abhorrent salvation; I am, I believe, alone of all our race, the only man in human memory to have been shipwrecked and cast up upon a deserted ship.

THUS, WITH UNABASHED conceits, wrote Roberto della Griva presumably in July or August of 1643.

How many days had he been tossed by the waves, feverish surely, bound to a plank, prone during the hours of light to avoid the blinding sun, his neck stiff, strained unnaturally so as not to imbibe the water, his lips burnt by the brine? His letters offer no answer to this question: though they suggest an eternity, the time cannot have been more than two days, for otherwise he would never have survived the lash of Phoebus (of which he so poetically complains), he, a sickly youth, as he describes himself, a creature condemned by a natural defect to live only at night.

He was unable to keep track of time, but I believe the sea grew calm immediately after the tempest swept him from the deck of the *Amaryllis,* on that makeshift raft a sailor had fashioned for him. Driven by the Trades over a serene sea, in a season when, south of the Equator, a temperate winter reigns, he was carried for not many miles, until the currents at last brought him into the bay.

It was night, he had dozed off, unaware that he was approaching a ship until, with a jolt, his plank struck against the prow of the *Daphne*.

And when—in the glow of the full moon—he realized he was floating beneath a bowsprit with a rope-ladder hanging from it not far from the anchor chain (a Jacob's ladder, Father Caspar would have called it), in an instant all his spirit returned. His desperation must have inspired him: he tried to reckon whether he had enough breath to cry out (but his throat was all an arid fire) or enough strength to free himself from the bonds that had cut livid furrows into his skin, and then to essay the climb. I believe that at such moments a dying man can become a very Hercules, and strangle serpents in his cradle. In recording the event, Roberto seems confused, but we must accept the idea that if, finally, he reached the forecastle, he must somehow have grasped that ladder. Perhaps he climbed up a bit at a time, exhausted at every gain, until he flung himself over the bulwarks, crawled along the cordage, found the forecastle door open . . . And instinct no doubt led him, in the darkness, to touch that barrel, pull himself up its side, until he found a cup attached to a little chain. And he drank as much as he could, then collapsed, sated, perhaps in the fullest meaning of the word, for that water probably contained enough drowned insects to supply him with food as well as drink.

He must have slept twenty-four hours. This is only an approximate calculation: it was night when he woke, but he was as if reborn. So it was night again, not night still.

He thought it was night still; for if not, a whole day had

to have passed, and someone should have found him by now. The moonlight, coming from the deck, illuminated that place, apparently a kind of cook-room, where a pot was hanging above the fireplace.

The room had two doors, one towards the bowsprit, the other opening onto the deck. And he looked out at the latter, seeing, as if by daylight, the rigging in good order, the capstan, the masts with the sails furled, a few cannon at the gun ports, and the outline of the quarterdeck. He made some sounds, but not a living soul replied. He gazed over the bulwarks, and to his right he could discern, about a mile away, the form of the Island, the palm trees along its shore stirred by a breeze.

The land made a kind of bend, edged with sand that gleamed white in the pale darkness; but, like any shipwrecked man, Roberto could not tell if it was an island or a continent.

He staggered to the other side of the ship and glimpsed— but distant this time, almost on the line of the horizon—the peaks of another mass, defined also by two promontories. Everything else was sea, giving the impression that the ship was berthed in an anchorage it had entered through a channel separating the two stretches of land. Roberto decided that if these were not two islands, one was surely an island facing a vaster body of land. I do not believe he entertained other hypotheses, since he had never known bays so broad that a person in their midst could feel he was confronting twin lands. Thus, in his ignorance of boundless continents, Roberto had chanced upon the correct answer.

A nice situation for a castaway: his feet solidly planted and dry land within reach. But Roberto was unable to swim. Soon he would discover there was no longboat on board, and the current meanwhile had carried away the plank on which he had arrived. Hence his relief at having escaped death was now accompanied by dismay at this treble solitude: of the sea, the neighboring Island, and the ship. Ahoy! he must have tried to shout on the ship, in every language he knew, discovering how weak he truly was. Silence. As if on board everyone was dead. And never had he—so generous with similes—expressed himself more literally. Or almost—and this is what I would fain tell you about, if only I knew where to begin.

For that matter, I have already begun. A man drifts, exhausted, over the ocean, and the complaisant waters bring him to a ship, apparently deserted. Deserted as if the crew has just abandoned it, for Roberto struggles back to the cook-room and finds a lamp there and a flint and steel, as if the cook set them in their place before going to bed. But the two berths beside the furnace, one above the other, are both empty. Roberto lights the lamp, looks around, and finds a great quantity of food: dried fish, hardtack, with only a few patches of mold easily scraped away with a knife. The fish is very salty, but there is water in abundance.

He must have regained his strength quickly, or else he was strong when he was writing this, for he goes into—highly literary—detail about his banquet, never did Olympus see such a feast as his, Jove's nectar, to me sweet ambrosia from farthest Pontus. But these are the things Roberto writes to the Lady of his heart:

Sun of my shadows, light of my darkness.

Why did Heaven not unmake me in that tempest it had so savagely provoked? Why save from the all-devouring sea this body of mine, only to wreck my soul so horribly in such mean and even more ill-starred solitude?

Perhaps, if merciful Heaven does not send me succor, you will never read this letter I now indite, and, consumed like a torch by the light of these seas, I will become dark to your eyes, as to some Selene, who, rejoicing too much in the light of her Sun, gradually consumes her journey beyond the far curve of our planet, bereft of the beneficent rays of her sovereign star, first growing thin to recall the sickle that severs the thread of life, then ever-paler, she is completely dissolved in that vast cerulean shield where ingenious nature forms heroic heraldry, mysterious emblems of her secrets. Bereft of your gaze, I am blind for you see me not, dumb for you address me not, oblivious for you forget me.

And, alone, I live, burning dullness and tenebrous flame, vague specter that in this adverse conflict of opposites my mind imagines ever the same, and so would convey to yours. Saving my life in this wood fortress, in this rocking bastion that defends me, prisoner of the sea, from the sea, punished by the clemency of Heaven, hidden in this deep sarcophagus open to every sun, in this airy dungeon, in this impregnable prison that offers me everywhere escape, I despair of seeing you more.

My Lady, I write you as if to offer, unworthy tribute, the withered rose of my disheartenment. And yet I take pride withal in my humiliation, and as I am to this privilege condemned, almost I find joy in an abhorrent salvation; I am, I believe, alone of all our race, the only man in human memory to have been shipwrecked and cast upon a deserted ship.

But is this really possible? To judge by the date of his first letter, Roberto begins writing immediately after his arrival, as soon as he finds pen and paper in the captain's quarters, before exploring the rest of the ship. And yet he must have required some time to recover his strength, reduced as he was to the condition of a wounded animal. Or perhaps, with a little amorous ruse, after first trying to ascertain his whereabouts, he then writes, pretending to write her before giving any thought to other things. But why, inasmuch as he knows, assumes, fears that these letters will never arrive and that he is writing them only for his own torment (tormenting solace, he would say, but we must not fall into his literary habits)? It is difficult to reconstruct the actions and feelings of a character surely afire with true love, for you never know whether he is expressing what he feels or what the rules of amorous discourse prescribe in his case—but then, for that matter, what do we know of the difference between passion felt and passion expressed, and who can say which has precedence? So Roberto was writing for himself: this was not literature, he was there truly, writing like an adolescent pursuing an impossible mirage, streaking the page with his tears, not because of the absence of the lady, pure image even when she was present, but out of fondness of himself, enamored of love. . . .

The situation is the stuff of a novel, but, once more, where to begin?

I say he wrote this first missive later, and before writing it, he had a look around; and in subsequent letters he will relate what he saw. But those, too, raise the question of how to treat the diary of a man with poor vision, who roams during the night, relying on his weak eyes.

Roberto will tell us that his eyes had been affected since the days of the siege of Casale, when that bullet grazed his temple. And this may be true, but elsewhere he hints that the weakness was caused by the plague. Roberto was certainly frail, and I infer he was also a hypochondriac—though in moderation: half of his photophobia must have been due to black bile, and half to some form of irritation, perhaps exacerbated by Monsieur d'Igby's salves.

It seems certain that during the voyage of the *Amaryllis* he remained below deck, since the role of photophobe—if it was not his true nature—was the part he had to play to keep an eye on what happened in the hold. Several months in total darkness or in dim lamplight—and then the time on the plank, dazzled by the equatorial or tropical sun, whichever it was. When he lands then on the *Daphne,* sick or not, he hates the sun, spends the first night in the cook-room, recovers his strength and attempts a first inspection the night following, and then things proceed virtually of themselves. Day frightens him; not only will his eyes not tolerate it, but neither will the burns he must surely have on his back. So he goes to ground. The beautiful moon he describes on those nights reassures him, during the day the sky is the same as everywhere else, at night he discovers new constellations (heroic heraldry and mysterious emblems, in fact); it is like being in a theater. He is convinced that this will be his life for a long time, perhaps until his death; he refashions his Lady on paper so as not to lose her, and he knows he has not lost much more than the little he had before.

At this point he takes refuge in his nightly vigils as in a maternal womb, and becomes thus more determined to elude the sun. Perhaps he has read of those Resurgents of Hungary, of Livonia or Walachia, who wander restless between sunset and dawn, hiding then in their graves at cock-crow: the role could lure him. . . .

Roberto must have begun his survey on the second night. By then he had shouted enough to be sure that there was no one else on board. But—and this he feared—he might find corpses, or some sign that explained their absence. He moved cautiously, and from his letters it is hard to tell in which direction: he names the ship's parts, the objects inexactly. Some are familiar to him and he has heard them from the sailors; others are unknown, and he describes them as they appear to him. But even of the familiar objects—an indication that on the *Amaryllis* the crew probably represented the dregs of the seven seas—he must have heard one in French, another in Dutch, and another in English. Thus he says *staffe*—as Dr. Byrd must have taught him—for the Jacob's staff; at times it is hard to understand how he could be one moment on the poop deck or the quarterdeck, and another on the *galliard d'arrière,* which is the Frenchified way of saying the same thing; for gun-port he uses *sabordo,* and I allow him the word gladly because it recalls the seafaring books most of us read as children; he talks about the *parrocchetto,* which for us is a fore-topsail, but since the French *perruche* is the topgallant, there is no telling what he is referring to when he says he was under the *parrucchetta.* Furthermore, sometimes he calls the mizzen the *artimon,* in the French way, but what can he mean then when he writes *misaine,* which is how the French identify the foremast (but, alas, not the English, for whom the *mezzana* is the mizzen, God help us)? And when he says eaves, he is probably referring to what we would call scuppers. So I have come to a decision here: I will try to decipher his intentions, then use the terms most familiar to us. If I am mistaken, too bad: the story remains the same.

This said, we will assume that on the second night, after finding a store of food in the cook-room, Roberto somehow proceeded in the moonlight to cross the deck.

Recalling the foredeck and the curved sides vaguely glimpsed the night before, judging now by the slim deck, the shape of the castle and the narrow, convex poop, and comparing all this with the *Amaryllis,* Roberto concluded that the *Daphne* was a Dutch *fluyt,* or flute, or flûte, or fluste, or flyboat, or fliebote, as they are variously called, those trading vessels of medium displacement, usually armed with about ten cannons to ease the conscience in the event of a pirate attack. Given its dimensions, it could be handled by a dozen seamen, and could carry many more passengers if it renounced comforts (scarce to begin with), cramming the space with pallets, until the men tripped over them. Gradually, their number would be reduced by epidemic deaths from miasmas of every kind if there were not enough sanitary provisions. So a flute it was, then, but larger than the *Amaryllis*, yet with a deck reduced, almost, to a single hatchway, as if the captain had been anxious to ship water at every over-lively wave.

In any case, it was a good thing the *Daphne* was a flute. Roberto could move about with some knowledge of how the space was divided. For example, in the center of the deck there should have been a longboat big enough to contain the entire crew; the fact that it was not there suggested the crew was elsewhere. But this did not reassure Roberto: an entire crew never leaves the ship unmanned, at the mercy of the sea, even if that ship is at anchor, its sails struck, in a calm bay.

That evening he promptly headed for the aft quarters and opened the door of the castle shyly, as if he should have asked somebody's permission. . . . Set next to the tiller, the compass told him that the channel between the two stretches of land ran from south to north. Then he found himself in what today would be called the wardroom, an L-shaped cabin, from which another door admitted him to the captain's quarters, with its large porthole over the rudder and lateral accesses to the gallery. On the *Amaryllis* the wardroom was not connected to the cabin where the captain slept, but here it looked as if they had tried to save space in order to make room for something else. And, in fact, while to the left of the wardroom there were two little cubbyholes for junior officers, on the right another cabin had been created, almost wider than the captain's, with a plain bunk at the end, but otherwise arranged as a work space.

The table was cluttered with maps, more numerous, it seemed to Roberto, than those a ship normally requires for navigation. This room seemed a scholar's study. Among the papers he saw some spyglasses lying, a handsome copper nocturlabe that cast tawny glints as if it were itself a source of light, an armillary sphere fastened to the surface of the table, more papers covered with calculations, and a parchment with circular drawings in red and black, which he recognized—having seen various copies of the same on the *Amaryllis* (though of cruder facture)—as a reproduction of the Ephemerides of Regiomontanus.

He went back into the wardroom: stepping out into the gallery, he could see the Island, he could stare—Roberto wrote—with lynx eyes at its silence. In other words, the Island was there, as it had been before.

He must have arrived at the ship nearly naked: I believe that, first of all, besmirched as he was by the sea's brine, he washed in the cook-room, not pausing to wonder if that water was all there was on board; then, in a chest, he found a handsome suit of clothing of the captain's, the outfit reserved for the final coming ashore. Roberto may even have swaggered a bit in his commander's garb, and pulling on the boots must have made him feel in his element once again. Only at this point can a decent man, suitably clad—and not an emaciated castaway—officially take possession of an abandoned ship. With no sense of committing a violation, but rather as if exercising a right, Roberto examined the tabletop until he found, lying open, apparently left interrupted, beside the goose-quill pen and the inkwell, the ship's log. The first page told him the name of the ship, but for the rest it was an incomprehensible sequence of *anker, passer, sterre-keyker, roer,* and it was of little help for him to learn that the captain was Flemish. Still, the last line bore a date, now a few weeks past, and after a few meaningless words an expression in proper Latin stood out, underlined, *pestis quae dicitur bubonica.*

It was a clue, a hint of explanation. An epidemic had broken out on board. This news did not trouble Roberto; he had had his bout of plague thirteen years earlier, and as all know, whoever has had the sickness gains a kind of grace, as if that serpent does not dare introduce itself a second time into the loins of one who has previously tamed it.

For the rest, the hint did not explain much, and prompted other worries. So they were all dead. But in that case he should have found, scattered in disorder on the deck, the corpses of the last, since the first to die must have been given Christian burial at sea.

There was the absence of the longboat: the last men—or all of them—had left the ship. What makes a ship of plague victims a place of invincible menace? Rats, perhaps? Roberto seemed to decipher, in the captain's Ostrogothic writing, the word *rottenest*, which he took to mean rats' nest—and he immediately turned, raising the lamp as he glimpsed something slithering along the wall and heard the squeaking that on the *Amaryllis* had made his blood run cold. With a shudder he recalled an evening when a hairy creature had grazed his face as he was falling asleep, and his cry of terror had brought Dr. Byrd running. The others then taunted him: even without the plague, there are as many rats on a ship as there are birds in a forest, and you must become accustomed to them if you want to sail the seas.

But in the aftercastle, at least, there was not a whiff of rats. Perhaps they had collected in the bilge, their red eyes glowing in the darkness, waiting for fresh meat. Roberto told himself that if they were on board, he had to know it at once. If they were ordinary rats, in an ordinary number, he could live with them. And what else could they be, anyway? He asked himself this question, and preferred not to answer it.

He found a musket, a sword, and a knife. He had been a soldier: he picked up the musket, a *caliver,* as the English called them, which could be aimed without a rest; he examined it, more for reassurance than with any notion of wiping out a pack of rats by shooting them, and he also slipped the knife into his belt, though knives are of scant use against rats.

He had decided to explore the hull from prow to poop. Back in the cook-room, by a little ladder set against the bowsprit he descended into the larder (or pantry, I believe), where provisions for a long voyage had been stored. The crew, since they could not store enough for the duration of the journey, had only recently replenished supplies at some friendly shore. There were baskets of fish, just smoked, and pyramids of coconuts, and barrels of tubers of an unfamiliar shape but apparently edible. And there were fruits such as Roberto had seen on the *Amaryllis* after its first tropical ports of call, fruits that resisted the seasons, prickly and scaly but with a pungent aroma that promised well-defended pulp, sweet hidden humors. And some island crop must have produced those sacks of gray flour that smelled of tufa and also of the loaves whose taste recalled the insipid warty shapes that the Indians of the New World call potatoes.

In the corner he saw also about a dozen little kegs with bung-holes. He tapped the first, and tasted water not yet putrid, indeed, only recently collected and treated with sulphur to make it last longer. There was not a great deal, but considering that the fruit, too, would slake his thirst, he could survive on the ship for a long time. And yet these discoveries, which should have made him realize he would not die of starvation on board, made him all the more uneasy—as is the way of melancholic spirits, to whom every sign of good fortune forebodes dire consequences.

To be shipwrecked on a deserted ship was in itself an unnatural circumstance; but if the ship had at least been abandoned by men and by God as a worthless relic, with no objects of nature or of art to make it an attractive refuge, this would have been in the order of things, and of the chronicles of seamen. But to find it like this, arranged as if to welcome an expected guest like a subtle offering, smacked of sulphur even more than did the water. Roberto was reminded of fairy tales his grandmother used to tell him, and other tales in finer prose read in the Paris salons, where princesses lost in the forest entered a castle and found sumptuously furnished chambers with canopied beds and cupboards filled with luxurious dresses, and even tables laid. . . . And, of course, the last room would contain the sulphurous revelation of the malignant mind that had set the trap.

He touched a coconut at the base of the pile, disturbing the balance of the whole, and those bristled forms came down in an avalanche, like rats waiting, mute, on the ground (or like bats that hang upside down from the beams of an attic), ready now to climb up his body and sniff his face salty with sweat.

Roberto had to make sure that this was not a spell: he had learned in his travels how to deal with foreign fruits. Using his knife as a hatchet, he cracked the nut open with one blow, gnawing at the manna concealed beneath the husk. It was all so sweetly good that the sensation of a snare grew stronger. Perhaps, he told himself, he was already a victim of illusion, he tasted coconuts but in reality was biting into rodents, he was already absorbing their quiddity, soon his hands would grow thinner, taloned, hooked, his body would be covered with a sour fuzz, his back would bend in an arc, and he would be received in the sinister apotheosis of the shaggy inhabitants of this vessel of Acheron.

But—to conclude this account of the first night—another signal of horror was to surprise our explorer. As if the collapse of the coconuts had wakened sleeping creatures, he heard coming nearer, beyond the partition that separated the larder from the rest of the lower deck, not a squeaking but a cheeping, a chirping, and the scratching of paws. So this was truly a trap: night animals were holding their council in some lair.

Roberto wondered if, musket in hand, he should confront immediately that Armageddon. His heart beat irregularly, he called himself a coward, knowing that, whether it was this night or another, sooner or later he would have to face Them. He havered, climbed up on deck again, and fortunately glimpsed the dawn already casting a waxy light on the metal of the cannons, until then caressed by the moon's beams. Day was breaking, he told himself with relief, and he was duty-bound to flee it.

Like a Resurgent of Hungary he ran along the deck to regain the aftercastle, he entered the cabin that was now his, barred the door, closed the accesses to the gallery, placed his weapons within reach, and prepared to sleep so as not to see the Sun, that executioner who with the axe of his rays severs the necks of shadows.

Restless, he dreamed of his shipwreck, and dreamed it as a man of wit, who even in dreams, or especially in them, must take care that as propositions embellish a conception, so reservations make it vital, while mysterious connections give it density; considerations make it profound; emphases uplift, allusions dissimulate, transmutations make subtle.

I imagine that in those days, and on those seas, more ships were wrecked than returned safely home; but to one shipwrecked for the first time the experience must have been a source of recurrent nightmares, which the habit of expressing in appropriate conceits must have made as picturesque as a Last Judgement.

Since the evening before, it was as if the air had sickened with catarrh, and it seemed that the eye of Heaven, brimming with tears, could support no longer the sight of the expanse of waves. The brush of nature had now diluted the line of the horizon and was sketching distances of indefinite provinces.

Roberto, whose viscera have already predicted an imminent catastrophe, flings himself on his pallet, rocked now by a nurse of giants, dozes amid uneasy dreams of which he dreams the dream he relates, and beholds before his very eyes a host of galactic wonders. He wakes to the bacchanal of thunder and the cries of the sailors, then streams of water invade his berth, Dr. Byrd looks in and, running, cries to him to come up on deck and cling firmly to anything more firm than himself.

On deck, confusion, groans, and bodies, as if lifted, all, by a divine hand and flung into the sea. For a moment Roberto grasps the spanker boom (if I have understood correctly), until the sail is rent, shredded by thunderbolts, the boom and the gaff both start emulating the curved course of the stars, and Roberto is flung at the foot of the mizzenmast. There a good-hearted sailor, unable to make room for him, throws him a rope and tells him to tie himself to a door torn from its hinges and hurled here from the castle, and luckily for Roberto the door, with him as its parasite, then slides to the bulwarks, for in the meanwhile the mast snaps in two, and a yard crashes down and splits open the head of his erstwhile Samaritan.

From a breach in the flank Roberto sees, or dreams he is seeing, cyclades of accumulated shadows as thunderbolts dart and roam over the fields of waves; and to me this seems excessive indulgence of a taste for precious quotation. But in any event, the *Amaryllis* tilts in the direction of the castaway ready to be cast away, and Roberto on his plank slides into an abyss above which he glimpses, as he sinks, the ocean freely rising to imitate cliffs; in the delirium of his eyelids he sees fallen Pyramids rise, he finds himself an aquatic comet fleeing along the orbit of that turmoil of liquid skies. As every wave flashes with lucid inconstancy, here foam bends, there a vortex gurgles and a fount opens. Bundles of crazed meteors offer the counter-subject to the seditious aria shattered by thundering; the sky is an alternation of remote lights and downpours of darkness; and Roberto writes that he saw foaming Alps within wanton troughs whose spume was transformed into harvests; and Ceres blossomed amid sapphire glints, and at intervals in a cascade of roaring opals, as if her telluric daughter Persephone had taken command, exiling her plenteous mother.

And, among errant, bellowing beasts, as the silvery salts boil in stormy tumult, Roberto suddenly ceases to admire the spectacle, and becomes its insensate participant, he lies stunned and knows no more of what happens to him. It is only later that he will assume, in dreams, that the plank, by some merciful decree of heaven or through the instinct of a natant object, joins in that gigue and, as it descended, naturally rises, calmed in a slow saraband—then in the choler of the elements the rules of every urbane order of dance are subverted—and with ever more elaborate periphrases it moves away from the heart of the joust, where a versipellous top spun in the hands of the sons of Aeolus, the hapless *Amaryllis* sinks, bowsprit aimed at the sky. And, with it, sinks every other living soul in its hold, the Jew destined to find in the Heavenly Jerusalem the terrestrial Jerusalem he would reach no longer, the Knight of Malta parted forever from the island Escondida, Dr. Byrd from his acolytes and—finally rescued by merciful Nature from the comforts of the physician's art—from that poor, infinitely ulcerated dog that, as it happens, I have not yet been able to mention because Roberto does not write of him until later.

But, in fine, I presume that dream and tempest made Roberto's sleep so uneasy that it was limited to a very brief time, to be followed by a bellicose wakefulness. In fact, accepting that outside it was day, but reassured that faint light penetrated the large opaque windows of the castle, and confident that he could go below by some interior stair, he mustered his courage, collected his weapons, and with audacious fear set out to find the source of those nocturnal noises.

Or, rather, he does not set out at once. I must crave indulgence, but it is Roberto who, in telling this to the Lady, contradicts himself—an indication that he does not tell in complete detail what has happened to him, but instead tries to construct his letter like a story or, more, like a sketch for what could become both letter and story, and he writes without deciding what things he will select later; he drafts, so to speak, the pieces of his chessboard without immediately establishing which to move and how to deploy them.

In one letter he says he went off to venture below. But in another he writes that, barely wakened at the morning light, he was struck by a distant concert. Sounds coming surely from the Island. At first Roberto imagined a horde of natives cramming into long canoes to raid the ship, and he clenched his musket, but then the concert sounded to him less combative.

It was dawn, and the sun did not yet strike the panes: he stepped into the gallery, caught the smell of the sea, opened the window slightly, and with his eyes half-closed he tried to make out the shore.

Aboard the *Amaryllis,* where he never went out on deck during the day, Roberto had heard the passengers tell of fiery dawns as if the sun were impatient to shoot its arrows at the world, whereas now, with no tears, he saw pastel hues: a sky foaming with dark clouds faintly edged in pearl, while a tinge, a memory, of pink was rising behind the Island, which seemed colored turquoise on rough paper.

But that almost nordic palette was enough for him to understand that the outline, which at night had seemed homogeneous, was created by the lines of a wooded hill that ended in a steep slope over a stretch covered with tall trees, down to the palms that lined the white beach.

Slowly the sand grew more luminous, and along the edges, at the sides, he could discern what seemed gigantic embalmed spiders as they were moving their skeletal limbs into the water. Roberto, from the distance, conceived of them as "ambulant vegetables," but at that moment the glare of the sand, now too bright, made him withdraw.

He discovered that where his eyes might fail, his hearing would not betray him, and he entrusted himself to that sense, closing the window almost completely and lending an ear to the noises from land.

He was accustomed to the dawns of his native hill, but he realized that for the first time in his life he was hearing birds really sing, and he had never heard so many, so various.

By the thousands they hailed the sunrise; it seemed to him that he could recognize, among the parrots' cries, the nightingale, the blackbird, the calander, an infinite number of swallows, and even the shrill sound of the cicada and the cricket, and he wondered if the animals he heard were actually of those species and not some antipodal cousin of theirs. . . . The Island was distant, and yet he had the impression that those sounds carried a scent of orange blossoms and basil, as if the air of all the bay were steeped in perfume—and for that matter M. d'Igby had told him how, in the course of one of his voyages, he had recognized the nearness of land by a waft of odorous atoms borne by the winds. . . .

He sniffed and listened to that invisible throng, as if looking from the battlements of a castle or the slit-windows of a fort at an army vociferously fanning out along the slope of the hill and the plain below, and along the river that protected the walls. He had the impression of having already experienced what he was imagining; and in the face of the immensity that besieged him, he felt besieged, and he almost aimed his musket. He was at Casale again, and before him was spread out the Spanish army, with the noise of its wagons, the clash of arms, the tenor voices of the Castilians, the shouting of the Neapolitans, the harsh grunts of the Landsknechts, and in the background some trumpet blasts that, however, reached him muted, above the muffled sounds of an occasional arquebus, *klok, paff, taa-boom,* like the fireworks on the feast day of the local saint.

As if his life had been spent between two sieges, one the image of the other—with the sole difference that now, at the conclusion of this circle of two full lustra, this river was too broad and also encircling, so any sortie was impossible—Roberto lived again the days of Casale.

CHAPTER 2

An Account of Events
in the Monferrato

ROBERTO TELLS US very little about the sixteen years of his life preceding that summer of 1630. He refers to episodes of the past only when they seem to have some connection with his present on the *Daphne,* and the chronicler of his turbulent annals must read between the lines of the story. To judge by his quirks, he is the sort of author who, to postpone the unmasking of the murderer, gives the reader only the scantiest of clues. And so I must wrest hints from him, as if from a delator.

The Pozzo di San Patrizio family belonged to the minor nobility, lords of the vast estate of La Griva along the border of the province of Alessandria (in those days a part of the duchy of Milan, and hence Spanish territory); but whether for geographical reasons or because of temperament, they considered themselves vassals of the marquis of Monferrato. Roberto's father spoke French with his wife, the local dialect with his peasants, and Italian with foreigners; to his son he expressed himself in various ways, depending on whether he was teaching the boy a secret of swordsmanship or taking him on a ride through the fields, cursing the birds that were ruining the crops. For the rest, the young Roberto spent his time without friends, daydreaming of distant lands as he wandered, bored, through the vineyards, or of falconry if he was hunting swallows, or combating dragons as he played with his dogs, or hidden treasure as he explored the rooms of their little castle or fort, as it could also be called. His mind was inspired to wander thus by the dusty volumes of romances and chivalric poems he found in the south tower.

So he was not uneducated, and he even had a tutor, if only seasonally: a Carmelite who had supposedly traveled in the Orient, where, it was murmured—the boy's mother would repeat, blessing herself—he had become a Mussulman. Once a year he would arrive at the castle with a manservant and four little mules laden with books and other scribblings, and he would be housed there for three months. What he taught his pupil I cannot say, but when Roberto turned up in Paris, he made a favorable impression; in any case he was quick to learn whatever he was told.

Of this Carmelite only one thing is known, and it is no accident that Roberto mentions it. One day old Pozzo cut himself while polishing a sword, and whether because the weapon was rusty, or because he had injured a sensitive part of his hand or fingers, the wound provoked severe pain. Then the Carmelite took the blade and sprinkled on it some powder that he kept in a little box; immediately old Pozzo swore he felt relief. In fact, the next day the wound was already healing.

The Carmelite enjoyed the general amazement, and he told father and son how the secret of this substance had been revealed to him by an Arab; it was a medicine far more powerful than the one Christian spagyrists called *unguentum armarium*. When they asked him why the powder was put not on the wound but, rather, on the blade that had produced it, he answered that such is the working of nature, among whose strongest forces is a universal sympathy, which governs actions at a distance. And he added that if this seemed hard to believe, they had only to think of the magnet, which is a stone that draws metal filings to itself, or of the great iron mountains, which cover the northern part of our planet and attract the needle of the compass. And so the unguent, adhering firmly to the sword, drew out those virtues of iron that the sword had left in the wound, impeding its healing.

Any man who in youth witnesses something of this sort cannot but remain marked by it for the rest of his life, and we shall soon see how Roberto's destiny was sealed by his attraction towards the attractive power of powders and unguents.

This, however, is not the episode that left the greatest mark on Roberto's boyhood. There is another, though properly speaking it is not an episode; it is more like a refrain, of which the boy preserved a suspect memory. It seems that his father, who was surely fond of his son even if he treated him with the taciturn roughness characteristic of the men of those lands, sometimes—and precisely in the first five years of Roberto's life—would lift him from the ground and shout proudly: "You are my firstborn!" Nothing strange, to be sure, beyond the venial sin of redundance, since Roberto was an only child. But, as he grew up, Roberto began to remember (or convinced himself that he remembered) how, at these outbursts of paternal joy, his mother's face would assume an expression of pleasure mingled with uneasiness, as if the father did well to say those words, though their repetition stirred in her an anxiety never completely eased. Roberto's imagination had long leaped and danced around the tone of that exclamation, concluding that his father did not utter it as if it were an assertion of the obvious but, rather, as an odd investiture, underlining the *you,* as if to say, "You, and not another, are my firstborn son."

Not another, or not *that* other? In Roberto's letters there appears always some reference to an Other, who haunts him; and the idea seems to have been born in him during those very years, when he became convinced (and what else could a little boy brood over, isolated as he was among bat-infested turrets, vineyards, lizards and horses, awkward in dealing with the big peasant boys his age, his unequal peers, a boy who when he was not listening to the fairy tales of his grandmother listened to those of the Carmelite?), convinced that somewhere an unrecognized brother was at large, who must have been of an evil nature, as their father had repudiated him. Roberto was at first too little and then too modest to wonder if this brother was his on his father's side or on his mother's (in either case one of his parents would have been living under the cloud of an ancient, unpardonable sin): a brother in some way (perhaps supernaturally) guilty of the rejection he had suffered, and because of it he surely hated him, Roberto, the favorite.

The shadow of this enemy brother (whom he would have liked to know, all the same, in order to love him and be loved) had troubled his nights as a boy; later, in adolescence, he leafed through old volumes in the library, hoping to find hidden there—what?—a portrait, a certificate from the curate, a revelatory confession. He wandered through the garrets, opening old chests full of great-grandparents' clothes, rusted medals, a Moorish dagger; and he lingered to question, with puzzled fingers, embroidered dresses that had certainly clad an infant, but whether that was years or centuries ago, there was no knowing.

Gradually he had also come to give this lost brother a name, Ferrante, and had begun attributing to him the little crimes of which he himself was wrongfully accused, like the theft of a cake or the improper liberation of a dog from his chain. Ferrante, privileged by his banishment, acted behind Roberto's back, and Roberto in turn hid behind Ferrante.

Indeed, little by little the habit of blaming the nonexistent brother for what he, Roberto, could not have done, became transformed into the habit of inculpating him with what Roberto had done, and of which he repented.

It was not that Roberto told others a lie: rather, with a lump in his throat, silently assuming the punishment for his own misdeeds, he managed to convince himself of his innocence and to feel the victim of an injustice.

Once, for example, to try out a new axe that the smith had just delivered to him, also partly out of spite for some abuse or other that he felt he had endured, Roberto chopped down a little fruit tree that his father had only recently planted with great hopes for future seasons. When Roberto realized the gravity of his foolishness, he imagined atrocious consequences: being sold to the Turks, at the very least, so they could set him rowing for life in their galleys. He was preparing to attempt flight, ready to end his life as an outlaw in the hills. Seeking a justification, he quickly persuaded himself that the person who had cut down the tree was Ferrante.

But, discovering the crime, his father assembled all the boys of the estate and said that, to avert his indiscriminate wrath, the guilty party would be wise to confess. Roberto felt mercifully generous: if he blamed Ferrante, the poor boy would suffer another repudiation; and after all the unhappy child misbehaved as if to confirm his orphaned abandonment, offended as he was by the sight of his parents smothering another in caresses. . . . Roberto took a step forward and, trembling with fear and pride, declared that he wanted no one else to be blamed in his stead. This statement, though it was not a confession, was taken for one. Twisting his moustache and looking at the boy's mother, the father said, harshly clearing his throat several times, that to be sure the crime was very serious, and punishment was inevitable, but he could not help but appreciate that the young "master of La Griva" had honored the family tradition and this was how a gentleman should always act, even if he was only eight years old. Then he announced that Roberto would not be allowed to participate in the mid-August visit to his cousins at San Salvatore, which was a grievous punishment (at San Salvatore there was Quirino, a vintner who could hoist Roberto to the top of a dizzyingly tall fig tree), but less grievous, certainly, than the galleys of the Sultan.

To us the story seems simple: the father, proud to have an offspring who does not lie, looks at the mother with ill-concealed contentment and administers a mild punishment to save face. But Roberto then embroidered this event at length, arriving at the conclusion that his father and mother had no doubt guessed the culprit was Ferrante, had appreciated the fraternal heroism of their preferred son, and had felt relieved not to have to bare the family secret.

Perhaps it is I who am embroidering, from meager clues, but the presence of the absent brother will have its importance in our story. We will find traces of this puerile game in the behavior of the adult Roberto—or at least of Roberto at the moment we find him on the *Daphne,* in a plight that, to tell the truth, would have ensnared anyone.

But I digress; we have still to establish how Roberto arrived at the siege of Casale. And here we must give fantasy free rein and imagine how it might have happened.

It took time for news to reach La Griva, but for at least two years they had known that the succession to the dukedom of Mantua was causing the Monferrato region much trouble, and a bit of a siege had already taken place. To be brief (and this is a story that others have already told, though in a fashion even more fragmentary than mine): in December of 1627 the duke Vincenzo II of Mantua is dying, and around the deathbed of the old rake who has been unable to produce sons there is a ballet of four claimants, with their agents and their protectors. The victor is the marquis of Saint-Charmont, who manages to convince Vincenzo that the inheritance should go to a cousin in the French line, Charles de Gonzaga, duke of Nevers. Old Vincenzo, between one dying gasp and the next, forces or allows Nevers to marry in great haste his niece Maria Gonzaga, then he dies, leaving his new nephew the dukedom.

Now Nevers was French, and the duchy he was inheriting comprised also the march of Monferrato with Casale, its capital, the most important fortress in Northern Italy. Situated as it was, between Spanish Milan and the lands of the Savoys, Monferrato controlled the upper course of the Po, the passes between the Alps and the south, the road from Milan to Genoa, and it acted as a cushion between France and Spain; for neither of the two powers could trust that other cushion-state, the duchy of Savoy, where Charles Emmanuel I was playing a game that it would have been kind to call duplicitous. If Monferrato went to Nevers, practically speaking it would go to Richelieu; so Spain obviously preferred someone else inherit, say, the duke of Guastalla, ignoring the fact that the duke of Savoy also had some claim to the succession. But since a will existed, and it designated Nevers, the other pretenders could only hope that the germanic Holy Roman Emperor, whose feudatory the duke of Mantua formally was, would refuse to ratify the succession.

But the Spanish were impatient and, while all were waiting for the Emperor to come to a decision, Casale had already been besieged once by Gonzalo de Córdoba and now, for the second time, an imposing army of Spaniards and imperials commanded by Spinola was surrounding it. The French garrison was preparing to resist, expecting a French army to come to its aid, but that army was still engaged in the north, and only God knew if it would arrive at Casale in time.

This was more or less the situation when old Pozzo, in mid-April, assembled before the castle the younger men of his household and the most keen of his peasants, and distributed the arms in his possession; then he called Roberto and to all made this speech, which he must have spent the whole night rehearsing: "Now listen to me, the lot of you. This land of ours, La Griva, has always paid tribute to the lord of Monferrato, who for quite a while has also been, practically speaking, the duke of Mantua. Now the duke is this Nevers, and if anybody comes and tells me that Nevers is not a Mantuan or a Monferrino, I'll kick his backside, because you're nothing but a bunch of ignoramuses, incapable of understanding these things, so best you keep your mouths shut and leave everything to your master, who at least knows what honor is. For most of you, I know, honor is not worth spitting on, but let me tell you something: if the imperials enter Casale—they are not men with scruples—your vineyards will go to hell and as for your women, better not think about it. So we are off to defend Casale. I am not forcing anybody. If there is some lazy, lily-livered lout who does not agree with me, he should speak up right now, and I will have him hanged from that oak." None of those present could yet have seen the etchings of Callot with clumps of people like these hanging from other oaks, but there must have been something in the air: they all raised their weapons, muskets or pikes or simple poles with a sickle tied to the top, and they yelled, "Viva Casale, down with the imperials." In one voice.

"My son," Pozzo said to Roberto as they were riding over the hills, their little army following them on foot, "that Nevers isn't worth one of my balls, and old Vincenzo, when he passed on the dukedom, not only had a limp prick but a limp brain as well. But he gave it to Nevers and not to that blockhead Guastalla, and the Pozzos have been vassals of the legitimate lords of Monferrato since the beginning of time. So we're going to Casale and, if we have to, we'll get ourselves killed because, God damn it, you can't stick with somebody when things go well and then drop him when he's up to his neck in the muck. But if we manage not to get ourselves killed, all the better. So keep your eyes open."

The journey of those volunteers, from the border of the Alessandria country to Casale, was surely one of the longest in recorded history. Old Pozzo's reasoning was in itself exemplary: "I know Spaniards," he said, "they're people who like to take their time. They'll head for Casale by way of the plains to the south, where wagons and cannons and various contraptions can pass more easily. So if we turn west, just before Mirabello, and follow the road through the hills, we'll take a day or two longer, but we'll get there without running into trouble, and we'll still be ahead of the Spaniards."

Unfortunately, Spinola had more tortuous ideas about the preparation of a siege and, when he was to the southeast of Casale, he began by ordering the occupation of Valenza and Occimiano; several weeks previously he had sent the duke of Lerma, Ottavio Sforza, and the count of Gemburg to the west of the city, with about seven thousand foot-soldiers, to try to take immediately the castles of Rosignano, Pontestura, and San Giorgio, thinking to block any possible support that might come from the French army, as, scissor-like, from the north, crossing the Po and heading south, the governor of Alessandria, Don Geronimo Augustin, was advancing with another five thousand men. And all were deployed along the path that Pozzo believed to be felicitously deserted. Nor, when our gentleman learned as much from some peasant, could he change his route, for to the east, by now, there were more imperials than to the west.

Pozzo said simply: "We'll stick to our plan. I know these parts better than they do, and we'll slip past like weasels." Which meant altering the plan considerably. And they even encountered the French from Pontestura, who meanwhile had surrendered and, on condition that they did not return to Casale, had been allowed to proceed towards Finale, where they could set out for France by sea. The Griva men came upon them around Otteglia, and they were close to firing, each side believing that the other was an enemy; from their commander Pozzo learned that, among the terms of the surrender, it was established that the Pontestura wheat should be sold to the Spanish, who would send the money to the people of Casale.

"The Spaniards are gentlemen, my son," Pozzo said, "and it's a pleasure to fight against such people. Luckily we are no longer living back in the times when Charlemagne fought the Moors, who, when they were at war, it was all killing here, there, and yonder. These new wars are between Christians, thank God! Now that they have their hands full at Rosignano, we'll pass behind them, slip between Rosignano and Pontestura, and we'll be at Casale in three days."

Having spoken these words at the end of April, Pozzo with his men arrived in sight of Casale on the 24th of May. It was —at least in Roberto's recollection—a fine journey, as they always abandoned roads and trails to cut across the fields. Makes no difference, Pozzo said, in wartime everything goes to hell anyway, and if we don't ruin the crops, the others will. In their concern to survive they had a high old time in vineyards, orchards, and chicken-runs. Why not? Pozzo said, this was Monferrato land and it should nourish its defenders. When a Mombello peasant objected, Pozzo had the men give him thirty lashes, saying that if you don't maintain a bit of discipline, it's the other side that wins the war.

Roberto began to see war as a splendid experience; from wayfarers he heard edifying tales, like the one about the French knight wounded and captured at San Giorgio, who complained that he had been robbed by a soldier of a portrait that was very dear to him; and the duke of Lerma, on hearing this, had the portrait returned to him, treated his wounds, then gave him a horse and sent him back to Casale. Yet, despite spiraling deviations that made them lose all sense of direction, old Pozzo had seen to it that his band did no real fighting.

Thus it was with great relief, but also with the impatience of those who want to participate in a long-awaited festivity, that one fine day, from the top of a hill, they saw the city below their feet and before their eyes, guarded to the north at their left by the broad stripe of the Po, which just in front of the fortress was divided by two great islands in the midst of the river, which curved sharply towards the south at the great star-shaped bulk of the citadel. Merry with towers and campaniles inside, Casale seemed impregnable on the outside, all bristling as it was with saw-toothed bastions, which made it resemble one of those dragons you see in storybooks.

It was a grand sight. All around the city, soldiers in vari-colored garb dragged obsidional machines among groups of tents bedecked with banners and among knights wearing many-plumed hats. Now and then you could see, against the green of the woods or the yellow of the fields, a sudden flash that wounded the eye, and it was a gentleman's silver cuirass joking with the sun, nor could you guess in which direction he was going, perhaps he was cantering along just for show.

Beautiful for everyone else, the spectacle seemed less happy to Pozzo, who said: "Men, this time we're truly buggered."

And to Roberto, who asked why, he added with a slap on the nape: "Don't play stupid, those are imperials; you surely don't believe there are that many Casalesi or that any of them would come outside their walls for the fun of it. The Casalesi and the French are inside, piling up bales of straw, and fouling their pants because there aren't even two thousand of them, whereas those men down there must number at least a hundred thousand. Look over at those hills opposite us, too." He was exaggerating: Spinola's army counted only eighteen thousand foot and six thousand cavalry, but that was enough, more than enough.

"What will we do, Father?" Roberto asked.

"What we'll do," his father replied, "is be careful to see where the Lutherans are, and bear in mind there's no getting past them: *in primis,* we can't understand one thing they say; *in secundis,* they kill you first and ask who you are afterwards. Look sharp and discover where the Spaniards are. As I've told you, they're people you can reason with. Make sure they're Spaniards of good family. What counts in these matters is breeding."

They picked their way along an encampment identified by banners of their most Catholic majesties, where more cuirasses glittered than elsewhere, and they moved downhill, commending their souls to God. In the confusion they were able to proceed a long way into the enemy's midst, for in those days only select corps, like the musketeers, had uniforms, and with the rest you could never tell who was on your side. But at a certain point, and just when they had only to cross a stretch of no-man's-land, they encountered an outpost and were stopped by an officer, who urbanely asked who they were and where they were going, while behind him, a squad of soldiers stood, alert.

"Sir," Pozzo said, "be so kind as to make way for us, for

we must go and take up our proper position in order to fire on you."

The officer doffed his hat, bowed with a salute that would have swept dust two meters before him, and said: "Señor, no es menor gloria vencer al enemigo con la cortesía en la paz que con las armas en la guerra." Then, in good Italian, he added: "Proceed, sir. If a fourth of our men prove to have one half of your courage, we will win. May Heaven grant me the pleasure of meeting you on the field of battle, and the honor of killing you."

"Fisti orb d'an fisti secc," muttered Pozzo, using an expression in the language of his lands that is even today an optative, wishing, more or less, that the interlocutor be first blinded and immediately afterwards seized with fatal choking. But aloud, calling on all his linguistic resources and his knowledge of rhetoric, he said: "Yo también!" He also doffed his hat, spurred his mount gently, not as much as the theatricality of the moment demanded, for he had to allow his men time to follow him on foot as he rode on towards the walls.

"Say what you like, they're polite people," Pozzo said to his son, and it was well that he turned his head, for thus he avoided the shot of an arquebus from the bastions. "Ne tirez pas, conichons! On est des amis. Nevers! Nevers!" he cried, raising his hands; then he addressed Roberto again: "You see what ungrateful people these are. Better the Spaniards, if you ask me."

They entered the city. Someone must have promptly reported their arrival to the commander of the garrison, Monsieur de Toiras, one-time comrade in arms of old Pozzo. Hearty embraces preceded a first stroll along the ramparts.

"My dear friend," Toiras was saying, "according to the rolls in Paris I am commanding five regiments of infantry of ten companies each, a total of ten thousand foot-soldiers. But Monsieur de La Grange has only five hundred men, Monchat has two hundred fifty, and in all I can count on one thousand seven hundred men on foot. Then I have six companies of light cavalry, a total of only four hundred men, however well-equipped they may be. The Cardinal knows I have fewer men than I should, but he insists I have three thousand eight hundred. I write him, sending proof to the contrary, and His Eminence pretends not to understand. I have had to recruit a regiment of Italians as best I could, Corsicans and Monferrini, but—forgive me for saying so—they are poor soldiers. Imagine! I had to order the officers to assign their valets to a separate company. Your men will join the Italian regiment, under Captain Bassiani, a good man. We'll send young La Grive there too, so when he comes under fire he will understand the orders. As for you, dear friend, you will join a group of excellent gentlemen who have come to us of their own free will, as you have, and are in my suite. You know the country and can give me good advice."

Jean de Saint-Bonnet, lord of Toiras, was tall, dark, with blue eyes, in the full maturity of his forty-five years, choleric but generous and naturally conciliatory, brusque in manner but generally affable, also with his soldiers. He had distinguished himself as defender of the Ile de Ré in the war against the English, but apparently he was not liked by Richelieu and the court. His friends repeated in whispers a dialogue between him and the Chancelier de Marillac, who had contemptuously said that in France two thousand gentlemen could have been found equally capable of handling the Ile de Ré matter as well as Toiras, and Toiras had replied that four thousand could be found capable of keeping the seals better than Marillac. His officers attributed a second bon mot to him (though others gave the credit for it to a Scottish captain): in a war council at La Rochelle, the future gray eminence Père Joseph, who prided himself on a knowledge of strategy, had put his finger on a map, saying, "We will cross here," and Toiras had rebutted coldly, "Unfortunately, Reverend Father, your finger is not a bridge."

"This is the situation, cher ami," Toiras was saying, pointing to the landscape as they walked along the bastion. "The theater is splendid, and the actors are the best of two empires and many seigneuries; among our adversaries we have even a Florentine regiment, commanded by a Medici. We count on Casale as a city: the castle, from which we control the side towards the river, is a fine fort, defended by a good moat, and at the walls we have made a fine gun platform that will allow the defenders to work well. The citadel has sixty cannon and solidly built bastions. There are some weak points, but I have reinforced them with demilunes and batteries. All this is excellent for withstanding a frontal assault, but Spinola is no novice: look at those men at work down there, they are preparing tunnels for mines, and when they arrive here below, at the wall, it will be as if we had opened the gates to them. To stop their work we would have to confront them in the open field, but there we are weaker. And as soon as the enemy has brought those cannons closer, he will start bombarding the city, and here the mood of the Casale civilians becomes important, and I don't trust them very far. For that matter I can understand them: the safety of their city means more to them than does M. de Nevers, and they are not yet convinced that dying for the lilies of France is a good thing. They must be made to understand that with Savoy or with the Spanish they would lose their freedom and Casale would no longer be a capital but simply another ordinary fortress, like Susa, which Savoy is ready to sell for a handful of gold pieces. In any case we will improvise: after all, this is an Italian comedy. Yesterday

I went out with four hundred men towards Frassineto, where the imperials are concentrating, and they retreated. But while I was engaged down there, some Neapolitans encamped on that hill, in precisely the opposite direction. I had them battered by the artillery for a few hours and I believe there was a fine slaughter, but they haven't cleared out. So who won the day? I swear by our Lord I don't know, and neither does Spinola. But I know what we'll do tomorrow. You see those hovels in the plain? If they were ours, we would have many enemy positions within range. A spy tells me they are empty, and this report gives me good reason to fear that men are hiding there—my dear young Lord Roberto, don't look so outraged. Learn this prime rule: a good commander wins a battle by using informers well, and this second rule: an informer, since he is a traitor, is prompt to betray those who pay him to betray. In any case, tomorrow our infantry will go and occupy those houses. Rather than keep the troops inside the walls to rot, better to expose them to fire, which is good training. Don't be impatient, Lord Roberto, it is not yet your turn; but the day after tomorrow, Bassiani's regiment must cross the Po. You see those walls over there? They are part of a little outwork the local men began before the enemy arrived. My officers don't agree, but I believe it is best to occupy it before the imperials do. We must keep them within range on the plain, in order to harass them and impede the construction of the tunnels. In short, there will be glory for all. Now let us go to supper. The siege has only begun and provisions are still plentiful. It will be a while before we start eating the rats."

CHAPTER 3

The Serraglio of Wonders

To SURVIVE THE siege of Casale, where, as it turned out, he had not been reduced to eating rats, only to arrive on the *Daphne,* where perhaps the rats would eat him. . . . Timorously meditating on this nice contrast, Roberto was finally prepared to explore those places from which, the evening before, he had heard vague noises.

He decided to descend from the quarterdeck and, if all proved to be as it had been on the *Amaryllis,* he knew he would find a dozen cannons on the two sides, and the pallets or hammocks of the crew. From the helmsman's room he reached the space below, divided by the tiller, which shifted with a slow creaking, and he should have been able to leave immediately by the door that opened into the lower deck. But, as if to gain familiarity with those deeper areas before facing his unknown enemy, he lowered himself further, through a trapdoor, into a space where on another ship there would have been more stores. Instead he found a room organized with great economy, paillasses for a dozen men. So the larger part of the crew slept down here, as if the rest of the space had been reserved for other functions. The pallets were all in perfect order. If there had been an epidemic, when the first men died, the survivors would surely have tidied up systematically. But, come to think of it, who could say whether all the sailors had died, or even any of them? And once again that thought failed to reassure him: a plague killing an entire crew is a natural event, sometimes providential, according to certain theologians; but an event that causes the crew to flee, leaving the ship in this state of unnatural order, might be far more worrisome.

Perhaps the explanation was to be found on the lower deck; he had to muster his courage. Roberto climbed back up and opened the door leading to the feared place.

He learned now the purpose of those vast gratings that perforated the main deck. Thanks to them, this lower deck had been transformed into a kind of nave, illuminated through the hatches by the full daylight that fell obliquely, intersecting the light that came from the gun-ports, colored by the reflection, now ambered, of the cannons.

At first Roberto perceived only shafts of sunlight, in which infinite corpuscles could be observed swirling, and as he saw them, he could not help but recall (and how he indulges himself with this play of learned memories, to dazzle his Lady, rather than confine himself to bald narration) the words with which the Canon of Digne invited him to observe the cascades of light that spread through the darkness of a cathedral, stirring within themselves a multitude of monads, seeds, indissoluble natures, drops of incense that exploded spontaneously, primordial atoms engaged in combat, battles, skirmishes by squadrons, amid numberless conjunctions and separations— obvious proof of the composition of this universe of ours, made of nothing but prime bodies teeming in the void.

Immediately thereafter, as if to confirm the fact that all creation is the work only of that dance of atoms, he had the impression of being in a garden, and he realized that from the moment he entered this place, he had been assailed by a host of odors, far stronger than those that had come to him earlier, from the shore.

A garden, an indoor orchard, is what the men from the *Daphne* had created in this space, to carry home flowers and plants from the islands they were exploring. The gratings allowed the sun, the winds, and the rains to keep the vegetation alive. Whether the vessel would have been able to preserve its sylvan booty through months of voyaging, or whether the first storm would have poisoned all with salt, Roberto could not say, but surely the mere fact that these plants were still alive indicated that the store, like the food, had been only recently collected.

Flowers, shrubs, saplings had been brought here with their roots and earth, and set in baskets and makeshift cases. But many of the containers had rotted; the earth had spilled out to create, from one container to the next, a layer of damp humus, where the shoots of some plants were already taking root. It was like being in an Eden sprouting from the very planks of the *Daphne*.

The light was not so strong as to trouble Roberto's eyes, but strong enough to heighten the colors of the foliage and make the first flowers open. Roberto's gaze rested on two leaves that had at first seemed like the tail of a crayfish, from which white jujubes blossomed, then on another pale-green leaf where a sort of half-flower was emerging from a clump of ivory lilies. A disgusting stench drew him to a yellow ear into which a little corncob seemed to have been thrust, while near it hung festoons of porcelain shells, snowy, pink-tipped, and from another bunch hung some trumpets or upturned bells with a faint odor of borage. He saw a lemon-colored flower which, as the days passed, would reveal to him its mutability, for it would turn apricot in the afternoon and a deep red at sunset, as others, saffron in the center, faded then to lilial white. He discovered some rough fruits that he would not have dared touch, if one of them, falling to the ground and splitting open in its ripeness, had not revealed a garnet interior. He ventured to taste others, and judged them more with the tongue that speaks than with the tongue that tastes, since he defines one as a bag of honey, manna congealed in the fertility of its stem, an emerald jewel brimming with tiny rubies. Now, reading between the lines, I would venture to suggest he had discovered something very like a fig.

None of those flowers or those fruits was known to him; each seemed generated by the fancy of a painter who had wanted to violate the laws of nature and invent convincing absurdities, riven delights and sapid falsehoods: such as that corolla covered with a whitish fuzz that blossomed into a tuft of violet feathers, but no, it was a faded primrose that extruded an obscene appendage, or a mask that covered a hoary visage with goat's beards. Who could have conceived this bush, its leaves dark green on one side, with wild red-yellow decorations, and the other side flaming, surrounded by other leaves of the most tender pea-green, of meaty consistency, conch-shaped to hold the water of the latest rain?

Overwhelmed by the spell of the place, Roberto did not reflect on the residue of rain that the leaves were holding, though it surely had not rained for at least three days. The perfumes that stunned him led him to consider any enchantment natural.

It seemed to him natural that a flaccid, drooping fruit should smell like a fermented cheese, and that a sort of purplish pomegranate with a hole at the bottom, when shaken, should give off a faint rattle as a seed danced about inside it, as if this were not a flower at all but a child's toy; nor was he amazed by a cusp-shaped blossom, hard and round at the base. Roberto had never seen a weeping palm, like a willow, but he had one before him, its multiple roots forming a paw from which rose a trunk that ended in a single clump, while the fronds of that plaintive plant sagged, exhausted by their own floridness. He had not yet reached another bush that produced broad and pulpy leaves, stiffened by a central nerve that seemed of iron, ready to be used as dishes or trays, while nearby grew other leaves in the form of limp spoons.

Uncertain if he was wandering in a mechanical forest or in an earthly paradise hidden in the bowels of the earth, Roberto roamed in that Eden that provoked odorous deliriums.

Later, when he tells all this to the Lady, he speaks of rustic frenzies, gardens of caprice, Protean bowers, cedars (cedars?) mad with lovely fury. . . . Or else he re-experiences it as a floating cavern rich in deceitful automata where, girded with horribly twisted cables, fanatic nasturtiums billow, wicked stolons of barbarous forest. . . . He will write of the opium of the senses, a whirl of putrid elements that, precipitating into impure extracts, led him to the antipodes of reason.

At first he attributed to the song reaching him from the Island the impression of feathered voices audible among the flowers and plants: but suddenly his flesh crawled at the passage of a bat that grazed his face, and immediately afterwards he had to duck to avoid a falcon that flung itself on its prey, felling it with a blow of its beak.

Moving farther into the lower deck, still hearing the distant birds of the Island, and convinced he was hearing them through the openings of the hull, Roberto now realized those sounds were much closer. They could not come from shore: so other birds, and not far away, were singing, beyond the plants, towards the prow, in the direction of that storeroom from which he had heard noises the night before.

It seemed to him, as he proceeded, that the garden ended at the foot of a tall trunk that went through the upper deck, then he realized that he had arrived more or less at the center of the ship, where the mainmast rose from the very bottom of the keel. But by now artifice and nature were so confused that we can justify also our hero's confusion. For, at that very point, his nostrils began to perceive a mixture of aromas, earthy molds, and animal stench, as if he were moving slowly from a flower garden to a sheepfold.

He was passing the trunk of the mainmast, heading for the prow, when he saw the aviary.

He could think of no other definition for that collection of wicker cages with solid boughs run through them to serve as perch, inhabited by flying creatures striving to discern that dawn of which they had only a beggared light, and to reply with distorted voices to the call of their similars singing in freedom on the Island. Set on the ground or hanging from the hatch of the deck above, the cages were arranged along this other nave like stalagmites and stalactites, creating another grotto of wonders, where the fluttering animals made their dwellings rock beneath the sun's rays, in a glitter of hues, a flurry of rainbows.

If until that day he had never heard birds really sing, neither could Roberto say he had ever seen birds, at least not in such guises, so many that he asked himself if they were in their natural state or if an artist's hand had painted them and decorated them for some pantomime, or to feign an army on parade, each foot-soldier and horseman cloaked in his own standard.

An embarrassed Adam, he could give no names to these creatures, except the names of birds of his own hemisphere: That one is a heron, he said to himself, that a crane, a quail. . . . But it was like calling a goose a swan.

Here prelates with broad cardinal's trains and beaks shaped like alembics spread grass-colored wings, swelling a rosy throat and revealing an azure breast, chanting in almost human sound; there multiple squads performed in great tourney, venturing assaults on the depressed domes that circumscribed their arena, among dove-gray flashes and red and yellow thrusts, like oriflammes that a squire threw and caught. Grouchy light cavalry, with long nervous legs in a cramped space, neighed indignantly *cra-cra-cra,* at times hesitating on one foot and peering around suspiciously, shaking the tufts on their elongated heads . . . Only in one cage, built to his measure, a great captain in a bluish cloak, his jerkin as vermilion as his eye and a cornflower plume on his helmet, emitted a dove's lament. In a small coop nearby, three foot-soldiers remained on the ground, without wings, little skipping clumps of muddied wool, mouse-muzzles moustached at the root of long curved beaks equipped with nostrils the little monsters used to sniff as they pecked the worms encountered in their path. . . . In a cage that wound like a narrow alley, a small stork with carrot legs, aquamarine breast, black wings, and flushed beak moved hesitantly, followed by its offspring in Indian file and, as its path ended, it croaked with vexation, first stubbornly trying to break what seemed to it a tangle of withes, then stepping back, reversing direction, with its young bewildered, not knowing whether to go forward or backward.

Roberto was divided between excitement at his discovery, pity for the prisoners, and the desire to release them and see his cathedral invaded by those heralds of an airy army, to save them from the siege to which the *Daphne,* besieged in her turn by the others, their similars outside, had constrained them. He imagined they were hungry, and saw that in the cages there were only crumbs of food, and the dishes and bowls that should have contained water were empty. But not far off he found sacks of grain and shreds of dried fish, prepared by those who meant to take this booty to Europe, for a ship does not go into the seas of the opposite south without bringing back to the courts or academies evidence of those worlds.

Proceeding further, he found also a pen made of planks with a dozen animals scratching inside it, belonging, he decided, to the poultry species, even though at home he had never seen any with such plumage. They too seemed hungry, but the hens had laid (and were glorifying the event like their sisters all over the world) six eggs.

Roberto seized one immediately, pierced it with the tip of his knife, and sucked it as he had done as a child. Then he placed the others inside his shirt and, to compensate the fecund mothers and fathers who were staring at him with great outrage, shaking their wattles, he distributed water and food; and he then did the same, cage by cage, wondering by what providence he had landed on the *Daphne* just as the animals were about to starve. In fact, by now he had been on the ship two nights, so someone had tended the aviaries the day before his arrival at the latest. He felt like a guest who arrives at a feast, tardy, to be sure, but while the last of the other guests are just leaving and the tables have not yet been cleared.

For that matter, he said to himself, it is an established fact that someone was here earlier and now is here no longer. Whether it was one day or ten days before my arrival, my fate remains unchanged, or, at most, it becomes more of a mockery: being shipwrecked a day earlier, I could have joined the sailors of the *Daphne*, wherever they have gone. Or perhaps not, I could have died with them, if they are dead. He heaved a sigh (at least it had nothing to do with rats) and concluded that he had at his disposal also some chickens. He reconsidered his thought of freeing the bipeds of nobler lineage and decided that if his exile were to last long, they might even prove edible.

The hidalgos before Casale were beautiful and varicolored, too, and yet we fired on them, and if the siege had lasted, we would even have eaten them. Anyone who soldiered in the Thirty Years' War (that is what I call it, but those alive at the time did not call it that, and perhaps they did not even understand that it was one long war in the course of which, every now and then, somebody signed a peace treaty) learned how to harden his heart.

CHAPTER 4

Fortification Display'd

WHY DOES ROBERTO evoke Casale when describing his first days on the ship? His taste for parallels is one reason, of course: besieged then, besieged now. But from a man of his century we demand something better. If anything, what should have fascinated him in the similarity are the differences, fertile in elaborate antitheses: Casale he had entered of his own choice, to prevent others from entering; he had been cast up on the *Daphne,* and yearned only to leave it. But I would say, rather, that while he lived a life of shadows, he recalled a story of violent deeds performed in broad daylight, so that the sun-filled days of the siege, which his memory restored to him, would compensate for this dim roaming. And perhaps there was something more to it. In the first part of Roberto's life, there had been only two periods in which he learned something of the world and of the ways of inhabiting it; I refer to the few months of the siege and to the later years in Paris. Now he was going through his third formative period, perhaps the last, at the end of which maturity might coincide with dissolution, and he was trying to decipher its secret message, seeing the past as a figure of the present.

Casale, at the beginning, was a story of sorties. Roberto
tells this story to the Lady, transfiguring it, as if to say that,
unable as he had been to storm the castle of her intact snow,
shaken but not undone by the flame of his two suns, in the
flame of that earlier sun he had still been able to pit himself
against those who laid siege to his Monferrato citadel.

The morning after the men from La Griva arrived, Toiras
sent some single officers, carbines on their shoulder, to observe
what the Neapolitans were installing on the hill conquered the
previous day. The officers approached too closely, and shots
were exchanged: a young lieutenant of the Pompadour regiment was killed. His comrades carried him back inside the
walls, and Roberto saw the first slain man in his life. Toiras
decided to have his men occupy the hovels he had mentioned
the day before.

From the bastions it was easy to observe the advance of
the ten musketeers, who at a certain point separated in an
attempt to seize the first house, as if with pincers. Cannon fire
from the walls passed above their heads and tore the roof off
the house: like a swarm of insects, Spaniards dashed out and
fled. The musketeers let them escape, took the house, barricaded themselves inside, and began laying down a harassing
fire towards the hill.

It seemed advisable to repeat the operation against the
other houses: even from the bastions it was clear that the
Neapolitans had begun digging trenches, edging them with
fagots and gabions. But these did not circumscribe the hill,
they ran towards the plain. Roberto learned that this was how
the enemy started constructing mine tunnels. Once these
reached the walls, they would be packed, along their final
stretch, with kegs of powder. It was thus necessary to prevent
the initial digging from reaching a depth sufficient to allow

further digging underground, otherwise the enemy from that point on could work under cover. This was the whole game: to anticipate from outside, in the open, the construction of the tunnels, and to dig countermine-tunnels of one's own from the other direction, until the relief army arrived and while provisions and ammunition lasted. In a siege there is nothing else to do: harry the other side, and wait.

The following morning, as promised, it was the turn of the outwork. Roberto found himself grasping his caliver in the midst of an unruly bunch of men who back in Lù or Cuccaro or Odalengo had never wanted to work. With some surly Corsicans, they were all crammed into boats to cross the Po, after two French companies had already touched the other shore. Toiras and his staff observed from the right bank, and old Pozzo saluted his son before waving him on with one hand, then put his forefinger to his cheekbone and pulled the skin down, as if to say, "Keep your eyes open!"

The three companies made camp in the outwork. Construction had not been completed, and part of the finished walls had already collapsed. The men spent the day barricading the gaps. The position was well protected by a ditch, beyond which some sentries were posted. When night fell, the sky was so bright that the sentries dozed off, and not even the officers considered an attack possible. But suddenly they heard the charge sounded, and they saw the Spanish light cavalry appear.

Roberto had been set by Captain Bassiani behind some bales of straw that patched a fallen part of the outer wall: he had no time to realize what was happening. Each cavalryman had a musketeer behind him and, as they arrived at the ditch, the horses began to follow it, surrounding the post while the musketeers fired, eliminating the few sentries. Then each musketeer jumped from his horse's back, rolling into the ditch. As the horsemen formed a semicircle before the entrance, opening heavy fire and forcing the defenders to seek cover, the musketeers, unharmed, reached the gate and the more vulnerable breaches.

The Italian company, which was on guard, had emptied its weapons and then scattered, seized with panic, and they would long be reviled for this; but the French companies could do no better. Between the first attack and the scaling of the walls only a few minutes had passed, and the rest of the men were surprised by the attackers, who were inside the walls before the defenders could even grab their weapons.

The enemy, exploiting this surprise, were slaughtering the garrison, and they were so numerous that while some continued felling the defenders still on their feet, others had already begun despoiling the fallen. Roberto, after firing on the musketeers, was reloading painfully, his shoulder sore from the recoil; he was unprepared for the charge of the cavalry. As the charge passed over his head through the breach, a horse's hoofs buried him under the collapsing barricade. It was a stroke of luck: protected by the fallen bales, he survived the first, murderous impact, and now, glancing from beneath his rick, he saw with horror the enemies finishing off the wounded, hacking at a finger in order to steal a ring, or a whole hand for a bracelet.

Captain Bassiani, to compensate for the shame of his men's rout, fought on bravely; but he was surrounded and had to surrender. From the riverbank they saw that the situation was critical, and Colonel La Grange, who had left the outwork after an inspection and was regaining Casale, wanted to rush to the assistance of the defenders, but he was restrained by his officers, who advised him rather to ask the city for reinforcements. From the right bank more boats set out, while Toiras, having been wakened abruptly, now arrived at full tilt. It quickly became clear that the French were routed, and the only thing to do was to lay down some covering fire to help the survivors reach the river.

In this confusion old Pozzo could be seen impatiently galloping back and forth between the staff and the jetty, seeking Roberto among those who had escaped. When it was almost certain that no more boats were coming, he was heard to utter "Oh cripes!" Then, as a man who knew the whims of the river, making a fool of those who had till then heaved and rowed, he chose a spot opposite one of the sandbars and spurred his horse into the water. Crossing a bar, he was on the other shore without even having made the animal swim, and he dashed like a madman, sword upraised, towards the outwork.

As the sky was already growing light, a group of enemy musketeers surrounded him, having no idea who this solitary rider was. The solitary rider rode through them, eliminating at least five with unerring downward blows; he encountered two cavalrymen, made his horse rear, bent to one side, avoiding a thrust, and suddenly sat erect, swinging his blade in a circle: the first adversary slumped over his saddle with his guts slipping down into his boots as the horse ran off; the second remained with his eyes wide, his fingers seeking one ear which, while still attached to his cheek, was hanging below his chin.

Pozzo arrived at the outwork. The invaders, busy stripping the last to fall—fugitives shot in the back—had no idea where this man had come from. He entered the compound, calling his son in a loud voice; he swept away another four people as he described a circle, jabbing his sword at all the cardinal points. Emerging from the straw, Roberto saw him at a distance and, before recognizing his father, he recognized Pagnufli, his father's mount and his own playmate for years. He stuck two fingers into his mouth and let out a whistle the animal knew well, and in fact Pagnufli reared, pricked up his ears, and began carrying the father towards the breach. Pozzo saw Roberto and shouted, "What are you doing in a place like that? Mount, you lunatic!" And as Roberto sprang onto the horse's back and clung to his father's waist, Pozzo said, "God's truth, you're never where you should be." Then, spurring Pagnufli again, he galloped off towards the river.

Now some of the looters realized that this man in this place was out of place, and they pointed at him, shouting. An officer wearing a dented cuirass and with three soldiers following him tried to block Pozzo's path. The old man saw him, started to swerve, then pulled on the reins and cried, "Talk about fate!" Roberto looked ahead and realized that this was the Spaniard who had let them pass three days before. The officer, too, had recognized his prey, and he advanced, eyes gleaming, sword upraised.

Old Pozzo rapidly shifted his sword to his left hand, drew his pistol from his belt, and held out his arm, all so quickly that the Spaniard was surprised; in his impetuosity he was now almost facing Pozzo, who however did not fire at once. He allowed himself the time to say, "Sorry about the pistol. But you're wearing a breastplate, so I have every right—" He pressed the trigger and felled the man with a bullet in his mouth. The soldiers, seeing their leader fall, took flight, and Pozzo replaced the pistol, saying, "We'd better go on before they lose their temper. . . . Move, Pagnufli!"

In a great cloud of dust they crossed the ground and, amid violent spray, the river, while in the distance some men were still emptying their weapons after them.

They reached the right bank, to applause. Toiras said: "Très bien fait, mon cher ami," then added, to Roberto, "La Grive, today all of them ran off, and only you remained. What's bred in the bone . . . You're wasted in that company of cowards. You will join my staff."

Roberto thanked him and then, climbing down from the saddle, held out a hand to his father, to thank him. Pozzo clasped it absently, saying, "I'm sorry for that Spaniard, such a fine gentleman. Well, war's an ugly animal, that's sure. Anyway, my son, never forget: always be good, but if somebody comes at you and means to kill you, then he's in the wrong. Am I right?"

They re-entered the city, and Roberto heard his father still muttering to himself, "I didn't go looking for him. . . ."

CHAPTER 5

The Labyrinth of the World

ROBERTO RECALLS THAT episode, caught up in a moment of filial devotion, daydreaming of a happy time when a protective figure could save him from the confusion of a siege, but he cannot help recalling what happened afterwards. And this does not seem to me a simple accident of memory. I have said before that Roberto apparently connects those distant events with his experiences on the *Daphne,* as if to find motives, reasons, signs of destiny. Now I would say that harking back, on the ship, to the Casale days helps him retrace the stages through which, as a youth, he slowly learned that the world was composed of alien architectures.

As if, on the one hand, finding himself now suspended between sky and sea could be only the most consequent development of his three lustra of peregrinations in a territory made up of forked paths; and, on the other hand, I believe that in reconstructing the history of his misfortunes he was seeking consolation for his present state, as if the shipwreck had restored him to that earthly paradise he had known at La Griva and had left behind on entering the walls of the besieged city.

———

Now Roberto no longer deloused himself in the soldiers' quarters but sat at Toiras's table amid gentlemen from Paris, and he listened to their boasts, their recollections of other campaigns, their fatuous or brilliant talk. In these conversations—beginning on the very first evening—he was given reason to believe that the siege of Casale was not the enterprise he had thought he was to take part in.

He had come here to bring to life his dreams of chivalry, nourished by the poems he had read at La Griva: to come from good stock and to have finally a sword at his side meant becoming a paladin who might cast away his life for a word from his king, or for the rescue of a lady. After his arrival, the devout host he had joined proved to be a mob of slothful peasants ready to turn and run at the first sign of a fight.

Now he was admitted to an assembly of heroes who welcomed him as one of their own. He knew that his heroism was the result of a misunderstanding: he had stayed in the outwork, all right, but only because he was even more frightened than those who had fled it. And, worse, after Monsieur de Toiras retired, and the others stayed up all night gossiping freely, Roberto came to realize that the whole siege was nothing but one more chapter in a meaningless history.

True, Don Vincenzo of Mantua had died and left the dukedom to Nevers, but if someone else had been present at the old man's deathbed, the story could have turned out quite differently. For example, Charles Emmanuel also boasted some claim to Monferrato through a niece or a granddaughter (sovereigns all married among themselves), and for some time he had wanted to lay hands on that marquisate that was a thorn in the side of his duchy, penetrating to within a few dozen miles of Turin. So, immediately after the naming of Nevers, Gonzalo de Córdoba, exploiting the ambitions of the Savoy duke to frustrate those of the French, suggested joining the Spaniards in taking Monferrato, dividing the territory afterwards. The Emperor, who already had his share of troubles with the rest of Europe, did not consent to the invasion, but neither did he pronounce himself against Nevers. Gonzalo and Charles Emmanuel acted promptly, and one of the two started by taking Alba, Trino, and Moncalvo. A good man but not a stupid one, the Emperor sequestered Mantua, entrusting it to an imperial commissioner.

This truce was to apply to all claimants, but Richelieu took it as an insult to France. Or else it suited him to take it as such. He did not act, however, for he was still besieging the Protestants of La Rochelle. Spain looked favorably on that massacre of a handful of heretics, and allowed Gonzalo to exploit it to muster eight thousand men and lay siege to Casale, defended by little more than two hundred soldiers. That was the first siege of Casale.

But as the Emperor showed no sign of giving way, Charles Emmanuel sensed the bad turn things were taking and, while still collaborating with the Spanish, he sent secret messages to Richelieu. In the meantime La Rochelle was taken, Richelieu was congratulated by the court of Madrid on this fine victory of the faith, he expressed his thanks, reassembled his army and, with Louis XIII at its head, he sent it across the Monginevro Pass in February of '29, and deployed it before Susa. Charles Emmanuel realized that by playing a double game, he risked losing not only Monferrato but also Susa, so—trying to sell what they were taking from him—he offered Susa in exchange for a French city.

One of Roberto's table companions recalled the affair in an amused tone. Richelieu, with fine sarcasm, inquired whether the duke preferred Orléans or Poitiers, and at the same time a French officer presented himself to the Susa garrison and requested lodging for the King of France. The Savoy commander, a man of wit, replied that His Highness the duke would no doubt be happy to welcome His Majesty, but inasmuch as His Majesty had come with such a large suite, they should allow the commander first to inform His Highness. With equal elegance the marshal of Bassompierre, cantering over the snow, doffed his hat before his king and, after informing him that the violins had entered and the mummers were at the door, asked his permission to open the dance. Richelieu celebrated a field mass, the French infantry attacked, and Susa was conquered.

Seeing how things then stood, Charles Emmanuel decided that Louis XIII was a most welcome guest and came out to receive him, asking him only not to waste time at Casale, which was already being dealt with, but to help him take Genoa instead. He was courteously invited not to talk nonsense and was given a handsome goose quill to sign a treaty allowing the French freedom of action in Piedmont. Charles Emmanuel managed to retain Trino as a consolation and was authorized to exact an annual rent from the duke of Mantua for Monferrato. "And so Nevers," the officer said, "to keep what was his, agreed to pay rent to someone who had never been its owner."

"And he paid!" Another man laughed. "Quel con!"

"Nevers has always had to pay for his follies," said an abbé, who had been introduced to Roberto as Toiras's confessor. "Nevers is a jester of God, convinced that he is Saint Bernard. He has always been dominated solely by the idea of assembling the Christian princes for a new crusade. These are times when the Christians are killing one another: who gives a thought to the infidels these days? Gentlemen of Casale, if a stone or two is left of this city, you must expect your new lord to invite all of you to Jerusalem!" The abbé smiled, amused, stroking his well-trimmed blond moustache, as Roberto was thinking: So it goes: this morning I was about to die for a madman, and this madman is called mad because he dreams, as I used to dream, of the days of the fair Melisende and the Leper King.

Nor did subsequent events allow Roberto to untangle the motives behind this story. Betrayed by Charles Emmanuel, Gonzalo de Córdoba realized that he had lost the campaign, recognized the Susa agreement, and led his eight thousand men back into Milanese territory. A French garrison was installed at Casale, another at Susa, the rest of Louis's army crossed the Alps again to wipe out the last Huguenots in Languedoc and the valley of the Rhone.

But none of those gentlemen had any intention of honoring pacts, and the officers seated around the table told the whole story as if it was all entirely natural, indeed some agreed and remarked, "La Raison d'Estat, ah, la Raison d'Estat." For reasons of state Olivares—Roberto gathered that he was some sort of Spanish Richelieu, but less blessed with luck—realized he had cut a sorry figure, unceremoniously dismissed Gonzalo, and put Ambrogio Spinola in his place, repeating that the insult offered to Spain was detrimental to the Church. "Rubbish," the abbé interjected. "Urban VIII favored the succession of Nevers." And Roberto wondered what the Pope had to do with matters not involving questions of faith.

Meanwhile the emperor—and there was no telling the thousand different ways Olivares put pressure on him—remembered that Mantua was in the hands of a commissioner, and Nevers could neither pay nor not pay for something that was still not his due; the emperor lost patience and sent twenty thousand men to besiege the city. The pope, seeing Protestant mercenaries running about Italy, immediately imagined another sack of Rome and sent troops to the Mantuan border. Spinola, more ambitious and determined than Gonzalo, decided to besiege Casale again, but seriously this time. In short, Roberto privately concluded, if you would avoid wars, never make treaties of peace.

In December of '29 the French again crossed the Alps. According to their pacts, Charles Emmanuel should have let them pass, but—evidence of his reliability—he reiterated his claims to the Monferrato and demanded six thousand French soldiers to besiege Genoa, which was really an obsession of his. Richelieu, who considered him a snake, said neither yes nor no. A captain, who dressed at Casale as if he were at court, described one day of the past February: "A marvelous feast, my friends! The musicians of the royal palace were missing, but the fanfares were there! His Majesty, followed by the army, rode before all Turin in a black suit worked in gold, a plume in his hat, and his cuirass gleaming!"

Roberto was expecting an account of a great attack, but no, this occasion was merely another parade. The King did not attack; he made a surprise diversion to Pinerolo and appropriated it, or reappropriated it, since a few hundred years earlier it had been a French city. Roberto had a vague idea of where Pinerolo was, and he could not understand how taking it would relieve Casale. Are we also under siege at Pinerolo perhaps, he wondered.

The Pope, worried by the turn things were taking, sent his representative to Richelieu, urging him to return the city to the Savoys. At table then they gossiped abundantly about that envoy, one Giulio Mazzarini, a Sicilian, a Roman plebeian— no, no, the abbé insisted, the natural son of an obscure officer from the mountains south of Rome. Somehow this Mazzarini had become a captain in the service of the pope; but he was doing everything he could to win the confidence of Richelieu, whose great favorite he now was. And he was someone to keep an eye on; for at that moment he was at Ratisbon, or on his way there, which is at the end of the earth, but it was in Ratisbon that the fate of Casale would be decided, not in some mine or countermine.

Meanwhile, as Charles Emmanuel was trying to cut lines of communication with the French troops, Richelieu also took Annecy and Chambéry, and Savoyards and French were fighting at Avigliana. In this slow game, the imperials were entering Lorraine to threaten France. Wallenstein was moving to help the Savoys, and in July a handful of imperials, transported on barges, took by surprise a lock at Mantua, the whole army had overrun the city, sacked it for seventy hours, emptying the ducal palace from top to bottom and, to reassure the pope, the Lutherans of the imperial army had despoiled every church in the city. Yes, those same Landsknechts that Roberto had seen arriving to lend Spinola a helping hand.

The French army was still engaged in the north, and no one could say if it would arrive in time, before Casale fell. They could only hope in God, the abbé said. "Gentlemen, it is political wisdom to realize that human means must always be sought, as if divine means did not exist; and divine means sought, as if human means did not exist."

"So let us hope in divine means," one gentleman exclaimed, but with an expression anything but devout, waving his cup until he had spilled some wine on the abbé's cassock. "Sir, you have stained me with wine," the abbé cried, blanching, which was the form indignation took in those days. "Pretend," the other replied, "that the mishap occurred during the Consecration. Wine is wine."

"Monsieur de Saint-Savin," the abbé cried, rising and putting his hand to his sword, "this is not the first time you have dishonored your own name by taking Our Lord's in vain! You would have done better, God forgive me, to stay in Paris dishonoring the ladies, as is the custom with you Pyrrhonians!"

"Come, come," Saint-Savin replied, obviously drunk, "we Pyrrhonians went about at night to provide music for the ladies, and the men of courage who wanted to enjoy some fine jest would join us. But when the lady failed to come to her window, we knew she preferred to remain in the bed the family confessor was warming for her."

The other officers had risen and were restraining the abbé, who tried to draw his sword. Monsieur de Saint-Savin is in his cups, they said to him, allowances had to be made for a man who had fought well those recent days, out of respect for the comrades who had just died.

"So be it," the abbé concluded, leaving the hall. "Monsieur de Saint-Savin, I invite you to end the night reciting a De Profundis for our fallen friends, and I will then consider myself satisfied."

The abbé went out, and Saint-Savin, who was sitting next to Roberto, leaned on his shoulder and commented: "Dogs and river birds make less noise than we do shouting a De Profundis. Why all the bell-ringing and all the Masses to resuscitate the dead?" He abruptly drained his cup, admonished Roberto with a raised finger, as if to direct him to a proper life and to the supreme mysteries of our holy religion. "Sir, be proud: today you came close to a happy death; and behave in future with the same nonchalance, knowing that the soul dies with the body. Go then to death after having savored life. We are animals among animals, all children of matter, save that we are the more disarmed. But since, unlike animals, we know we must die, let us prepare for that moment by enjoying the life that has been given us by chance and for chance. Let wisdom teach us to employ our days in drinking and amiable conversation, as is proper to gentlemen scorning base spirits. Comrades, life is in our debt! We are rotting at Casale, and we were born too late to enjoy the times of the good King Henry, when at the Louvre you encountered bastards, monkeys, madmen and court buffoons, dwarfs and legless beggars, castrati and poets, and the king was amused by them. Now Jesuits lascivious as rams fulminate against the readers of Rabelais and the Latin poets, and would have us all be virtuous and kill the Huguenots. Lord God, war is a beautiful thing, but I want to fight for my own pleasure and not because my adversary eats meat on Friday. The pagans were wiser than we. They had their three gods, but at least their mother Cybele did not claim to give birth and yet remain a virgin."

"Sir!" Roberto protested, as the others laughed.

"Sir," Saint-Savin replied, "the first quality of an honest man is contempt for religion, which would have us afraid of the most natural thing in the world, which is death; and would have us hate the one beautiful thing destiny has given us, which is life. We should rather aspire to a heaven where only the planets live in eternal bliss, receiving neither rewards nor condemnations, but enjoying merely their own eternal motion in the arms of the void. Be strong like the sages of ancient Greece and look at death with steady eye and no fear. Jesus sweated too much, awaiting it. Why should he have been afraid, for that matter, since he was going to rise again?"

"That will do, Monsieur de Saint-Savin," an officer virtually ordered him, taking him by the arm. "Do not scandalize this young friend of ours, as yet unaware that in Paris nowadays blasphemy is the most exquisite form of *bon ton;* he might take you too seriously. And you, Monsieur de la Grive, go to bed, too. Remember that the Good Lord, in His mercy, will forgive even Monsieur de Saint-Savin. As that theologian said, strong is a king who destroys all, stronger still is a woman who obtains all, but strongest is wine, which drowns reason."

"You quote by halves, sir," Saint-Savin mumbled as two of his comrades were dragging him out almost bodily. "That phrase is attributed to the Tongue, which added: Stronger still, however, is Truth and I who speak it. And my tongue, even if it now moves with difficulty, will not be silent. The wise man must attack falsehood not only with his sword but also with his tongue. My friends, how can you call merciful a divinity that desires our eternal unhappiness only to appease his rage of an instant? We must forgive our neighbor, and he need not? And we should love such a cruel being? The abbé calls me Pyrrhonian, but we Pyrrhonians, if he must so call us, are concerned with consoling the victims of imposture. Once three companions and I distributed rosaries with obscene medals among some ladies. If you only knew how devout they became immediately thereafter!"

He went out, accompanied by the laughter of the whole company, and the officer remarked, "If God will not pardon his tongue, at least we will, for he has such a beautiful sword." Then he said to Roberto, "Keep him as your friend, and don't vex him any more than necessary. He has felled more Frenchmen in Paris over a point of theology than my whole company has run through Spaniards here. I would not want him next to me at Mass, but I would consider myself fortunate to have him beside me on the field."

Thus introduced to his first doubts, Roberto was to acquire more the following day. Returning to collect his pack in that wing of the castle where he had slept the first nights with his Monferrini, he had trouble orienting himself among the corridors and courtyards. He was going along a passage when he realized he had taken a wrong turn, and at the end of the hall he saw a mirror dulled with dirt, in which he spied himself. But as he approached, he realized that this self had, certainly, his face, but wore gaudy Spanish-style clothing, and his hair was gathered in a little net. Further, this self, at a certain point, no longer faced him, but withdrew to one side.

It was not a mirror. It was in fact a window with dusty

panes overlooking an external rampart from which a stairway descended towards the courtyard. So he had seen not himself but someone very like him, whose trail he had now lost. Naturally he thought at once of Ferrante. Ferrante had followed him to Casale, or had preceded him, and perhaps belonged to another company of the same regiment, or to one of the French regiments, and while Roberto was risking his life at the outwork, the other was reaping God knows what advantages from the war.

At that age Roberto tended to smile at his boyhood imaginings of Ferrante, and reflecting on his vision, he quickly convinced himself that he had seen only someone who vaguely resembled him. He chose to forget the incident. For years he had brooded over an invisible brother, and that evening he thought he had seen him, but (he told himself, trying with his reason to contradict his heart) if he had seen someone, it was not a figment, and since Ferrante was a figment, the man seen could not have been Ferrante.

A master of logic would have refuted that paralogism, but for the present it satisfied Roberto.

CHAPTER 6

The Great Art
of Light and Shadow

AFTER DEVOTING HIS letter to the first memories of the siege, Roberto found some bottles of Spanish wine in the captain's quarters. We can hardly reproach him if, having lit the fire and cooked himself a pan of eggs with bits of smoked fish, he opened a bottle and permitted himself a regal supper on a table laid almost to perfection. If he was destined to remain a castaway for a long time, he had to maintain good manners and not become bestialized. He remembered how at Casale, when wounds and sickness were causing even the officers to behave like castaways, Monsieur de Toiras requested that, at table at least, each should bear in mind what he had learned in Paris: "To appear in clean clothes, not to drink after each mouthful, but first to wipe moustache and beard, not to lick one's fingers or spit in the plate, not to blow one's nose into one's napkin. We are not imperials, gentlemen!"

He woke the next morning at cockcrow, but he dawdled at length. When in the gallery he again opened the window a crack, he realized he had risen later than the day before, and dawn was already becoming sunrise: behind the hills now the pink of the sky was more intense, as the clouds drifted away.

Since the first rays would soon strike the beach, making it intolerable to his sight, Roberto thought of looking to where the sun was not yet predominant, and he moved along the gallery to the other side of the *Daphne*, towards the western land. It immediately appeared to him as a jagged turquoise outline, which in a few minutes' time was divided into two horizontal strips: a brush of greenery and pale palm trees already blazing below the dark area of the mountains, over which the clouds of night obstinately continued to reign. But slowly these clouds, still coal-black in the center, were shredding at the edges in a medley of white and pink.

It was as if the sun, rather than confront them, was ingeniously trying to emerge from inside them, though the light unraveled at their borders as they grew dense with fog, rebelling against their liquefaction in the sky in order that it become the faithful mirror of the sea, now wondrously wan, dazzled by sparkling patches, as if shoals of fish passed, each fitted with an inner lamp. Soon, however, the clouds succumbed to the lure of the light, and yielded, abandoning themselves above the peaks, while on one side they adhered to the slopes, condensing and settling like cream, soft where it trickled down, more compact at the summit, forming a glacier, and on the other side making snow at the top, a single lava of ice exploding in the air in the shape of a mushroom, an exquisite eruption in a land of Cockaigne.

What he saw was perhaps enough to justify his shipwreck: not so much for the pleasure that this fickle, attitudinizing nature afforded him, but for the light that this light cast on words he had heard from the Canon of Digne.

Until now, in fact, he had often asked himself if he was not dreaming. What was happening to him did not usually happen to humans; at best it evoked the novels of childhood.

Like dream-creatures were the ship and the animals he had encountered on it; of the same substance as dreams were the shadows that for three days had enfolded him. On cold consideration he realized also that even the colors he had admired in the garden and in the aviary appeared dazzling to his amazed eyes alone, that in reality they were heightened only thanks to that patina, like an old lute's, that covered every object on the ship, a light that had already enveloped beams and casks of seasoned wood encrusted with paint, pitch, oils. . . . Could not, then, the great theater of celestial crews, which he now thought he saw on the horizon, be likewise a dream?

No, Roberto told himself, the pain that this light now causes my eyes informs me that I am not dreaming: I see. My pupils are suffering because of the storm of atoms that like a great warship bombards me from that shore; for vision is nothing but the encounter of the eye with the powder of matter that strikes it. To be sure, as the Canon had said to him, it is not that objects from a distance send you, as Epicurus had it, perfect simulacra that reveal both the exterior form and the concealed nature. You receive only signals, clues, and you arrive at the conjecture we call vision. But the very fact that Roberto, a moment before, had named through various tropes what he believed he saw, creating in the form of words what the still formless something suggested to him, now confirmed for him that he was indeed seeing. Among the many certainties whose lack he complained of, one alone is present, and it is that all things appear to us as they appear to us, and it is impossible for them to appear otherwise.

Whereby, seeing and being sure he was seeing, Roberto had the unique sureness on which senses and reason can rely: the certainty that he was seeing something; and this something was the sole form of being of which he could speak, for it was nothing but the great theater of the visible arranged in the basin of Space. Which conclusion tells us much about that bizarre century.

He was alive, awake, and an island lay over there, or perhaps a continent. What it was he did not know, for colors depend on the object that affects them, on the light that is refracted in them, and on the eye that fixes them, thus even the most distant land appeared real to his excited and afflicted eyes, in their transient marriage to that light, to those winds, and clouds. Perhaps tomorrow, or in a few hours' time, that land would be different.

What he saw was not just the message the sky was sending him but the result of a friendship among sky, earth, and the position (and the hour, the season, the angle) from which he was observing. Surely, if the ship were anchored along another line crossing the rhombus of the winds, the spectacle would have been different. The sun, the dawn, the sea and land would have been another sun, another dawn, a sea and land twins but distorted. That infinity of worlds of which Saint-Savin spoke to him was to be sought beyond the constellations, in the very center of this bubble of space of which he, pure eye, was now the source of infinite parallaxes.

We must grant Roberto one thing: in all his vicissitudes then, he did not press his speculations beyond that point, whether in metaphysics or in the physics of bodies; though, as we will see, he was to do so later, and go farther than he should have; but here we find him already reflecting that if there could be a single world in which appeared different islands (for many Robertos who observed them from many ships positioned at different degrees of the meridian), then in that single world many Robertos and many Ferrantes could appear and mingle. Perhaps on that day at the castle he had moved, without realizing it, a few yards with respect to the highest hill on the Isla de Hierro and had seen the Universe inhabited by another Roberto, a Roberto not sentenced to the conquest of the outwork beyond the walls or saved by another father who did not kill the polite Spaniard.

But Roberto surely recurred to these considerations rather than confess that the distant body, made and unmade in voluptuous metamorphoses, had become for him the anagram of another body, which he would have liked to possess; and as this land smiled languidly at him, he would have liked to join it and commingle with it, blissful pygmy on the bosom of a lovely giantess.

I do not believe, however, that it was modesty that prompted him to retire, but, rather, the fear of excessive light—and perhaps another summons. He had, in fact, heard the hens announcing a new provision of eggs, and he had the thought of treating himself that evening to a pullet roasted on a spit. But he took the time to trim, with the captain's scissors, his moustache, beard, and hair, all still a castaway's. He had decided to enjoy his shipwreck like a holiday in a country villa, which offered him an extended suite of dawns, daybreaks, and (he savored in anticipation) sunsets.

So less than an hour after the hens' cackling, he went below and immediately realized that while they must have laid their eggs (for their cackling could not have been a lie), there was not an egg to be seen. And, further, all the birds had fresh feed, neatly distributed, still untouched.

Curious as it may seem, his first feeling was of jealousy. Someone else was master of his ship and stole from him those cares and those perquisites to which he was entitled. Losing the world to gain an abandoned vessel only to find that someone else inhabited it seemed to him as unbearable as the fear that his Lady, inaccessible goal of his desire, might become prey to the desire of another.

Then a more rational concern ensued. Just as the world

of his childhood had been inhabited by an Other who preceded him and followed him, clearly the *Daphne* had holds and quarters he did not yet know, where a hidden guest lived, who followed his steps the moment he had gone, or took them a moment before he did.

He ran to hide, too, in his berth, like the African ostrich that, hiding his head, thinks to erase the world.

To reach the quarterdeck he passed the top of a ladder that descended to the hold: what could be hidden down there, considering that on the lower deck he had found a miniature island? Was that the realm of the Intruder? You see, he was already acting towards the ship as towards an object of love which, once it is discovered and you discover you desire it, makes all who had previously possessed it seem usurpers. And it is at this point that Roberto confesses, writing to the Lady, that when he saw her for the first time, and he saw her because his eyes followed another man's gaze addressed to her, he felt the revulsion of one who espies a caterpillar on a rose.

Such an access of jealousy for a vessel redolent of fish, smoke, and faeces might almost provoke a smile, but by now Roberto was becoming lost in a shifting maze where every junction led him back always to a single image. He suffered doubly, because of the Island he did not have and because of the ship that had him—both unattainable, one through its distance, the other through its enigma—and both stood for a beloved who eluded him, blandishing him with promises that he made to himself alone. I cannot otherwise explain this letter in which Roberto pours out embellished laments only to say, basically, that Someone had deprived him of his morning meal.

My Lady,

How can I expect mercy from one who is destroying me? And yet to whom, if not to you, can I confide my suffering, seeking solace, if not in your listening, at least in my unlistened-to words? If love is a medicine that heals every pain with a yet greater pain, can I not perhaps conceive of it as a suffering that kills through excess every other suffering, until it becomes a balm for all save itself? For if ever I saw beauty and wanted it, it was only in the dream of you, and why should I lament that another beauty is for me equally a dream? It would be worse if I made that beauty mine and were sated with it, no longer suffering with the image of you: for scarce balm would I enjoy, and the sickness would increase in the remorse for that infidelity. Better to trust in your image, the more so now that I have glimpsed once again an enemy whose features I do not know and perhaps wish never to know. To ignore this hated phantom, may your beloved phantom sustain me. May love make of me at least an insensitive fragment, a mandragora, a fountain of stone that weeps away every anguish. . . .

But, tormenting himself as he does, Roberto does not become a fountain of stone, and he promptly connects the anguish he is feeling to the other anguish he felt at Casale, this with effects—as we shall see—far more dire.

CHAPTER 7

Pavane Lachryme

THE STORY IS as clear as it is dark. While little skirmishes
followed one another, as in a game of chess where not a move
but the mere expression that accompanies the hint of a move
works to make the opponent renounce a winning opportunity,
Toiras concluded that a more substantial sortie had to be attempted. Clearly the game was being played between spies and
counterspies: at Casale rumor had it that the relief army was
near, led by the king himself, while Monsieur de Montmo-
rency was coming from Asti and the marshals de Créqui and
La Force from Ivrea. Falsehoods, as Roberto learned from the
wrath of Toiras when he received a courier from the north:
in this exchange of messages Toiras informed Richelieu that
he was now without victuals, and the cardinal replied that
Monsieur Agencourt had in due course inspected the storerooms and determined that Casale could hold out excellently
throughout the summer. The army would move in August,
taking advantage along the way of the harvests just reaped.

Roberto was amazed when Toiras instructed some Corsicans to desert and go over to Spinola, reporting that the army
was not expected until September. But then he heard the com-

mander explain to his staff: "If Spinola believes he has time, he will take time to dig his tunnels, and we will have time to dig our own tunnels against his mines. But if he thinks reinforcements are about to arrive, what course is left him? Surely not to confront the French army, because he knows he hasn't sufficient troops; not to wait for it, because then he himself would be besieged; not to return to Milan and prepare a defense of that region, because honor forbids retreat. So the only thing left for him is to conquer Casale at once. But since he cannot do that with a frontal attack, he will have to spend a fortune in purchasing betrayal. And from that moment on, every friend will become for us an enemy. So we will send spies to Spinola, to convince him of the delay of our relief, we will allow him to dig his tunnels for mines where they will not bother us too much, and we will destroy those that are really a threat to us, and we will let him wear himself out in this game. Signor Pozzo, you know the land. Where should we leave him undisturbed and where should we thwart him at all costs?"

Old Pozzo, without looking at the maps (which seemed to him too ornate to be accurate) and pointing with one hand out of the window, explained how in certain areas the terrain was notoriously treacherous, infiltrated by the waters of the river, and there Spinola could dig as long as he pleased and his sappers would choke to death on snails. Whereas in other areas digging tunnels was child's play, and there they should hammer with the artillery and make sorties.

"Very well," said Toiras. "Tomorrow we will force them to move and defend their positions outside the San Carlo bastion, and then we'll surprise them outside the San Giorgio bastion." The game was well prepared, with detailed instructions to all companies. And since Roberto had proved good at writing, Toiras kept him busy from six in the evening till two in the morning, dictating messages, then asked him to sleep, dressed, on a bench outside his room and receive and look over the replies, waking him if there were any contretemps. Which there were, and more than once, between two o'clock and dawn.

The next morning the troops were in readiness on the covered way above the counterscarp and inside the walls. At a signal from Toiras, who was overlooking everything from the citadel, the first contingent, fairly numerous, moved in the deceitful direction: a vanguard of pikemen and musketeers, with a reserve of fifty arquebuses closely following, and after them, shamelessly, an infantry corps of five hundred men and two companies of cavalry. It was a fine parade, and later everyone realized that this was precisely how the Spaniards had taken it.

Roberto saw thirty-five men who, obeying Captain Columbat, scattered and attacked a ditch; the Spanish captain emerged from the barricade and gave them a great salute. Columbat and his men, out of politeness, stopped and responded with equal courtesy. After which, the Spaniards seemed ready to withdraw and the French marked time. Toiras ordered his cannon to fire at the trench from the walls, Columbat took the hint, ordered the attack, the cavalry followed him, assailing the ditch from both flanks, the Spaniards reluctantly resumed their position and were overrun. The French seemed crazed and some, as they fought, shouted the names of friends killed in previous engagements, "This is for Bessières, this for the Bricchetto farm!" Their furor was such that when Columbat wanted to reassemble the squad, he failed. Some of the men were still fiercely striking the fallen, others turned towards the city, shaking earrings, belts, scalps, and other trophies on their raised pikes.

There was no immediate counterattack, and Toiras made

the mistake of considering that an error of the enemy, whereas it was calculated. Believing that the imperials were bent on sending more troops to contain that assault, Toiras goaded them with more cannonades, but the men merely fired into the city, and one ball damaged the church of Sant'Antonio, quite near staff headquarters.

Toiras was content, and ordered another group to move out from the San Giorgio bastion. Only a few companies, but they were commanded by Monsieur de la Grange, lively as a stripling despite his fifty-five years. Sword extended before him, La Grange ordered a charge against a little abandoned church, alongside which the construction of a tunnel was already far advanced; but suddenly, from behind a gulley, the main body of the enemy army appeared, having waited hours for this rendezvous.

"Betrayal!" Toiras shouted, rushing down to the gate, where he ordered La Grange to fall back.

A little later, an ensign of the Pompadour regiment brought before Toiras a boy of Casale, his wrists bound by a cord. He had been caught in a little tower near the castle, signaling with a white cloth to the besiegers. Toiras had him laid on the ground; he stuck the thumb of the boy's right hand into the raised cock of his pistol, pointing the barrel towards the boy's left hand. After putting his own finger on the trigger, Toiras asked, "Et alors?"

The boy quickly realized the bad turn things were taking, and began to talk: the previous evening, towards midnight, outside the church of San Domenico, a certain Captain Gambero had promised him six pistoles, three in advance, if he would do what he then had done, at the moment when the French troops moved from the San Giorgio bastion. Indeed, not having grasped the military art, the boy seemed to demand the outstanding three pistoles, as if Toiras should be pleased with his service. At a certain point he saw Roberto and started shouting that this was the notorious Gambero.

Roberto was stunned, the older Pozzo fell on the slanderous wretch and would have strangled him if some gentlemen of the staff had not restrained him. Toiras immediately pointed out that Roberto had been all night at his side and that, though he was surely a fine-looking youth, nobody could mistake him for a captain. In the meantime others had ascertained that a Captain Gambero really did exist, in the Bassiani regiment, and they haled him, kicking and shoving, into Toiras's presence. Gambero protested his innocence, and in fact the boy prisoner did not recognize him, but Toiras prudently had the officer locked up anyway. Capping the disorder, someone came to report that as La Grange's troops were retreating, a man had fled from the San Giorgio bastion, reaching the Spanish lines, to be greeted with manifestations of joy. Not much could be said about him except that he was young, dressed in the Spanish style with a net over his hair. Roberto thought at once of Ferrante. But what made the deepest impression on him was the suspicion with which the French commanders looked at the Italians in Toiras's train.

"Can one little rascal stop a whole army?" he heard his father ask, nodding towards the retiring French. "Forgive me, dear friend," Pozzo said, addressing Toiras, "but here the idea is growing that, in our parts, we are all a bit like that rogue Gambero, or am I mistaken?" And when Toiras protested esteem and friendship, but in an absent tone, Pozzo went on: "Let it go. It seems to me everyone's shitting his pants, and this business is more than I can take. I've had a bellyful of those lousy Spaniards, and if you don't mind, I'll knock off two or three just to show we can dance the galliard when we have to. And if we feel like it, we don't bow down before anybody, *mordioux!*"

He then rode outside the gate and galloped like a fury, his sword raised, against the enemy host. He obviously didn't mean to put them to flight, but it seemed proper to him to act on his own, just to show the others.

As proof of his courage, it was good; as a military action, very bad. A ball struck his forehead and he slumped onto the withers of his Pagnufli. A second volley rose against the rampart, and Roberto felt a violent blow to the temple, like a stone; he staggered. He had been grazed, but he freed himself from the arms of the man supporting him. Shouting his father's name, he stood erect and glimpsed Pagnufli, bewildered, galloping with his master's lifeless body across the empty field.

Once again Roberto thrust his fingers into his mouth and emitted his whistle; Pagnufli heard and came back towards the walls, but slowly, at a solemn little trot, so as not to unsaddle his rider, no longer imperiously pressing his flanks. The horse came in again, neighing his pavane for his dead master, returning the body to Roberto, who closed those still-wide eyes and wiped clean that face spattered with blood now clotted, while his own blood, alive, striped his cheek.

That shot may have touched a nerve. The next day, as soon as he came out of the cathedral of Sant'Evasio, where Toiras had decreed the solemn obsequies of the lord Pozzo di San Patrizio della Griva, Roberto could hardly tolerate the light of day. Perhaps his eyes were red from tears, but the fact remains that from then on, they continued to ache. Today students of the psyche would say that because his father had entered the shadows, Roberto also wanted to enter the shadows. He knew little of the psyche, but this figure of speech might have appealed to him, in the light—or in the shadows—of what happened later.

I consider that Pozzo died of punctilio, which seems superb to me, but Roberto was unable to appreciate it. All praised his father's heroism to him; he should have borne his bereavement with pride, and here he was sobbing. Recalling how his father had told him that a gentleman must learn to bear, dry-eyed, the blows of adverse fortune, he apologized for his weakness to his parent, who could no longer call him to account, and repeated to himself that this was the first time he had been orphaned. He thought he would become accustomed to the idea, not yet understanding that it is useless to become accustomed to the loss of a father, for it will never happen a second time: might as well leave the wound open.

But to give some sense to what had happened, he could not help falling back, once again, on Ferrante. Ferrante, following him closely, had sold to the enemy the secrets he knew and then shamelessly had joined the adversary's ranks to enjoy the well-earned reward. His father, who had realized this, wanted thus to cleanse the stained escutcheon of the family, and to bathe Roberto in the glow of his own courage, to purify him of that aura of suspicion just cast on him, who was blameless. To make sure his father's death was not in vain, Roberto owed to him the conduct that all at Casale expected of the hero's son.

He could not do otherwise: he found himself now the legitimate lord of La Griva, heir to the family name and possessions, and Toiras no longer dared employ him for little tasks—nor could he call on him for big ones. And so, left alone to sustain his new role of illustrious orphan, Roberto found himself still more alone, lacking even the comfort of action: at the heart of a siege, released from all duties, he asked himself how he should spend his days as a besieged soldier.

CHAPTER 8

The Curious Learning
of the Wits of the Day

ARRESTING FOR A moment the wave of memories, Roberto realized he had evoked his father's death not with the pious intention of keeping open that Philoctetes' wound, but by mere accident, as he was summoning up the specter of Ferrante, elicited by the specter of the Intruder of the *Daphne*. The two now appeared to him as such obvious twins that he decided to eliminate the weaker in order to overpower the stronger.

In the final analysis, he said to himself, during those days of siege did I ever have any other hint of Ferrante? No. What happened then? I was convinced of his nonexistence by Saint-Savin.

Roberto had in fact made friends with Monsieur de Saint-Savin. He had seen him again at the funeral, and had received a demonstration of affection from him. When not prey to wine, Saint-Savin was an accomplished gentleman. Small of stature, nervous, brisk, and though his face was perhaps marked by the Parisian dissipation of which he spoke, he could not have been thirty.

He apologized for his excesses at that supper: not for what

he had said, but for his uncivil way of saying it. He inquired about Monsieur Pozzo, and Roberto was grateful to him for at least feigning interest. Roberto told how his father had taught him what he knew of fencing; Saint-Savin asked various questions, waxed enthusiastic at the mention of a certain thrust, drew his sword right in the middle of a square and insisted that Roberto illustrate the action. Either Saint-Savin already knew it or he was very quick, because he parried it with dexterity, though admitting that it was an invention worthy of the haute école.

In gratitude he indicated only one stratagem of his own to Roberto. He put him on guard, they traded a few feints, he awaited the first attack, suddenly he seemed to slip to the ground, and when Roberto dropped his guard, speechless, Saint-Savin rose as if by miracle and snipped a button off his tunic—showing that he could have wounded him had he thrust harder.

"You like that, my friend?" he said, as Roberto saluted, conceding defeat. "It's the coup de la mouette, the seagull thrust, as it's called. If you go to sea one day, you will observe how those birds dive abruptly as if they were falling, but when they have barely grazed the water, they soar up again with their catch in their beaks. It is a move that requires long practice, and it is not infallible. In my experience, it failed once— for the braggart who invented it. And so he made me a gift both of his life and of his secret. I believe he was sorrier to part with the second than with the first."

They would have gone on at length if a little crowd of civilians had not collected. "Shall we stop?" Roberto said. "I would not want someone to say I have forgotten I am in mourning."

"You honor your father better now," Saint-Savin said, "by remembering his teachings, than you did before, listening to that execrable Latin in church."

"Monsieur de Saint-Savin," Roberto said to him, "are you not afraid of ending up at the stake?"

Saint-Savin frowned for a moment. "When I was more or less your age, I admired a man who had been an older brother to me. Like an ancient philosopher I called him Lucretius, for he, too, was a philosopher, and moreover a priest. He ended up at the stake in Toulouse, but first they tore out his tongue and strangled him. And so you see that if we philosophers are quick of tongue, it is not simply, as that gentleman said the other evening, to give ourselves *bon ton*. It is to put the tongue to good use before they rip it out. Or, rather, jesting aside, to dispel prejudice and to discover the natural cause of Creation."

"So you truly do not believe in God?"

"I find no reason to, in nature. Nor am I the only one. Strabo tells us that the Galicians had no notion of a higher being. When the missionaries wanted to talk of God with the natives of the West Indies, Acosta recounts (and he was also a Jesuit), they could use only the Spanish word *Dios*. You will not believe it, but no suitable term existed in the local language. If the idea of God is unknown in the state of nature, it must then be a human invention. . . . But do not look at me as if I lacked sound principles and were not a faithful servant of my king. A true philosopher never seeks to subvert the order of things. He accepts it. He asks only to be allowed to cultivate the thoughts that comfort a strong spirit. For the others, luckily there are both popes and bishops to restrain the crowd from revolt and crime. The order of the state demands a uniformity of conduct, religion is necessary for the people, and the wise man must sacrifice a part of his independence so that society will remain stable. As for me, I believe I am an upright man: I am loyal to my friends, I do not lie, except when I make a declaration of love, I love knowledge, and they say I write good verses. So the ladies consider me charming. I would like to write romances, which are so much in fashion, but though I think of many, I never sit down to write one. . . ."

"What romances do you think of?"

"Sometimes I look at the Moon, and I imagine that those darker spots are caverns, cities, islands, and the places that shine are those where the sea catches the light of the sun like the glass of a mirror. I would like to tell the stories of their kings, their wars, and their revolutions, or of the unhappiness of lovers up there, who in the course of their nights sigh as they look down at our Earth. I would like to tell about war and friendship among the various parts of the body, the arms that do battle with the feet, and the veins that make love with the arteries, or the bones with the marrow. All the stories I would like to write persecute me. When I am in my chamber, it seems as if they are all around me, like little devils, and while one tugs at my ear, another tweaks my nose, and each says to me, 'Sir, write me, I am beautiful.' Then I realize that an equally beautiful story can be told, inventing an original duel, for example, a man fighting and convincing his adversary to deny God, then running him through so that he dies damned. Stop, Monsieur de la Grive, draw your sword once again, like that, parry, there! You set your heels along the same line: a mistake, for you jeopardize the steadiness of your legs. The head must not be held erect, because the space between the shoulder and the neck exposes an excessive surface to the blows of the adversary. . . ."

"But I protect my head with the sword in my extended hand."

"Wrong, in that position you are weaker. Besides, I opened with the German stance, and you placed yourself in the Italian position. Bad idea. When a ready position has to be countered, you should imitate it as closely as possible. But you have told me nothing of yourself, of your experiences before you turned up in this valley of dust."

More than anyone, an adult able to dazzle with perverse paradoxes can fascinate a youth, who immediately wants to emulate him. Roberto opened his heart to Saint-Savin, and to make himself interesting since the first sixteen years of his life offered scant material—he recounted his obsession with his unknown brother.

"You have read too many romances," Saint-Savin said to him, "and you try to live one. But the purpose of a story is to teach and please at once, and what it teaches is how to recognize the snares of the world."

"And what might I be taught by what you consider the romance of Ferrante?"

"A romance," Saint-Savin explained to him, "must always have at its base a misconception—of a person, action, place, time, circumstance—and from that fundamental misconception episodic misconceptions must arise, developments, digressions, and finally unexpected and pleasant recognitions. By misconception I mean things like a living person's reported death, or one person's being killed in place of another, or a misconception of quantity, as when a woman believes her lover dead and marries another, or of quality, when it is the judgement of the senses that errs, when someone who appears dead is then buried, while actually he is under the influence of a sleeping potion; or else a misconception of relation, as when one man is wrongly believed the murderer of another; or of instrument, as when one man pretends to stab another using a weapon whose tip, while seeming to wound, does not pierce the throat but retracts into the sleeve, pressing a sponge soaked in blood. . . . Not to mention forged letters, assumed voices, messages not delivered in time or delivered to the wrong place or into the wrong hands. And of these stratagems the most celebrated, but too common, is that involving the mistaking of one person for another, the mistake being explained by the Double . . . The Double is a reflection that the character pulls behind himself or that precedes him in every situation. A fine machination, whereby the reader identifies with the main character, sharing his fear of an Enemy Brother. But you see how man is also machine, and it suffices to turn one wheel on the surface and other wheels then turn inside: the brother and the enmity are merely the reflection of the fear that each man has of himself, of the recesses of his own soul, where unconfessed desires lurk, or, as they are saying in Paris, unconscious concepts. For it has been demonstrated that imperceptible thoughts exist, affecting the soul without the soul's being aware of them, clandestine thoughts whose existence is demonstrated by the fact that, however little each of us examines himself, he will not fail to remark that in his heart he bears love or hatred, joy or sorrow, while remaining unable to remember distinctly the thoughts that generated it."

"Then Ferrante——" Roberto began, and Saint-Savin concluded: "Ferrante stands for your fears and your shame. Often men, rather than admit they are the authors of their fate, see this fate as a romance narrated by a fanciful and scoundrel author."

"But what would this parable, which I have unwittingly constructed, mean for me?"

"Who knows? Perhaps you did not love your father as much as you think, you feared the harshness with which he wanted to punish your virtue, so for him you invented a sinner, to punish him not with your own sins but with those of another."

"Sir, you are speaking to a son who is still mourning his most beloved parent! I believe it is a greater sin to teach contempt of fathers than contempt of Our Lord!"

"Come, come, my dear La Grive! The philosopher must have the courage to criticize all the false teachings that have been inculcated in us, and among these is the absurd respect for old age, as if youth were not the greatest good and the highest merit. Tell me frankly: when a young man is capable of conceiving, judging, and acting, is he not perhaps more skillful in managing a family than some sexagenarian dullard, with snow on his head that has frozen his imagination? What we honor as prudence in our elders is simply panic in action. Would you be subject to them when laziness has weakened their muscles, hardened their arteries, evaporated their spirits, and sucked the marrow from their bones? If you adore a woman, is it not perhaps because of her beauty? Do you continue your genuflections after age has made a phantom of that body, now apt to remind you of the imminence of death? And if you behave thus with your mistresses, why should you not do the same with your old men? You will say that this old man is your father and that Heaven promises you long life if you honor him. Who said so? Some ancient Jews who realized they could survive in the desert only by exploiting the fruit of their loins? If you believe that Heaven grants you a single additional day of life because you have been your father's lapdog, you are deceived. Do you believe a respectful greeting that causes the plume of your hat to sweep the ground at your parent's feet can heal a malignant abscess or help you pass a stone? If that were so, physicians would not then prescribe their ghastly potions, but to rid you of the Italian sickness they would instead suggest four bows before supper to your lord father, and a kiss to your lady mother at bedtime. You will say to me that without that father you would not exist, nor he without his, and so on back to Melchizedek. But it is he who owes something to you, not you to him: you pay with many years of weeping for his momentary tickle of pleasure."

"You cannot believe what you are saying."

"Well, no. Hardly ever. But the philosopher is like the poet.

The latter composes ideal letters for an ideal nymph, only to plumb with his words the depths of passion. The philosopher tests the coldness of his gaze, to see how far he can undermine the fortress of bigotry. I would not have your respect for your father diminished, for you say he taught you well. But do not let memory make you melancholy. I see you weeping. . . ."

"Oh, that is not sorrow. It must be my head wound, which has affected my eyes. . . ."

"You should drink coffee."

"Coffee?"

"I swear that in a short while it will be the fashion. It is a panacea. I will procure you some. It dries the cold humors, dispels wind, strengthens the liver, it is the sovereign cure for hydropsy and scabies, it restores the heart, relieves bellyache. Its steam, in fact, is recommended for fluxions of the eyes, buzzing in the ears, catarrh, rheum or heaviness of the nose, as you will. And then bury with your father the cumbersome brother you created for yourself. And, above all, fall in love."

"Love?"

"Better even than coffee. Suffering for a live being, you will allay the pain for a dead one."

"I have never loved a woman," Roberto confessed, blushing.

"I did not say a woman. It could be a man."

"Monsieur de Saint-Savin!" Roberto cried.

"It is obvious you come from the provinces."

At the height of embarrassment, Roberto took his leave, saying his eyes were too painful; and he put an end to that encounter.

To explain to himself all he had heard, he decided that Saint-Savin had been teasing him: as with duelling, Saint-Savin had wanted to show how many artifices they knew in Paris.

And Roberto had indeed come out looking like a provincial. And worse, in taking seriously that talk, he had sinned: which would not have happened if he had taken everything in jest. He drew up a list of the sins he had committed by listening to those many propositions against faith, morals, the state, familial respect. And, thinking of his lapse, he was seized by further anguish: he remembered that, dying, his father had uttered a blasphemy.

CHAPTER 9

The Aristotelian Telescope

AND SO THE next day he went back to pray in the cathedral of Sant'Evasio. He was also seeking refreshment: on that early June afternoon the sun beat down on half-deserted streets—as, at this moment, on the *Daphne,* he felt the heat spreading over the bay, the sides of the ship absorbed it, and the wood seemed red-hot. But then he had felt the need to confess both his own sin and his father's. In the nave he stopped a religious, who first said he was not of this parish but, seeing the look in the youth's eyes, consented and sat in a confessional to hear the penitent.

Padre Emanuele cannot have been very old, perhaps forty, and according to Roberto he was "florid, pink of face, regal, and affable," and Roberto felt encouraged to confide all his sufferings. He told first of all about the paternal blasphemy. Was this sufficient reason to keep his father from reposing now in the bosom of the Father, to make him moan in Hell? The confessor asked a few questions and led Roberto to admit that no matter when old Pozzo died, that event would most likely have occurred while he was taking the name of the Lord in vain: cursing was a bad habit you pick up from the peasants, and the lords of the Monferrato countryside considered it a sign of superiority to speak, in the presence of their equals, with the words of their villeins.

"You see, my son," the confessor concluded, "your father died while he was performing one of those grand & noble Acts through which a Man is said to enter the Paradise of Heroes. Now, while I do not believe such a Paradise exists, for I believe that in the Kingdom of Heaven both Beggars & Sovereigns, Heroes & Cowards live together in holy accord, surely our Almighty King will not have denied His Kingdom to your Father only because his Tongue slipped a bit at a moment when he had a great Enterprise on his mind, and I would dare say that at such moments a similar Ejaculation can even be a way of calling God as Witness & Judge of the great Deed. If you are still tormented, pray for the Soul of your Parent & have some Masses said for him, not so much to persuade the Lord to change his Verdict—as He is not a Vane that turns as the bigots blow—but, rather, for the good of your own Soul."

Roberto told him then about the seditious talk of a friend to whom he had listened, and the priest opened his arms in a disconsolate gesture: "My Son, I know little of Paris, but from what I have heard I learn how many Malefactors, Climbers, Abjurers, Spies, Intriguers exist in that new Sodom. And among them there are False Witnesses, Robbers of Ciboria, Tramplers on Crucifixes, & those who bribe Beggars to make them deny God, & even people who in Mockery have baptized Dogs. . . . And this is considered following the Fashion of the Time. In the Churches they no longer say Prayers, but stroll and laugh, wait in ambush behind columns to entrap Ladies; there is constant Noise even during the Elevation. They claim to philosophize & they assail you with malicious Whys; why has God given Laws to the World, why is Fornication prohibited, why was the Son of God made Flesh; & they distort your every Reply to transform it into a Proof of Atheism. These are the Fine Wits of the Time: Epicureans, Pyrrhonians, Diogenians, & Libertines! So you must not lend your Ear to such Seductions, which come from the Evil One."

As a rule Roberto does not abuse those capital letters in which the writers of his day excelled: but when he attributes sayings to Padre Emanuele, he employs many, as if the priest not only wrote but also spoke them, enforcing his words with special dignity——a sign that he was a man of great and attractive eloquence. And in fact, thanks to those words Roberto felt so relieved that, coming out of the confessional, he chose to linger awhile with the older man. He learned that the priest was a Savoyard Jesuit and surely not a negligible figure, for he was resident in Casale as observer and envoy of the duke of Savoy: a normal mission during a siege in those days.

Padre Emanuele carried out his mission gladly: the gloomy siege afforded him opportunity to conduct in a leisurely way some studies that could not have tolerated the distractions of a capital city like Turin. And, questioned as to his occupation, he said that he, too, like the astronomers, was constructing a telescope.

"You must have heard some talk about that Florentine Astronomer who used the Telescope, or Spyglass, that hyperbole of the eyes, to explain the Universe, & how with the Telescope he saw what the eyes had only imagined. I have great respect for this use of Mechanical Instruments to understand, as they say nowadays, the Res Extensa. But to understand the Res Cogitans, that is to say our way of knowing the World, we can use only another Telescope, the same that Aristotle formerly used, and which is neither a tube nor a lens, but a Weft of Words, Perspicacious Idea, because it is only the gift of Artful Eloquence that allows us to understand this Universe."

Speaking thus, Padre Emanuele led Roberto out of the church and, strolling, they climbed up to the bastion, to a place that was calm that afternoon, as a muffled sound of cannon fire arrived from the opposite side of the city. They had before them the imperial encampments in the distance, but for a long stretch the fields were empty of troops and wagons, and the meadows and hills shone in the spring sun.

"What do you see, my boy?" Padre Emanuele asked Roberto, who, still lacking eloquence, replied, "Fields."

"To be sure, anyone can see Fields down there. But you well know that, depending on the position of the Sun, the color of the Sky, the hour of the day & the season of the year, those fields can appear to you in varying Guise & inspire different Feelings. To the peasant, weary after his work, they appear as Fields & nothing more. Similar is the case of the savage fisherman terrified by those nocturnal Images of Fire sometimes visible in the Sky & frightening to behold; but as soon as the Meteorists, who are also Poets, dare call them Crined Comets, Bearded & Tailed, Goats, Beams, Shields, Torches & Thunderbolts, these figures of speech clarify for you the clever Symbols through which Nature means to speak, as she uses these Images as Hieroglyphics, on the one hand referring to the Signs of the Zodiac & on the other to past Events. And the Fields? You see how much you can say of Fields & how, as you speak, you see & comprehend more: Favonius blows, the Earth opens, the Nightingales weep, the leaf-crowned Trees swagger, & you discover the wondrous genius of the Fields in the variety of their strains of Grasses nourished by the Streams that play in happy puerility. The festive Fields rejoice with jaunty merriment, at the appearance of the Sun they open their countenance & in them you observe the arc of a smile, & they celebrate the return of the Star, intoxicated with the gentle Austral kisses & laughter on the Earth itself that expands in dumb Happiness, & the matutinal warmth so fills them with Joy that they shed tears of Dew. Crowned with Flowers, the Fields submit to their Genius & compose subtle Hyperboles of Rainbows. But their Youth soon learns it must hasten to death, their laughter is troubled by a sudden pallor, the sky fades & lingering Zephyr already sighs over a languishing Earth, so that on the arrival of the winter heavens' first frowns, the Fields sadden & reveal skeletons of Frost. There, my son: if you had said simply that the Fields are pretty, you would have done nothing but depict for me their greening— which I already know of—but if you say the Fields laugh, you show me the Earth as Animate & reciprocally I will learn to observe in human Countenances all the refinements that I have perceived in the fields. . . . And this is the office of the supreme Figure of all: Metaphor. If Genius, & therefore Learning, consists in connecting remote Notions & finding Similitude in things dissimilar, then Metaphor, the most acute and farfetched among Tropes, is the only one capable of producing Wonder, which gives birth to Pleasure, as do changes of scene in the theater. And if the Pleasure produced by Figures derives from learning new things without effort & many things in small volume, then Metaphor, setting our mind to flying betwixt one Genus & another, allows us to discern in a single Word more than one Object."

"But one must know how to invent metaphors, which is not something for a rustic like me, who in all his life has seen fields only as the place for shooting at birds. . . ."

"You are a Gentle Man, & it will not be long before you become what in Paris they call an Honest Man, skilled in verbal joust as in that of the sword. And knowing how to conceive Metaphors, & thus to see a World immensely more various than it appears to the uneducated, is an Art that is learned. For, I must tell you, in this world where today all lose their minds over many & wondrous Machines—some of which, alas, you can see also in this Siege—I construct Aristotelian Machines, that allow anyone to see with Words. . . ."

In the days that followed, Roberto made the acquaintance of Signor della Saletta, who represented the city fathers in their dealings with Toiras. The commander was complaining, Roberto had heard, about the Casalesi, in whose loyalty he had little faith. "Do they not understand," Toiras said, irritated, "that even in times of peace Casale is in no condition to allow one simple foot-soldier or a mere basket of victuals to enter without asking leave of the Spanish ministers? That the protection of the French is the city's only guarantee of being respected?" But, now, from Signor della Saletta Roberto learned that Casale was not exactly comfortable with the dukes of Mantua either. Gonzaga policy had always been to put down any Casale opposition, and for sixty years the city had suffered the progressive reduction of many privileges.

"You understand, Signor della Griva?" Saletta said. "First we complained of too many taxes, and now we are bearing the expense of maintaining the garrison. We do not love having the Spanish in our midst, but are we expected really to love the French? Are we dying for our own sake, or for theirs?"

"And for whom did my father die?" Roberto asked. Signor della Saletta was unable to answer him.

Weary of political talk, Roberto went back to see Padre Emanuele a few days later, in the convent where he was staying. There, they directed Roberto not to a cell but an apartment reserved for the priest under the arches of a silent cloister. He found Padre Emanuele conversing with two gentlemen, one sumptuously dressed in purple with gold braid, a cloak with gilded trimming and lined with short fur, a doublet edged with a crocheted red stripe and a ribbon of little gems. Padre Emanuele introduced him as the ensign Don Gaspar de Salazar, but from his haughty tone and the style of his moustache and hair Roberto had already identified him as a gentleman from the enemy army. The other visitor was Signor della Saletta. For a moment Roberto suspected he had fallen into a den of spies, then he realized, as I realize on this occasion, that the etiquette of sieges allowed a representative of the besiegers access to the besieged city for meetings and negotiations, just as Signor della Saletta had free access to Spinola's camp.

Padre Emanuele said that he was just preparing to show the two guests his Aristotelian Machine, and he led all three into a room where the strangest imaginable piece of furniture was standing—nor am I sure I can reconstruct its form exactly from Roberto's description of it to his Lady, as it was surely something never seen before or since.

The base consisted of a great chest or case whose front held eighty-one drawers—nine horizontal rows by nine vertical, each row in both directions identified by a carved letter (BCDEFGHIK). On the top of the chest, to the left stood a lectern on which a great volume was placed, a manuscript with illuminated initials. To the right of the lectern were three concentric cylinders of decreasing length and increasing breadth (the shortest being the most capacious, designed to contain the two longer ones); a crank at one side could then, through inertia, make them turn, one inside the other, at different speeds according to their weight. Each cylinder had incised at its left margin the same nine letters that marked the drawers. One turn of the crank was enough to make the cylinders revolve independently of one another, and when they stopped, one could read triads of letters aligned at random, such as CBD, KFE, or BGH.

Padre Emanuele set about explaining the concept that governed his Machine.

"As the Philosopher has taught us, Genius is simply the ability to perceive objects under ten Categories, and these are Substance, Quantity, Quality, Relation, Action, Affection, Position, Time, Place & State. The substances are the very subject of all reasoning & their ingenious Correlatives must be predicated. What the Substances are is noted in this book under the letter A, nor would my whole life suffice to make a complete List of them. In any case I have already collected several Thousands, taking them from the books of Poets and of wise men, and from that wondrous Regestus that is the *Fabric of the World* of Francesco Alunno. Thus among the Substances we may place, under Supreme Being: Divine Persons, Ideas, Gods of Fable, greater, middle & lesser, Celestial Deities, and the Aerial, Marine, Terrestrial & Infernal, the deified Heroes, Angels, Demons, Sprites, the Heavens and the wandering Stars, celestial Signs and Constellations, the Zodiac, the Circles & Spheres, the Elements, Vapors, Exhalations, and then—making no attempt to mention everything—Subterranean Fires & Sparks, Meteors, Seas, Rivers, Springs & Lakes & Cliffs. . . . And so on and so on through the Artificial Substances, with the works of each Art, Books, Pens, Inks, Globes, Compasses, Squares, Palaces, Temples & Hovels, Shields, Swords, Drums, Paintings, Brushes, Statues, Axes & Saws, and finally the Metaphysical Substances such as Genus, Species, Properties & Accidentals & similar Notions."

He pointed now to the drawers in his construction, and opening them, he showed how each contained square sheets of very thick parchment, the kind used for binding books, aligned in alphabetical order: "I must tell you, each vertical row refers, from B to K, to one of the other nine Categories, and for each of them one of the nine drawers has gathered families of Members. Verbi gratia, for Quantity is recorded the family of the Quantity of Volume, whose Members comprise the Small, the Great, the Long or the Short; or the family of

Numeral Quantity, whose members are Naught, One, Two &c., and Many or Few. Under Quality you will find the family of the qualities associated with seeing, such as Visible, Invisible, Beautiful, Deformed, Clear, Obscure; or with Smell, such as Aroma & Stink; or the Qualities of Affection, such as Happiness & Sadness; and so on for each category. And each sheet represents a Member. I then consider all the things affected by it. Is that clear?"

All nodded with awe, and the priest continued. "Now we will open at random the great Book of Substances, and we will pick any one at all. . . . Here: Dwarf. What could we say, before initiating any scholarly discussion, of the Dwarf?"

"Que es pequeño, little, petit," ventured don Gaspar de Salazar, "y que es feo, e infeliz, y ridículo . . ."

"True," Padre Emanuele granted, "but still I do not know what to choose, and if I were required to speak not of a Dwarf but rather, say, of Corals, could I be sure of finding equally salient features so promptly? And besides, Smallness has to do with Quantity, Ugliness with Quality, and where then should I begin? No, better to trust in Fortune, whose Ministers my Cylinders are. Now I make them move & I obtain, as random dictates, the triad BBB. B in the first Position is Quantity, B in the second Position bids me look along the line of Quantity, in the drawer of Volume, and there, at the very beginning of the B sequence, I find Small. And in this sheet devoted to Small I find that the Angel is small, as it stands on a pin, & so is the Pole small, the fixed point of the Sphere, & among elementary small things are the Spark, the Drop of water & the Scruple of Stone, & the Atom, of which, according to Democritus, all things are composed. In Human Things here is the Embryo, the Pupil, the Astragal; for Animals the Ant & the Flea, for Plants the Twig, the Mustard Seed & the Crumb; for the Mathematical sciences the Minimum Quod Sic, the

Letter I, the book bound in 16°, or the Apothecary's Dram; for Architecture the Coffer or the Pivot; or for Fables the Psychapax general of Mice against the Frogs & the Myrmidons born of Anto. . . . But we must stop here, for I could already call our Dwarf a Coffer of Nature, Puppet of a Youth, Crumb of a Man. And pray note that if we try turning the Cylinders again and obtain instead—here we are—CBF, the letter C would refer me to Quality, the B would send me to look for my Members in the drawer of that which affects Sight, and then the letter F would have me encounter as Member the being Invisible. And among the Invisible Things I would find —ah, wondrous conjunction—the Atom & the Point, which would allow me now to define my Dwarf as Atom of Man or Point of Flesh."

Padre Emanuele turned his cylinders and searched through his drawers, fast as a conjuror, so the metaphors seemed to arise for him as if by enchantment, without anyone's noticing the mechanical gasping that produced them. But he was still not satisfied.

"Gentlemen," he continued, "the Ingenious Metaphor has to be far more complex! Every Thing that I have found so far must be analyzed in its turn from the aspect of the ten Categories, and as my Book explains, if we consider a Thing that depends on Quality, we should see if it is visible & and at what distance, what Deformity or Beauty it has & what Color; how much Sound, how much Odor, how much Taste; if it is sensible or tactile, if it is rarefied or dense, hot or cold, & of what Form, what Affection, Love, Art, Learning, Health, Infirmity, & if any Science of it exists. And I call these questions Particles. Now I know that our first essay has led us to deal with Quantity, which includes Smallness among its Members. Now I turn the cylinders again and I obtain the triad BKD. The letter B, we have already determined, must refer to Quantity; if I consult my book, it tells me that the first Particle apt to express a Small Thing is to establish With What it is Measured. If I consult the book to find to what Measure refers, it sends me back to the Quantity drawer, under the Family of Quantities in General. I go to the page for Measure & there choose the thing K, which is the Measure of the Geometric Finger. And here I would be able to compose a quite clever Definition, as, for example, that wanting to measure that Puppet of Youths, that Atom of Man, a Geometric Finger would be an Immeasurable Measure, which, uniting to Metaphor also Hyperbole, tells me much of the Misfortune & Ridiculousness of the Dwarf."

"What a marvel," Signor della Saletta said, "but, in the second triad obtained, you have not yet used the last letter, the D. . . ."

"I expected no less of your perception, sir," Padre Emanuele said smugly, "but you have touched the Wonderful Point of my invention! This letter is left over (and I could discard it if it bored me, or if I considered I had already achieved my aim); it allows me to resume my search! This D allows me to begin again the cycle of the Particles, looking into the category of State (exempli gratia, what garb befits them, or if they can serve as emblem of something), & from there start over, as I did earlier with Quantity, turning the cylinders again, using the first two letters & retaining the third for yet another trial, and so on ad infinitum, for millions of Possible Conjugations, though some may seem more clever than others, and it will be my Wisdom that distinguishes those more apt to generate Amazement. But I would not lie to you, Gentlemen, I had not chosen Dwarf at random; only last night I applied myself with the greatest care to deriving the maximum possible advantage from this Substance."

He waved a page and began to read the series of definitions

with which he was suffocating his poor dwarf, a little man
shorter than his name: embryo, fragment of homunculus,
such that the corpuscles that arrive with the light from the
window seem much greater, a body that with millions of his
similars could tell the hours through the neck of an hourglass,
the complection in which the foot is close to the head, the
carnal appendage that begins where it ends, the line that clots
in a point, the tip of a needle, a subject to be spoken to with
caution for fear that your breath would blow it away, a substance so small that it is not penetrable by color, a mustard
spark, a bodikin that has nothing more or less than what it
never had, matter without form, body without body, pure
being of reason, invention of wit so minute that no blow could
ever find it in order to wound it, able to escape through every
fissure and feed for a year on a single barley seed, to be so
epitomized that there is never any telling whether it is seated,
prone, or erect, capable of drowning in a snail's shell, seed,
granule, grape, dot of i, mathematical individual with arithmetical nothing. . . .

And he would have continued, for he possessed the material, if those present had not stopped him with applause.

CHAPTER 10

Geography and Hydrography Reformed

ROBERTO UNDERSTOOD NOW that Padre Emanuele behaved essentially as if he were a follower of Democritus or of Epicurus: he accumulated atoms of concepts and composed them in various guises to make many objects of them. And as the Canon sustained that a world made of atoms was not in conflict with the idea of a divinity who disposed them according to reason, so Padre Emanuele from that powder of concepts accepted only the truly acute compositions. Perhaps he would have done the same if he had taken up creating scenes for the theater: do not playwrights derive improbable and clever events from passages of probable but insipid things, so that they may be satisfied with unexpected hircocervi of action?

And if this was so, did it not perhaps happen that in the concurrence of circumstances creating both his shipwreck and the condition in which he found himself on the *Daphne*—the smallest detail being lifelike: the reek and creak of the hull, the smell of the plants, the cries of the birds—all collaborated in forming the impression of a presence that was nothing but the effect of a phantasmagory perceived only by the mind, like the laughter of the fields and the tears of dew? So the phantom of a hidden intruder was a composition of atoms of action, like that of the lost brother, both formed with fragments of his own countenance and of his desires or thoughts?

And as he began to hear against the panes a light rain cooling the noonday heat, he said to himself: It is only natural, I—and no other—am the one who has climbed aboard this ship as an intruder, I disturb this silence with my footsteps, and so it is that, as if afraid of having violated another's sanctum, I constructed another self who roams beneath the same decks. What evidence have I of his existence? A few drops of water on the leaves? But is it not possible that, as it is raining now, it rained last night, however briefly? The feed? But could not the birds, pecking at what was already there, have scattered it, making me think someone had thrown new grain? The absence of eggs? Why, only yesterday I saw a gyrfalcon devour a flying mouse! I am populating a hold I have not yet visited, and I am doing this perhaps for reassurance, as I am terrified at finding myself abandoned between sky and sea. Signor Roberto della Griva, he repeated to himself, you are alone and you may remain alone until the end of your days, and this end may also be near. The food on board is plentiful, but for a period of weeks, not months. Go therefore and set on the deck some vessel to collect all the rainwater you can, and learn to fish from the bulwarks, tolerating the sun. And one of these days you must find a way to reach the Island, and live there as its sole inhabitant. This is what you should be thinking about, not stories of Intruders and Ferrantes.

Braving the light, now filtered through clouds, he collected some empty barrels and arranged them on the bridge. In performing this task, he realized he was still very weak. He went below again, lavished the animals with food (perhaps so that no one else would be tempted to do it in his stead), and once again gave up the idea of descending still farther. He came back, spent a few hours lying down, while the rain showed no sign of letting up. There were gusts of wind, and for the first time he realized that he was in a floating house, which rocked like a cradle, as a slamming of doors enlivened the considerable bulk of that wooden womb.

He savored this metaphor and wondered how Padre Emanuele would have read the ship as a source of Enigmatic Devices. Then he thought of the Island and defined it as unattainable proximity. This fine conceit showed him, for the second time that day, the dissimilar similitude between the Island and the Lady, and he stayed awake into the night to pen the pages I have drawn on for this chapter.

The *Daphne* pitched all night, but its motion, like the waves of the bay, grew calm at first dawn. Through the window Roberto saw the signs of a cold but clear morning. Remembering those Hyperboles of the Eyes recalled the day before, he reminded himself that he could observe the shore through the spyglass he had seen in the adjoining cabin; the lens itself and the narrow field would temper the sun's glare.

He set the instrument on the frame of a window in the gallery and boldly gazed at the farthest confine of the bay. The Island seemed pale, its peak tufted with a patch of wool. As he had learned on the *Amaryllis,* ocean islands retain the humidity of the Trades and condense it in cloudy puffs, so that sailors often recognize the presence of land before they can see the shores, from the clumps of the airy element that it holds as if they were anchored there.

It had been Dr. Byrd who told him about the so-called Trade Winds, in French *les alisées.* Over those seas there are great winds that decree hurricanes and calms, but the Trades joke with them, capricious winds whose movement is depicted on maps in the form of a dance of curves and currents, raving carols and graceful deviations. They penetrate the course of the greater winds and disrupt them, cut across them, race with them. They are lizards that dart along unexpected paths, as if in the Sea of the Contrary only the rules of art count, not those of nature. They have the form of artful things, and resemble not the harmonious arrangements of Nature, such as snow or crystal, but, rather, those volutes that architects impose on domes, capitals, and columns.

That this was a sea of artifice Roberto had long suspected, and it explained why down here cosmographers had always imagined creatures contrary to nature, who walked with their feet in the air.

To be sure, the artists of the courts of Europe, who built grottoes encrusted with lapis lazuli, fountains operated by secret pumps, had not inspired nature in her invention of the lands of those seas; any more than it was the nature of the Unknown Pole that inspired those artists. The fact is, Roberto said to himself, both Art and Nature are fond of machination, and that is simply what the atoms themselves do when they aggregate in this way or in another. Is there any more artificed wonder than the tortoise, work of a goldsmith of thousands and thousands of years past, who fashioned this Achilles' shield patiently nielloed, imprisoning a serpent with its feet?

At home, he continued his musing, everything that is vegetal life has the fragility of a leaf with its veins and of the flower that lasts the space of a morning; whereas here the vegetal is like leather, a thick and oily matter, a scaly sheath prepared to resist the rays of mad suns. Every leaf—in these lands where the wild inhabitants surely do not know the art of metals or of clays—could become instrument, blade, goblet, spatula, and the petals of the flowers are of lacquer. Everything vegetal here is strong, while everything animal is weak, to judge by the birds I have seen, spun from varicolored glass, while at home we have the strength of the horse, the stubborn sturdiness of the ox. . . .

And what of fruits? At home the complexion of the apple, ruddy with health, denotes its friendly taste, whereas the livid mushroom betrays its hidden venom. Here, on the contrary, as I saw yesterday and during the voyage of the *Amaryllis,* there is the witty play of opposites: the mortuary white of one fruit guarantees vivid sweetness, whereas the more russet fruits may secrete lethal philters.

With the spyglass he studied the shore and glimpsed between land and sea some climbing roots that seemed to leap towards the open sky, and clumps of oblong fruits that revealed their treacly ripeness by appearing as unripe berries. And he recognized on some other palms coconuts yellow as summer melons, whereas he knew they would proclaim their maturity by turning the color of dead earth.

So to live in this terrestrial Beyond—he had to remember, if he was to come to terms with its nature—he should proceed in the direction opposite to his instinct, for instinct was probably a discovery of the first giants, who tried to adapt themselves to the nature of the other side of the globe. Believing the most natural nature was that to which they had become adapted, they thought nature naturally born to adapt herself to them. Hence they were sure the sun was small, as it seemed to them, whereas certain leaves of grass were immense, if they looked at them through eyes close to the ground.

To live in the Antipodes, then, means reconstructing instinct, knowing how to make a marvel nature and nature a marvel, to learn how unstable the world is, which in one half follows certain laws, and in the other half the opposite of those laws.

He heard again the birds waking, over there, and—unlike the first day—he realized how artful those songs sounded if compared to the chirping of his native land: whistles, gurgles, crackles, grumblings, cluckings, whimperings, muffled musket shots, whole chromatic scales of pecking; and sometimes he heard something like a croaking of frogs squatting among the leaves of the trees, in Homeric parley.

The spyglass allowed him to see spindles, feathery bullets, black shudders or other shudders of indistinct hue, who flung themselves from a taller tree aiming at the ground with the insanity of an Icarus eager to hasten his own destruction. Suddenly it seemed to him even that one tree, perhaps a kumquat from China, shot one of its fruits into the air, a skein of bright crocus that quickly vanished from the round eye of the glass. He convinced himself it was the effect of a glint and gave it no further thought, or so at least he believed. We shall see later that when it came to unconscious concepts, Saint-Savin was right.

He thought those birds of unnatural nature were the emblem of the Parisian coteries he had left behind many months past. In this universe without humans, where, if not the only living creatures, certainly the only speaking creatures were the birds, he found himself as in that salon where, on first entering, he had caught only a vague chattering in an unknown language, whose scent he shyly perceived—though I would say he must have finally absorbed the sense of that scent, otherwise he would not have been able to reason about it as he now did. But, remembering that it was there he had met the Lady—and hence if one place stood supreme above all others, it was there and not here—he concluded that they did not there imitate the birds of the Island, but, rather, here on the Island the animals tried to equal that most human Language of Birds.

Thinking of the Lady and of her distance, which the day before he had compared to the insuperable distance to the land westward, he looked once more at the Island, of which the spyglass revealed to him only wan and circumscribed hints, yet like those images seen in convex mirrors, which, reflecting a single side of a small room, suggest a spherical cosmos, infinite and stupefying.

How would the Island seem to him if he were to reach it one day? To judge by the landscape he saw from his vantage-point, and by the specimens which he had found on the ship, was it perhaps the Eden where milk and honey flow in streams, amid abundant trophies of fruit and flocks of meek animals? What more, in those islands of the opposing south, were the brave men seeking as they navigated there, defying the tempests of an illusory pacific ocean? Was this not what the Cardinal had wanted, in despatching him on a mission to discover the secret of the *Amaryllis:* the possibility of taking the lilies of France to a Terra Incognita that would finally renew the offerings of a vale untainted by the sin of Babel or by the Flood or by Adam's Fall? The human beings there must be loyal, dark of skin but pure of heart, caring nothing for the mountains of gold and the balms of which they were the heedless custodians.

But if this was so, would he not be repeating the error of the first sinner if he chose to violate the virginity of the Island? Perhaps Providence had rightly wanted him to be a chaste witness to a beauty that he should never disturb. Was this not the manifestation of the most perfect love, such as he professed to his Lady, loving from afar, renouncing the pride of dominion? Is aspiration to conquest love? If the Island were to be one with the object of his love, he owed the same nicety to it that he had shown to her. The same frenzied jealousy he had felt every time he feared another's eye threatened that sanctuary of reluctance was not to be interpreted as a claim to any right of his own, no, it was a denial of rights to anyone, a duty his love imposed on him, the guardian of that Graal. And to that same chastity he must feel bound with regard to the Island: the more he wished it to be rich in promises, the less he should want to touch it. Far from the Lady, far from the Island, he should only speak of them, wanting them immaculate as long as they could keep themselves immaculate, touched only by the caress of the elements. If there was beauty somewhere, its purpose was to remain purposeless.

Was the Island he saw really like that? Who was encouraging him to decipher the hieroglyph in this way? It was known that from the time of the first voyages to these islands, situated vaguely on the maps, mutineers were abandoned there, and the islands became prisons with bars of air, in which the condemned were their own jailers, punishing one another reciprocally. Not to arrive there, not to discover the secret, was, more than a duty, a right, a reprieve from endless horrors.

Or perhaps not. The only reality of the Island was that in its center stood, tempting in delicate hues, the Tree of Oblivion, whose fruit, if Roberto ate it, could give him peace.

To disremember. So he spent the day, apparently slothful but highly energetic in his effort to become tabula rasa. And, as happens to those who set themselves to forgetting, the more effort he made, the more his memory was fired.

He tried to put into practice all the suggestions he had formerly heard. He imagined himself in a room crammed with objects that reminded him of something: his Lady's veil, the pages where he had made her image present through his laments on her absence, the contents of the palace where he met her; and he pictured himself throwing all those things out of the window, until the room (and, with it, his mind) became bare and empty. He made immense efforts, dragging to the windowsill crockery, tapestries, cupboards, chairs, and panoplies, but—contrary to what he had been told—as he gradually wore himself out in this labor, the figure of the Lady was multiplied, and from different corners she followed him in his spasms with a sly smile.

Thus, passing the day in dragging furniture, he forgot nothing. Quite the opposite. These were days when he thought of his own past, his eyes staring at the one scene he had before him, that of the *Daphne;* and the *Daphne* was transformed into a Theater of Memory, as such theaters were conceived in his day, where every feature recalled to him an episode, remote or recent, in his story: the bowsprit, his arrival after the wreck, when he realized he would never see his beloved again; the furled sails, his long hours of staring at them and dreaming of her lost, lost; the gallery, from which he explored the distant Island, and Her distance. . . . But he had dedicated to her so many meditations that, as long as he remained there, every corner of that seagoing house would remind him, moment by moment, of everything he wanted to forget.

He realized this truth as he came out on deck to seek distraction in the wind. This was his forest, where he went as unhappy lovers go into forests; here was his invented nature, plants planed by the shipwrights of Antwerp, rivers of rough canvas in the wind, tarred caverns, astrolabe-stars. And as a lover, revisiting a place, recognizes the beloved in every flower, in every rustling of leaves, every path, here, now, he could die of love, caressing the mouth of a cannon. . . .

Did poets not celebrate their lady, praising her lips of ruby, her eyes of coal, her breasts of marble, her heart of diamond? Then he, too—locked in that mine of now-fossil firs—would have only mineral passions, hawsers beringed with knots would seem to him her locks, shining bosses her forgotten eyes, the sequence of eaves her teeth dripping scented saliva, a creaking capstan her neck adorned with necklaces of hemp, and he would find peace in the illusion that he had loved the work of a master of automata.

Then he regretted his hardness in imagining her hardness; he told himself that in petrifying her features he was petrifying his desire—which, on the contrary, he wanted living and unsatisfied—and, as evening fell, he turned his eyes to the broad conch of the sky dotted with undecipherable constellations. Only in contemplating celestial bodies could he think the celestial thoughts proper to one who, by celestial decree, was sentenced to love the most celestial of human creatures.

The queen of the forest, who in snowy dress whitens the woods and silvers the countryside, had not yet appeared above the peak of the Island, covered in mourning. The rest of the sky was ablaze and visible, and, at its southwestern extremity, almost level with the sea beyond the greater land, he discerned a clot of stars that Dr. Byrd had taught him to recognize: it was the Southern Cross. And, in the words of a forgotten poet, some of whose verses his Carmelite tutor had made him memorize, Roberto recalled a vision that had fascinated his childhood, that of a pilgrim in the realms of the Beyond who, emerging into that same Terra Incognita, saw those four stars, never glimpsed before unless by the first (and last) inhabitants of the Earthly Paradise.

CHAPTER 11

The Art of Prudence

WAS HE SEEING them because he had truly been shipwrecked at the edge of the Garden of Eden, or was it because he had emerged from the belly of the ship as from a hellish funnel? Both perhaps. That shipwreck, restoring him to the spectacle of another nature, had rescued him from the Hell of the World which he had entered, losing the illusions of boyhood, in the Casale days.

He was still there when, having seen history now as a place rich in whims and incomprehensible plots for Reasons of State, he learned from Saint-Savin how treacherous was the great machine of the world, plagued by the iniquities of Chance. In a few days his adolescent dream of heroic feats was ended, and from Padre Emanuele he had learned that one should be excited by Heroic Enterprises—and that a life can be well spent not in fighting a giant but in giving too many names to a dwarf.

Leaving the convent, he accompanied Signor della Saletta, who in turn was accompanying Señor de Salazar beyond the walls. And to reach what Salazar called Puerta de Estopa, they walked along the ramparts for a while.

The two gentlemen were praising Padre Emanuele's machine, and Roberto ingenuously asked how all that knowledge could affect the destiny of a siege.

Señor de Salazar laughed. "My young friend," he said, "we are all here, serving different monarchs, in order to resolve this war as justice and honor dictate. But the days are long gone when the sword could alter the course of the stars. The time is past when gentlemen created kings; now it is kings who create gentlemen. Now all the gentlemen you can see down there," and he pointed to the Spanish tents, "and down here," and he indicated the French camps, "are engaged in this war in order to return to their natural setting, which is the court, and at court, my friend, no one competes any longer to equal the king in merit, but only to gain his favor. Today in Madrid you see gentlemen who have never drawn their sword, and they never leave the city: for to cover themselves with dust on the field of glory they would have to abandon the city to the hands of moneyed burghers and a noblesse de robe that nowadays even a monarch holds in great esteem. The warrior may abandon valor only to follow prudence."

"Prudence?" Roberto asked.

Salazar suggested he look over the plain. The two sides were engaged in listless skirmishes, and clouds of dust could be seen rising from the mouths of the tunnels where the cannonballs fell. To the northwest the imperials were pushing a mantelet: a sturdy cart, its sides armed with scythes, while the front was an oak wall reinforced with studded bars of iron. In that wall there were slits from which mortars extended, and colubrines, and arquebuses, and from the side you could see the Landsknechts barricaded inside. Bristling with muzzles in front and with blades on the flanks, chains creaking, the machine emitted occasional puffs of smoke from one of its mouths. The enemy clearly did not intend to employ it immediately, for it was a device to be brought beneath the walls when the mines had done their work; but it was equally clear that it was being displayed now to terrify the besieged.

"You see," Salazar said, "the war will be decided by machines, whether armored wagons or mine-tunnels, as may be. Some of our fine companions, on both sides, who have bared their breast to the enemy, unless they died by mistake, acted as they did not to conquer but to win a reputation to be exploited on their return to court. The most valiant among them were wise enough to choose enterprises that attracted attention, but only after they had calculated the balance between what they risked and what they stood to gain. . . ."

"My father—" said Roberto, orphan of a hero who had calculated nothing. Salazar interrupted him. "Your father was, in fact, a man in the old style. Believe me, I mourn him; but can it still be worthwhile to perform a brave deed when people will talk more of a fine retreat than of a bold attack? Have you not observed, just now, a war machine ready to resolve the fate of a siege more swiftly than swords did in their day? And have not swords, these many years, yielded to arquebuses? We still wear a cuirass, but a pikeman could learn in a day how to pierce the cuirass of the great Bayard."

"Then what does a gentleman have left?"

"Wisdom, Signor della Griva. Success no longer has the color of the sun, but grows in the light of the moon, and no one has ever said that this second luminary was displeasing to the creator of all things. Jesus himself meditated, in the garden of Olivet, at night."

"But then he came to a decision inspired by the most heroic of virtues, and without prudence. . . ."

"But we are not the firstborn Son of the Eternal One, we are the children of our century. When this siege ends, if a machine has not taken your life, what will you do, Signor della Griva? Will you perhaps return to your lands, where no one will give you an opportunity to prove yourself worthy of your father? After a few days of association with Parisian gentlemen, you already seem won over by their ways. You will want to try your fortune in the great city, and you well know that it is there that you must make use of that halo of bravery that your long inaction among these walls will have gained you. You too will seek your fortune, and you must be keen in obtaining it. If here you have learned to dodge a musket ball, there you must learn to elude envy, jealousy, greed, using those same weapons to combat your adversaries, namely, everyone. Hear me out. For half an hour you have been interrupting me to say what you think and, under the guise of questioning me, you would show me I am mistaken. Never do this again, especially with the powerful. Occasions will arise when confidence in your own perspicacity and the impulse to tell the truth will enable you to give sound advice to someone of higher station. Never do it. Every victory produces hatred in the vanquished, and if the victory is over one's own master, then it is foolish or harmful. Princes wish to be assisted, not outstripped. But you must be prudent also with your equals. Do not humiliate them by your merits. Never speak of yourself: either you will praise yourself, which is vanity, or you will denigrate yourself, which is stupidity. Rather, let others discover in you some venial sin, which envy can gnaw on without doing you too much harm. Be much but seem little. The ostrich never aspires to fly, and thus risk an exemplary fall: he allows the beauty of his feathers to be revealed gradually. And above all, if you have passions, never display them, however noble they may appear. Not everyone must be granted access to your heart. A prudent, cautious silence is the cabinet of wisdom."

"Sir, you are telling me that a gentleman's first duty is to learn simulation!"

Signor della Saletta intervened with a smile. "Come, my dear Roberto, Señor de Salazar is not saying the wise man must simulate. He is suggesting, if I have understood rightly, that the wise man must learn to dissimulate. It is a virtue above virtue to dissimulate virtue. Señor de Salazar is teaching you a prudent way of being virtuous, or how to be virtuous prudently. When the first man opened his eyes and discovered he was naked, he tried to conceal himself even from the sight of his Maker: so diligence in hiding was born almost when the world was born. Dissimulating means drawing a veil composed of honest shadows, which does not constitute falsehood but allows truth some respite. The rose seems beautiful because at first sight it dissimulates, pretending to be so fleeting, and although it is frequently said of mortal beauty that it seems not of this earth, it is simply a corpse dissimulated by the favor of youth. In this life it is not always best to be open-hearted, and the truths that mean most to us must always be uttered by halves. Dissimulation is not fraud. It is an effort not to show things as they are. And it is a difficult effort: when we excel, others must not recognize our excellence. If someone were to become famous for his ability to disguise himself, as actors do, all would know that he is not what he pretends to be. But concerning the true, excellent dissimulators, who have existed and exist still, we have no information."

"And note further," added Señor de Salazar, "that while you are being invited to dissimulate, you are not invited to remain dumb as a fool. On the contrary. You will learn to do with a clever word what you cannot do with open speech: to move in a world that favors appearance, and with all the rapidity of eloquence to be the weaver of words of silk. If arrows can pierce the body, words can pierce the soul. Make natural in yourself what in Padre Emanuele's machine is mechanical art."

"But, sir," Roberto said, "Padre Emanuele's machine seems to me an image of Genius, which does not aim at striking or seducing but at discovering and revealing connections between things, and therefore becoming a new instrument of truth."

"This is for philosophers. But for fools use Genius to awe, and you will earn acceptance. Men love to be awed. If your fate and your fortune are decided not on the field but in the halls of the court, a good point scored in conversation will be more fruitful than a victorious attack in battle. The prudent man with an elegant phrase extricates himself from any complication, and can use his tongue with the lightness of a feather. Most things can be paid for with words."

"You are expected at the gate, Salazar," said Saletta. And so ended for Roberto that unexpected lesson in life and wisdom. He was not edified by it, but he was grateful to his two teachers. They had explained to him many of the era's mysteries, never mentioned at La Griva.

CHAPTER 12

The Passions of the Soul

As ALL HIS illusions collapsed, Roberto fell prey to an amorous obsession.

It was now the end of June, and it was quite hot; for about ten days the first rumors had been spreading about a case of plague in the Spanish camp. Munitions were growing scarce in the city; the soldiers were being issued only fourteen ounces of black bread daily, and for a pint of wine from the Casalesi you had to pay three florins, that is to say twelve reales. Salazar from the camp and Saletta from the city had alternated visits to arrange the ransoming of officers captured by both sides in the course of combat, and the ransomed had to swear an oath not to take up arms again. There was more talk of that captain rising in the diplomatic world, Mazzarini, to whom the pope had entrusted negotiations.

Some hopes, some sorties, and the game of the reciprocal destruction of tunnels: thus the indolent siege progressed.

While waiting for the negotiations or for the relief army, the bellicose spirits grew calmer. Some Casalesi decided to go outside of the walls to harvest those fields of wheat spared by horses and wagons, heedless of the weary musket fire from the distant Spaniards. But not all were unarmed: Roberto saw a young peasant woman, tall and tawny, who at intervals interrupted her work with the sickle, crouched among the rows of grain, and raised a culiver, holding it like a veteran soldier, pressing the butt against her red cheek, to fire at the trouble makers. The Spaniards, irked by the shots of that warrior Ceres, returned fire, and a ball grazed the girl's wrist. Bleeding now, she fell back, but did not cease firing or shouting at the enemy. When she was finally almost below the walls, some Spaniards apostrophized her: "Puta de los franceses!" To which she replied, "Yes, I'm the Frenchmen's whore, but I'm not yours!"

That virginal figure, that quintessence of ripe beauty and martial fury, joined to the hint of shamelessness with which the insult had crowned her, kindled the boy's senses.

That day he combed the streets of Casale, eager to renew the vision: he questioned the peasants, learned that the girl's name according to some was Anna Maria Novarese, according to others Francesca, and in one tavern they told him she was twenty, she came from the country, and was carrying on with a French soldier. "She's a good girl, that Francesca, a very good girl," they said with a knowing leer, and to Roberto his beloved seemed all the more desirable as she was again praised in licentious tones.

A few evenings later, passing a house, he glimpsed her in a dark room on the ground floor. To enjoy the faint breeze that barely mitigated the Monferrino sultriness, she was seated at the window, in the light of an unseen lamp placed near the sill. At first he failed to recognize her because her lovely hair was wound around her head; just two locks escaped, falling over her ears. Only her face could be seen: bent slightly, a single, pure oval beaded with a few drops of sweat, it seemed the real lamp in that penumbra.

At a little low table she was occupied with some sewing,

on which her intent gaze rested, so she did not notice the youth, who stepped back to peer at her from a corner, crouching against the wall. His heart pounding in his breast, Roberto noticed that her lip was shaded by blond down. Suddenly she raised a hand even more luminous than her face, to hold a length of dark thread to her mouth: placing it between her red lips, she bared her white teeth, severing it with one bite, the act of a gentle animal happily smiling in her domestic cruelty.

Roberto could have remained there all night; he barely breathed, in his fear of being discovered and in the ardor that froze him. But after a while the girl blew out the lamp, and the vision was dissolved.

He passed along that street in the days that followed, not seeing her again, save once, and even then he was not sure, because she, if it was she, sat with her head bowed, her nape bare and rosy, a cascade of hair covering her face. An older woman stood behind her, navigating through those leonine waves with a shepherdess's comb, which she sometimes laid aside to seize with her fingers a little fleeing creature, which her nails snapped with a sharp click.

Roberto, no novice to the rites of delousing, discovered however its beauty for the first time, and he imagined being able to plunge his hands into those silken waves, to kiss those furrows, being himself the destroyer of those bands of infesting myrmidons.

He had to move away from the enchantment because of the arrival of some noisy rabble in that street, and this was the last time that window offered him an amorous tableau.

On other afternoons and other evenings he saw the older woman there, and another girl, but not his. He concluded this was not her house, but the woman's, a relative, to whom she went occasionally to perform some chore. Where she was for days, he no longer knew.

An amorous yearning is a liquor that becomes stronger when decanted into a friend's ear. While he fruitlessly scoured Casale and became thin in his search, Roberto was unable to hide his condition from Saint-Savin. He revealed it out of vanity, for every lover bedecks himself with the beauty of his beloved—and of this beauty Roberto was certain.

"Love her, then," Saint-Savin responded negligently. "It is nothing new. It seems humans derive pleasure from it, unlike animals."

"Animals do not love?"

"No, simple machines do not love. The wheels of a wagon, what is it they do along a slope? They roll towards the bottom. The machine is a weight, and the weight hangs, dependent on the blind need that impels it downwards. So it is with an animal: it is weighted towards intercourse and is not appeased until it has had it."

"But did you not tell me yesterday that men are machines?"

"True, but the human machine is more complex than the mineral and the animal, and it enjoys an oscillatory motion."

"So?"

"So you love, and therefore you desire and do not desire. Love makes us the enemy of ourselves. You fear that attaining your end will disappoint you. You have pleasure *in limine*, as the theologians put it, you enjoy delay."

"That's not so. I . . . I want her at once!"

"If that were the case, you would be still only a rustic. But you have wit. If you wanted her, you would already have taken her—and you would be a beast. No, you want your desire to be set aflame, and you want hers to be stirred as well. If her desire were to blaze to such a degree that she was impelled to surrender herself to you at once, probably you would no longer want her. Love flourishes in expectation. Expectation strolls through the spacious fields of Time towards Opportunity."

"But what am I to do in the meantime?"

"Court her."

"But . . . she knows nothing yet, and I must confess I have difficulty approaching her. . . ."

"Write her a letter and tell her of your love."

"But I have never written a love-letter! Indeed, I am ashamed to say, I have never written any letter."

"When nature fails, we turn to art. I will dictate to you. A gentleman often enjoys writing letters to a lady he has never seen, and I am equal to the task. As I do not love, I can speak of love better than you, who are struck dumb by love."

"But I believe each person loves in a different way. . . . It would be artificial."

"If you revealed your love to her in tones of sincerity, you would seem awkward."

"But I would tell her the truth. . . ."

"The truth is a young maiden as modest as she is beautiful, and therefore she is always seen cloaked."

"But I want to tell her of my love, not of the love you would describe!"

"Well, if you would be believed, feign. There is no perfection without the splendor of machination."

"But she would understand that the letter is not speaking of her."

"Never fear. She will believe that what I dictate to you was made to her measure. Come now, sit down and write. Just allow me to summon my inspiration."

Saint-Savin moved about the room as if, Roberto tells us,

he were imitating the flight of a bee returning to the honey-comb. He was almost dancing, his eyes restless; he seemed to read in the air the message that did not yet exist.

Then he began: "My lady   "

"Lady?"

"Well, how would you address her? Perhaps: Holà, little hussy of Casale?"

"Puta de los franceses," Roberto couldn't help murmuring, alarmed as Saint-Savin had in jest come so close, if not to the truth, at least to the insult.

"What did you say?"

"Nothing. Very well. Lady. Then what?"

"My lady, in the wondrous architecture of the Universe, it has been written since the natal day of Creation that I would encounter you and love you. But with the first line of this letter, I feel that my soul has already so poured forth that it will abandon my lips and my pen before this is concluded."

". . . concluded. But I don't know if that will be comprehensible to a—"

"The truth is all the more appreciated when it is barbed with difficulties, and a revelation is more respected if it has cost us dearly. Let us raise the tone, in fact. Let us say then: My lady . . ."

"Again?"

"Yes. Lady. For a woman beautiful as Alcidiana, an unassailable dwelling is without doubt necessary, as it was for that Heroine. And I believe that by enchantment you have been transported elsewhere and that your province has become a second Floating Island that the wind of my sighs causes to retreat as I attempt to advance, the province of the Antipodes, a land where ice-floes bar my approach. You look puzzled, La Grive: does it still seem commonplace to you?"

"No, the fact is . . . I would say quite the contrary."

"Have no fear," Saint-Savin said, misunderstanding, "there will be no lack of the counterpoint of contradictions. Let us proceed: Perhaps your charms entitle you to remain distant as is proper for the gods. But do you not know that the gods receive with favor at least the fumes of incense we burn to them here below? Do not then refuse my worship: as you possess beauty and splendor to the highest degree, you would make me impious if you prevented me from adoring in your person two of the greatest divine attributes. . . . Does that sound better?"

At this point Roberto was thinking that the problem now was whether or not La Novarese could read. Once this barrier was overcome, what she read would surely intoxicate her, as he was becoming intoxicated, writing.

"My God," he said, "she should go mad."

"She will. Continue. Far from having lost my heart when I entrusted my freedom to your hands, I find it has grown larger since that day, multiplied, as if, since one heart alone is not enough for my love of you, it were reproducing itself in all my arteries, where I feel it throbbing."

"Good Lord . . ."

"Keep calm. You are speaking of love, you are not loving. Forgive, my Lady, the raving of a desperate man, or, better, pay no heed to it. Sovereigns have never been held to account for the death of their slaves. Ah yes, I should consider my fate enviable if you take the trouble to cause my destruction. If you will deign at least to hate me, this will tell me I am not indifferent to you. Thus death, with which you think to punish me, will be for me a cause of joy. Yes, death. If love means understanding that two souls were created to be united, when one realizes that the other does not feel this union, he can only die. And this—while my body still lives, though not for long—is the message that my soul, departing from it, sends you."

". . . departing from it?"

". . . sends you."

"Let me catch my breath. My head is spinning."

"Control yourself. Do not confuse love with art."

"But I love her! You understand? I love her!"

"And I do not. For this reason you have come to me. Write without thinking of her. Think of—let me see—Monsieur de Toiras."

"Monsieur!"

"Do not look like that. He is a handsome man, after all. But write: Lady . . ."

"Again?"

"Again. Lady, I am fated moreover to die blind. Have you not made of my eyes two alembics, wherein my life must evaporate? And so it happens that the more my eyes are moistened, the more I burn. Perhaps my father did not mold my body from the same clay that gave life to the first man, but, rather, from lime, since the water I shed consumes me. And how does it happen that I still live, though consumed, finding yet more tears to be consumed further?"

"Are you not exaggerating?"

"On grand occasions thought must also be grand."

Now Roberto protested no longer. He felt as if he had become La Novarese and was feeling what she should feel on reading these pages. Saint-Savin continued dictating.

"Abandoning my heart, you have left in it an insolent creature who is your image and who boasts of having the power of life and death over me. And you have gone from me as sovereigns leave the torture chamber for fear of being importuned with pleas for mercy. If my soul and my love are composed of two pure sighs, when I die I will beseech my

Agony that the breath of my love be the last to leave me, and I will have achieved—as my last gift—a miracle of which you should be proud, and for one instant at least you will draw a sigh from a body already dead."

"Dead. Is that the end?"

"No, let me think. We need a closing with a *pointe.* . . ."

"A what?"

"Yes, an act of the intellect that expresses the inconceivable correspondence between two objects, beyond all belief, so that in this pleasant play of wit any concern for substance is happily lost."

"I do not understand. . . ."

"You will. Here: let us reverse for the moment the direction of the appeal. In fact, you are not yet dead: let us give her the possibility of hastening to succor this moribund lover. Write: You could perhaps, my Lady, yet save me. I have given you my heart. But how can I live without the very motor of life? I do not ask you to give it back to me; for only in your prison does it enjoy the most sublime of freedoms, but I beg you to send me, in exchange, your own, that could find no tabernacle more prepared to welcome it. To live you have no need of two hearts, and mine beats so hard for you that it can assure you of the most eternal of fervors."

Then, half-turning and bowing like an actor anticipating applause, he asked: "Beautiful, is it not?"

"Beautiful? Why, I find it—how can I say?—ridiculous. Do you see this lady running around Casale delivering hearts, like a sort of page?"

"Would you expect her to love a man who speaks like any ordinary citizen? Sign it and seal it."

"But I am not thinking of the lady. I am thinking that if she were to show it to anyone, I would die of shame."

"She will never do that. She will keep the letter in her

bosom, and every night she will light a candle beside her bed to read it, and cover it with kisses. Sign and seal."

"But let us imagine, for the sake of argument, that she cannot read. She will have to find someone to read it to her. . . ."

"Monsieur de la Grive! Are you telling me you have been captivated by a peasant? That you have squandered my inspiration to embarrass a rustic? You must give me satisfaction."

"It was just a hypothesis. A jest. But I was taught that the prudent man must consider situations, circumstances, and along with the possible also the impossible. . . ."

"You see? You are learning to express yourself properly. But you have considered badly and chosen the most risible among possibilities. In any case, I would not wish to force you. Strike out the last sentence and continue now as I say. . . ."

"But if I strike it out, then I will have to rewrite the letter."

"So you are lazy, into the bargain. But the wise man must exploit misfortune also. Strike it out. . . . Done? Now then." Saint-Savin dipped one finger into a pitcher, then he allowed a drop to fall on the cancelled line, making a little damp spot, its edges irregular, growing gradually darker as the water caused the black ink, diluting it, to flow back on the sheet. "Now write. Forgive me, my Lady, if I lack the heart to allow the survival of a thought that, stealing from me a tear, has frightened me with its boldness. Thus may an Aetnaean fire generate the loveliest stream of brackish water. But ah, my Lady, my heart is like a seashell that, imbibing the beautiful sweat of dawn, generates the pearl and grows to be one with it. At the thought that your indifference would take from my heart the pearl it has so jealously fed, my heart flows from my eyes. . . . Yes, La Grive, this is unquestionably better, we have restrained the excesses. Better to end by reducing the

vehemence of the lover, to increase the emotion of the beloved. Sign, seal, and send. Then wait."

"Wait for what?"

"The north of the Compass of Prudence consists in un-
furling the sails to the wind of the Favorable Moment. In these
affairs waiting never does any harm. Presence takes the edge
off hunger, and distance sharpens it. Maintaining your distance, you will be considered a lion, while being present, you
could become a mouse born of the mountain. You are certainly rich in fine qualities, but qualities lose their luster if
touched too often, whereas fancy travels farther than sight."

Roberto thanked him and rushed home, concealing the
letter in his bosom as if he had stolen it. He feared someone
might rob him of the fruit of his theft.

I will find her, he told himself, I will bow and hand her
the letter. Then he tossed in his bed, thinking how she would
read it with her lips. By now he was imagining an Anna Maria
Francesca Novarese endowed with all those virtues Saint-Savin
had attributed to her. Declaring, even if in another's voice, his
love, he had felt more than ever a lover. Doing something
uncongenial, he had been enticed by Genius. He now loved La
Novarese with the exquisite violence he described in his letter.

A few days later, setting out to find the one from whom
he had been so prepared to remain distant, heedless of the
danger as cannon fire rained down on the city, he saw her at
a street corner, laden with sheaves like a mythological figure.
With great inner tumult he ran to her, not knowing quite
what he would do or say.

Having approached her, trembling, he stood before her and
said, "Young lady . . ."

"Me?" the girl answered, laughing, and said, "Well?"

". . . well," Roberto could think of nothing better to say. "Could you tell me which direction I should take for the Castle?" And the girl, throwing back her head and the great mass of her hair, said, "Oh, that way, of course." And she turned the corner.

At that corner, as Roberto was uncertain whether or not to follow her, a whistling cannon ball fell, knocking down a garden wall and raising a cloud of dust. He coughed, waited till the dust settled, and realized that by ambling too hesitantly through the spacious fields of Time he had missed the Favorable Moment.

To punish himself, he scrupulously tore up the letter and turned towards home, while the shreds of his heart lay crumpled on the ground.

His first, imprecise, love convinced him forever that the beloved object must dwell in the distance, and I believe this conviction sealed his fate as a lover. During the next days he went back to every corner (where he had received information, where he had found a trail, where he had heard her mentioned, where he had seen her) to reconstruct a landscape of memory. He thus laid out a Casale of his own passion, transforming alleys, fountains, squares into the River of Inclination, the Lake of Indifference, or the Sea of Hostility: he made the wounded city into the Land of his personal unsated Tenderness, an island (presage even then) of his solitude.

CHAPTER 13

The Map of Tenderness

ON THE NIGHT of June 29th a great noise wakened the besieged, followed by a rolling of drums: the enemy had managed to explode the first mine beneath the walls, blowing up a lunette and burying twenty-five soldiers. The next day, towards six in the evening, something like a storm was heard to the west, and in the east a cornucopia appeared, whiter than the rest of the sky, with a tip that extended and retracted. It was a comet, which upset the soldiers and led the local inhabitants to lock themselves in their houses. Over the next weeks other parts of the wall were blown up, while from the ramparts the defenders fired back in vain, for now the enemy moved underground, and the countermines were unable to dislodge him.

Roberto lived in this wreck like an alien passenger. He spent long hours discussing with Padre Emanuele the best way to describe the fires of the siege, and he saw more and more of Saint-Savin to develop with him similarly appropriate metaphors to depict the fires of his love—whose failure he had not dared confess. Saint-Savin provided him with a stage whereon his amorous story would be happily enacted; in silence he submitted to the ignominy of drafting, with his friend, further letters, which he then pretended to deliver, rereading them every night instead, as if the diary of all those longings were addressed to him from her.

He envisaged situations in which La Novarese, pursued by Landsknechts, fell overcome into his arms as he routed the assailants and led her, exhausted, into a garden where he enjoyed her wild gratitude. On his bed he abandoned himself to such thoughts, recovered his senses after long swoons, and composed sonnets for his beloved.

He showed one to Saint-Savin, who remarked, "I consider it of an extreme repugnance, if I may say so, but console yourself: in Paris the majority of those who are called poets produce worse. Do not poetize about your love; passion deprives you of that divine coldness that was the glory of Catullus."

Roberto found himself of melancholic humor, and said as much to Saint-Savin. "Rejoice," his friend remarked. "Melancholy is not the lees but the flower of the blood, and it generates heroes because, on the border of madness, it spurs them to the bravest of actions." But Roberto did not feel spurred to anything, and he became melancholy because he was not melancholic enough.

Deaf to cries and cannon fire, he heard rumors of relief (the Spanish camp is in turmoil, they say the French army is advancing), and he rejoiced because in mid-July a countermine had finally succeeded in slaughtering many Spaniards; but meanwhile many lunettes were being evacuated, and in mid-July the enemy vanguard could already fire directly into the city. He learned that some Casalesi were afraid to fish in the Po, and, not worrying that he might be taking streets exposed to enemy fire, he ran to look, afraid the imperials might shoot at La Novarese.

He forced his way among the soldiers, who were discontent because their contract said nothing about the digging of trenches; but the Casalesi refused to do it for them, so Toiras had to promise his men extra pay. Like all the others, Roberto was delighted to learn that Spinola had fallen ill of the plague, and pleased to see a group of Neapolitan deserters enter the city, abandoning in fear the hostile camp threatened by the disease, though he heard Padre Emanuele say that the arrivals could themselves become a source of contagion. . . .

In mid-September, when the plague appeared in the city, Roberto still paid no attention, except to fear that La Novarese might fall ill. Then he woke one morning with a high fever. He managed to send someone to inform Padre Emanuele, and was secretly borne to his convent, avoiding one of those makeshift lazarettoes where the sick died without fuss so as not to distract the others engaged in dying of pyrotechnics.

Roberto did not think of death: he mistook his fever for love and dreamed of touching the flesh of La Novarese, while he rumpled the folds of his pallet or fondled the sweating, aching parts of his body.

In the grip of an exuberant memory, that evening on the *Daphne,* as night advanced, as the sky performed its slow motions, and the Southern Cross disappeared on the horizon, Roberto no longer knew whether he was burning with revived love for the warrior Diana of Casale or for the Lady equally far from his sight.

Yearning to know where she could have fled, he rushed into the cabinet of nautical instruments, where he seemed to recall there was a map of those seas. He found it: large, colored, and incomplete, as many maps then were incomplete out of necessity; the navigator, coming upon a new land, drew the shores he could see but left the rest unfinished, never

knowing how and how much and whither that land extended.
Hence the maps of the Pacific often seemed arabesques of
beaches, hints of perimeters, hypotheses of volumes, and only
the few circumnavigated islands were defined there, like the
course of the winds learned from experience. Some cartogra-
phers, to make an island recognizable, simply drew with great
precision the form of the peaks and the clouds hanging over
them, to render them identifiable, as you might recognize a
man by his hat brim or his halting gait.

Now, on this map, the outlines of the two facing shores
were visible, divided by a channel running from south to
north. One of the two shores, with irregular curves, practically
defined an island, and it could be his Island; but beyond a
broad stretch of sea there were other groups of presumed islands of very similar formation, which could equally represent
the place where he was.

We would err if we thought that Roberto was gripped by
a geographer's curiosity. Padre Emanuele had trained him only
too well to reverse the visible through the lens of his Aristotelian telescope; and Saint-Savin had taught him too well to
foment desire through language, which can turn a maiden into
a swan or a swan into a maiden, the sun into a ladle or a ladle
into the sun! Late in the night we find Roberto daydreaming
over the map now transformed into the desired female body.

If it is a lover's error to write on the sands of the shore
the beloved name, which is only to be washed away then by
the waves, how prudent a lover Roberto felt himself, having
entrusted his beloved's body to the arcs of grottoes and gulfs,
her hair to the flow of the currents through mazy archipela-
goes, the summer moisture of her face to the glint of the
waters, the mystery of her eyes to the blue of a vast desert—
and the map repeated many times the features of that beloved
body, in various attitudes of bays and promontories. Desirous,

he was wrecked with his mouth on the map, he sucked in that ocean of voluptuousness, tickled a cape, hesitated to penetrate a strait; his cheek pressed against the page, he breathed the breath of the winds, he would have liked to savor the pools and the springs, fling himself thirsting to drink the streams dry, become sun to kiss the banks, tide to caress the secret estuaries. . . .

However, he was to enjoy not possession but, rather, privation. While, raving, he touched that vague prize of an erudite pen, Others perhaps, on the real Island—where it reclined in charming poses the map had not yet been able to capture—were biting into its fruits, bathing in its waters. . . . Others, stupefied and ferocious giants, extended at that moment a rough hand to its breast; misshapen Vulcans possessed that delicate Venus, grazed her mouths with the same ignorance of the fisherman of the Island Not Found who, beyond the last horizon of the Canaries, foolishly discards the rarest among pearls. . . .

She in another's loving hands. . . . This thought was the supreme intoxication, in which Roberto writhed, howling his rapier impotence. And in this frenzy, as he groped on the table as if to seize at least the hem of a skirt, his gaze slipped away from the depiction of that softly waved pacific body to another map, where the unknown author had sought perhaps to portray the fiery conduits of the volcanoes of the western land: it was a portulan of our entire globe, all plumes of smoke at the summits of projections of the crust or inside a tangle of dried veins; and he felt suddenly the living image of that globe, he moaned, exuding lava from every pore, the lymph of his unsatisfied satisfaction erupting, as he lost also his senses— destroyed by arid hydropsy (so he writes)—over that longed- for austral flesh.

CHAPTER 14

A Treatise on the Science of Arms

AT CASALE, TOO, he dreamed of open spaces, and of the broad valley where he had seen La Novarese for the first time. But now that he was no longer ill, he concluded, more lucidly, that he would never find her again, either because he would soon be dead, or because she was dead already.

Actually, he was not dying; indeed he was gradually recovering, but he did not realize this and mistook the languors of convalescence for the languishing of life. Saint-Savin came often to visit him, supplying him with a gazette of events if Padre Emanuele was present (the priest kept an eye on the visitor, as if he were about to steal Roberto's soul), but when the older man had to leave (for in the convent negotiations were intensifying), Saint-Savin philosophized on life and death.

"My friend, Spinola is dying. You are already invited to the great festivities we will hold for his decease."

"My friend, next week I shall also be dead. . . ."

"That is not true. I would recognize the face of a dying man. But it would not be right for me to distract you from the thought of death. Indeed, take advantage of your sickness to perform that admirable exercise."

"Monsieur de Saint-Savin, you talk like an ecclesiastic."

"Not at all. I am not urging you to prepare for the next life, but to use well this, the only life that is given you, in order to face, when it does come, the only death you will ever experience. It is necessary to meditate early, and often, on the art of dying, to succeed later in doing it properly just once."

Roberto wanted to get up, but Padre Emanuele forbade it, not believing that Roberto was yet ready to return to the confusion of the war. Roberto hinted that he was impatient to find a certain person again; Padre Emanuele considered it foolish that his body, so wasted, should allow itself to be further weakened by the thought of another body, and he tried to make the female species seem contemptible to him. "That most vain Womanly World," he said, "that certain modern female Atlases carry on their back, revolves around Dishonor and has the Signs of the Crab & Capricorn for its Tropics. The Mirror, which is its Primum Mobile, is never so murky as when it reflects the Stars of those lewd Eyes, transformed, through the exhalation of the Vapors of stultified Lovers, into Meteors heralding disaster for Honesty."

Roberto did not appreciate the astronomical allegory, nor did he recognize his beloved in the portrait of those society sorceresses. He remained in bed, though still exhaling the Vapors of his infatuation.

More news reached him meanwhile from Signor della Saletta. The Casalesi were wondering if they should not grant the French access to the citadel: they had realized by now that if the enemy was to be denied entry, citizenry and garrison had to join forces. But Signor della Saletta implied that now more than ever, while the city seemed on the point of falling, its inhabitants made only a show of collaborating, while in their hearts they laughed at the pact of alliance. "It is necessary," he said, "to be innocent as the dove with Monsieur de

Toiras, but also sly as the serpent in the event that his king wishes them to sell Casale. We must fight in such a way that if Casale is saved, we can share in the merit; but without going too far, so that if it falls, the blame will be attributed entirely to the French." And he added, for Roberto's instruction: "The prudent man must never harness himself to a single wagon."

"But the French say that you are merchants: no one notices when you fight, and all see when you are selling at high prices!"

"To live much it is best to be worth little. The cracked pot is never entirely broken, and in the end its very endurance becomes wearing."

One morning, at the beginning of September, a liberating downpour struck Casale. The healthy and the convalescent all went outside to enjoy the rain, which would wash away every trace of contagion. But it was more a refreshment than a cure, and the disease continued to rage even after the storm. The only consoling news was the equally destructive job the plague was doing in the enemy camp.

Able now to stand on his feet, Roberto ventured out of the convent, and at a certain point, at the threshold of a house marked with a green cross designating it as a place of infection, he saw Anna Maria or Francesca Novarese. She was wan as a figure in the Dance of Death. Once snow and garnet, she was reduced to a sallow uniformity, though her haggard features had not lost their former charms. Roberto recalled the words of Saint-Savin: "Would you continue your genuflections after old age has turned that body into a phantom, able only to remind you of the imminence of death?"

The girl was weeping on the shoulder of a Capuchin, as if she had lost someone dear, perhaps her Frenchman. The Capuchin, his face grayer than his beard, was supporting her, one bony finger pointed at the sky, as if to say, "One day, up there . . ."

Love becomes a matter for the mind only when the body desires and that desire is suppressed. If the body is weak and unable to desire, the mental aspect vanishes. Roberto discovered he was so weak that he was incapable of loving. Exit Anna Maria (Francesca) Novarese.

He went back to the convent and to bed, determined to die really: he suffered too much at not suffering more. Padre Emanuele recommended he take fresh air. But the news arriving from outside did not encourage him to live. Now, besides the plague, there was famine, or, rather, something worse: a frenzied hunt for the food that the Casalesi were still hiding and did not want to give to their allies. Roberto said that if he could not die of the plague, he wanted to die of starvation.

Finally Padre Emanuele got the better of him and sent him out. Turning the corner, Roberto came upon a group of Spanish officers. He started to flee, but they saluted him ceremoniously. He realized that as various bastions had been breached, the enemy was now installed in various parts of the town, whence it could be said that it was not the country besieging Casale, but Casale that was besieging its own castle.

At the end of the street he encountered Saint-Savin. "My dear La Grive," he said, "you fell ill a Frenchman and you are healed a Spaniard. This part of the city is now in enemy hands."

"And we may pass?"

"Do you not know that a truce has been signed? And, in any case, the Spanish want the castle, not us. In the French sector wine is growing scarce, and the Casalesi bring it up from their cellars as if it were the Most Precious Blood. You will not be able to keep good Frenchmen from frequenting certain taverns in this quarter, where the tavern-keepers are now bringing in excellent wine from the country. And the Spaniards receive us like great gentlemen. Except that the proprieties must be respected: if you want to brawl, you must brawl in your own quarter and with compatriots, for in this area we must behave politely, as is correct between enemies. So I confess the Spanish quarter is less amusing than the French, for us at least. But do join us. This evening we want to serenade a lady who had concealed her charms from us until the other day, when I saw her look out of a window for an instant."

And so that evening Roberto found again five familiar faces from the court of Toiras. Even the abbé was of the company, and for the occasion had decked himself out in laces and furbelows, with a satin sash. "The Lord forgive us," he said with flaunted hypocrisy, "but the spirit must yet be appeased if we are still to perform our duty. . . ."

The house was in a square in what was now the Spanish part of the city, but the Spanish at that hour must all have been in the pothouses. In the rectangle of sky outlined by the low roofs and the crowns of the trees flanking the square, the moon reigned serene, only slightly pocked, and was reflected in the water of a fountain murmuring in the center of that rapt quadrangle.

"O fairest Diana," Saint-Savin said, "how calm and peaceful must your cities and your villages be, that do not know war, for the Selenites live in their own natural felicity, ignorant of sin. . . ."

"No blasphemy, Monsieur de Saint-Savin!" the abbé said. "For even if the moon were inhabited, as Monsieur de Moulinet has fancied in that recent romance of his, and as the Scriptures do not teach us, those inhabitants would be most unhappy, as they would not know the Incarnation."

"And it would have been most cruel of the Lord God to deprive them of that knowledge," Saint-Savin rebutted.

"Do not seek to penetrate divine mysteries. God had not vouchsafed the preaching of His Son even to the natives of the Americas, but in His goodness He now sends missionaries there, to carry the light to them."

"Then why does Monsieur the Pope not send missionaries also to the moon? Are the Selenites perhaps not children of God?"

"Do not talk foolishness!"

"I will ignore your having called me a fool, Monsieur l'Abbé, but you must know that beneath this foolishness lies a mystery, which certainly our Lord Pope does not wish to reveal. If the missionaries were to discover inhabitants on the moon, and saw them looking at other worlds within the range of their eyes but not of ours, they would see them wondering if on those other worlds there are not other creatures living, similar to us. And the Selenites would then ask themselves if the fixed stars also are not so many suns surrounded by their moons and by their other planets, and if the inhabitants of those planets also see other stars unknown to us, which would be that many more suns with as many planets, and so on and on, to infinity. . . ."

"God has made us incapable of conceiving the infinite, so be content, human races, with the *quia*."

"The serenade, the serenade," the others were whispering. "That is the window." The window was bathed in a rosy light that came from the interior of an imagined chamber. But the two debaters were by now aroused.

"And further," Saint-Savin insisted, mocking, "if the world were finished and surrounded by the Void, God would also be finished: since His task, as you say, is to dwell in Heaven and on earth and in every place; He could not dwell where there is nothing. The Void is a non-place. Or else, to enlarge the world He would have to enlarge Himself, and be born for the first time where before He was not, and this would contradict His proclaimed eternity."

"Enough, sir! You are denying the eternity of the Eternal One, and this I cannot allow. The moment has come for me to kill you, so that your so-called wit can no longer weary us!" And he drew his sword.

"If that is your wish," Saint-Savin said, saluting and putting himself on guard. "But I will not kill you: I do not wish to subtract soldiers from my king. I will simply disfigure you, so that you will live wearing a mask, as the Italian comedians do, a fitting distinction for you. I will draw a scar from your eye to your lip, and I will give you this neat pig-castrator's cut, but only after having taught you, between a feint and a parry, a lesson in natural philosophy."

The abbé attacked, trying to strike home at once with great slashes, shouting at his opponent that he was a poisonous insect, a flea, a louse to be crushed mercilessly. Saint-Savin parried, then pressed him, driving him back against a tree, but philosophizing at every move.

"Aha! What wild slashes and thrusts, the vulgar chops of one blinded by rage! You lack any Idea of fencing. But you also lack charity, in your contempt for fleas and lice. You are too small an animal to be able to imagine the world as a big animal can, as the divine Plato displays it to us. Try to imagine the stars as worlds with other lesser animals, and remember that lesser animals in turn serve as worlds to still lesser breeds: then you will not find it contradictory to think that we—and also horses and elephants—are whole worlds for the fleas and the lice that inhabit us. They do not perceive us because of our bigness, as we do not perceive larger worlds because of our smallness. Perhaps there is now a population of lice that takes your body for a world, and when one of them has traveled there from forehead to nape, his fellows say of him that he has dared venture to the confines of the known earth. This little populace considers your hair the forests of their country, and when I have struck you, they will see your wounds as lakes and seas. When you use your comb, they believe this agitation is the flux and reflux of the ocean, and it is their misfortune to inhabit such a changeable world, because of your inclination to comb your hair constantly like a female, and now that I snip off that tassel, they will take your cry of anger for a hurricane. There!" And he snipped off an ornament, almost ripping the abbé's embroidered jacket.

The abbé foamed with rage. He had moved to the center of the square, looking behind him to make sure there was room for the movements he was now essaying, then retreating so that the fountain would protect his back.

Saint-Savin seemed to dance around him, without attacking. "Raise your head, Monsieur l'Abbé. Look at the moon, and reflect that if your God was able to make the soul immortal, He could easily have made the world infinite. But if the world is infinite, it will be so in time as well as in space, and therefore it will be eternal, and when there is an eternal world, which has no need of creation, then it will be unnecessary to conceive the idea of God. Oh, what a fine joke, Monsieur l'Abbé. If God is infinite, you cannot curtail His power: He could never *ab opere cessare,* and therefore the world will be infinite; but if the world is infinite, then there will no longer be God, just as there will soon be no more tassels on your jacket!" And suiting the deed to the word, he snipped off a few more appendages of which the abbé was so proud, then he shortened his guard, lifting the tip slightly; and as the abbé tried to close the distance, Saint-Savin sharply struck the flat of his opponent's blade. The abbé almost dropped his sword, clutching with his left hand his aching wrist.

He cried: "I must finally cut you open, you villain, you blasphemer! Holy womb! By all the damned saints of Paradise, by the blood of the Crucified!"

The lady's window was opened, someone looked out and shouted. By now all present had forgotten the purpose of their enterprise and were moving around the two duellers, who shouted as they skirted the fountain, while Saint-Savin confounded his enemy with a series of circular parries and feints on the tip of his weapon.

"Do not call on the mysteries of the Incarnation for help, Monsieur l'Abbé," he quipped. "Your holy Roman church has taught you that this ball of mud of ours is the center of the Universe, which turns around it, acting as its minstrel and strumming the music of the spheres. Be careful, you are allowing yourself to be driven too close to the fountain, you are getting your hem wet, like an old man suffering from stones. . . . But what if, in the great Void, infinite worlds are moving, as a great philosopher said before your similars burned him in Rome, and very many of them are inhabited by creatures like us, and what if all had been created by your God, where does the Redemption then fit?"

"What will God do with you, sinner!" the abbé cried, parrying a cut with some effort.

"Was Christ perhaps made flesh only once? Was Original Sin committed only once, and on this globe? What injustice! Both for the other worlds, deprived of the Incarnation, and for us, because in that case the people of all the other worlds would be perfect, like our progenitors before the Fall, and they would enjoy a natural happiness without the weight of the Cross. Or else infinite Adams have infinitely committed the first error, tempted by infinite Eves with infinite apples, and Christ has been obliged to become incarnate, preach, and suffer Calvary infinite times, and perhaps He is still doing so, and if the worlds are infinite, His task will be infinite, too. Infinite

His task, then infinite the forms of His suffering: if beyond the Galaxy there were a land where men have six arms, as in our own Terra Incognita, the Son of God would be nailed not to a cross but to a wooden construction shaped like a star— which seems to me worthy of an author of comedies."

"Enough! I will put an end to your comedy!" the abbé screamed, beside himself, and he flung himself at Saint-Savin, wielding his final blows.

Saint-Savin parried them effectively, then there was a static instant. While the abbé had his sword raised after a prime parry, Saint-Savin moved towards him as if to attack, and pretended to fall forward. The abbé stepped to one side, hoping to strike him as he fell. But Saint-Savin, who had not lost control of his legs, sprang up like lightning, supporting himself with his left hand on the ground as the right darted upwards: it was the coup de la mouette. The tip of the sword marked the abbé's face from the base of the nose to the upper lip, slicing off the left half of his moustache.

The abbé was cursing as no Epicurean would ever have dared to, while Saint-Savin stood erect and saluted, and the witnesses applauded his master stroke.

But at that very moment, from the end of the square, a Spanish patrol arrived, attracted perhaps by the noise. Instinctively, the French put their hands to their swords, the Spanish saw six armed enemies and cried betrayal. A soldier aimed his musket and fired. Saint-Savin fell, struck in the chest. The officer saw that four men, rather than engage in fighting, rushed to the fallen man, throwing aside their weapons. He looked at the abbé, covered with blood, realized that he had interrupted a duel, gave a command to his patrol, and all of them disappeared.

Roberto bent over his poor friend. "Did you see," Saint-

Savin murmured with an effort, "did you see, La Grive, my mouette? Ponder it and practice it. I would not have the secret die with me. . . ."

"Saint-Savin, my friend"—Roberto was weeping "you must not die in such a foolish way!"

"Foolish? I defeated a fool and I am dying on the field, and by enemy lead. In my life I have observed a wise mean . . . To speak always seriously provokes irritation. To be always witty, contempt. To philosophize always, sadness. To jest always, uneasiness. I have played every role, according to the time and the occasion, and once in a while I have also been court jester. But this evening, if you tell the story well, it will not have been a comedy but, rather, a fine tragedy. And do not grieve at my dying, Roberto." He called him by name for the first time. "Une heure après la mort, notre âme évanouie, sera ce qu'elle estoit une heure avant la vie. . . . Lovely verses, are they not?"

He died. Deciding on a noble lie, to which the abbé consented, all said that Saint-Savin died in a clash with some Landsknechts who were approaching the castle. Toiras and all the officers mourned him as a hero. The abbé told how in the clash he, too, had been wounded, and he prepared to receive an ecclesiastical benefice on his return to Paris.

In a brief period of time Roberto lost father, beloved, health, friend, and probably the war.

He could find no consolation in Padre Emanuele, who was too taken up with his councils. Roberto returned to the service of Monsieur de Toiras, last familiar image, and bearing his orders, he witnessed the final events.

On September 13th envoys of the King of France, the duke of Savoy, and Captain Mazzarini arrived at the castle. The relief army was also negotiating with the Spanish. Not the least bizarre note in that siege: the French sought a truce in order to arrive in time to save the city; the Spanish granted it because their camp, devastated by the plague, was also in a critical state, desertions were increasing, and Spinola was by now clinging to life with his teeth. Toiras found himself forced to accept the terms of the agreement imposed by the newcomers, which allowed him to continue defending Casale after Casale was already taken. The French would establish themselves in the citadel, abandoning the city and the castle itself to the Spanish, at least until the 15th of October. If by that date the relief army had not arrived, the French would abandon the citadel, too, truly defeated. Otherwise the Spanish would relinquish both city and castle.

Meanwhile, the besiegers had to provide the besieged with victuals. This is surely not the way we might feel a siege should have gone in those days, but such was the agreement. This was not waging war, it was playing dice, interrupting the game when the opponent had to go and urinate. Or perhaps it was like betting on a winning horse. And the horse was that approaching army, whose dimensions increased gradually on the wings of hope, though no one had seen it. Living in Casale, in the citadel, was like living on the *Daphne:* imagining a distant Island, and with intruders in the house.

The Spanish vanguards had behaved well, but now the main body of the army was entering the city, and the Casalesi had to deal with bullies who requisitioned everything, raped the women, clubbed the men, and treated themselves to the pleasures of city life after months in the woods and fields. Equally distributed among conquerors, conquered, and those shut up in the citadel: the plague.

On September 25th there was a rumor that Spinola had died. Rejoicing in the citadel and bewilderment among the conquerors, orphaned, too, like Roberto. These were days

more colorless than those on the *Daphne*, until October 22nd
when the relief army was announced, already at Asti. The
Spanish started arming the castle, and lining up cannons on
the banks of the Po, not respecting (while Toiras cursed) the
agreement that at the army's arrival they were to abandon
Casale. The Spanish, through the words of Señor de Salazar,
recalled that the agreement set the 15th of October as the final
date; if anything it was the French who should have relin-
quished the citadel a week since.

On October 24th, from the ramparts of the citadel great
movements of enemy forces were observed; Toiras prepared to
support the arriving French with his cannons. In the next few
days the Spanish began to load their baggage onto river barges
to ship it to Alessandria, and to those in the citadel this seemed
a good sign. Then the enemies on the river began also constructing boat bridges to prepare for the retreat. To Toiras this
looked so inelegant that he began firing his cannons on them.
Out of pique, the Spanish arrested all the French still to be
found in the city, and why there were any left, I confess I
have no idea, but this is what Roberto reports, and at this
point, where that siege is concerned, I am ready to believe
anything.

The French were near, and it was known that Mazzarini,
acting on the Pope's orders, was doing everything possible to
prevent the clash. The captain moved from one army to the
other, he returned to confer in Padre Emanuele's convent,
rode off again to carry counterproposals to this side and that.
Roberto saw him only and always from a distance, covered
with dust, doffing his hat abundantly to all. Both sides meanwhile were blocked, because the first to move would be check-
mated. Roberto even wondered if by chance the relief army
was not an invention of young Mazzarini, who was making
besieged and besiegers dream the same dream.

In fact since June a meeting of the imperial electors had been in session at Ratisbon, and France had sent her ambassadors there, including Père Joseph. And, as they shared out cities and regions, an agreement on Casale was reached as early as October 13th. Mazzarini learned of it quite quickly, as Padre Emanuele said to Roberto, and it was only a matter of convincing both those who were arriving and those who were waiting for them. The Spanish had received abundant news, but each despatch contradicted the others; the French knew something, too, but they feared Richelieu was not in agreement—and, for that matter, he was not, but from those days on, the future cardinal Mazarin studied how to make things go his way and behind the back of the man who would later become his patron.

This is how things stood when on October 26th the two armies found themselves face-to-face. To the east, along the hills towards Frassineto, the French army was deployed; opposite, with the river to the left, in the plain between the walls and the hills, was the Spanish army, which Toiras was cannonading from behind.

A line of enemy wagons was coming from the city; Toiras assembled what little cavalry he had left and sent it outside the walls to stop them. Roberto had begged to take part in this action, but permission was not granted. Now he felt as if on the bridge of a ship from which he could not go ashore, watching a vast stretch of sea and the mountains of an Island denied him.

Firing was suddenly heard, perhaps the two vanguards were coming to grips: Toiras had decided on a sortie to engage the men of His Catholic Majesty on two fronts. The troops were about to emerge from the walls, when Roberto, from the bastions, saw a black rider, heedless of the first bullets, galloping between the two armies just along the line of fire, waving a paper and shouting, as those present later recalled, "Peace! Peace!"

It was Captain Mazzarini. In the course of his last pilgrimages between one shore and the other, he had convinced the Spanish to accept the agreements of Ratisbon. The war was over. Casale remained with Nevers, the French and Spanish pledged to leave it. While the ranks were breaking up, Roberto leaped onto the trusty Pagnufli and sped to the scene of the failed conflict. He saw gentlemen in gilded armor exchanging elaborate salutes, formalities, and dance-steps as some little makeshift tables were being set up for the signing of the treaties.

The next day departures began, first the Spanish and then the French, but with confusion, casual encounters, exchanges of gifts, offers of friendship, while in the city corpses of the plague victims rotted in the sun, widows sobbed, some burghers found themselves enriched with both ready money and the French disease, having lain with no women save their wives.

Roberto tried to find his peasants again. But of La Griva's army there was no word. Some must have died of the plague, others were simply missing. Roberto thought they had gone home, and from them his mother had probably learned of her husband's death. He asked himself if he should not be close to her at this moment, but he no longer understood where his duty lay.

It is hard to say if his faith had been shaken most by the infinitely small and infinitely big worlds, in a void without God and without rule, that Saint-Savin had made him glimpse, or by the lessons of prudence from Saletta and Salazar, or by the art of Heroic Devices that Padre Emanuele bequeathed him as the sole science.

From the way he recalls it on the *Daphne* I tend to believe that at Casale, while he lost both his father and himself in a war of too many meanings and of no meaning at all, Roberto learned to see the universal world as a fragile tissue of enigmas, beyond which there was no longer an Author; or if there was, He seemed lost in the remaking of Himself from too many perspectives.

If there Roberto had sensed a world now without any center, made up only of perimeters, here he felt himself truly in the most extreme and most lost of peripheries; because, if there was a center, it lay before him, and he was its immobile satellite.

CHAPTER 15

Horologium Oscillatorium

WHY, THE READER may ask, have I been speaking, for a hundred pages at least, of so many events that preceded Roberto's being wrecked on the *Daphne,* while on the *Daphne* itself I have made nothing happen. But if the days on board a deserted ship are empty, I cannot be held responsible, for it is not yet certain this story is worth transcribing, nor can Roberto be blamed. At most we can reproach him for having spent a day (what with one thing and another, it is barely thirty hours since he discovered the theft of his eggs) suppressing the thought of the one possibility that might have given his sojourn more flavor. As would soon be clear to him, it was a mistake to consider the *Daphne* too innocent. On that vessel there was someone or something, roaming or lurking in ambush, and not Roberto alone. Not even on that ship could a siege be conceived in its pure state. The enemy was inside the gates.

Roberto should have suspected it the very night of his cartographical embrace. Coming to, he felt thirsty, the pitcher was empty, so he went off to seek a keg of water. Those he had set out to collect rain were heavy, but there were smaller ones, in the larder. He went there, seized the closest to hand

—on later reflection, he conceded that it was too close to hand—and, once in his cabin, he set it on the table, putting his mouth to the bung.

It was not water and, coughing, he realized that the keg contained aqua vitae. He did not know what kind, but good country boy that he was, he could tell it was not made from wine or juniper. He did not find the beverage unpleasant, and with sudden merriment he indulged to excess. It did not occur to him that if the kegs in the larder were all like this one, he should be worrying about his supply of drinking water. Nor did he ask himself why on the second evening he had drawn from the first keg of his store and found it filled with fresh water. Only later was he convinced that Someone had placed, afterwards, that insidious gift where he would grab it at once. Someone who wanted him in a state of intoxication, to have him in his power. But if this was the plan, Roberto followed it with excessive enthusiasm. I do not believe he drank much, but for a catechumen of his kind, a few glasses were already too many.

From the tale that follows we deduce that Roberto experienced the successive events in an unnatural state, and he would be in that state also during the days to come.

As is normal with the intoxicated, he fell asleep, but was tortured by an even greater thirst. In this thick sleep a last image of Casale returned to his mind. Before leaving, he had gone to say good-bye to Padre Emanuele and had found him in the process of dismantling and crating his poetic telescope, to return to Turin. But, having left Padre Emanuele, he encountered the wagons on which the Spanish and the imperials were piling the pieces of their obsidional machines.

It was those cogged wheels that peopled his dream: he heard a creaking of rusty locks, a scraping of hinges, and they were sounds that this time could not have been produced by a wind, since the sea was smooth as oil. Irritated, like those who, waking, dream they are dreaming, he forced himself to open his eyes and heard again that sound, which came from the lower deck or from the hold.

Rising, he felt a terrible headache. To treat it he could think of nothing better than to avail himself again of the keg, and when he left it, he was worse off than before. He armed himself, failing several times before he succeeded in thrusting his knife into its sheath, made numerous signs of the Cross, and staggered below.

Beneath him, as he already knew, was the tiller. He went farther down, to the end of the steps: if he turned towards the prow, he would enter the garden. Astern there was a closed door that he had never breached. From that place now came, very loud, a ticking, multiple and unsynchronized, like a superimposition of many rhythms, among which he could distinguish a tick-tick and a tock-tock and a tack-tack, but the general impression was of a tickety-tock-tackety-tick. It was as if beyond that door there was a legion of wasps and hornets, and all were flying furiously along different trajectories, slamming against the walls and ricocheting one into another. So he was afraid to open the door, fearing he might be struck by the crazed atoms of that hive.

After much hesitation, he made up his mind. He used the butt of his musket, broke the lock, and entered.

The storeroom received light from another gun-port, and it contained clocks.

Clocks. Water clocks, sand clocks, solar clocks propped against the walls, but especially mechanical clocks arrayed on various shelves and chests, clocks moved by the slow descent of weights and counterweights, by wheels that bit into other wheels, as those bit into still others, until the last wheel nipped the two unequal blades of a vertical staff, causing it to make two half-revolutions in opposing directions, its indecent wiggle moving, as balance, a horizontal bar fixed at its upper extremity. Spring clocks, too, where a fluted conoid played out a chain drawn by the circular movement of a little barrel that devoured it link by link.

Some of the clocks concealed their works behind rusted ornament and corroded chasing, displaying only the slow movement of their hands; but the majority exhibited their gnashing hardware, and recalled those dances of Death where the only living things are grinning skeletons that shake the scythe of Time.

All these machines were active, the largest hourglasses still gulping sand, the smaller now almost filled in their lower part, and for the rest a grinding of teeth, an asthmatic chewing.

To anyone entering for the first time, this place must have seemed to go on to infinity: the far wall of the little room was covered by a canvas that depicted a suite of rooms inhabited only by other clocks. But even after overcoming that spell, and considering only the clocks present, so to speak, in flesh and blood, there was enough to stun.

It may seem incredible—to you who read this with detachment—but imagine a castaway, amid the fumes of aqua vitae, on an uninhabited vessel, finding a hundred clocks almost all in unison telling the tale of his interminable time; he must think of the tale before thinking of its author. And this is what Roberto did as he examined those toys one by one, those playthings for the senile adolescence of a man sentenced to a very long death.

The thunder of Heaven came afterwards, as Roberto writes, when emerging from that nightmare he bowed to the necessity of discovering a cause for it: the clocks were functioning, thus someone must have set them in motion, even if their winding had been designed to last a long time. And if they had been wound before his arrival, he would have heard them already, passing by that door.

If it had been a single mechanism, he could have thought that it had been somehow set and needed only a starting tap; this tap could have been provided by a movement of the ship, or else by a sea bird entering through the gun-port and lighting on a lever, on a crank, initiating a sequence of mechanical actions. And does not a strong wind sometimes stir church bells, and has it not happened that bolts have snapped backwards when not pushed forward to their full length?

But a bird cannot in one blow wind dozens of clocks. No. Ferrante may or may not have once existed, but on the ship an Intruder did exist.

He had entered this room and had wound the mechanisms. Why he had done so was the first but less urgent question. The second was where had he then taken refuge.

So it was necessary to descend into the hold. Roberto told himself he now could no longer postpone it, though in reasserting his firm proposal, he further delayed its execution. He realized he was not entirely himself; he climbed up on deck to bathe his head in rainwater, and with a clearer mind set to pondering the identity of the Intruder.

The Intruder could not be a savage come from the Island or a surviving sailor, either of whom might have done anything (attack him in broad daylight, try to kill him in the dark, beg for mercy) but not feed chickens and wind clockworks. So on the *Daphne* a man of peace and learning was concealed, perhaps the occupant of the room with the maps. Then—if he was here, and since he had been here first—he was a Legitimate Intruder. But this nice antithesis did not allay Roberto's angry anxiety.

If the Intruder was Legitimate, why was he hiding? In fear of the illegitimate Roberto? And if he was hiding, why then was he making his presence obvious by creating this horological concert? Was he perhaps a man of perverse mind who, afraid of Roberto and unable to face him, wanted to destroy him by driving him to madness? But to what end would he do this, inasmuch as, equally shipwrecked on this artificial island, he could derive only advantage from an alliance with a companion in misfortune? Perhaps, Roberto said further to himself, the *Daphne* concealed other secrets that He was unwilling to reveal to anyone.

Gold, then, and diamonds, and all the riches of the Terra Incognita, or of the Islands of Solomon of which he had heard Colbert speak . . .

It was the evocation of the Islands of Solomon that brought Roberto a kind of revelation. Why, of course, the clocks! What were so many clocks doing on a ship headed for seas where morning and evening are defined by the course of the sun, and nothing else need be known? The Intruder had come to this remote parallel also to seek, like Dr. Byrd, *el Punto Fijo!*

Surely this was it. By an extraordinary coincidence, Roberto, having set out from Holland to follow, as the Cardinal's spy, the secret maneuvers of an Englishman, almost clandestine on a Dutch ship, in search of the *Punto Fijo,* now found himself on the (Dutch) ship of Another, from God knows what country, bent on discovering the same secret.

CHAPTER 16

Discourse on the Powder of Sympathy

How HAD HE got himself into this imbroglio?

Roberto allows only brief glimpses of the years between his return to La Griva and his entrance into Parisian society. From scattered hints we deduce that he stayed home to care for his mother until he was almost twenty, reluctantly arguing with stewards about sowing and harvests. Once his mother had followed her husband to the grave, Roberto discovered he was alien to that world. He must then have entrusted the land to a relative, retaining for himself a substantial income, after which he set off to travel the world.

He had remained in correspondence with some men he met at Casale, whose acquaintance had prompted him to extend his knowledge. I do not know how he arrived at Aix-en-Provence, but certainly he was there, for he recalls gratefully two years spent with a local gentleman versed in every science, possessor of a library rich not only in books but in art objects, antiquities, and embalmed animals. While a guest in Aix, he must have met that master to whom he refers often, with devout respect, as the Canon of Digne and sometimes as le doux prêtre. It was with the Canon's letters of introduction that, at an uncertain date, Roberto finally confronted Paris.

Here he immediately got in touch with the Canon's friends, and was enabled to frequent one of the most distinguished places of the city. He often mentions a cabinet of the brothers Dupuy and recalls how, every afternoon there, his mind opened more and more, stimulated by men of learning. But I find references to other cabinets he visited in those years, boasting rich collections of medals, Turkish knives, agate stones, mathematical rarities, shells from the Indies. . . .

We can tell the sort of circle in which he moved during the happy April (or perhaps May) of his youth by his frequent quotation of teachings that to us seem dissonant. He spent his days learning from the Canon how a world made of atoms could be conceived, just as Epicurus had taught, and yet willed and governed by Divine Providence; but, attracted by that same love for Epicurus, he spent his evenings with friends who called themselves Epicureans and could combine debate about the eternity of the world with the society of beautiful ladies of scant virtue.

He often mentions a band of friends, carefree but still not ignorant at twenty of things that others would be proud of knowing at fifty: Linières, Chapelle, Dassoucy, a philosopher and poet who went around with a lute slung over his shoulder, Poquelin, who translated Lucretius but dreamed of becoming the author of comedies, and Hercule Savinien, who had fought valiantly at the siege of Arras, composed declarations of love for fantastic lovers, and made a show of affectionate intimacy with young gentlemen, from whom he boasted of having acquired the Italian disease, while at the same time he mocked a comrade in vice "qui se plasoit à l'amour des masles" and said tauntingly that the man had to be forgiven for his shyness, which led him always to hide behind the backs of his friends.

Feeling welcome in a society of keen wits, Roberto became—if not a sage—a scorner of the insipid, which he found both in gentlemen of the court and in certain enriched bourgeois who ostentatiously displayed empty boxes bound in morocco leather from the Levant with the names of the greatest authors printed in gold on the spine.

In short, Roberto had entered the circle of those honnêtes gens who, even if they did not come from the nobility of the blood but, rather, from the noblesse de robe, represented the cream of this world. But he was young, eager for new experiences and, despite both his erudite company and his libertine routs, he did not remain insensitive to the fascination of the aristocracy.

For a long time, as he strolled at evening along rue Saint-Thomas-du-Louvre, he had admired from the outside the Palais Rambouillet, its handsome façade adorned with cornices and friezes, architraves and pilasters, in a play of red brick, white stone, and dark slate. He looked at the lighted windows, he saw the guests enter, and he imagined the loveliness, already famous, of the inner garden. He pictured the salons of that little court, celebrated in all Paris, established by a woman of taste who considered the other court coarse, subject to the whim of a king incapable of appreciating the refinements of the spirit.

Finally Roberto sensed that as a Cisalpine he would enjoy some credit in the house of a lady born of a Roman mother, from a line more ancient than Rome itself, stemming from a family of Alba Longa. Not by chance, about fifteen years earlier an honored guest in that house, Cavalier Marino, had led the French to the paths of a new poetry destined to make the art of the ancients pale.

Roberto managed to gain admittance to this temple of elegance and intellect, of gentlemen and *précieuses* (as they were

then called), sages without pedantry, gallants without libertin-
ism, wits without vulgarity, purists without absurdity. He
found himself at his ease in that atmosphere: it seemed to him
that he was allowed to breathe the air of the great city and of
the court without having to bow to those dictates of prudence
inculcated in him at Casale by Señor de Salazar. He was not
asked to conform to the will of a potentate, but, rather, to
show his distinction. Not to simulate, but to test himself—
though always observing the rules of good taste—against persons superior to him. He was not asked to be a courtier but
to be bold, to exhibit his skill in good and courteous conversation, and to be able to utter profound thoughts lightly. . . .
He did not feel a servant but a dueller, of whom courage,
totally intellectual, was demanded.

He was learning to avoid affectation, to use in every circumstance his ability to conceal art and effort so that what he
did or said would seem a spontaneous gift, as he tried to become master of that studied ease of manner that in Spain was
called *despejo* and in Italy *sprezzatura*.

Accustomed to the spaces of La Griva redolent of lavender,
after entering the hôtel of Arthénice, Roberto moved among
cabinets where the perfume of countless corbeilles wafted always, as in an eternal spring. The few aristocratic houses he
had known had consisted of cramped rooms around a central
staircase; but at Arthénice's the stairs had been placed in a
corner at the end of the courtyard, so that all the rest was a
succession of salons and cabinets, with tall doors and windows,
one facing the other; the chambers were not tiresomely red
or the color of tanned leather but of various hues, and the
Chambre Bleue of the Guest had walls of that color, trimmed
in gold and silver.

Arthénice received her friends recumbent in her chamber,
among screens and thick tapestries to protect guests from the

cold: she could suffer neither the light of the sun nor the heat of braziers. Fire and daylight overheated the blood in her veins and made her swoon. Once she forgot a brazier under her bed and came down with erysipelas. She was like certain flowers that, if their freshness is to be preserved, must neither be always in the light nor always in the shade and require gardeners to create for them a special season. Umbratile, Arthénice received in bed, her legs in a bearskin bag, and she covered her head with so many nightcaps that, as she wittily said, she went deaf at Martinmas and recovered her hearing at Easter.

And yet, even if no longer young, this Hostess was the very portrait of grace, large and well-made, with admirable features. The light in her eyes was beyond description, yet it did not instill improper thoughts: it inspired a love tempered by awe, purifying the hearts it enflamed.

In those rooms, the Hostess conducted, without imposition, debates on friendship and love, but they touched with equal levity on matters of morality, politics, philosophy. Roberto discovered the qualities of the other sex in their most tender expression, worshipping at a distance unapproachable princesses, like the beautiful Mademoiselle Paulet, known as "La Lionne" because of her proud mane, and ladies who could enhance their beauty with a wit that the venerable Academies attributed only to men.

After a few years of this school he was ready to meet the Lady.

He saw her for the first time one evening when she appeared in dark garb, veiled like a modest moon hiding behind clouds of satin. Le bruit, that unique mode which in Parisian society took the place of truth, told him contradictory things about her: that she had suffered a cruel widowhood, at the loss not of a husband but of a lover, and she glorified that loss to reaffirm her dominion over it. Some whispered to Roberto that she concealed her face because she was a splendid Egyptian, come from Morea.

Whatever the truth might have been, at the mere movement of her dress, at the light progress of her footsteps, at the mystery of her hidden face Roberto's heart was hers. He was illuminated by those radiant shadows, he imagined her a dawn bird of night, he thrilled at the miracle by which light became dark and darkness radiant, ink turned to milk, ebony to ivory. Onyx flashed in her hair, and the delicate fabric that revealed, concealing, the outlines of her face and her body had the same silvery atrament of the stars.

But suddenly, and on that same evening of their first encounter, her veil dropped for an instant from her brow, and he was able to glimpse under that sickle moon the luminous abyss of her eyes. Two loving hearts looking at each other say more things than all the tongues of this Universe could express in a day—Roberto flattered himself, sure that she had looked at him and, in looking, had seen him. And, on returning to his house, he wrote her.

My Lady,

The fire with which you burned me exhales such fine smoke that you cannot deny having been dazzled by it, though you may find blame in those blackening fumes. The sole power of your gaze made me abandon the weapons of pride and leads me to implore you to demand of me my life. How much I myself have fostered your victory, I who began fighting as one who wishes to be defeated, offering to your attack the most vulnerable part of my body: a heart already weeping tears of blood, proof that you have deprived my house of water to make it prey to the fire whose victim I am, through your so brief regard!

He found the letter so splendidly informed by the dictates of the Aristotelian machine of Padre Emanuele, so apt to reveal to the Lady the nature of the one person capable of such tenderness, that he did not consider it necessary to affix his signature. He did not yet know that the précieuses collected love letters as they did geegaws and bangles, more interested in their conceits than in their author.

In the weeks and months that followed he received no sign of reply. The Lady meanwhile had abandoned first her black garb, then the veil, and finally appeared to him in all the whiteness of her skin, not moorish, in her blond locks, in the triumph of her pupils, no longer elusive, windows of Aurora.

But now that his gaze could freely meet hers, he learned how to intercept her looks while they were directed at others; he basked in the music of words not addressed to him. He could not live save in her light, but he was condemned to remain in the penumbra of another body absorbing her rays.

One evening he caught her name, hearing someone call her Lilia; it was certainly the precious name of a précieuse, and he knew well that such names are given in jest: the marquise herself had been called Arthénice as an anagram of her real name, Cathérine—but it was said that the masters of that *ars combinatoria,* Racan and Malherbe, had also excogitated Eracinthe and Carinthée. And still he felt that Lilia and no other name could be given to his Lady, lily-like in her scented whiteness.

From that moment on the Lady was for him Lilia, and it was to Lilia that he dedicated amorous verses, which he then promptly destroyed, fearing they were an inadequate tribute: *Ah sweetest Lilia | hardly had I plucked a flower when I lost it! | Do you scorn to see me? | I pursue you and you flee | I speak to you and you are mute. . . .* But he didn't speak to her, save with his gaze full of querulous love, for the more one loves, the more one tends to rancor, shivering with cold fire, aroused by sickly health, the soul uplifted like a leaden feather, swept away by love's dear effects without affection; and he went on writing letters that he sent unsigned to the Lady, and verses for Lilia, which he jealously kept for himself, to reread them every day.

Writing (but not sending) *Lilia, Lilia, where art thou? Where dost thou hide? | Lilia, splendor of Heaven, an instant in thy presence | and I was wounded, as thou didst vanish*, he multiplied her presence. Following her at night as she returned to her house with her maid (*Through the darkest forests | along the darkest streets, | I shall enjoy following, though in vain | the fleeting prints of thy airy foot . . .*), he discovered where she lived. He lay in wait near that house at the hour of her daytime stroll, and he fell in behind her when she came out. After some months he could repeat by heart the day and the hour she changed the style of her hair (poetizing on those beloved bonds of the soul that encircled the snowy brow like lascivious serpents), and he remembered that magic April when she first essayed a little cape the color of wild broom, which gave her the prim gait of a solar bird as she walked in the first breezes of spring.

Sometimes, after following her like a spy, he retraced his steps in a great hurry, running around a palace and slowing only at the corner where, as if by chance, he would find her facing him; then he would pass her with a timid bow. She would smile at him discreetly, surprised by this unexpected encounter, and would give him a brief sign, as propriety demanded. He would stand in the middle of the street, a pillar of salt spattered by water as the carriages passed, exhausted after that battle of love.

Over the course of many months Roberto contrived to produce five of these victories; he suffered over each as if it were the first and the last, and he convinced himself that frequent as they had been, they could not have occurred at random, and perhaps it was not he but she who had assisted chance.

Pilgrim of this elusive holy land, ever mutable lover, he wanted to be the wind that stirred her hair, the matutinal water that kissed her body, the gown that fondled her at night, the book that charmed her during the day, the glove that warmed her hand, the mirror that could admire her in every pose. . . . Once he learned that she had been given a squirrel, and he dreamed of being the curious little animal that, at her caresses, thrust its innocent muzzle between the virgin breasts, while its tail teased her cheek.

He was troubled by the audacity to which his doting drove him, he translated impudence and remorse into restless verses, then told himself that a man of honor may love madly but not foolishly. It was only by giving evidence of wit in the Chambre Bleue that his destiny as a lover would be decided. A novice to those amiable rites, he yet understood that a précieuse is won only with words. He listened then to the talk in the salons, where gentlemen engaged in a kind of tournament, but he did not feel ready.

It was his familiarity with the learned men of the Dupuy cabinet that suggested to him how the principles of the new learning, though they were still unknown in society, could become similes of the emotions of the heart. And it was the meeting with Monsieur d'Igby that inspired the speech that was to lead to his ruin.

Monsieur d'Igby—at least that was what he was called in Paris—was an Englishman Roberto had met at the Dupuys', then found again one evening in a salon.

Less than three lustra had passed since the Duc de Bouquinquant had shown that an Englishman could have le roman en teste and be prone to well-bred madness. Informed that there was in France a queen beautiful and haughty, to the dream of winning her he devoted his life, until he died of it. Living for a long time on a ship, he erected an altar to his beloved. When it was learned that d'Igby, actually as Bouquinquant's envoy, had fought a privateering war against Spain, the universe of the précieuses found him fascinating.

In the Dupuys' circle the English were not popular: they were identified with characters like Robertus a Fluctibus, Medicinae Doctor, Eques Auratus et Armiger Oxoniensis, against whom various pamphlets had been written, deprecating his excessive faith in the occult operations of nature. But in that same circle they welcomed an eccentric churchman like Monsieur Gaffarel, who, when it came to believing in unheard-of curiosities, was the equal of any Briton. D'Igby, on the other hand, had proved capable of discussing with great erudition the necessity of the Void—in a group of natural philosophers who were horrified by anyone suffering from horror vacui.

If anything, his prestige suffered a blow among some gentlewomen to whom he had recommended a beauty cream of his own invention; it caused one lady blisters, and others murmured that his beloved wife, Venetia, had actually died, a few years earlier, victim of a viper wine he had concocted. But these were certainly calumnies of the envious, piqued by the fame of other remedies of his, including one for kidney stone, derived from a liquid of cow dung and hares slaughtered by hounds. Talk that could not win much acclaim in circles where, for conversation with the ladies, words were carefully avoided if they contained even a syllable that might, however vaguely, sound obscene.

D'Igby, in a salon one evening, quoted some verses of a poet from his country:

If they be two, they are two so
*   As stiffe twin compasses are two,*
Thy soule the fixt foot, makes no show
*   To move, but doth, if th'other doe.*

And though it in the center sit,
*   Yet when the other far doth rome,*
It leanes, and hearkens after it,
*   And growes erect, as that comes home.*

Such wilt thou be to mee, who must
*   Like th'other foot, obliquely runne;*
Thy firmnes drawes my circle just,
*   And makes me end, where I begunne.*

Roberto listened, his eyes fixed on Lilia, who had her back to him, and he decided that through all eternity he would be for Lilia the other foot of the compass, and that he would learn English in order to read other works by this poet, who so well interpreted his tremors. In those days no one in Paris would have wanted to learn so barbarous a language, but accompanying d'Igby back to his inn, Roberto realized that the foreigner had difficulty expressing himself in good Italian despite his travels on the Peninsula, and felt humiliated at not having sufficient mastery of a tongue essential to every educated man. They determined to frequent each other and to make each reciprocally fluent in the other's native language.

Thus a firm friendship was born between Roberto and this man, who proved to be rich in medical and naturalist knowledge.

D'Igby had had a dreadful childhood. His father, involved in the Gunpowder Plot, had been executed. Through an uncommon coincidence, or perhaps the consequence of impenetrable emotions, d'Igby had devoted his life to the study of another powder. He had traveled much, first for eight years in Spain, then for three in Italy where, another coincidence, he had known Roberto's Carmelite tutor.

D'Igby was also, evidence of his corsair past, a good swordsman, and a few days later he was to amuse himself fencing with Roberto. That day there was also a musketeer with them, who began by challenging an ensign of the company of cadets: it was all in fun, and the fencers were very careful, but at a certain point the musketeer essayed a prime with too much vigor, forcing his opponent to react with a beat, and so he was wounded in the arm, a very ugly wound.

Immediately d'Igby, with one of his garters, bound the arm to keep the veins closed, but in a few days' time the wound threatened to turn gangrenous, and the surgeon said the arm would have to be cut off.

At this point d'Igby offered his services, warning them, however, that they might consider him a meddler, though he asked all to trust him. The musketeer, who did not know where to turn, replied with a Spanish proverb: "Hágase el milagro, y hágalo Mahoma."

D'Igby then asked him for something stained with the blood from the wound, and the musketeer gave him a piece of the cloth that had protected his arm until that day. D'Igby had them bring him a basin of water, and into it he poured a vitriol powder, which quickly dissolved. Then he put the cloth in the basin. Suddenly the musketeer, who had been distracted in the meanwhile, gave a start, clutched his wounded arm, and said that the burning had ceased, and he was actually feeling a cool sensation on the wound.

"Good," d'Igby said. "Now you have only to keep the wound clean, bathing it every day in salt water, so that it may receive the correct influence. And I will expose this basin, during the day at the window, and at night at the corner of the hearth, so that it will remain at a moderate temperature."

When Roberto attributed the sudden improvement to some other cause, d'Igby, with a knowing smile, took the cloth and held it at the fire, and immediately the musketeer resumed his groans, until the cloth was again soaked in the solution.

The musketeer's wound healed in a week.

I believe that, in a time when disinfection was perfunctory, the mere fact of washing the wound daily was itself sufficient cause of healing, but Roberto cannot be reproached if he spent the next days questioning his friend about that treatment, which moreover reminded him of the Carmelite's feat he had witnessed as a child. Except that the Carmelite had applied the powder to the weapon that had caused the harm.

"True!" d'Igby replied. "The dispute about the *unguentum armarium,* the weapon salve, has been going on for a long time, and the great Paracelsus was the first to speak of it. Many use a thick grease, and insist that it acts best on the weapon. But, as you can understand, a weapon that has wounded and a cloth that has bound the wound are the same thing, because the powder must be applied where there are traces of the blood. Many, seeing the weapon treated in order to alleviate the effects of the blow, think of some magical operation, whereas my Powder of Sympathy derives from the operations of nature!"

"Why is it called Powder of Sympathy?"

"Again, the name itself could be misleading. Many have spoken of a conformity or sympathy that connects things among themselves. Agrippa says that to excite the power of a star, you must recur to things similar to it, which therefore receive its influence. And he uses the word *sympathy* to define this mutual attraction. As with pitch, with sulphur, and with oil you prepare wood to receive the flame, thus employing things that conform to the operation of the star, a particular benefit is reflected on the matter properly arranged through the soul of the world. To influence the sun you must act on gold, which is solar by nature, and on those plants that follow the sun, or that fold their leaves and droop at sunset, reopening them at sunrise, like the lotus, the peony, the celandine. But these are old wives' tales, an analogy of this sort is not enough to explain the operations of nature."

D'Igby shared his secret with Roberto. The orb or, rather, the sphere of air is full of light, and light is a material and corporeal substance; a notion Roberto accepted willingly, because in the Dupuys' he had heard that light also was merely a very fine powder of atoms.

"It is obvious that light," d'Igby said, "issuing incessantly from the sun and shooting off in all directions along straight lines, when it encounters some obstacle in its path, an opposition of solid and opaque bodies, is deflected *ad angulos aequales,* following another route until it deviates at another angle upon encountering another solid body, and so it continues until it is extinct. As in the royal game of tennis, where a ball driven against a wall rebounds from it to strike the wall opposite and often makes a complete circuit, returning to the point from which it set out. Now what happens when light strikes a body? Its rays rebound, detaching some atomies, some tiny particles, as a ball might carry with it pieces of the fresh plaster from the wall. And as these atomies are formed by the four Elements, the light with its heat incorporates the viscous parts and carries them far off. The proof lies in the fact that if you attempt to dry a wet cloth at a fire, you will see that the rays which the cloth reflects carry with them a kind of watery mist. These vagrant atomies are like riders on winged chargers that go through space until the sun, setting, withdraws its Pegasuses and leaves the riders without a mount. And then they fall again in a mass towards the earth, whence they came. But such phenomena occur not only with reference to light but also, for example, with wind, which is nothing but a great river of similar atomies attracted by the solid terrestrial bodies. . . ."

"And smoke," Roberto suggested.

"Of course. In London they obtain fire from the coal of the earth brought from Scotland, which contains a great deal of very sharp volatile salt; this salt, transported by smoke, is dispersed into the air, defacing walls, beds, and all light-colored furnishings. When you keep a room closed for some months, afterwards you will find a black dust that covers everything, as you find a white dust in mills and in bakers' shops. And in spring all flowers seem stained with grease."

"But how is it possible that so many corpuscles are scattered in the air, while the body that emanates them betrays no diminishment?"

"There is diminishment perhaps, as you are aware when you cause water to evaporate, but with solid bodies we are not aware of it, as we are unaware with musk or other fragrant substances. Any body, however small, can always be divided into smaller parts, thanks to which our English dogs, guided by their sense of smell, are able to follow the track of an animal. Does the fox perhaps, at the end of his race, seem smaller to us? Now, it is precisely thanks to such corpuscles that the phenomenon of attraction occurs, which some celebrate as Action at a Distance, which is not distant and therefore not magic but takes place through the constant intercourse of atomies. And so it is with attraction by suction, such as that of water or wine through a syphon, or the attraction of the magnet on iron, or attraction by filtration, as when you put a strip of cotton in a vessel filled with water, allowing a good length of the strip to hang outside the vessel, and you see the water rise beyond the rim and drip on the ground. And the last attraction is that which takes place through fire, which attracts the surrounding air with all the corpuscles whirling in it, as the water of a river carries along the soil of its bed. And since air is wet and fire is dry, they become attached one to the other. So then, to occupy the space of what is carried away by the fire, more air must come from the vicinity, otherwise a void would be created."

"Then you deny the Void?"

"Not at all. I say that as soon as it is encountered, nature tries to fill it with atomies, in a battle to conquer its every region. If this were not the case, my Powder of Sympathy could not act, whereas, on the contrary, experience has shown you that it does. Fire with its action provokes a constant affluxion of air, and the divine Hippocrates cleansed an entire province of the plague by having great bonfires set everywhere. Always in time of plague, cats and pigeons are killed and other hot animals, which constantly transpire spirits, so that air will fill the place of the spirits liberated in the course of that evaporation, causing the plague atomies to attach themselves to the feathers and fur of those animals, as the bread taken from an oven attracts to itself the foam of barrels and as wine spoils if you put bread on the top of the barrel. As, for that matter, when you expose to the air a pound of salt with calcinated and duly fired tartar, which will produce ten pounds of good oil of tartar. The physician of Pope Urban VIII told me the story of a Roman nun who, after too many fasts and prayers, had so heated her body that her bones all dried up. That internal heat, indeed, attracted air that was incorporated in the bones as it does in the salt of tartar, and the air emerged at the point that controls the discharge of the serosity, hence through the bladder, so the poor saint released more than two hundred pounds of urine in twenty-four hours, a miracle that all accepted as proof of her sanctity."

"But if everything attracts everything, then for what reason do elements and bodies remain separate without the collision of any force with another?"

"Good question. Bodies that have equal weight are more easily joined, and thus oil joins more easily with oil than with water, so we must conclude that what keeps atomies of the same nature firmly together is their rarity or density, as the philosophers you frequent could also easily tell you."

"And so they have told me, proving it with various kinds of salt, which, however you grind or coagulate them, always resume their natural form, and common salt is always found in cubes with squared facets, and soda niter in columns with six facets, and ammoniacal salt in hexagons, six-pointed, like snow."

"And the salt of urine forms pentagons, and thus Mr. Davidson explains the form of each of the eighty stones found in the bladder of Monsieur Pelletier. But if bodies of analogous form mingle with more affinity, it is logical that they should attract one another with greater strength. Hence if you burn your hand, you will obtain relief of your suffering by holding it for a bit in front of the fire."

"My tutor once, when a peasant was bitten by a viper, held the head of the viper to the wound . . ."

"Of course. The venom, which was seeping towards the heart, returned to its chief source, where there was a greater quantity of it. If in time of plague you carry a jar of toad powder, or perhaps a live toad or spider, or even some arsenic, that poisonous substance will attract the infection of the air. And dried onions ferment in the larder when those of the garden begin to grow."

"And this explains also birthmarks, when the mother craves something and . . ."

"Here I would proceed with greater caution. Sometimes analogous phenomena may have different causes, and a man of science must not lend credence to old superstitions. But to return to my powder. What happened when, for a few days, I subjected the cloth stained with our friend's blood to the action of the Powder? First of all, the sun and the moon, from a great distance, attracted the spirits of the blood found on the bandage, thanks to the heat of the room, and the spirits of vitriol with the blood could not avoid following the same path. On the other hand, the wound continued to expel a great abundance of hot and igneous spirits, thus attracting the circumambient air. This air attracted more air and this attracted still more, until the spirits of the blood and the vitriol, dispersed at a great distance, were finally conjoined with that air, which carried with it other atomies of the same blood. Thus the atomies of the blood coming from the cloth met those coming from the wound, expelling the air as a useless encumbrance, and they were attracted to their prime seat, the wound, and, united to them, the spirits of the vitriol penetrated the flesh."

"But could you not have applied the vitriol directly to the wound?"

"I could have, as I had the wounded man before me. But what if he had been at some distance? Consider further: if I had applied the vitriol directly to the wound, its corrosive strength would have increased the irritation, whereas transported by the air, it releases only its gentle and balmy component, capable of arresting the blood. It is used also in collyria for the eyes."

Roberto listened intently, as in the future he would make good use of that advice, which certainly explains the worsening of his condition.

"On the other hand," d'Igby added, "you must surely not use normal vitriol, as was formerly the practice, doing more harm than good. For myself I procure a vitriol from Cyprus, and first calcine it in the sun: calcination removes the superfluous moisture, as if reducing it to a concentrated broth; and further, the calcination makes the spirits of this substance suitable for transportation by the air. Finally I add some gum tragacanth, which closes the wound more rapidly."

I have dwelt on what Roberto learned from d'Igby because this discovery was to mark his fate.

It must also be said, to the shame of our friend, that he was fascinated by this revelation not because of any interest in natural science, but only—again and always—through love. In other words, that description of a universe crowded with spirits that unite according to their affinity seemed to him an allegory of falling in love, and he took to frequenting private libraries to seek everything he could find on the weapon salve, which at that time was a great deal, and it would be even more in the years that followed. Advised by Monsieur Gaffarel (in whispers, so the other habitués of the Dupuys, who gave scant credence to these things, could not overhear), he read the *Ars Magnesia* of Kircher, the *Tractatus de magnetica vulnerum curatione* of Goclenius, the work of Fracastoro, the *Discursus de unguento armario* of Fludd, and the *Hopolochrisma spongus* of Foster. He became learned in order to translate his learning into poetry and to be able one day to shine, eloquent messenger of the universal sympathy, in the same forum where the eloquence of others humiliated him.

For many months (the duration of his stubborn research, in which time he did not advance a single step along the path of conquest), Roberto practiced a sort of principle of double —indeed, multiple—truth, an idea that in Paris many considered at once foolhardy and prudent. During the day he discussed the possible eternity of matter, and at night he wore out his eyes on the little treatises that promised him—albeit in terms of natural philosophy—occult miracles.

In great enterprises we must seek not so much to create opportunities as to take advantage of those that are offered us. One evening at Arthénice's, after a heated debate on *Astrée,* the Hostess urged her guests to consider what love and friendship have in common. Roberto then took the floor, observing that the principle of love, whether between friends or between lovers, was not unlike the action of the Powder of Sympathy. At the first sign of interest, he repeated the stories of d'Igby, excluding only that of the urinating sainted nun, then he began discoursing on the theme, ignoring friendship and speaking only of love.

"Love obeys the same laws as the wind, and the winds are always influenced by the places from which they come. If they come from gardens of flowers or simples, they may have the scent of jasmine or of mint or of rosemary, and so they make sailors yearn to reach the land that sends so many promises. Not dissimilar are the amorous spirits that intoxicate the nostrils of the enamoured heart" (and we must forgive Roberto this unfortunate trope). "The loved heart is a lute, which causes the strings of another lute to sound in unison, as the ringing of bells acts on the surface of streams, especially at night, when in the absence of other sound the water generates the same movement that has been generated in the air. What happens to the loving heart is not unlike what happens to tartar, which generates the perfume of roses when it has been allowed to dissolve in the darkness of a cellar during the season of roses, for the air, filled with rose atoms changing into water by the attraction of the salt of tartar, perfumes the tartar. Nor does the beloved's cruelty avail. A barrel of wine, when the vineyards are in flower, ferments and sends to the surface its white flower, which remains there until the flowers of the vines fall. But the loving heart, more obstinate than wine, when it is bedecked at the flowering of the beloved heart, cultivates its blossom even when the source has dried up."

He seemed to catch a glance of tenderness from Lilia, and he continued: "Loving is like taking a moon bath. The rays coming from the moon are those of the sun reflected down to us. Concentrating the sun's rays in a mirror, you strengthen the calefactory force. Concentrating the moon's rays with a silver basin, you will see that its concave bottom reflects the refreshing rays through the gathering of dew they contain. It seems senseless to wash in an empty basin: and yet you find your hands moist, and it is an infallible remedy for warts."

"Monsieur de la Grive," someone said, "love is hardly a cure for warts!"

"No, certainly not," Roberto resumed, by now beyond arresting, "but I have given examples that come from base things to remind you that love, too, depends on the powder of corpuscles alone. Which is a way of saying that love obeys the same laws that govern both sublunary and celestial bodies, save that, of these laws it is the most noble manifestation. Love is born of sight, for it is at first sight that love is kindled: what is love, then, if not an access of the light reflected by the body beheld? Beholding it, my body is penetrated by the best element of the beloved body, the aerial, which through the meatus of the eyes arrives directly at the heart. And therefore to love at first sight is to drink the spirits of the beloved's heart. The great Architect of nature, when He composed our body, set internal spirits in it, like sentinels, so that they could report their discoveries to their general, namely, the imagination, which is the master of the corporeal family. And if it is struck by some object, the result is the same as when we hear viols playing, and we carry their melody in our memory and continue to hear it even in sleep. Our imagination constructs a simulacrum of the object, which delights the lover, if it does not lacerate him because it is, in fact, no more than a simulacrum. From this it follows that when a man is surprised by the sight of the lovable person, he changes color, flushes or pales according to whether those ministers, the internal spirits, proceed rapidly or slowly towards the object, to return thence to the imagination. These spirits do not travel only to the brain, but also straight to the heart along the great conduit that carries from it to the brain the vital spirits that there become animal spirits; and along this conduit the imagination also transmits to the heart some of the atomies it has received from the external object, and these atomies produce the ebullience of the vital spirits that sometimes expands the heart and sometimes brings it to syncope."

"You tell us, sir, that love proceeds like a physical movement, not differently from the way wine flowers; but you do not tell us why love, unlike other phenomena of matter, is an elective virtue, which chooses. For what reason, then, does love make us slaves of one creature and not of another?"

"This is the very reason why I compared the qualities of love with the principle of the Powder of Sympathy, namely that atomies which are equal and of the same form attract equal atomies! If I were to dust the weapon that wounded Pylades with that powder, I would not heal the wound of Orestes. Thus love unites only two beings who in some way already possess the same nature, unites a noble spirit to a spirit equally noble, and a vulgar spirit to one equally vulgar—as it happens that villeins also love, as do shepherdesses, and we are so instructed by the admirable story of Monsieur d'Urfé. Love reveals a harmony between two creatures that was ordained since the beginning of time, as Destiny had always decided that Pyramus and Thisbe would be united in a single mulberry tree."

"What of unhappy love?"

"I do not believe there is truly an unhappy love. There are only loves that have not yet arrived at perfect fruition, if for some reason the beloved has not received the message coming to her from the eyes of the lover. And yet the lover knows to such a degree which similarity of nature has been revealed to him that, because of this knowledge, he is able to wait, even all his life. He knows that the revelation to both, and their conjunction, can take place even after death, when, the atomies of the two bodies having evaporated as they dissolve in the earth, the lovers will be united in some heaven. And perhaps, as a wounded man, even unaware that someone is scattering the Powder on the weapon that struck him, enjoys a new health, so countless loving hearts may enjoy a sudden relief of the spirit, unaware that their happiness is the work of the beloved heart, which in its turn has become loving and has thus set in motion the unification of the twin atomies."

I must say that all this complex allegory held only up to a certain point, and perhaps the Aristotelian Machine of Padre Emanuele would have demonstrated its instability. But that evening everyone became convinced of the kinship between the Powder, which heals a sickness, and love, which can heal but more often causes sickness.

The story of this speech on the Powder of Sympathy and the Sympathy of Love spread through all of Paris, for some months and perhaps longer, with results that we will narrate in due course.

And Lilia, at the end of the speech, smiled again at Roberto. It was a smile of congratulation, or at most of admiration, but nothing is more natural than to believe that one is loved. Roberto interpreted the smile as an acknowledgment of all the letters he had sent. Too accustomed to the torments of absence, he abandoned the gathering, content with that victory. It was an error, and we will see why later. From then on, to be sure, he dared speak to Lilia, but the replies he received were always contradictory. Sometimes she would murmur, "Just as we said a few days ago." Sometimes, on the contrary, she murmured, "And yet you said something quite different." Other times, leaving, she would promise, "But we will talk of it later. Keep your word."

Roberto could not decide if she was absently attributing to him the words and deeds of another, or if she was coyly provoking him.

What later befell him drove him to compose those few episodes into a far more disturbing story.

CHAPTER 17

Longitudinum Optata Scientia

IT WAS—AT last a firm date—the evening of the 2nd of December, 1642. They were leaving a theater, where Roberto spent every evening in the role of an ardent wooer. Lilia, on coming outside, furtively pressed his hand, whispering, "Monsieur de la Grive, you were not shy that evening. Until tomorrow then, again, on the same stage."

He left in mad turmoil, bidden to such a tryst at a place he could not know, urged to repeat what he had never dared say. And yet she could not have mistaken him for another, because she had called him by his name.

Oh—he writes of having said to himself—today the streams flow back to their source, white chargers scale the towers of Our Lady of Paris, a fire smiles glowing in the ice, for it has truly happened that she has invited me. Or perhaps not, today blood flows from the rock, a grass snake couples with a bear, the sun has turned black, because my beloved has offered me a cup that I will never be able to drain, for I do not know where we are to meet. . . .

Just a step short of happiness, he ran home in despair. The one place where he was sure she could not be.

Lilia's words can be interpreted in a far less mysterious fashion: she was simply reminding him of his remote discourse on the Powder of Sympathy, was urging him to say more, in that same salon of Arthénice where he had already spoken. Since then she had seen him silent and adoring, and this did not correspond to the rules of the game of seduction, so severely regulated. She was recalling him, we would say today, to his social duty. "Come," she was saying to him. "That evening you were not shy, tread again that same stage, I am waiting to see you there." Nor could we expect any other challenge from a précieuse.

But Roberto, on the contrary, had understood: "You are shy, and yet a few evenings ago you were not, and with me you were——" (I suspect that jealousy forbade and at the same time encouraged Roberto to imagine the rest of that sentence). "So tomorrow, again, on that same stage, in that same secret place."

It is natural that—his fancy having taken the most thorny path—he should immediately conceive a case of mistaken identity, of someone who had passed himself off as Roberto and in such guise received from Lilia that for which Roberto would have bartered his life. So, then, Ferrante had reappeared, and all the threads of the past were knotted once more. Maleficent alter ego, Ferrante had thrust himself into this story, playing on Roberto's absences, his delays, his early departures, and at the right moment had garnered the reward for Roberto's speech on the Powder of Sympathy.

And in his distress, Roberto heard a knocking at the door. Ah, Hope! dream of wakeful men! He rushed to open, convinced he would see her on the threshold: it was instead an officer of the Cardinal's guards, with two men as escort.

"Monsieur de la Grive, I presume," he said. Then, identifying himself as Captain de Bar, he went on: "I am sorry to have to do what I am now obliged to do. But you, sir, are under arrest, and I must beg you to give me your sword. If you come with me now in a mannerly fashion, we will board the carriage awaiting us, like two friends, and you will have no cause for embarrassment." He indicated that he did not know the reason for the arrest, and hoped it was all a misunderstanding. Roberto followed him in silence, formulating the same wish, and at the end of the journey, consigned with many apologies to a sleepy guard, he found himself in a cell of the Bastille.

He spent two very cold nights there, visited only by a few rats (a provident preparation for his voyage on the *Amaryllis*) and by a guard who to every question replied only that this place had housed so many illustrious guests that he had long since given up wondering why they had fetched up here; and considering that a great gentleman like Bassompierre had been here for seven years, it was not Roberto's place to start complaining after a few hours.

Having left Roberto for those two days to anticipate the worst, on the third evening de Bar returned, arranged for him to wash, and announced that he was to appear before the Cardinal. Roberto understood at least that he was a prisoner of State.

They reached the palace late in the evening, and already from the stir at the door it was evident that this evening was exceptional. The stairs were crowded with people of every condition scurrying in opposite directions; gentlemen and ecclesiastics came into the antechamber, breathless, and politely expectorated against the frescoed walls, assuming a doleful expression, then entered another hall, from which members of the household emerged, in loud voices calling servants who could not be found and motioning all the others to be silent.

Roberto was also led into that hall, where he saw only people's backs, while all peered in at the door of yet another room, on tiptoe, making not a sound, as if to witness some sad spectacle. De Bar looked around, apparently seeking someone; finally he motioned Roberto to remain in a corner, and went off.

Another guard was trying to make many of those present leave the room, his courtesy varying according to their rank; he saw Roberto unshaven, his clothing disheveled after his detention. When the guard asked him roughly what he was doing there, Roberto answered that the Cardinal was expecting him, to which the guard replied that the Cardinal, to everyone's misfortune, was himself expected by Someone of far greater importance.

In any case, the man left Roberto where he was, and little by little, when de Bar (by now the only friendly face he knew) did not return, Roberto moved closer to the gathering, and after waiting a bit and then pushing a bit, he reached the threshold of the inner room.

There he saw and recognized, in a bed at the far end, resting on a snowbank of pillows, the shadow of the man that all France feared and very few loved. The great Cardinal was surrounded by doctors in black robes, who seemed to be interested chiefly in their own debate; an acolyte wiped the prelate's lips as weak fits of coughing formed a reddish spume; under the covers you could see the painful respiration of a now exhausted body, one hand emerged from a nightshirt, clutching a crucifix. Suddenly a sob escaped the acolyte. Richelieu with effort turned his head, tried to smile, murmuring, "Did you believe I was immortal?"

As Roberto was asking himself who could possibly have summoned him to the bed of this dying man, there was a great confusion behind him. Some whispered the name of the pastor of Saint-Eustache, and as all stood aside, a priest entered with his suite, bearing the holy oil.

Roberto felt someone touch his shoulder; it was de Bar. "Come," he said, "the Cardinal is awaiting you." Bewildered, Roberto followed him along a corridor. De Bar led him into a room, signaling him again to wait, then withdrew.

The room was spacious, with a great globe in the center and a clock on a little table in one corner against red drapery. To the left of the drapery, under a full-length portrait of Richelieu, Roberto finally saw a man with his back to him, in cardinal's robes, standing at a lectern and writing. The Cardinal moved his head slightly, motioning Roberto to approach, but as Roberto did so, the older man bent over the inclined board, placing his left hand as a screen along the margin of the page even though, at the respectful distance where Roberto still stood, he could have read nothing.

Then the personage turned, in an unfolding of purple, and stood for a few seconds erect, as if to reproduce the pose of the great portrait behind him, his right hand resting on the lectern, the left at his breast, affectedly, the palm held upwards. At last he sat on a stool beside the clock, coyly stroked his moustache and goatee, and asked, "Monsieur de la Grive?"

Monsieur de la Grive until this moment had been convinced he was dreaming, in a nightmare of this same Cardinal's dying a dozen yards away, but now he saw him rejuvenated, with features less sharp, as if on the pale aristocratic face of the portrait someone had shadowed the complexion and redrawn the lip with more defined and sinuous lines. Then that voice with the foreign accent wakened in him the long-forgotten memory of the captain who twelve years before had galloped between the opposing forces at Casale.

Roberto was facing Cardinal Mazarin, and he realized that

slowly, during the death-agony of his protector, this man had been assuming his functions. Already the guard referred to "the" Cardinal, as if there were no longer any other.

Roberto was about to answer the question, but he soon became aware that the Cardinal only made a show of interrogating: actually he was asserting, and his interlocutor could only agree.

"Monsieur de la Grive," the Cardinal, in fact, affirmed, "Lord Pozzo di San Patrizio. We know the castle, as we know the Monferrato region well. So fertile, it could even be France. Your father, in the days at Casale, fought with honor and was more loyal to us than others of your compatriots." He said *us* as if at that time he was already the creature of the King of France. "You also acted bravely on that occasion, we are told. Will you believe, then, that we are all the more, and paternally, sorry that as a guest in this country you have not observed the rules of hospitality? Did you not know that in this kingdom laws are applied equally to citizens and to guests? Naturally, naturally we will not forget that a gentleman is always a gentleman, whatever crime he may have committed: you will enjoy the same advantages granted Cinq-Mars, whose memory you apparently do not execrate as you should. You will also die by the axe and not by the rope."

Roberto could not be ignorant of a question that had all France talking. The Marquis de Cinq-Mars had tried to convince the King to dismiss Richelieu, and Richelieu had convinced the King that Cinq-Mars was conspiring against the throne. In Lyons the condemned man attempted to behave with bold dignity before the executioner, but the latter made such an appalling mess of the victim's neck that the indignant crowd had then massacred him.

As Roberto, aghast, was about to speak, the Cardinal forestalled him with a gesture. "Come now, San Patrizio," he said, and Roberto inferred that this name was being used to remind him he was a foreigner; though the Cardinal was speaking to him in French when he could have spoken in Italian. "You have succumbed to the vices of this city and this country. As His Eminence the Cardinal is accustomed to saying, the innate frivolity of the French brings them to desire change because of the tedium caused by the present. Some of these light-minded gentlemen, whom the King has taken care to make still lighter by relieving them of their head, seduced you with their subversive propositions. Your case is not the sort that need disturb any tribunal. The States, whose preservation is of necessity extremely dear to us, would quickly be ruined if in matters of crime that tend to their subversion we demanded proofs of the sort required in common law. Two evenings ago you were seen in the company of friends of Cinq-Mars, who uttered yet again sentiments highly treasonable. The witness who saw you in their midst is worthy of trust, for he was there under our orders. And that is enough. No," he again anticipated, bored, "we did not have you brought here to make us listen to protests of innocence, so remain calm and listen yourself."

Roberto was not calm, but he had arrived at some conclusions: at the very moment Lilia was touching his hand, he was seen elsewhere conspiring against the State. Mazarin was so convinced of this that the thought had become fact. It was everywhere murmured that the wrath of Richelieu was not yet sated, and many feared being chosen as further examples. However he may have been chosen, Roberto was in any case doomed.

He could have reflected that, not only two nights previously but often, he had participated in some conversation on leaving the Rambouillet salon; that it was not impossible that among those interlocutors there had been an intimate of

Cinq-Mars; that if Mazarin, for reasons of his own, wanted to ruin him, he needed only to interpret maliciously any phrase reported by a spy. . . . But naturally Roberto's reflections were different, and they confirmed his fears: someone had taken part in a seditious gathering, boastfully assuming his name and his face.

All the more reason to attempt no defense. What remained inexplicable to him was why—if he was already condemned —the Cardinal was taking the trouble to inform him of his fate. Roberto had not been the recipient of any message but was himself the cipher, the riddle that others, still dubious of the king's decisiveness, would have to solve. In silence he awaited an explanation.

"You see, San Patrizio, if we were not honored by the ecclesiastical dignity with which the pope, and the King's wish, invested us a year ago, we would say that Providence was guiding your imprudence. For some time you have been under surveillance, while we wondered how we could ask you to render us a service which you were in no way obliged to perform. We receive your misstep of three evenings ago as a singular gift of Heaven. Now you could be in our debt, and our position changes, to say nothing of yours."

"In your debt?"

"For your life. Naturally it is not in our power to pardon you, but we have the power to intercede. Let us suppose you manage to avoid the rigor of the law through escape. After a year, or even more, the memory of the witness would no doubt be clouded, and he could swear, with no blot on his honor, that the man of three evenings ago was not you; and it could be verified that at that hour you were elsewhere playing tric-trac with Captain de Bar. Then—we do not decide, mind you, we presume, and the opposite could also happen, but we are confident that we are correct—you would be accorded full vindication and unconditional freedom. Be seated, please," he said. "I have a mission to propose to you."

Roberto sat down. "A mission?"

"And a delicate one. In the course of which—we will not shirk the fact—you might risk losing your life. But this is a transaction: you are saved from the certitude of the executioner, and are allowed many chances of returning safe and sound, if you are alert. A year of hardship, shall we say, in exchange for a whole life."

"Your Eminence," Roberto said, seeing the image of the executioner at least fading, "from what I gather, it is pointless for me to swear, on my honor or on the Cross, that—"

"We would be lacking in Christian charity if we absolutely denied the possibility of your innocence or of our being victim of a misunderstanding. But the misunderstanding so coincides with our plans that we see no reason to examine it. For that matter, you would not wish to insinuate that we are proposing to you a dishonest exchange, as if to say either you are innocent and to the block with you, or self-confessed guilty and, by perjury, in our service. . . ."

"Far be it from me to make any such disrespectful suggestion, Your Eminence."

"Very well, then. We offer you some possible danger, but certain glory. And we will tell you how we happened to have our eye on you, even before your presence in Paris was known. The city, you see, talks much of what happens in the salons, and all Paris has gossiped about an evening not long ago during which you shone in the eyes of many ladies. Yes, all Paris: do not blush. We refer to that evening when you passionately expounded the virtues of a so-called Powder of Sympathy, and when in discoursing (as is said in those places, am I not right?), your ironies gave that subject spice, as your paronomasias lent it grace; your assertions, solemnity; hyperbole, richness; and comparisons, perspicuity. . . ."

"Ah, Your Eminence, I was merely repeating things I had learned . . ."

"I admire modesty, but it seems to me that you revealed a thorough knowledge of certain natural secrets. Now I need a man of such learning, who is not French and who, without compromising the crown, can discreetly board a ship sailing from Amsterdam with the intention of discovering a new secret, connected in a way with the use of that powder."

He forestalled another objection from Roberto: "Never fear, we require you to know well what we are seeking, so that you can interpret even the vaguest signs. We would have you thoroughly instructed in the subject, as we see you now so disposed to satisfy us. You will be assigned a gifted master, and do not be deceived by his youth." He reached out and pulled a rope. No sound was heard, but the act must have made a bell ring somewhere or given some other signal—or so Roberto deduced, in those days when great lords still yelled for their servants in loud voices.

In fact, a short time later, a young man deferentially entered; he looked to be slightly over twenty.

"Welcome, Colbert, this is the person of whom we were speaking today," Mazarin said to him, then turned to Roberto. "Colbert, who is being initiated in a promising fashion into the secrets of the administration of the State, has for some time been considering a problem that means much to Cardinal de Richelieu, and consequently to me. You may know, San Patrizio, that before the Cardinal took the helm of this great vessel of which Louis XIII is captain, the French navy was nothing compared to the navies of our enemies, in war as in peace. Now we can be justly proud of our ship-builders, of our eastern fleet and of the western, and you will recall with what success, no more than six months past, the marquis de Brézé commanded off Barcelona forty-four galleons, fourteen galleys, and I do not recall how many other vessels. We have consolidated our conquests in New France, we have won dominion over Martinique and Guadeloupe, and many of those Islands of Peru, as the Cardinal likes to say. We have begun establishing commercial companies, though not yet with complete success. While in the United Provinces, in England, Portugal, and Spain, there is no noble family that does not have one son off at sea making his fortune, in France, alas, this is not so. The proof is that whereas we know enough perhaps of the New World, we know little of the Very New. Colbert, show our friend how empty of lands the other part of that globe still appears."

The young man turned the globe, and Mazarin smiled sadly: "This expanse of waters is not empty because of a grudging Nature; it is empty because we know all too little of Nature's generosity. And yet, after the discovery of a western passage to the Moluccas, this whole vast unexplored zone is at hazard, extending from the western shores of the American continent to the last eastern outcrops of Asia. I refer to the ocean called the Pacific, as the Portuguese have named it, in which surely lies the Austral Terra Incognita, of which only a few islands are known, a few hazy coasts, but still enough for us to assume that it conceals fabulous riches. And now, for some time, too many adventurers who do not speak our language have been swarming over those waters. Our friend Colbert, with something I consider more than just youthful caprice, cherishes the idea of a French representation in those seas. The more plausible, as we presume that the first to set foot on an Austral land was a Frenchman, Monsieur de Gonneville, sixteen years before the voyage of Magellan. And yet that worthy gentleman, or ecclesiastic as he might be, neglected to record on maps the place where he landed. Can we

imagine a good Frenchman being so imprudent? No, surely
not. The fact is that in those remote days there was one problem he did not know how to solve completely. And this
problem—you will be amazed to learn what it is—remains a
mystery even for us."

He paused, and Roberto understood that since both the
Cardinal and Colbert knew, if not the solution, at least the
name of the mystery, the pause was solely for his benefit. He
thought it wise to play the part of fascinated listener, and he
said: "And what is this mystery, if I may ask?"

Mazarin exchanged a knowing look with Colbert and said:
"It is the mystery of longitude." Colbert gravely nodded his
assent.

"For the solution of this problem of the *Punto Fijo*," the
Cardinal continued, "seventy years ago Philip II of Spain offered a fortune, and later Philip III promised six thousand duc-
ats of perpetual income and an annuity of another two
thousand, while the Estates General of Holland offered thirty
thousand florins. . . . By the way, Colbert, we've been keeping
that Dr. Morin waiting for eight years. . . ."

"Your Eminence, you yourself have expressed your conviction that this business of the lunar parallax is a chimera. . . ."

"Yes, but to sustain his quite dubious hypothesis the man
has effectively studied and criticized the others. Let us allow
him to take part in this new project; he could enlighten Monsieur de San Patrizio. Offer him a pension; there is nothing
like money to stimulate good inclinations. If his idea contains
a seed of truth, we will be enabled better to ensure it for
ourselves and at the same time we will avoid his feeling abandoned by his own country, and hence succumbing to the lures
of the Dutch. It seems to me that it is indeed the Dutch who,
seeing the hesitation of the Spaniards, have started negotiating
with that Galilei, and we would be wise not to remain outside
the matter. . . ."

"Your Eminence," Colbert said hesitantly, "you will be pleased to recall that Galilei died at the beginning of this year. . . ."

"Really? Let us pray God he is happy, more so than he was in life."

"And in any case his solution seemed for a long time definitive, but it is not. . . ."

"You have felicitously anticipated us, Colbert. But let us assume that Morin's solution, too, is worthless. Nevertheless, we will support it, cause it to rekindle the debate around his ideas, stimulate the curiosity of the Dutch, see that he allows himself to be tempted, and thus we will have set our adversaries on the wrong track for a while. It will be money well spent in any case. But we have talked enough of this. Continue, please; as San Patrizio learns I will learn with him."

"Your Eminence taught me everything I know," Colbert said, blushing, "but your kindness encourages me to speak." With this, he must now have felt he was on friendly terrain: he raised his head, which he had kept bowed, and moved nonchalantly to the globe. "Gentlemen, on the ocean—where even if you encounter land, you do not know what it is, and if you go towards a known land, you must proceed for days and days amid an expanse of water—the navigator has no points of reference save the stars. With instruments that made the ancient astronomers illustrious, the altitude of a star above the horizon is established, its distance from the zenith is deduced; and knowing its declination, and since zenith distance plus or minus declination determines latitude, you know immediately on which parallel you are, that is, how much you are north or south of a known point. That is clear, I think."

"A child could understand it," Mazarin said.

"We must believe," Colbert went on, "that in similar fashion it can be established also how far to the east or to the west of the same point you are, in short, at what longitude, or on what meridian. As Sacrobosco says, the meridian is a circle that passes through the poles of our world and through the zenith directly above our head. And it is called meridian because wherever a man is and at whatever time of the year, when the sun reaches his meridian, for that man in that place it is noon. Alas, through a mystery of nature, every means conceived to establish longitude has always proved faulty. How much does it matter, the profane might ask? It matters a great deal."

Gaining confidence, he turned the globe, pointing to the outline of Europe. "Fifteen degrees of meridian, approximately, separate Paris from Prague, a little more than twenty separate Paris from the Canaries. What would you say to the commander of a land army who thought he was fighting at the White Mountain, and instead of killing Protestants he slaughtered the doctors of the Sorbonne at Mont-Sainte-Geneviève?"

Mazarin smiled, holding out his hands, as if to convey the expectation that such things would happen only on the correct meridian.

"The tragedy," Colbert continued, "is that errors of such dimensions are made with the means used to determine longitude. And thus dreadful things happen: almost a century ago, that Spaniard Mendaña discovered the Islands of Solomon, lands blessed by Heaven with fruits of the soil and gold beneath the soil. This Mendaña fixed the position of the land he had discovered, came home to announce the event, and in less than twenty years ships had been fitted out for him four times to return to the islands and definitively assert the rights of Their Most Catholic Majesties, as they are called in their country, and what happened? Mendaña was never able to find those islands again. The Dutch did not remain idle: at the beginning of this century they set up their Dutch East India Company, they created in Asia the city of Batavia as point of departure

for many expeditions to the east, and they reached a New
Holland; while other lands probably to the east of the Solomon
Islands were discovered by English pirates, to whom the court
of Saint James's quickly granted charters of nobility. But of
the Solomon Islands no one was to find a trace, and it is
understandable that some are now inclined to consider them
a legend. Legendary or not as they may be, Mendaña actually
found them, but, while he fixed their latitude properly, he
mistook their longitude. And even if, through celestial help,
he had established it correctly, other navigators seeking that
longitude (and he himself, on his second voyage) did not know
clearly what their own longitude was. And even if we knew
where Paris was but could not establish whether we were in
Spain or among the Persians, you see well, sir, that we would
be proceeding like blind men leading the blind."

"Truly," Roberto ventured, "I can scarcely believe, with all
I have heard about the advancement of learning in this century
of ours, that we still know so little."

"I will not give you a list of the methods proposed, sir,
from the one based on lunar eclipses to the one considering
the variations of the magnetic needle, on which our Le Tellier
labored even recently, not to mention the *loch* method, which
our Champlain guaranteed with many promises. . . . But all
proved insufficient, and they will continue to be so until
France has an observatory where all these many hypotheses
can be tested. There is of course one sure method: keep on
board a clock that always tells the time of the Paris meridian,
then determine the local time at sea, and from the difference
in times deduce the difference of longitude. This is the globe
on which we live, and you can see how the wisdom of the
ancients divided it into three hundred sixty degrees of longitude, usually starting from the meridian that crosses the Isla
de Hierro in the Canaries. In its celestial course, the sun (and

whether it is the sun that moves or, as they have it nowadays, the earth, is a question of little consequence in this instance) covers fifteen degrees of longitude in one hour, so when in Paris it is midnight, as it is at this moment, then at one hundred eighty degrees of meridian from Paris it is noon. So if you know for sure that in Paris the clocks say, for example, noon, and you can determine that in the place where you are now it is six in the morning, you calculate the difference in time, translate every hour into fifteen degrees, and you will learn that you are ninety degrees from Paris, and hence more or less here. . . ." He turned the globe and indicated a point on the American continent. "But while it is not hard to determine the time in the place where you are making your calculation, it is quite difficult to keep a clock that will continue to tell the correct time after months of navigation on board a ship tossed by the winds, such movement causing error even in the most ingenious of modern instruments, not to mention hourglasses and water clocks, which to function properly must rest on an immobile plane."

The Cardinal interrupted him: "We do not believe that Signor di San Patrizio need know any more for the present, Colbert. You will see to it that he is given further enlightenment during the journey to Amsterdam. After which it will no longer be we who teach him, but he, we trust, who teaches us. In fact, my dear San Patrizio, the Cardinal, whose eye has seen and will see—for a long time, let us hope—farther than ours, provided in the past for a network of trusted informants, who would journey to other countries, frequent the ports, question captains setting out on a voyage or just returning from one, to learn what the other governments were doing and what they knew that we did not, for—and this seems to me obvious—the State that discovers the secret of longitude, and manages to prevent word of it from spreading, will obtain a great advantage over the others. Now . . ." And here Mazarin paused again, once more smoothing his moustache, then folded his hands as if to concentrate and at the same time implore the support of Heaven. "Now we have learned that an English physician, one Dr. Byrd, has devised a new and prodigious means to determine the meridian, based on the use of the Powder of Sympathy. How, dear San Patrizio, do not ask us, for I barely know the name of this deviltry. We are certain that this powder is employed, but we know nothing of the method Byrd plans to adopt, and our informant is most surely not versed in natural magic. However, it is certain that the English admiralty has agreed to fit out a ship to brave the seas of the Pacific. The matter is of such moment that the English have chosen not to have the ship appear as one of their own. It belongs to a Dutchman, who pretends to be eccentric and claims that he wants to repeat the course of his compatriots who, about twenty-five years ago, discovered a new passage between the Atlantic and the Pacific, beyond the straits of Magellan. But since the cost of the venture could prompt suspicion of secret financing, the Dutchman is overtly loading cargo and seeking passengers, as if he were concerned with meeting expenses. Seemingly by chance, Dr. Byrd will also be on board, with three assistants, to collect exotic flora, they say. In fact they will be in complete charge of the expedition. And among the passengers there will be you, San Patrizio: our agent in Amsterdam will take care of everything. You will be a Savoyard gentleman who, pursued by a warrant in every land, feels it is wise to disappear for a long period at sea. Obviously, you will not even have to lie. Your health will be delicate—and the fact that you have an eye affliction, as we have heard, is a touch that perfects our plan. You will be a passenger who spends almost all his time indoors, with some poultice or other on his face, and for the rest you will not see beyond your nose. But, vague vagabond, you will seem to divagate, while in reality you will keep both eyes open and your ears pricked. We know you understand English, but you will pretend not to, so the enemies will speak freely in your presence. If someone on board understands Italian or French, you will ask questions and remember what you are told. Do not disdain to engage common men in conversation, who for a few coins will disclose anything. But let the sum be small, and it must appear a gift, not a bribe, else they will grow suspicious. You will never ask anything directly, and after questioning someone one day, you will ask the same questions on the morrow in different terms, so that if the man at first lied, he will be led to contradict himself: foolish men forget the tales they tell, and the next day they invent an opposite story. You will recognize liars: when they laugh, they have dimples in their cheeks, and they keep their fingernails closely trimmed; similarly, beware of men of short stature, who utter falsehoods out of vainglory. In any case keep your dialogues with them brief, and do not appear content: the person with whom you must speak is Dr. Byrd, and it will be natural for you to crave the company of the only passenger who is your equal in education. He is a man of learning, he will speak French, perhaps Italian, certainly Latin. You are ill, and you will seek advice and solace from him. You will not behave like those who eat berries or red earth and pretend to spit blood, but you will have your pulse taken after supper, for always at that hour one seems to have a fever, and you will tell him you never close your eyes at night; thus you will have an excuse if you are surprised somewhere, wide awake, which is bound to happen if their experiments involve the stars. This Byrd must be a man possessed, as for that matter are all men of science: invent some fancies and talk to him about them, as if you were confiding a secret, thus he will be led to talk about the obsession that is his secret. Show interest, but pretending to understand little or nothing, so he will tell it to you better a second time. Repeat what he says, as if you have understood, and make some mistakes, so that out of vanity he is prompted to correct you, explaining in detail what he should remain silent about. Never affirm, always allude: allusions are made to test the spirit and probe the heart. You must inspire trust in him: if he laughs often, laugh with him, if he is bilious, be bilious also, but always admire his knowledge. If he is choleric and insults you, tolerate the insult, knowing you began punishing him even before the insult was uttered. At sea the days are long and the nights endless, and there is nothing that consoles an Englishman in his boredom better than many beakers of that *cervisia,* or beer, as they call it, of which the Dutch always carry a supply in their hold. You will pretend to be a devotee of that beverage, and you will encourage your new friend to partake of it more than you do. One day he might become suspicious and have your cabin searched: for this reason you will put no observation in writing, but you may keep a diary in which you complain of your ill-luck, or implore the Virgin and the Saints, and pour out your despair of seeing your Beloved again; and in this diary there must appear notes on the doctor's virtues, praising him as the one friend you have found on board. You will not quote any of his words pertinent to our object, but only pompous pronouncements, no matter how trite they may be: if he uttered them, he did not consider them so and will be grateful to you for having recorded them. In short, we are not here to offer you a breviary of the good secret informant: a man of the church is not versed in such matters. Trust your talent, be keenly on guard and guardedly keen, let the penetration of your gaze be the opposite of its reputation and in proportion to your alacrity."

Mazarin stood, to indicate to his guest that their conversation had ended, and to stand over him for a moment before he also rose. "You will follow Colbert. He will give you instructions and entrust you to the persons who will accompany you to Amsterdam for your embarkation. Go now and good fortune attend you."

They were about to leave the room when the Cardinal called them back: "Ah, I had almost forgotten, San Patrizio. You must have realized that from now until you sail you will be followed at every step, but you may ask yourself why we do not fear that later, at the first port of call, you will be tempted to escape and hide. We do not fear this because it would not be in your best interest. You could not return here, where you would remain an outlaw, or go into exile in some land down there, with the constant menace of being found by our agents. We do not for a moment entertain the suspicion that a man of your qualities would sell himself to the English. What would you sell, after all? Your being a spy is a secret that, in order to sell, you would first have to reveal, and once revealed, it would be of no further worth, unless it was worth a stab in the back. Whereas, returning, with even modest information, you will have earned our gratitude. We would be wrong to dismiss a man who has proved capable of carrying out such a difficult mission well. The rest, then, depends on you. The favor of the great, once won, must be jealously guarded if it is not to be lost, and nourished with services if it is to be perpetuated. You will decide at that point if your loyalty to France is such as to counsel you to devote your future to her king. It is said that other men, born elsewhere, have succeeded in making their fortune in Paris."

The Cardinal was proposing himself as a model of loyalty rewarded. But for Roberto surely at that point it was not a question of rewards. The Cardinal had given him a glimpse of adventure, new horizons, and had infused him with a wisdom of living he had not known before, an ignorance that may have lowered him in the esteem of others. Perhaps it was best to accept the invitation of destiny, which would carry him away from his sufferings. As for the other invitation, that of three evenings before, everything had become clear as the Cardinal was beginning his discourse. If an Other had taken part in a conspiracy, and all believed it was he, then an Other had surely conspired to inspire in Her the words that had tormented him with joy and enamored him of jealousy. Too many Others between him and reality. And so, all the better to be isolated on the seas, where he could possess his Beloved in the only way permitted him. After all, the perfection of love is not being loved, but being Lover.

He bent one knee, and said: "Eminence, I am yours."

Or at least that is what I would have liked to happen, for it does not seem to me civil to give him a safe-conduct that says, "C'est par mon ordre et pour le bien de l'état que le porteur du présent a fait ce qu'il a fait."

CHAPTER 18

Unheard-of Curiosities

IF THE *DAPHNE*, like the *Amaryllis,* had been sent out to seek the *Punto Fijo,* then the Intruder was dangerous. By now Roberto knew of the relentless struggle among the nations of Europe to gain that secret. He had to prepare himself carefully and play his cards with skill. Obviously the Intruder had acted at night first, then had come out into the open during the day, when Roberto remained awake in his cabin. Should he now revise his plans, giving the impression of sleeping in the daytime and staying awake at night? Why? The other would simply alter his strategy. No, Roberto should instead be unpredictable, make the other unsure, pretend to be asleep when he was awake and awake while he was asleep. . . .

He had to try to imagine what the other thought he thought, or what the other thought he thought the other thought he thought. . . . Thus far the Intruder had been his shadow; now Roberto would become the shadow of the Intruder, learn to follow the trail of the man walking behind his. But that reciprocal ambush could not continue to infinity, one man scrambling up a ladder while the other descended the opposite side, one in the hold while the other was active on deck, one rushing below while the other was perhaps climbing up the flank of the ship.

Any sensible person would have immediately decided to proceed in the exploration of the rest of the ship, but we must bear in mind that Roberto was not sensible. He had succumbed again to aqua vitae, and had convinced himself he was doing so to gain strength. For a man in whom love had always inspired delay, that nepenthe could not inspire decision. So he moved slowly, believing himself a thunderbolt. He thought he was making a leap, when he crawled. Especially since he still did not dare go out during the day, and he felt strong at night. But at night he drank, and dragged his feet. Which was what his enemy wanted, he told himself in the morning. And to muster courage, he clung to the keg.

In any case, towards the evening of the fifth day, he decided to venture into that part of the hold that he still had not visited, below the hatchway of the storeroom. He realized that on the *Daphne* all space had been exploited to the utmost, and between the second deck and the hold partitions and false bottoms had been installed, in order to create closets reached by rickety ladders. He first entered the hawser locker, stumbling over coils of ropes of every kind, soaked in salt water. Then he descended still farther and found himself in the secunda carina, among chests and cases of various description.

He found more food and more barrels of fresh water. He should have rejoiced, and he did, but only because he could now carry on his hunt forever, with the pleasure of delaying it. Which is the pleasure of fear.

Behind the kegs of water he found four others of aqua vitae. He climbed back to the larder and once more examined the kegs there. All contained water, a sign that the keg of aqua vitae he had found the day before had been carried up from below deliberately, to tempt him.

Rather than worry about ambush, he went back down into the hold, brought up another keg of liquor, and drank some.

Then he returned below, we can imagine in what condition; but he stopped, catching the rotten smell of bilge. He could go no lower.

So he went aft, towards the poop, but his lamp was failing and he stumbled on something, realized he was moving through the ballast, at the very point where on the *Amaryllis* Dr. Byrd had devised the cabin for the dog. But here in the hold, among puddles of water and scraps of stored food, he discovered the print of a foot.

He was now so sure an Intruder was on board that his first thought was this: Finally he had proof he was not drunk. Which is, after all, the proof drunks constantly seek. In any case, the evidence was incontrovertible, clear as day, if that is the appropriate phrase to describe his progress between the darkness and the glimmer of his lantern. Convinced now that the Intruder existed, Roberto did not think that in all this coming and going he could have left the print himself. He climbed up again, determined to fight.

It was sunset. It was the first sunset he had seen, after five days of nights, twilights, and dawns. A few black clouds, almost parallel, flanked the more distant island, condensing along the peak, from whence they diminished into arrows aimed southwards. The shore stood dark against the sea now the color of pale ink, while the rest of the sky was a wan and weary camomile, as if the sun were not behind the scene, celebrating his sacrifice, but, rather, dozing off slowly while asking sky and sea to accompany his repose with a murmur.

Roberto, on the contrary, experienced a return of the fighting spirit. He decided to confound the enemy. He went to the clock room and carried as many clocks as he could up on deck, arranging them like the pins in a game of billiards, one by the mainmast, three on the quarterdeck, one against the capstan, still others around the foremast, and one at each hatch and port, so that anyone trying to pass in the dark would trip.

Then he wound the mechanical ones (not considering that in so doing he made them audible to the enemy he wished to surprise) and turned over the hourglasses. He gazed at the deck covered with machines of Time, proud of their noise, sure that it would overwhelm the Other and retard his progress.

Having set out those innocuous snares, he was their first victim. As night fell over a calm sea, he went from one to another of those metal mosquitoes, to listen to their buzz of lifeless essence, to watch those drops of eternity suffer one by one, and fear those terminal termites toothless but gluttonous (these are the very words he wrote), those cogged wheels that shredded the day into bits of instants and consumed life in a music of death.

He remembered some words of Padre Emanuele: "What a jocund Spectacle it would be if through a Crystal at the Breast the motions of the Heart could be seen like the movement of a Clock!" He followed by starlight the slow rosary of those grains of sand muttered by a glass, and he philosophized on those little bundles of moments, those successive anatomies of time, those fissures through which the hours trickled in a fine line.

The cadence of passing time carried a presage of his own demise, which was nearing, one movement after another. He looked close with his myopic eye to decipher that puzzle of fugues, with trepid trope he transformed a water machine into a fluid coffin, and in the end he inveighed against those charlatan astrologers capable of heralding to him only the hours that had passed.

And who knows what else he would have written if he

had not felt the need to abandon his poetic mirabilia, as before he had abandoned his chronometric mirabilia—and not of his own volition but because, having in his veins more liquor than ichor, he had allowed that tick-tock gradually to become a toxical lullaby.

On the morning of the sixth day, wakened by the last machines still gasping, he saw among the clocks, all of them shifted, two little cranes scratching (were they cranes?). Pecking nervously, the birds upset and shattered one of the most beautiful of the hourglasses.

The Intruder, not in the least frightened (and why should he be, knowing perfectly well who was on board?), playing absurd trick for absurd trick, had freed the two animals from below. To create havoc on *my* ship—Roberto was in tears—to show he is more powerful than I. . . .

But why those cranes, he wondered, accustomed to seeing every event as a sign and every sign as a Device. What did he intend them to mean? Roberto tried to recall the symbolic meaning of cranes, what he remembered from Picinelli or Valeriano, but he could find no answer. Now we know very well that there was neither a purpose nor a concept in that Serraglio of Stupefactions: the Intruder was now losing his mind as Roberto had. But Roberto could not know this, and he tried to read sense into something that was no more than a petulant scrawl.

I will catch you! I will catch you, damn you! he cried. And, still sleepy, he seized his sword and flung himself once more towards the hold, falling down the ladders and ending in a still unexplored area, among piles of fagots and newly hewn logs. But, falling, he struck the logs and, rolling with them, found himself with his face on a grating, again breathing the foul stink of the bilge. And at eye-level he saw scorpions crawling.

It was likely that, along with the wood, some insects also had been stored in the hold, and I am not sure they were actually scorpions, but that is how Roberto saw them—introduced by the Intruder, naturally, so that they would poison him. To escape this danger, Roberto began to scramble up the ladder; but, running on those moving logs, he remained where he was, or, rather, he lost his balance and had to cling to the rungs. Finally he climbed up and discovered a cut on his arm.

No doubt he had wounded himself with his own sword. Instead of thinking of the wound, he went back to the wood-pile and searched breathlessly among the logs for his weapon, which was stained with blood. He carried it to the aftercastle and poured aqua vitae on the blade. But finding no improvement, he abjured all the principles of his science and poured the liquor directly on his arm. He invoked some saints with excessive familiarity, ran outside where a great downpour was beginning, at which the cranes flew off and vanished. The downpour brought him to; he became worried about his clocks, ran here and there to carry them to shelter. He caught his foot in a hatchway, sprained it, hopped back inside on one leg, crane-like, undressed and—his response to all these meaningless events—set to writing while the rain first grew heavier, then abated. Some hours of sunshine returned, and finally night fell.

And it is good for us that he did write, for we are thus able to learn what happened to him on the *Amaryllis* and what he discovered in the course of that voyage.

CHAPTER 19

A New Voyage
Round the World

THE *AMARYLLIS* SAILED from Holland and called briefly at London. There, one night, it furtively took something on board, while the sailors formed a cordon between the deck and the hold, so Roberto was unable to see what the new cargo was. Then the ship sailed due southwest.

With amusement Roberto describes the company he found on board. It seemed the captain had taken the greatest care to choose wool-gatherers and eccentrics for his passengers, to serve as a pretext at departure, with no concern if he then lost them along the way. They fell into three categories: those who thought the ship would sail westwards, like the Galician couple who wanted to join a son in Brazil, or the old Jew who had made a vow to go to Jerusalem in pilgrimage by the longest route; those who as yet had no clear idea as to the extension of the globe, like some scapegrace youths determined to make their fortunes in the Moluccas, which they could have reached more comfortably by way of the Levant; and finally those who had been blatantly deceived, like the group of heretics from the Piedmont valleys who meant to join the English Puritans on the northern coast of the New World and did not know that, in fact, the ship would head straight south, making its next call at Recife. Before the heretics became aware of the fraud, they arrived at that colony—then in Dutch hands— and agreed to be put ashore, in any case, at this Protestant port, fearing even worse trouble later among the Catholic Portuguese. At Recife the ship took on a Knight of Malta with the face of a freebooter, whose aim was to find an island some Venetian had told him of: it had been christened Escondida, he did not know its position, and no one else on the *Amaryllis* had ever heard the name. The captain apparently knew how to pick his passengers.

Nor was anyone else concerned about the well-being of that little company packed below deck: while they were crossing the Atlantic, there had been no shortage of food, and some provisions were acquired on the American shores. But, after sailing among long tufted clouds and an azure sky beyond the Fretum Magellanicum, almost all the passengers, except the privileged guests of rank, for at least two months had drunk water that caused the staggers and eaten tack that stank of rat piss. And some men of the crew, as well as many passengers, died of scurvy.

In search of supplies, the ship sailed up the coast of Chile to the west and anchored at a desert island which the nautical charts called Más Afuera. They stayed there three days. The climate was salubrious and the vegetation luxuriant, inspiring the Knight of Malta to say it would be a great stroke of luck to be shipwrecked one day on those shores, and to live there happily, with no wish to return to one's native land—and he tried to persuade himself that this was Escondida. Escondida or not, if I had remained there—Roberto told himself on the *Daphne*—now I would not be here, afraid of an Intruder whose footprint I saw in the hold.

Later there were contrary winds, the captain said, and the

ship, against all reason, turned northwards. Roberto had felt no contrary winds, quite the opposite: when the change of course was announced, the ship had been proceeding under full sail, and thus it had to come hard about. Probably Dr. Byrd and his men needed to proceed along the same meridian to perform their experiments. The fact is that they reached the Galópegos Islands, where they amused themselves turning huge turtles on their backs, then cooking them in their shells. The Maltese consulted certain maps of his at length and decided that this was not Escondida.

Resuming their westward course, descending below the twenty-fifth-degree latitude south, they replenished their water at an island of which the maps gave no indication. It offered no attractive features beyond its solitude, but the Knight— who could not bear the food on board and harbored a strong aversion to the captain—said to Roberto how beautiful it would be if a small band of good men, brave and reckless, would take possession of the ship, put the captain and any who wanted to stay with him in the longboat, burn the Amaryllis, and settle on that land, far from every known world, to build a new society. Roberto asked him if this was Escondida; the man shook his head sadly.

Proceeding again northwest, abetted by the favoring Trades, they came upon a group of islands inhabited by savages with amber-colored skin, with whom they exchanged gifts, taking part in their merry festivities, animated by maidens who danced with the movements of the grasses that swayed on the beach almost at the water's edge. The Knight, who had taken no vow of chastity, on the pretext of drawing portraits of some of those creatures (and he was an artist of some skill), certainly had occasion to have carnal congress with them. The crew wanted to do the same, so the captain moved forward the ship's departure. The Knight hesitated about staying behind;

spending his days sketching here seemed to him a splendid
way to conclude his life. But then he decided this was not
Escondida.

Afterwards they again headed northwest and found an island with quite docile indigenes. In the two days and two
nights they stayed there, the Knight of Malta took to telling
stories: he told them in a dialect not even Roberto could understand, still less the natives, but the speaker assisted himself
by drawing in the sand, and he gesticulated like an actor,
stirring the enthusiasm of his audience, who hailed him with
cries of "Tusitala, Tusitala!" To Roberto the Knight said how
fine he thought it would be to end his days among those
people, telling them all the myths of the universe. "But is this
Escondida?" Roberto asked. The Knight shook his head.

He died in the wreck, Roberto reflected on the *Daphne,* and
perhaps I have found his Escondida, but I will never be able
to narrate it to him, or to anyone else. Perhaps this is why
Roberto wrote to his Lady. To survive, you must tell stories.

The Knight's last fantasy was heard one evening, only a
few days and no great distance from what would be the scene
of the wreck. They were skirting an archipelago, which the
captain had decided not to approach, inasmuch as Dr. Byrd
seemed anxious to continue once again towards the Equator.
In the course of the voyage it had been evident to Roberto
that the captain's behavior was not that of the navigators he
had heard of, who took careful note of all new lands, per-
fecting their maps, drawing cloud-shapes, tracing the line of
shores, gathering native artifacts. . . . The *Amaryllis* proceeded
as if she were the traveling lair of an alchemist bent only on
his Opus Nigrum, indifferent to the great world opening before
her.

It was sunset, the play between clouds and sky against
the shadow of the island drew on one side what looked like

emerald fishes drifting over the peak. On the other there were crumpled balls of fire. Above, gray clouds. Immediately afterwards, as a fiery sun disappeared behind the island, a broad pink stripe was reflected on the clouds, bloodied along the lower fringe. After a few seconds the fire behind the island spread, looming over the ship. The sky was all a brazier with only a few cerulean threads. And then blood everywhere, as if some impenitents had been devoured by a school of sharks.

"Perhaps it would be right to die now," the Knight of Malta said. "Are you not seized by the desire to hang from the mouth of a cannon and slide into the sea? It would be quick, and at that moment we would know everything. . . ."

"Yes, but at the instant we knew it, we would cease to know," Roberto said.

And the ship continued its voyage, moving through sepia seas.

The days flowed by, incommutable. As Mazarin had foreseen, Roberto could establish relations only with the gentlemen. The sailors were a gang of jailbirds: it was frightening to encounter one on deck at night. The passengers were starving, ill, praying. Byrd's three assistants never dared sit at his table, and they glided by silently, carrying out his orders. The captain might as well have been elsewhere: by evening he was drunk, and besides he spoke only Flemish.

Byrd was a thin, dry Briton with a great head of red hair that could have served as a ship's lantern. Roberto, who tried to wash whenever he could, taking advantage of the rain to rinse his clothes, had never seen the doctor change his shirt in all these months of sailing. Luckily, even for a young man accustomed to the drawing rooms of Paris, the stink of a ship was such that the stink of one's fellows was no longer perceptible.

A hearty drinker of beer Byrd was, and Roberto had learned to keep up with him, pretending to swallow while leaving the liquid in his glass always more or less at the same level. Byrd, it seemed, had been taught to fill only empty glasses. And since his own was empty always, he filled it, raising it for a toast. The Knight did not drink: he listened and asked an occasional question.

Byrd spoke decent French, like every Englishman who in those days wanted to travel beyond his own island, and he had been captivated by Roberto's stories about the growing of grapes in the Monferrato region. Roberto listened politely to how beer was made in London. Then they talked about the sea. Roberto was making his first voyage, and Byrd seemed not to want to talk too much about navigation. The Knight asked questions only about the possible location of Escondida, but as Byrd could offer no clue, he received no reply.

Since Byrd said he was making this voyage to study the flora, Roberto sounded him out on that subject. Byrd was not ignorant about botanical matters, and he could thus indulge in long explanations, which Roberto made a show of hearing with interest. At every landfall Byrd and his men actually collected plants, though not with the care of scholars who had undertaken the voyage for that purpose; still, many evenings were spent examining what they had gathered.

During the first days Byrd tried to learn about Roberto's past, and the Knight's as well, as if he suspected them. Roberto gave the version agreed on in Paris: a Savoyard, he had fought at Casale on the side of the imperials, had got into trouble first in Turin, then in Paris, after a series of duels; he had had the misfortune of wounding a favorite of the Cardinal, and thus had chosen the Pacific solution to put much water between himself and his persecutors. The Knight narrated many stories; some took place in Venice, others in Ireland, still others in South America, but it was not clear which were his and which were not.

Finally Roberto discovered that Byrd liked to talk about women. The young man invented furious loves with furious courtesans, and the doctor's eyes glistened as he vowed he would visit Paris one day. Then he recovered himself and observed that all papists were corrupt. Roberto pointed out that many Savoyards were practically Huguenots. The Knight made the sign of the Cross, and returned to the subject of women.

Until the landing at Más Afuera, the doctor's life seemed to unfold at a steady pace, and if he took any readings on board, it was while the others were ashore. When the ship was under sail, he lingered on deck during the day, sat up with his table companions till the small hours, and certainly slept at night. His cramped lodging adjoined Roberto's, a pair of narrow cubicles separated by a partition, and Roberto lay awake to listen.

But once they had entered the Pacific, Byrd's habits changed. After the call at Más Afuera, Roberto saw the doctor go off every morning from seven to eight, whereas before, they had fallen into the way of meeting at that hour for breakfast. Then throughout the period when the ship was heading north, until it reached the island of turtles, Byrd vanished at six in the morning. When the ship again turned its prow westwards, the doctor advanced his rising to five o'clock, when Roberto would hear an assistant come to wake him. Then by degrees the doctor took to rising at four, at three, at two.

Roberto was able to check on him because he had brought along a little sand clock. At sunset, as if idly strolling, he would pass by the helmsman, where next to the compass floating in its whale-oil there was a little stick on which the pilot, after taking the latest bearings, marked the position and the presumed time. Roberto took careful note, then went and turned over his hourglass, returning to repeat the operation when it seemed to him that the hour was about to end. And so, even lingering after supper, he could always calculate the hour with some assurance. In this way he became convinced that Byrd went off a little earlier each morning, and if he kept up that pace, one fine day he would rise at midnight.

After what Roberto had learned from Mazarin and Colbert and his men, it did not take long to deduce that Byrd's disappearances corresponded to the successive passing of the meridians. So, then, it was as if someone sent a signal from Europe, every day at the noon of the Canaries or at some other fixed hour, which Byrd went off to receive. Knowing the hour on board the *Amaryllis,* Byrd was thus able to learn their longitude.

It would have sufficed to follow Byrd as he slipped away. But that was not easy. When the doctor disappeared in the morning, it was impossible to follow him unobserved. When he began moving in the hours of darkness, Roberto could hear the man leave, but he could not go after him at once. So he waited a little, then tried to discover the path he had taken. But every effort proved futile. I refrain from mentioning the many times when, essaying a route in the dark, Roberto ended up among the hammocks of the crew, or stumbled over the pilgrims; but more and more often he would encounter someone who at that hour should have been asleep. So there were others keeping their eyes open.

When Roberto met one of these spies, he would mention his usual insomnia and go up on deck, managing not to arouse suspicion. For some time he had earned himself the reputation of an eccentric who dreamed at night, wide-eyed, and spent the day with his eyes closed. But when he found himself on deck, although he could exchange a few words with the sailor on watch, if they could make themselves understood, the night was lost.

So the months went by, Roberto was close to discovering the mystery of the *Amaryllis,* but had not yet found a way to stick his nose where he would have liked.

In addition, from the beginning he had tried to extract some confidences from Byrd. And he thought up a method that even Mazarin had not been capable of suggesting to him. To satisfy his curiosities, during the day he asked questions of the Knight, who was unable to answer. Roberto emphasized that the things he was asking were of great importance if the Knight was truly determined to find Escondida. And thus, at evening, the Knight would repeat the questions to the doctor.

One night on the bridge, they were looking at the stars, and the doctor remarked that it must be midnight. The Knight, prompted by Roberto a few hours earlier, said, "I won-der what time it is now in Malta."

"That is easy," the words escaped the doctor. Then he corrected himself, "Or, rather, that is very difficult, my friend." The Knight was amazed to learn it could not be deduced from calculation of the meridians: "Does the sun not take an hour to cover fifteen degrees of meridian? So it would be enough to say that we are so many degrees from the Mediterranean, divide by fifteen then, and knowing our own time as we do, we would discover what time it is there."

"You sound like one of those astronomers who have spent their lives poring over charts without ever navigating. Other-wise you would be aware that it is impossible to know on what meridian one is."

Byrd answered more or less what Roberto already knew but the Knight did not. On this subject, however, Byrd proved loquacious: "Our ancestors thought they had an infallible method, based on the eclipses of the moon. You know what a lunar eclipse is: it is a moment when the sun, the earth, and the moon are on a single line, and the shadow of the earth falls on the face of the moon. Since it is possible to predict the day and exact hour of future eclipses, and it is enough to have at hand the Tables of Regiomontanus, you presume you know that a given eclipse should take place in Jerusalem at midnight, and you will observe it at ten o'clock. You will then know that you are at two hours' distance from Jerusalem and therefore your observation point is thirty degrees west of that city."

"Perfect," Roberto said. "All praise to the ancients!"

"Yes, but this calculation is not always accurate. The great Columbus, in the course of his second voyage, calculated by an eclipse while he lay at anchor off Hispaniola, and he made an error of twenty-three degrees west, that is to say a difference of an hour and a half! And on his fourth voyage, again relying on an eclipse, he erred by two hours and a half!"

"Did he make a mistake or did Regiomontanus?" the Knight asked.

"Who knows? On a ship, which moves constantly even when it is at anchor, it is always hard to take bearings correctly. You may also know that Columbus wanted to prove at all costs that he had reached Asia, and therefore his wish led him to err, to show he had gone much farther than he really had. . . . And lunar distances? They have been very fashionable over the last hundred years. The idea had—how shall I say—a certain wit. During its monthly course the moon makes a complete revolution from west to east against the sky of the stars, and therefore it is like the hand of a celestial clock that moves over the face of the Zodiac. The stars move through the sky from east to west at about fifteen degrees per hour, whereas during the same period the moon moves fourteen and a half degrees. So the moon, with respect to the stars, is off by half a degree each hour. Now the ancients thought that the distance between the moon and a fixed star, as it is called, was the same for any observer from any point on the earth. So it sufficed to know, thanks to the usual tables or ephemerides, and observing the sky with the astronomer's Cross—"

"The staff?"

"Exactly, with this 'Jacob's Cross' you calculate the distance of the moon from that star at a given hour on the meridian of departure, and you know that at the hour of observation at sea, in such and such a city it is a certain hour. But . . . ah . . ." And Byrd paused, to enthrall his listeners even more. "There are the parallaxes, a highly complex matter I dare not explain to you. They are due to the difference of refraction of the celestial bodies at different altitudes above the horizon. Now with these parallaxes the distance found here would not be the same that our astronomers back in Europe would find."

Roberto remembered having heard from Mazarin and Colbert something about parallaxes, and about that Monsieur Morin who thought he had found a way of calculating them. To test Byrd's knowledge, he asked if astronomers could not calculate parallaxes. Byrd replied that it was possible but extremely difficult, and the risk of error was very great. "And besides," he added, "I am but a layman and know little of these things."

"So the only thing is to seek a surer method?" Roberto then ventured.

"You know what your Vespucci said? He said: 'As for longitude, it is a very perplexing thing that few people understand, except those capable of sacrificing sleep to observe the conjunction of the moon and the planets.' And he said: 'It is for this determination of longitudes that I have often renounced sleep and have shortened my life by ten years. . . .' A waste of time, I say. But look, the sky is overcast so let us hasten to our lodging, and end our talk."

Some evenings later, Roberto asked the doctor to point out the Pole Star to him. The doctor smiled: from that hemisphere it could not be seen, and other fixed stars had to be used. "Another defeat for the seekers of longitudes," he remarked. "This way, they cannot fall back even on the variations of the magnetic needle."

Then, at the urging of his friends, he broke again the bread of his learning.

"The needle of the compass should always point north, and therefore in the direction of the Pole Star. And yet, except on the meridian of the Isla de Hierro, in all other places it shifts from true north, moving now east, now west according to the climes and the latitudes. If, for example, from the Canaries you move towards Gibraltar, as any sailor knows, the needle turns more than six degrees of a rhomb towards northwest, and from Malta to Tripoli there is a variation of two thirds of a rhomb to the left, and you well know that the rhomb is one fourth of a wind. Now these deviations, it has been said, follow set rules according to the different longitudes. So with a good table of deviations you could know where you are. But . . ."

"Another but?"

"Yes, unfortunately. There are no good tables of the declinations of the magnetic needle. Those who attempted to make them all failed, and there are good reasons to suppose that the needle does not vary in a uniform way depending on the longitude. Furthermore, these variations are very slow, and at sea it is difficult to follow them, even when the ship is not pitching and thus disturbing the balance of the needle. Whoever trusts the needle is a madman."

Another evening, at supper, the Knight, brooding on a few

words Roberto had let fall with apparent nonchalance, said that perhaps Escondida was one of the Solomons, and he asked if they were close.

Byrd shrugged. "The Solomon Islands! Ça n'existe pas!"

"Did not the English Francisco Drako reach them?" the Knight asked.

"Nonsense! Drake discovered New Albion, in quite a different place."

"The Spaniards at Casale spoke of it as something well known, and said they had been the discoverers," Roberto said.

"It was that Mendaña who made the claim, some seventy years ago. But he said they lay between the seventh and eleventh degrees of latitude south. As if to say between Paris and London. But at what longitude? Queirós said that they were fifteen hundred leagues from Lima. Ridiculous. You could practically spit from the coast of Peru and hit them. Recently a Spaniard said that they lay seven thousand five hundred miles from that same Peru. Too far, perhaps. But be so kind as to look at these maps, some of them newly revised, though they but reproduce the older ones, as well as some offered to us as the latest discovery. You see? Some put the islands on the two-hundred-and-twelfth meridian, others on the two-hundred-and-twentieth, others on the two-hundred-and-thirtieth, not to mention those who imagine them on the hundred-and-eightieth. Even if one of these was right, others would err by as much as fifty degrees, which is more or less the distance between London and the lands of the Queen of Sheba."

"It is truly admirable, the number of things you know, doctor," the Knight said, answering the prayers of Roberto, who was about to say as much himself. "As if for your whole life you have done nothing but look for longitudes."

Dr. Byrd's face, dotted with pale freckles, suddenly flushed.

He filled his mug with beer, drained it without taking a breath. "Oh, a naturalist's curiosity. Actually, I would have no idea where to begin if I had to tell you our present position."

"But . . ." Roberto thought he could speak up at this point. "By the tiller, I saw a chart on which—"

"Oh, yes."—the doctor quickly recovered himself—"to be sure, a ship does not proceed at random. They prick the Card. They record the day, the direction of the needle and its declination, the direction of the wind, the hour of the clock on board, the miles traveled, the height of the sun and of the stars, and therefore the latitude, and from that they deduce a longitude. You will have seen sometimes at the poop a sailor throwing a rope into the sea with a little piece of wood attached to one end. It is the loch or, as some call it, the Dutchman's log. The rope is let out, knotted at intervals for measurement, then with a clock you can calculate how much time it takes to cover a given distance. In this way, if everything proceeds regularly, you can determine how many miles you have sailed from the last known meridian."

"You see? There is a method!" Roberto said triumphantly, already knowing what the doctor would reply. That the loch is something that is used only because there is nothing better, since it tells us how far a ship has gone only if it is proceeding in a straight line. But since a ship goes as the winds choose, when the winds are not favoring, it must move now to starboard, now to port.

"Sir Humphrey Gilbert," the doctor said, "more or less at the time of Mendaña, in the Terranova region, intending to proceed along the forty-seventh parallel, 'encountered winds always so scant,' winds—how shall I say it?—so lazy and frugal, that for a long time he sailed anywhere between the forty-first and the fifty-first, ranging over ten degrees of latitude, gentlemen, which would be as if an immense snake were to go from Naples to Portugal, first touching Le Havre with its head and Rome with its tail, then finding itself with its tail at Paris and its head at Madrid! So the deviations must be calculated before doing the sums, and one must be very careful —which a sailor never is. And you cannot have an astronomer ready at your side all day long. To be sure, estimates are possible, especially if you are following a familiar course and consider all the discoveries previously made by others. For this reason from the shores of Europe to those of the Americas the maps give meridians that are fairly reliable. And then, observation of the stars from land can produce some good results, and therefore we know the longitude of Lima. But even in this case, my friends," the doctor asked gaily, "what happens?" And he looked slyly at the other two. "It happens that this gentleman," and he tapped a finger on one of the maps, "places Rome on the twentieth degree east of the meridian of the Canaries, whereas this other," and he waved his finger as if to admonish paternally the other cartographer, "this other gentleman sets Rome at the fortieth degree! And this manuscript contains also the report of a very knowledgeable Fleming, who informs the King of Spain that there has never been agreement on the distance between Rome and Toledo, por los errores tan enormes, como se conoce por esta línea, que muestra la differencia de las distancias, et cetera et cetera. . . . And here is the line: if you fix the first meridian at Toledo (the Spanish always think they live at the center of the world), Mercator believes Rome is twenty degrees farther east, but for Tycho Brahe it is twenty-two, and almost twenty-five for Regiomontanus, and twenty-seven for Clavius, and twenty-eight for good old Ptolemy, and for Origanus thirty. All these errors, just to measure the distance between Rome and Toledo. Imagine what happens, then, on routes like this, where we are perhaps the first to reach certain islands, and the reports of other travelers are quite vague. And add that if a Dutchman has taken correct bearings, he will not tell them to the English, nor will they to the Spanish. On these seas the captain's nose counts most, as with his poor loch he calculates, say, that he is on the two-hundred-twentieth meridian, and perhaps he is thirty degrees ahead, or behind."

"But then," the Knight suggested, "the man who found a way of calculating the meridians would be master of the oceans!"

Byrd flushed again, stared to see if the Knight was speaking with some ulterior motive, and smiled, as if he would have liked to bite him. "Why do you not try, the two of you?"

"Alas, I give up," Roberto said, holding out his hands in a gesture of surrender. And that evening the conversation ended amid hearty laughter.

For many days Roberto did not consider it wise to steer the conversation again to the question of longitude. He changed the subject, and in order to do so he came to a brave decision. With his knife he wounded the palm of one hand. Then he bandaged it with strips of a shirt now worn threadbare by water and the winds. That evening he showed the wound to the doctor. "I am truly foolish. I had put my knife in my bag, unsheathed, and then as I was searching for something, I cut myself. And very painfully."

Dr. Byrd examined the wound with the eye of a specialist, while Roberto prayed he would bring a basin of water to the table and dissolve some vitriol in it. Instead, Byrd merely said it did not seem serious and that Roberto should cleanse it well every morning. But by a stroke of luck the Knight came to the rescue: "Ah, here what is needed is the *unguentum armarium!*"

"What the devil is that?" Roberto asked. And the Knight, as if he had read all the books Roberto knew, began praising the virtues of that substance. Byrd remained silent. After the Knight's superb throw, Roberto now cast the dice himself. "But those are old wives' tales! Like the story of the pregnant woman who saw her lover with his head cut off and then gave birth to a baby whose head was detached from his body. Or like the peasant wife who, to punish a dog that has soiled the kitchen, takes a hot coal and thrusts it into the feces, hoping the animal will feel the fire in his behind! Sir, no person of sense believes in these *historiettes!*"

He had struck the right note, and Byrd could not remain silent. "Ah no, my dear sir, the story of the dog and his shit is quite true. I know a gentleman who resorted to the same measure when a spiteful rival shat on his doorstep, and I assure you the offender learned his lesson." Roberto chuckled as if the doctor were joking, and then led him, piqued, to supply further arguments. Which proved to be more or less the same as d'Igby's. But the doctor grew heated: "Ah yes, my dear sir, you who play the philosopher so much and despise the learning of a mere chirurgeon. I will even say, since it is of shit we are speaking, that a man with bad breath should keep his mouth open over a dung-pit, and he will be finally cured: the stink there is much stronger than that of his throat, and the stronger attracts and carries away the weaker."

"Why, these are extraordinary revelations, Dr. Byrd, and I am awed by your learning!"

"I can tell you still more. In England, when a man is bitten by a dog, the animal is killed, even if it is not rabid. It could become so, and the yeast of canine madness, remaining in the body of the person who was bit, would draw to itself the spirits of hydrophobia. Have you ever seen peasant women pour milk on embers? After it, they immediately throw on a handful of salt. Great wisdom of the vulgar! Milk, falling on the coals, is transformed into steam, and through the action of light and

air, this steam, accompanied by the atoms of fire, spreads to
the place where the cow that gave the milk is kept. Now the
cow's udder is a very glandulous and delicate organ, and the
fire warms it, hardens it, produces ulcers and, since the udder
is near the bladder, it stimulates that as well, provoking the
anastomosis of the veins that flow into it, so the cow will piss
blood."

Roberto said: "The Knight mentioned this unguentum armarium as if it were some useful cure, but you lead us to
believe that it could also be used to do harm."

"Indeed, and that is why certain secrets should be kept
from the plebs, so that they are not put to evil use. Ah, dear
sir, the debate over what we English call the Weapon Salve is
full of controversy. The Knight spoke to us of a weapon that,
suitably treated, brings relief to the wound. But take the same
weapon and place it by a fire, and the wounded man, even if
miles away, will scream with pain. And if you immerse the
blade still stained with blood into icy water, the victim will be
seized with a fit of shivering."

This conversation told Roberto nothing he did not already
know, except that Dr. Byrd knew a great deal about the Powder of Sympathy. And yet the doctor's talk had dwelt largely
on the worst effects of the powder, and this could not be mere
chance. The connection between all this and the arc of the
meridian, however, was another story.

Finally one morning, taking advantage of a sailor's bad fall
from a yardarm, which fractured his skull, while there was
great confusion on the deck and the doctor was summoned
to treat the unfortunate man, Roberto slipped down into the
hold.

Almost groping, he managed to find the right path. Perhaps it was luck, or perhaps the animal was whimpering more

than usual that morning: Roberto, more or less at the point where later on the *Daphne* he would find the kegs of aqua vitae, was confronted by a horrid sight.

Well shielded from curious eyes, in an enclosure made to his measure, on a bed of rags, lay a dog.

He was perhaps of good breed, but his suffering and hunger had reduced him to mere skin and bones. And yet his tormentors showed their intention to keep him alive: they had provided him with abundant food and water, including food surely not canine, subtracted from the passengers' rations.

He was lying on one side, head limp, tongue lolling. On that exposed side gaped a broad and horrible wound. At once fresh and gangrenous, it revealed a pair of great pinkish lips, and in the center, as along the entire gash, was a purulent secretion resembling whey. Roberto realized that the wound looked as it did because the hand of a chirurgeon, rather than sew the lips together, had deliberately kept them parted and open, attaching them to the outer hide.

Bastard offspring of the medical art, that wound had not only been inflicted but wickedly treated so it would not form a scar and the dog would continue suffering—who knows for how long. Further, Roberto saw in and around the wound a crystalline residue, as if a doctor (yes, a doctor, so cruelly expert!) every day sprinkled an irritant salt there.

Helpless, Roberto stroked the wretch, now whimpering softly. He asked himself what he could do to help, but at a heavier touch, the dog's suffering increased. Moreover, Roberto's own pity was giving way to a sense of victory. There was no doubt: this was Dr. Byrd's secret, the mysterious cargo taken aboard in London.

From what Roberto had seen, from what a man with his knowledge could infer, the dog had been wounded in England, and Byrd was making sure he would remain wounded. Someone in London, every day at the same, agreed hour, did something to the guilty weapon, or to a cloth steeped in the animal's blood, provoking a reaction, perhaps of relief, but perhaps of still greater pain, for Dr. Byrd himself had said that the Weapon Salve could also harm.

Thus on the *Amaryllis* they could know at a given moment what time it was in Europe. And knowing the hour of their transitory position, they were able to calculate the meridian!

The only thing to do was obtain proof. At that period Byrd would always leave at around eleven: so they were nearing the antimeridian. Roberto would await him, hidden near the dog, at about that hour.

He was fortunate, if fortune can be associated with the unfortunate chance that would lead that ship, and all those aboard it, to the nadir of misfortune. That afternoon the sea was rough, and so Roberto could convincingly complain of nausea and stomach upset, and seek his bed, deserting the supper table. At first dark, when nobody yet thought of setting up the watch, he slipped furtively into the hold, carrying only a flint and a tarred rope to light his way. He reached the dog and saw, above his bed, a platform laden with bales of straw used to replace the infested pallets of the passengers. He picked his way through these bales and made himself a niche, from whence he could not see the dog but could see anyone standing beside him, and could certainly overhear all speech.

The waiting lasted hours, made longer by the moans of the hapless creature, but finally he heard other sounds and discerned lights.

A little later, he found himself witnessing an experiment taking place only a few steps from him, in the presence of the doctor and his three assistants.

"Are you taking notes, Cavendish?"

"Aye, aye, doctor."

"We will wait then. He is whining too much this evening."

"It is the sea."

"Good dog, good old Hakluyt," the doctor said, calming the animal with some hypocrite petting. "It was a mistake not to establish a set sequence of actions. We should always begin with the lenitive."

"Not necessarily, doctor. Some evenings he is asleep at the proper hour and has to be wakened with an irritant."

"Careful . . . he seems to be stirring. . . . Good dog, Hakluyt . . . Yes, he's upset!" The dog was emitting unnatural yelps. "They have exposed the weapon to the fire. Are you recording the time, Withrington?"

"It is almost half eleven."

"Look at the clocks. About ten minutes should go by."

The dog continued howling for an interminable time. Then he made a different sound, which after an arf arf grew gradually weaker until it was replaced by silence.

"Good," Dr. Byrd was saying. "Now what time is it, Withrington?"

"It should correspond. A quarter before midnight."

"We cannot cry victory yet. We must wait for the control."

Another interminable wait, and then the dog, who had apparently dozed off with relief, yowled again, as if someone had stamped on his tail.

"Time, Withrington?"

"The hour is past. Only a few grains of sand are left."

"The clock. already says midnight," a third voice announced.

"That seems enough to me. Now, gentlemen," Dr. Byrd said, "I hope they stop the irritation at once. Poor Hakluyt cannot bear it. Water and salt, Hawlse, and the cloth. Good dog, Hakluyt, now you're better. . . . Sleep . . . listen to your master . . . it's over. . . . Hawlse, the sleeping draught in the water."

"Aye, aye, doctor."

"There, drink this, Hakluyt. . . , Good boy, you . . . drink the nice water. . . ." A timid little whine, then again silence.

"Excellent, gentlemen," Dr. Byrd was saying. "If this cursed ship did not toss so indecently, we might say we have had a good evening. Tomorrow morning, Hawlse, salt on the wound, as usual. Let us sum up, gentlemen. At the crucial moment, here we were close to midnight, and from London they signaled us that it was noon. We are on the antimeridian of London, and therefore on the one-hundred-ninetieth of the Canarics. If the Islands of Solomon, as tradition has it, are on the antimeridian of the Isla de Hierro, and if we are at the correct latitude, sailing towards the west with a following wind, we should land at San Cristoval, or however we choose to rebaptize that ghastly island. We will have found what the Spaniards have been seeking for decades, and at the same time we will hold in our hand the secret of the *Punto Fijo*. Beer, Cavendish, we must drink a toast to His Majesty, may God keep him always!"

"God save the King!" the three said in one voice—and all four were obviously stout-hearted men, still loyal to a monarch who, in those days, had not yet lost his head though he was on the point of losing his throne.

Roberto put his mind to work. That morning, seeing the dog, he had noticed that the animal, when stroked, grew calmer but, touched more roughly, he yelped with pain. It took very little, on a ship tossed by the sea, to provoke various sensations in a sick body. Perhaps those villains believed they were receiving a message from far away, while on the contrary the dog suffered or experienced relief as the waves alternately jarred or lulled him. Or if, as Saint-Savin used to say, unconscious concepts existed, then Byrd by moving his hands caused the dog to react according to the doctor's own unconfessed wishes. Had he himself not said of Columbus that the man had erred, wishing to prove he had traveled farther? Was the destiny of the world thus affected by the way these madmen interpreted the language of a dog? Could a grumbling in the poor animal's belly make the villains decide they were approaching or moving away from a place desired by Spanish, French, Dutch, and Portuguese, all equally villainous? And was not he, Roberto, involved in this adventure in order one day to tell Mazarin and young Colbert how to populate the ships of France with tortured dogs?

The others by now had left. Roberto came out of his hiding place and stopped, in the light of his tarred rope, before the sleeping dog. He touched the creature's head gently. In that poor animal he saw all the suffering of the world, the furious tale told by an idiot. His slow education, from the Casale days to this moment, had brought him to this truth. Oh, if only he had remained a castaway on the desert island, as the Knight had wanted, or if only, as the Knight had also wanted, he had set fire to the *Amaryllis,* if only he had stopped at the third island, among those natives the color of burnt sienna, or on the fourth, where the Knight became the bard of that people. If only he had found Escondida, to hide there from all the assassins of this merciless world!

He did not know then that fate had in store for him, soon, a fifth island, perhaps the Last.

The *Amaryllis* seemed mad, and Roberto, clinging to everything along the way, returned to his cabin, forgetting the sickness of the world as he suffered instead the sickness of the sea. Then came the shipwreck, of which we have told. He had carried out his mission with success: sole survivor, he bore with him Dr. Byrd's secret. But he could no longer reveal it to anyone. And besides, it was perhaps a secret of no worth.

Was it not true that, having emerged from an unhealthy world, he had found true health? The wreck had granted him the supreme gift, exile, and a Lady whom no one could now take from him. . . .

But the Island did not belong to him and remained distant. The *Daphne* did not belong to him, and Another claimed possession of her. Perhaps in order to continue experiments no less brutal than those of Dr. Byrd.

CHAPTER 20

Wit and the Art of Ingenuity

ROBERTO STILL DID not act, allowing the Intruder space to play in order to discover his game. He put the clocks back on the deck, wound them daily, then ran to feed the animals to prevent the Other from doing it, then he tidied every room and everything on deck, so that if the Other moved, his passage would be noted. During the day Roberto remained inside but with the door ajar, so as not to miss a sound from outside or from below; he kept watch at night, drank aqua vitae, again went down into the depths of the *Daphne*.

He discovered two other storage spaces beyond the hawser locker towards the prow, one was empty, the other completely full, its walls covered with shelves that had raised edges to prevent objects, falling when the sea turned rough. He saw lizard skins dried in the sun, pits of fruit of forgotten identity, stones of various colors, pebbles polished by the sea, fragments of coral, insects pierced with a pin on a board, a fly and a spider in a piece of amber, a dried chameleon, jars filled with liquid in which young snakes or little eels floated, enormous bones (a whale's, he thought), the sword that must have adorned the snout of a fish, and a long horn which Roberto took for a unicorn's, though I believe it was a narwhal's. In short, a room revealing a taste for erudite collection, such as could be found in those days on the vessels of explorers and naturalists

In the center there was an open case, empty except for some straw on the bottom. What it must have contained Roberto realized when he returned to his lodging and, opening the door, found an animal awaiting him, erect, more terrible than if it had been the Intruder himself in flesh and blood.

A rat, a sewer rat, no, a demon more than half a man's height, eyes glaring, a long tail stretching over the floor, it stood motionless on its hind legs while the front ones were like little arms stretched out towards Roberto. Short-haired, it had a bag on its belly, an opening, a natural sac from which a little monster of the same species was peering. We know how much thought Roberto had devoted to rats on the first two evenings; he had expected them big and wild, like all rats that live on ships. But this one exceeded his most fearful expectations. He could not believe that human eye had ever seen a rat of such dimensions—and, with reason, for as we will later see, it was, I have deduced, a marsupial.

When the first moment of terror was past, it became clear, from the invader's immobility, that the animal was stuffed, badly embalmed or badly preserved in the hold: the skin emanated an odor of decomposed organs, and tufts of straw were already spilling from its back.

The Intruder, shortly before Roberto entered the cabinet of wonders, had removed its most effective piece, and as Roberto was admiring that museum, he had placed the animal in Roberto's lodging, perhaps hoping that Roberto, victim, losing his reason, would rush to the bulwarks and plunge into the sea. He would have me dead, he would have me insane,

Roberto muttered, but I will make him eat his rat in mouthfuls, I will stuff him and put him on those shelves. Where are you hiding, rogue, where are you, perhaps you are watching me to see if I lose my mind, but I will see you lose yours, scoundrel.

He pushed the animal onto the deck with the butt of his musket and, overcoming his revulsion, picked it up with his bare hands and flung it into the sea.

Determined to discover the hiding-place of the Intruder, he went back to the woodpile, taking care not to roll again on the logs now scattered over the floor. Beyond the wood he found a place that on the *Amaryllis* they called the soda (or *soute* or *sota*), for storing biscuit. Under a canvas there, carefully wrapped and protected, he found first of all a very large spyglass, more powerful than the one he had in his room, perhaps a Hyperbole of the Eyes intended for the exploration of the sky. The telescope was in a big basin of light metal, and beside the basin, also carefully wrapped, were instruments of uncertain nature, metallic arms, a circular cloth with rings along its circumference, a kind of helmet, and finally three rounded containers that, to his smell, seemed full of a thick, stagnant oil. What purpose this collection might serve, Roberto did not ask himself: at that moment what he sought was a living creature.

He examined the soda to see if, below it, yet another space opened. There was one, but it was very cramped, so that he could advance only on all fours. He explored it, holding the lamp low, watching out for scorpions and in fear of setting fire to the ceiling. After a brief crawl he reached the end, striking his head against hard larch, the Ultima Thule of the *Daphne,* beyond which he could hear the water slapping against the hull. So beyond that blind passage there could be nothing further.

Then he stopped, as if the *Daphne* could reveal no more secrets to him.

If it seems strange that during a week or more on board the ship Roberto had not succeeded in seeing everything, suffice it to recall what happens to a boy who climbs into the attics or the cellars of a great and ancient dwelling, irregular in its plan. At every step cases of old books appear, discarded clothing, empty bottles, and piles of fagots, ruined furniture, dusty and rickety cupboards. The boy advances, lingers on the discovery of some treasure, glimpses an entrance, a dark passage, and imagines some alarming presence there, postpones the search to a later occasion, and he proceeds always in tiny steps, on the one hand fearing to go too far, on the other in anticipation of future discoveries, yet daunted by the emotion of the recent ones, and that attic or cellar never ends, and can have in store for him enough new nooks and crannies to last through his boyhood and beyond.

And if the boy is frightened every time by new noises, or if—to keep him away from those labyrinths—he is daily told terrifying tales (and if that boy, in addition, is drunk), obviously the space will expand at each new adventure. Such was Roberto's life in the exploration of his still hostile territory.

It was early morning, and Roberto again was dreaming. He dreamed of Holland. It was while the Cardinal's men were conducting him to Amsterdam to put him on the *Amaryllis.* During the journey they stopped at a city, and he entered the cathedral. He was impressed by the cleanliness of the naves, so different from those of Italian and French churches. Bare of decorations, only a few standards hanging from the naked columns, the glass windows plain and without images: the sun created there a milky atmosphere dotted only by the few black forms of the worshippers below. In that peace a single sound was heard, a sad melody that seemed to wander through the ivory air, born from the capitals or the keystones. Then he noticed in one chapel, in the ambulatory of the choir, a man in black, alone in one corner playing a little recorder, his eyes staring into the void.

When the musician finished, Roberto went over to him, wondering if he should give him something; not looking into Roberto's face, the man thanked him for his praise, and Roberto realized he was blind. He was the master of the bells (der Musicyn en Directeur van de Klokwerken, le carillonneur, der Glockenspieler, he tried to explain), but it was also part of his job to delight with the sound of his flute the faithful who lingered at evening in the yard and the cemetery beside the church. He knew many melodies, and on each he developed two, three, sometimes even five variations of increasing complexity, nor was it necessary for him to read notes: born blind, he could move in that handsome luminous space (yes, he said luminous) of his church, seeing, as he said, the sun with his skin. He explained how his instrument was so much a living thing, that it reacted to the seasons, and to the temperature of morning and sunset, but in the church there was always a sort of diffuse warmth that guaranteed the wood a steady perfection—and Roberto reflected on the notion of diffuse warmth a man of the north might have, for he himself was growing cold in this clarity.

The musician played for him the first melody twice more, and said it was entitled "Doen Daphne d'over schoone Maeght." He refused any offering, touched Roberto's face and said, or at least Roberto understood him to say, that "Daphne" was something sweet, which would accompany Roberto all of his life.

Now, on the *Daphne,* Roberto opened his eyes and, without

doubt, heard coming from below, through the fissures in the wood, the notes of "Daphne," as if it were being played by a more metallic instrument which, not hazarding variations, repeated at regular intervals the first phrase of the tune, like a stubborn ritornello.

He told himself at once that it was a most ingenious emblem: to be on a *fluyt* named *Daphne* and to hear music for flute entitled "Daphne." It was pointless to persist in the illusion that this was a dream. It was a new message from the Intruder.

Once again he armed himself, once again he sought strength from the keg, then followed the sound. It seemed to originate in the clock room. But, since he had scattered those mechanisms over the deck, the space was now empty. He revisited it. Still empty, but the music was coming from its far wall. Surprised the first time by the clocks themselves, breathless the second time from the effort of carrying them off, he had never considered whether or not the room ran all the way to the hull. If so, the far wall should have been curved. But was it? The great canvas with that perspective of clocks created a deception of the eye, so at first sight there was no telling if the wall was flat or concave.

Roberto started to rip away the canvas, but he realized it was a running curtain, as in a theater. And behind the curtain there was another door, also closed with a chain and lock.

With the courage of the devotees of Bacchus, and as if with a spingard shot he could overpower all enemies, he aimed his gun, shouted in a loud voice (and God only knows why), "Nevers et Saint-Denis!," gave the door a kick, and flung himself forward, intrepid.

The object occupying the space was an organ, which was surmounted by about twenty pipes, from whose holes the notes of the melody issued. The organ was fixed to the wall and consisted of a wooden structure supported by an armature of little metal columns. On the upper level, the pipes were in the center, but at either side of them little automata moved. To the left, on a kind of circular base, stood an anvil certainly hollow inside, like a bell; around the base were four figures that moved their arms rhythmically, striking the anvil with little metal hammers. The hammers, of varying weight, produced silvery sounds in harmony with the tune sung by the pipes, commenting on it through a series of chords. Roberto recalled conversations in Paris with a Minim friar, who spoke to him of research into the Universal Harmony. Thanks more to their musical functions than to their features, he now recognized Vulcan and the three Cyclopes to whom, as legend had it, Pythagoras referred when he affirmed that the difference in musical intervals depended on number, weight, and measure.

To the right of the pipes an amorino tapped out (striking a wand upon a wooden book held in his other hand) the ternary rhythm on which the melody "Daphne" was based.

On a slightly lower level lay the console of the organ, its keys rising and falling according to the notes emitted by the pipes, as if an invisible hand were running over them. Below the keys, where as a rule the organist works the bellows with his feet, a cylinder had been set, in which teeth were fitted, large spikes, in an order unpredictably regular or regularly unpredictable, which suggested the way notes are arranged in rising and descending patterns, unforeseen breaks, vast white spaces and a density of crotchets, on the lines of a sheet of music.

Below the cylinder was a fixed horizontal bar supporting some little levers which, as the cylinder turned, successively touched the teeth and, through a play of half-hidden rods, operated the keys—as they operated the pipes.

But the most stupefying phenomenon was the reason why the cylinder rotated and the pipes received breath. To the side of the organ a glass syphon was fixed, whose form recalled the cocoon of a silkworm, inside which two perforated plates could be discerned, one above the other, dividing it into three separate chambers. The syphon received an influx of water from a pipe entering its lowest chamber from an open gun-port that also admitted light to this room, pouring in the liquid that through the action of some hidden pump was obviously sucked directly from the sea, but in such a way that, entering the cocoon, it was mixed with air.

The water entered the lowest part of the cocoon with force, as if it were boiling; spun in a vortex against the walls, it no doubt released the air, which was inhaled through the two plates. Thanks to a tube linking the upper part of the cocoon with the base of the organ pipes, the air was transformed into song through artful movements. The water, which meanwhile had gathered in the lower part, ran off through another tube and, moving the wheel of a little mill, then poured into a metal shell below, whence it was emptied, by another pipe, through the gun-port.

The wheel turned a bar that, connected to the cylinder, transmitted its own movement.

To the drunken Roberto all this seemed natural, so natural that he felt betrayed when the cylinder began to slow down, and the pipes whistled their tune as if it was dying in their throat, while the Cyclopes and the amorino relaxed their blows. Obviously—though in his day there was much talk of perpetual motion—the hidden pump that controlled the intake and flow of the water could operate only for a certain amount of time after being set in motion, and then its impetus came to an end.

Roberto did not know whether to be amazed more by this

feat of technasma—and he had heard talk of other similar feats, the making of little skeletons or winged cherubs dance —or more by the fact that the Intruder (since it could be none but he) had made the organ play on that morning and at that hour.

And to send what message? That Roberto was defeated from the beginning? That the *Daphne* could still conceal such and so many surprises, that he could spend his life trying to violate her, in vain?

A philosopher once told him that God knows the world better than we do because He made it. And that to approach divine knowledge, even slightly, it was necessary to conceive the world as a great building and try to construct it. This is what he had to do. To know the *Daphne,* he had to construct her.

He sat down at his table then and traced the outline of the ship, relying both on the remembered structure of the *Amaryllis* and on what he had seen so far of the *Daphne.* So, then, he said to himself, we have the cabins of the quarterdeck and, below, the guard-room. Even further below (but still at the level of the deck), the gun-room and the space where the tiller passes. It has to emerge at the stern, and there can be nothing more than that. All this is on the same level with the cook-room in the forecastle. After that, the bowsprit rests on another elevation, and there—if I am correctly interpreting Roberto's awkward paraphrases—is the place where, with but-tocks exposed, bodily functions were performed at that time. If you went down below the cook-room, you arrived at the stores. He had explored to the end of the bowsprit, and here, too, there could be nothing else. Below he had found the hawsers and the fossil collection. There was no going beyond that.

So he retraced his steps and crossed the whole lower deck, through the aviary and the greenhouse. Unless the Intruder could transform himself at will into animal or vegetable, he could not hide there. Beneath the tiller were the organ and the clocks. There, too, Roberto had gone all the way to the hull.

Descending still farther, he had found the broadest part of the hold, with additional provisions, ballast, wood; and he had knocked against the side to make sure there was no false wall that would give off a hollow sound. If this was a normal ship, the bilge would not allow other refuges. Unless the Intruder himself clung to the keel, underwater, like a leech, and crawled aboard at night; but of all the explanations—and he was prepared to consider many—this seemed to Roberto the least scientific.

Aft, more or less beneath the organ, there was the soda with the basin, the telescope, and the other instruments. Looking around it, he had not investigated to see if the space ended right at the helm; but from the drawing he was now making, it seemed to him that the paper did not allow him to imagine any other void—if he had drawn the curve of the stern correctly. Below, only the blind passage was left, and after that there was nothing, he was sure.

So, dividing the ship into compartments, he had filled it all and left no space for any other storage. Conclusion: the Intruder did not have a fixed place. He moved as Roberto moved, he was like the far side of the moon, which we know must exist though we never see it.

Who could see the other face of the moon? Only an inhabitant of the fixed stars: he could wait, not moving, and he would catch the concealed face by surprise. As long as Roberto moved with the Intruder or allowed the Intruder to base his movements on Roberto's, Roberto would never see him.

He had to become a fixed star and force the Intruder to move. And as the Intruder obviously was on deck when Roberto was below, and vice versa, he had to make the Intruder believe him below in order to surprise him on deck.

To mislead the Intruder, Roberto left a light burning in the captain's quarters, as if he were there, engaged in writing. Then he went and hid at the top of the forecastle, just behind the bell, so that, turning, he could survey the area below the bowsprit, while before him he dominated the deck and the aftercastle all the way to the lantern of the poop. He set his musket beside him—and, I fear, also a keg of aqua vitae.

He spent the night alert to any sound, as if he were still spying on Dr. Byrd, pinching his ears to stay awake, until dawn. In vain.

Then he went back to his berth, where meanwhile the light had gone out. And found his papers in disorder. The Intruder had spent the night there, perhaps reading the letters to the Lady, while Roberto was suffering the chill of the night and the morning's dew!

The Adversary had now penetrated his memories . . . Roberto recalled Salazar's warning: expressing his private passions had opened a breach in his spirit.

He rushed out on deck and fired a bullet at random, splintering a mast, then he shot again, until he realized that he was killing no one. Considering the time it took in those days to reload a musket, the enemy could take a stroll between shots, having a good laugh at that rumpus—which had impressed only the animals, clucking below.

The Intruder was laughing, then. But where was he laughing? Roberto went back to his drawing and told himself that he truly knew nothing about ship-building. The drawing showed only top, bottom, and length, not breadth. Seen in its length (we would now say, in cross-section), the ship revealed no other possible hiding-places, but seen in its breadth, other places could be lurking among those already discovered.

Roberto, pondering, realized only now that on this ship too many things were still missing. For example, he had found no other weapons. Very well: assume that the sailors had taken them away—if they had abandoned the ship of their own volition. But on the *Amaryllis* the hold had been crammed also with considerable lumber, for repairing masts, the helm, the sides, in the event of damage by the elements, whereas here he had found only enough firewood, recently dried, to supply the cook-stove, but nothing of oak or larch or seasoned fir. Also wanting, along with carpenter's wood, were carpenter's tools: saws, axes of various sizes, hammers, nails. . . .

Were there other storerooms? He drew the design over again, and tried to portray the ship not seen from a side but as if observed from the crow's nest. And he decided that in this beehive he was drawing there could still be inserted a nook beneath the organ, from which it was possible to descend farther, without a ladder, into the blind passage. Not big enough to contain everything that was missing, but an extra hole, in any case. If in the low ceiling of the blind passage there existed a trap through which to hoist oneself into that same newly conceived space, from there anyone could climb up to the clocks and then have the run of the entire vessel.

Now Roberto was sure that the Enemy could be only there. He hurried below, slipped into the passage, this time throwing light on its ceiling. And there was a trapdoor. He resisted the initial impulse to open it. If the Intruder was up there, he would wait for Roberto to stick his head through the opening, then overpower him. The Intruder had to be taken by surprise from the direction where he was not expecting an attack, as they had done at Casale.

If there was a chamber above, it was adjacent to that of the telescope, and Roberto could enter there.

He went up, passing through the soda, stepping over the instruments, to find himself at a wall that—only now did he realize it—was not of the same hard wood as the hull.

This wall was fairly thin. As before, on entering the place from which the music came, he gave a sturdy kick, and the wood splintered.

He was in the dim light of a rat's nest, with a little porthole in the rounded far wall. And there on a pallet, his knees almost against his chin, his outstretched arm clutching a big pistol, was the Other.

He was an old man, his pupils dilated, his desiccated face framed by a pepper-and-salt beard, his sparse white hair standing up on his head, his mouth almost toothless, the gums the color of blueberries. He was engulfed in some cloth that once might have been black but now was greasy, with pale stains.

Pointing the pistol, which he gripped in both hands as his arms trembled, he shouted in a weak voice. The first sentence was in German or Dutch, and the second, and surely he was repeating his message, was in halting Italian—a sign that he had deduced his interlocutor's nationality by looking at his papers.

"If you move, I kill you!"

Roberto was so surprised by the apparition that his reaction was slow. And just as well, for he had time to realize that the pistol was not cocked, and the Enemy therefore was not much versed in the military arts.

So he went over amiably, grasped the pistol by the barrel, and tried to slip it from those hands clenched around the butt, while the creature emitted wrathful Germanic cries.

With some effort Roberto finally managed to wrest the weapon from him. The man sank down, and Roberto knelt beside him, supporting the old man's head.

"Sir," he said, "I mean you no harm. I am a friend. You understand? Amicus!"

The man opened and closed his mouth, but could not speak: only the white of his eyes could be seen, or, rather, the red, and Roberto feared he was on the point of death. He took the man in his arms, frail as he was, and carried him to his room. He offered him water, made him sip some aqua vitae, and the man said, "Gratias ago, domine," raised his hand as if to bless Roberto, who at that point, taking a closer look at the man's dress, realized he was a cleric.

CHAPTER 21

Telluris Theoria Sacra

WE WILL NOT reconstruct the dialogue that followed over the next two days. For that matter, Roberto's papers become more laconic from now on. His confidences to the Lady having perhaps fallen under alien eyes (he never had the courage to seek confirmation from his new companion), he stops writing altogether for many days, then records in a far more curt style what he learns and what happens.

So Roberto found himself facing Father Caspar Wander-drossel, *e Societate Iesu, olim in Herbipolitano Franconiae Gymnasio, postea in Collegio Romano Matheseos Professor,* and, further, astronomer, and student of many other disciplines, at the General Curia of the Order. The *Daphne,* under a Dutch captain who had already ventured along those routes for the Vereenigde Oost-Indische Compagnie, had left the Mediterranean shores many months earlier, circumnavigating Africa with the aim of arriving at the Islands of Solomon. Precisely as Dr. Byrd had proposed to do on the *Amaryllis,* except that the *Amaryllis* sought the Islands by sailing west to reach the east, whereas the *Daphne* had done the opposite; but it matters little, the Antipodes can be reached from either direction. On the Island (and Father

Caspar motioned beyond the beach, beyond the trees), the Specula Melitensis was to be mounted. The nature of this Maltese Mirror was not clear, and Father Caspar, mentioning it, lowered his voice as if referring to a secret so famous that it was on the lips of the entire world.

To arrive here, the *Daphne* had taken its own good time. Everyone knows what it meant to navigate those seas in that period. After leaving the Moluccas, bound southeast for Porto Sancti Thomae in New Guinea, as it was necessary to call at the places where the Society of Jesus had its missions, the ship, driven by a storm, became lost in waters never before seen, arriving at an island inhabited by rats as big as boys, with very long tails and bags over their abdomen. Roberto had encountered a stuffed exemplar (indeed, Father Caspar reproached him for throwing away "a Wunder worth all Peru").

They were, Father Caspar told him, friendly animals, who surrounded the seamen, holding out their little hands to beg for food, or actually tugging at the men's clothes, but in the end they proved to be expert thieves and even stole hardtack from one sailor's pocket.

If I may be allowed to interject, to support Father Caspar's credibility, let me confirm that such an island exists, and cannot be mistaken for any other. Those pseudo-kangaroos are called Quokkas, and they live only there, on Rottenest Island, which the Dutch had then only recently discovered, calling it in fact the Island of Rats' Nests. But as the island is off Perth, the *Daphne* must have reached the western coast of Australia. If we consider that she was therefore on the thirtieth parallel south, and west of the Moluccas, whereas she was supposed to have gone east, just a bit below the Equator, we would be obliged to say that the *Daphne* was off course.

But that was the least of it. The men of the *Daphne* must have seen a coast not far from that island, and they probably thought it was some other little island with some other rodent on it. They were in search of something quite different, and who knows what Father Caspar's instruments were saying on board. Surely, the seamen were only a few oar strokes from that Terra Incognita et Australis that mankind had been dreaming of for centuries. What is hard to conceive—since the *Daphne* would finally reach (as we shall see) a latitude of seventeen degrees south—is how they managed to circumnavigate at least half of Australia without ever seeing it: either they sailed north and then passed between Australia and New Guinea, risking at every mile running aground on either one shore or the other; or else they sailed south, passing between Australia and New Zealand, seeing always open sea.

You would think I was narrating a romance, if Abel Tasman, setting out from Batavia more or less during the months of our story, had not also arrived at a land that he called Van Diemen, which today we know as Tasmania; but since he, too, was seeking the Solomon Islands, he kept the southern shore of that land on his left, never imagining that beyond it lay a continent a hundred times greater, and he ended up southeast of New Zealand, flanked it to the northeast and, abandoning it, reached the Tongas. Thus he arrived by and large where the *Daphne* was, I believe, but there, too, he passed between the coral reefs and headed for New Guinea. Which meant caroming like a billiard ball, but it seems that for many years afterwards navigators were fated to arrive within a hair's breadth of Australia and not see it.

So we can accept Father Caspar's story as authentic. Often following the whims of the Trades, the *Daphne* ended up in storm after storm and would be badly mauled, so they would have to stop at some God-forsaken island without trees, just sand forming a ring around a little central lake. There they would patch up the ship, and this explained why there was no longer a supply of carpenter's wood on board. Then they resumed navigating, and finally came to cast anchor in this bay. The captain sent a boat ashore with an advance guard, decided there were no inhabitants, but, just in case, he loaded and aimed his few cannon, then three operations—all fundamental—were set in motion.

First, the collection of water and provisions, which were by then almost exhausted; second, the capture of animals and uprooting of plants to take home to delight the naturalists of the Society; third, the felling of trees to provide a new supply of logs and planks, material against future misfortunes. The final operation was the installation, on a height of the Island, of the Specula Melitensis, and this proved the most laborious undertaking. From the hold they had to collect all the carpenter's tools and the various pieces of the Specula, then carry them ashore. All this consumed much time, particularly because they could not unload directly in the bay: between the ship and the shore, almost at the surface of the water and with only a few, too-narrow gaps, there extended a barbican, a curtain wall, a terreplein, an Erdwall made entirely of coral—in short, what today would be called a coral reef. After many unfruitful attempts they discovered that they would have to round the cape to the south of the bay each time; beyond it there was an inlet that allowed them to land. "And that is why that boat abandoned by the sailors we cannot see nunc, although it is still behind there, heu me miserum!" As can be deduced from Roberto's transcription, this Teuton had lived in Rome, speaking Latin with his brothers from a hundred countries, but he had had little practice in Italian.

When the Specula had been set up, Father Caspar began making his observations, which proceeded successfully for almost two months. What was the crew doing meanwhile? They were idling, and discipline on board was breaking down. The captain had taken on many kegs of aqua vitae, which were supposed to be used only as a restorative during storms, and then with great parsimony, or else to serve for barter with the natives; but instead, flouting all orders, the crew started bringing the kegs up on deck, and everyone drank to excess, including the captain. Father Caspar was working, the others were living like brutes, and from the Specula he could hear their lewd singing.

One day Father Caspar was working alone at the Specula. It was very hot, so he removed his cassock (thus, the good Jesuit said with shame, sinning against modesty, which God could now forgive since He had punished him promptly!), and an insect stung him on the chest. At first he felt only a little jab, but when he was ferried back on board that evening, he was attacked by a high fever. He told no one of what had happened to him, then in the night his ears rang and his head was heavy, so the captain unbuttoned the cassock, and what did he see? A pustule, such as wasps can cause, or even mosquitoes of great dimensions. But immediately that swelling became in the officer's eyes a carbunculus, an anthrax, a nigricant pimple—in short, a bubo, a most evident symptom of the *pestis, quae dicitur bubonica,* as was immediately noted in the log.

Panic spread through the ship. It was futile for Father Caspar to tell about the insect: plague victims always lied so as not to be segregated; this was well known. Futile for him to assure them that he knew the plague well, and this was not plague for many reasons. The crew was almost ready to cast him overboard, to avert contagion.

Father Caspar tried to explain that during the great pestilence that struck Milan and Northern Italy a dozen years before, he had been sent, with some of his brothers, to lend a hand in the lazarettoes, and to study the phenomenon closely.

And therefore he knew a great deal about that contagious lues. There are diseases that affect only individuals and in different places and times, like the Sudor Anglicus, others peculiar to a sole region, like the Dysenteria Melitensis or the Elephantiasis Aegyptia, and still others that, like the plague, strike over a long period all the inhabitants of many regions. Now, the plague is announced by sun spots, eclipses, comets, the appearance of subterranean animals emerging from their lairs, plants that wither because of mephitis: and none of these signs had appeared on board or on land, or in the sky or on the sea.

Secondly, the plague is certainly produced by fetid air that rises from swamps, from the decomposition of many cadavers during war, also by invasions of locusts that drown in swarms in the sea and are then washed up on shore. Contagion is caused, in fact, by those exhalations, which enter the mouth and the lungs, and through the vena cava reach the heart. But in the course of navigation, apart from the stink of the food and the water, which in any case causes scurvy and not plague, the sailors had suffered no malefic exhalation, indeed they had breathed pure air and the most healthful winds.

The captain argued that traces of such exhalations stick to clothing and to many other objects, and perhaps on board there was something that had retained the contagion at length and then transmitted it. And he remembered the story of the books.

Father Caspar had brought with him some good books on navigation, such as l'Arte de navegar of Medina, the Typhis Batavus of Snellius, and the De rebus oceanicis et orbe novo decades tres of Peter Martyr, and one day he told the captain he had acquired them for a trifle, and in Milan: after the plague, on the walls along the canals, the entire library of a gentleman prematurely deceased had been put out for sale. And this was the Jesuit's little private collection, which he carried with him even at sea.

For the captain it was obvious that the books, having belonged to a plague victim, were agents of infection. The plague is transmitted, as everyone knows, through venenific unguents, and he had read of people who died by wetting a finger with saliva as they leafed through works whose pages had in fact been smeared with a poison.

Father Caspar employed all his powers of persuasion: no, in Milan he had studied the blood of the diseased with a very new invention, a technasma that was called an *occhialino* or microscope, and in that blood he had seen some *vermiculi* floating, and they are precisely the elements of that *contagium animatum* and are generated by *vis naturalis* from all rot and then are transmitted, *propagatores exigui,* through the sudoriferous pores or the mouth, or sometimes even the ear. But this pullulation is a living thing, and needs blood for nourishment, it cannot survive twelve or more years amid the dead fibers of paper.

The captain would not listen to reason, and the small but lovely library of Father Caspar had finally been carried off on the tide. But that was not all: though Father Caspar was quick to say that the plague could be transmitted by dogs and flies but, to his knowledge, surely not by rats, the entire crew nevertheless fell to hunting rats, shooting in every direction, risking breaches in the hold. And finally, as Father Caspar's fever continued the next day, and his bubo showed no sign of going away, the captain came to a decision: they would all go to the Island and there wait until the priest either died or was healed, and the ship would be purified of every malignant flux and influx.

No sooner said than done. Everyone on the ship boarded the longboat laden with weapons and tools. And since it was foreseen that between the priest's death and the time when

the ship would be purified two or three months might have
to pass, they had decided to build huts on land, and everything
that could make the *Daphne* a manufactory was towed to shore.

Not to mention most of the butts of aqua vitae.

"However, they did not do a good thing," Caspar remarked
bitterly, grieved by the punishment that Heaven had wreaked
on them for having abandoned him like a lost soul.

For no sooner had they arrived than they promptly went
and killed some animals in the woods, then lighted great fires
that evening on the beach, and caroused for three days and
three nights.

Probably the fires attracted the attention of the savages.
Even if the Island itself was uninhabited, in that archipelago
there lived men black as Africans, who must have been good
navigators. One morning Father Caspar saw about ten pirogues
arrive from nowhere, beyond the great island to the west,
heading for the bay. They were boats hollowed from logs like
those of the Indians of the New World, but double: one contained the crew and the other glided over the water like a
sled.

Father Caspar first feared they would make for the *Daphne*,
but they seemed to want to avoid it and instead turned towards the little inlet where the sailors had gone ashore. He
tried shouting, to warn the men on the Island, but they were
in a drunken stupor. In short, the sailors found the savages
suddenly upon them, bursting from the trees.

The sailors sprang to their feet; the savages immediately
displayed their bellicose intentions, but none of the crew could
think clearly, still less remember where they had left their
weapons. Only the captain stepped forward and felled one of
the attackers with a pistol shot. On hearing the report and
seeing their comrade fall dead though no other human had
touched him, the natives made signs of submission, and one

of them approached the captain, holding out a necklace taken from around his own neck. The captain bowed, then was obviously seeking some object to give in exchange, and he turned to ask something of his men.

In doing so, he exposed his back to the natives.

Father Wanderdrossel thought that the natives, even before the shot, had been immediately awed by the bearing of the captain, a Batavian giant with a blond beard and blue eyes, features that they probably attributed to the gods. But as soon as they saw his back (since it is clear that those savage peoples do not believe a divinity has a back), the native leader, club in hand, promptly attacked him and bashed in his head, and the captain fell prone, moving no more. The black men attacked the sailors, who, unable to defend themselves, were massacred.

A horrible banquet ensued, and continued three days. Father Caspar, in his illness, followed all of it through his spyglass, impotent. The crew became so much butcher's meat: Caspar saw the men first stripped (with shrieks of joy, the savages divided clothes and objects), then dismembered, then cooked, and finally chewed with great calm, between gulps of a steaming beverage and some songs that to anyone would have seemed innocent, if they had not accompanied that ghastly kermess.

Then the natives, sated, began pointing at the ship. Probably they did not associate it with the presence of the sailors: majestic as it was with masts and sails, incomparably different from their canoes, they had not thought it the work of man. According to Father Caspar (who felt he understood the mentality of idolators throughout the world, for the Jesuit travelers, returning to Rome, would give accounts of them), they believed it an animal, and the fact that it had remained neutral while they indulged in their anthropophagic rites strengthened this conviction. For that matter even Magellan—Father Caspar insisted—had told how certain aborigines believed that ships, having come flying from the sky, were the natural mothers of the longboats, which they nursed allowing them to hang from their sides, then weaned them by flinging them into the air.

But now someone probably suggested that if this animal was meek and its flesh as tasty as the sailors', it was worth seizing. And they headed for the *Daphne*. At which point the peaceful Jesuit, to keep them at a distance (his Order imposed that he live ad majorem Dei gloriam and not die for the satisfaction of some pagan cujus Deus venter est), lit the fuse of a cannon already loaded, and turned it towards the Island, and fired a ball. With a great roar, while the *Daphne*'s flank was haloed with smoke as if the animal were snorting with wrath, the ball fell amid the pirogues, overturning two of them.

The portent was eloquent. The savages went back to the Island, vanishing into the woods, and they emerged a little later with wreaths of flowers and leaves which they cast on the water, making gestures of reverence before they vanished beyond the western island. They had paid what they considered a sufficient tribute to the great irritated animal, and surely they would never be seen again on these shores: they had decided that the area belonged to a peevish and vindictive creature.

This was the story of Father Caspar Wanderdrossel. For at least a week, before Roberto's arrival, he had felt ill again, but thanks to some preparations of his own making ("Spiritus, Olea, Flores, und andere dergleichen Vegetabilische, Animalische, und Mineralische Medicamenten"), he had already begun to enjoy his convalescence, when one night he heard footsteps on the deck.

From that moment, out of fear, he fell ill again, abandoned his room and took refuge in that cubbyhole, taking with him his medicines and a pistol, not knowing whether or not it was loaded. And from there he emerged only to seek food and water. At first he stole the eggs for nourishment, then he confined himself to consuming the fruit. He became convinced that the Intruder (in Father Caspar's account the Intruder was naturally Roberto) was a man of learning, curious about the ship and its contents, and he began to wonder if this man might not be, rather than just a castaway, the agent of some heretical country that wanted the secrets of the Specula Melitensis. This is why the good father had taken to behaving in such a childish fashion, intending to drive Roberto to abandon that vessel infested with demons.

Then it was Roberto's turn to tell his story, and not knowing how far Caspar had read in his writings, he dwelt in detail on his mission and his voyage on the *Amaryllis*. The narration took place while, at the end of that first day, they boiled a cock and opened the last of the captain's bottles. Father Caspar had to recover his strength and make new blood, and they celebrated what now seemed to each a return to the human community.

"Ridiculoso!" Father Caspar commented after hearing the incredible story of Dr. Byrd. "Such bestialitas have I never heard. Why did they do to him that harm? Of the longitude mysterium I thought to have heard all, but never that it could be sought by using the *unguentum armarium*! If that was possible, a Jesuit would have invented. This has no connection with longitudes, I will explain you how good I do my work, and you will see it is different. . . ."

"Now tell me," Roberto asked, "were you hunting for the Islands of Solomon or did you want to solve the mystery of longitudes?"

"Why, both, is it not? You find the Islands of Solomon and you have learned where is the hundred-eightieth meridian, you find the hundred-eightieth meridian and you know where are the Islands of Solomon!"

"But why must those islands lie on that meridian?"

"Ach mein Gott, the Lord forgive I take His Most Holy Name in vain. In primis, after Solomon the Temple had constructed, he made a great fleet, as the Book of Kings says, and this fleet arrives at the Island of Ophir, from where they bring him—how do you say?—quadrigenti und viginti . . ."

"Four hundred twenty."

"Four hundred twenty talents of gold, a very big richness: the Bible says very little to say very much, as if pars pro toto. And no land near Israel had such big riches, quod significat that the fleet to ultimate edge of the world had gone. Here."

"But why here?"

"Because here is the meridian one hundred eighty which is exactlich the one that divides the earth in two, and on the other side is the first meridian: you count one, two, three, for three hundred sixty degrees of meridian, and if you are at one hundred eighty, here it is midnight and in that first meridian, noon. Verstanden? You guess now why the Islands of Solomon are so named? Solomon dixit: Cut baby in two. Solomon dixit: Cut Earth in two."

"I understand, if we are on the one-hundred-eightieth meridian, we are at the Solomon Islands. But how do you know we are actually on the one-hundred-eightieth meridian?"

"Why, the Specula Melitensis, nichtwahr? If all my previous evidence is not enough to prove the one-hundred-eightieth meridian passes just there, the Specula also proved it." He dragged Roberto onto the deck, pointing to the bay. "You see that promontorium north there, where big trees stand with big paws walking on the water? Et hora you see the other promontorium south? You draw a line between the two promontoria, you see the line passes between here and the shore, a bit more apud the shore than apud the ship. . . . See the line, I mean a geistige line that you see with eyes of imagination? Gut, that line is the line of the meridian!"

The next day Father Caspar, who never lost track of time, informed Roberto it was Sunday. He celebrated Mass in his lodging, consecrating a crumb of one of the few hosts he had left. Then he resumed his lesson, first there, among globes and maps, then on deck. When Roberto remonstrated, unable to tolerate the full light of day, the priest from one of his cupboards produced a pair of spectacles, but with smoked lenses, which he had once used to explore profitably the mouth of a volcano. Roberto began to see the world in softer colors, finally very pleasant, and he began gradually to be reconciled to the severity of daylight.

To clarify what follows I must provide a gloss, for if I do not, I will not know where I am either. Father Caspar was convinced that the *Daphne* lay between the sixteenth and seventeenth degrees of latitude south and at one hundred eighty longitude. As far as latitude is concerned, we can trust him completely. But let us imagine he had also got the longitude right. From Roberto's confused notes it seems Father Caspar calculates precisely three hundred sixty degrees from the Isla de Hierro, eighteen degrees west of Greenwich, as tradition had required since the days of Ptolemy. Therefore if he considered that he was at the one-hundred-eightieth meridian, it meant that in reality he was at the one-hundred-sixty-second east (from Greenwich). Now the Solomons lie comfortably around the one-hundred-sixtieth east, but from five to twelve degrees latitude south. Therefore the *Daphne* would have been too low, west of the New Hebrides, in a zone where only some coral reefs appear, those that would later become the Recifs d'Entrecasteaux.

Could Father Caspar have calculated from another meridian? Certainly. As Coronelli, at the end of that century, was to say in his *Libro dei Globi*, the first meridian was established by "Eratosthenes at the Pillars of Hercules, by Martin of Tyr at the Isles of the Blest, and Ptolemy in his Geography accepted the same opinion, but in his Books of Astronomy he transferred it to Alexandria in Egypt. Among the moderns, Ishmael Abulfeda marks it at Cadiz, Alfonso at Toledo, Pigafetta and Herrera the same, Copernicus sets it at Fruemburg, Reinhold at Monte Reale or Koenigsberg, Longomontanus at Copenhagen, Lansbergis at Goes, Riccioli at Bologna, and the atlases of Iansonius and Bleau at Monte Pico. To continue the order of my Geography in this Globe I have set the Prime Meridian at the westernmost point of the Island of Iron, also to follow the decree of Louis XIII, who with the Council of Geography in 1634 fixed it at that same place."

But if Father Caspar had decided to ignore the decree of Louis XIII and had established his first meridian, say, at Bologna, then the *Daphne* would have been anchored more or less between Samoa and Tahiti. The natives there, however, do not have dark skin like those he says he saw.

For what reason should the tradition of the Isla de Hierro be accepted? We must start with the assumption that Father Caspar speaks of the Prime Meridian as of a fixed line established by divine decree from the days of the Creation. Where would God have considered it natural to have the line run? Through that place of uncertain location, surely Oriental, that was the Garden of Eden? Through ultima Thule? Jerusalem? No one so far had dared make a theological decision, and rightly: God does not reason as men do. Adam, for example, appeared on the earth after the sun was already there, and the moon, day and night, and hence the meridians.

The solution therefore had to be found not in terms of History but, rather, of Sacred Astronomy. It was necessary to make the dictates of the Bible coincide with what knowledge we had of the celestial laws. Now, according to Genesis, in the beginning God created the heaven and the earth. And the earth was without form, and void, and darkness was upon the face of the deep. And the Spirit of God moved upon the face of the waters. But these waters could not be those we know, which God separates only on the second day, dividing the waters that are above the firmament (from which we still receive rain) from those below, namely rivers and seas.

Which means that the first result of Creation was First Matter, without form or dimensions, qualities, properties, tendencies, lacking movement and repose, raw primordial chaos, *hyle,* which was yet neither light nor darkness. It was an undigested mass where the four elements were still mingled, as well as cold and hot, dry and wet, churning magma that exploded in glowing drops like a pot of beans, like a diarrhoeic belly, a clogged pipe, a stagnant pond where circles of water appear and disappear through the emersion and immersion of blind larvae. It was such that the heretics deduced that this matter, so resistant to every creative impulse, was at least as eternal as God.

But even so, a divine fiat was necessary if from it and in it and on it the alternating process of light and darkness was to be imposed, day and night. This light (and that day) which is mentioned in the second stage of Creation was not yet the light we know, that of the stars and of the two great luminaries, which were not created until the fourth day. This was creative light, divine energy in the pure state, like the ignition of a keg of powder, which at first is black granules compressed into an opaque mass, and then all of a sudden it is an expansion of flames, a concentrate of lightning that spreads to its own extreme confine, beyond which, in contraposition, darkness is created (even if the explosion occurs at day). It is as if from a held breath, from a coal reddening through an inner respiration, from that göldene Quelle des Universums was born a scale of luminous excellences gradually descending towards the most irreparable of imperfections; as if the creative afflatus came from the infinite and concentrated luminous power of the Divinity, so searing that it seems to us dark night, down through the relative perfection of the Cherubim and the Seraphim, through the Thrones and the Dominions, to the lowest waste where the worm crawls and the insensible stone survives at the very border of the Void. "And this was the Offenbarung göttlicher Mayestat!"

And if, on the third day, grasses and trees and meadows are already born, it is because the Bible does not yet speak of the landscape that cheers our sight, but of a dark vegetative power, the couplings of seed, the stir of suffering and twisted roots that seek the sun, which, however, on the third day has not yet appeared.

Life arrives on the fourth day, when the moon and sun and stars are created to give light to the earth and to separate day from night, as we understand them when we calculate the course of time. It is on this day that the circle of the heavens is arranged, from the Primum Mobile and the fixed stars to the moon, with the earth in the center, a hard gem barely lighted by the rays of the luminaries, and around it a garland of precious stones.

The sun and the moon, establishing our day and our night, were the first and unsurpassed model of all future clocks, which, monkeys of the firmament, mark human time on the Zodiac's face, a time that has nothing to do with cosmic time: it has a direction, an anxious respiration composed of yesterday, today, and tomorrow, and not the calm breathing of Eternity.

We will stop then at this fourth day, Father Caspar said.

God creates the sun, and when the sun is created—and not before, naturally—it begins to move. Well, at the moment when the sun begins its course never to stop again, in that Blitz, in that flash before it takes its first step, it is directly above a precise line that vertically divides the earth in two.

"And the Prime Meridian is that on which it is suddenly noon," Roberto commented, believing he had understood everything.

"Nein!" his teacher reproached him. "You think God is dumb like you? How can He make the first day of Creation at noon begin? Do you perhaps begin, in beginning des Heyls, the Creation with an aborted day, a Leibesfrucht, a foetus of a day with only twelve hours?"

No, certainly not. On the Prime Meridian the course of the sun would have to begin by the light of the stars, when it was midnight plus a scrap, and before that there was Non-Time. On that meridian began, at night, the first day of Creation.

Roberto objected that if on *that* meridian it was night, an aborted day would have to begin somewhere else, where the sun appeared suddenly, without it or anything else having been before, only dark chaos, without time. Father Caspar said that the Holy Book does not tell us the sun appeared suddenly as if by magic, and that he was not displeased to think (as all logic, natural and divine, demanded) that God had created the sun, causing it to proceed in the sky, through the first hours, like an unignited star, that would bit by bit come alight like green wood touched by the first spark from a flint. The wood at first barely smolders and then, as the puffing encourages it, it begins to crackle and finally agrees to a lively, blazing fire. Was it not beautiful to imagine the Father of the Universe blowing on that still-green ball, urging it to celebrate its victory twelve hours after the birth of Time, right here on the Antipodal Meridian where they stood at this moment?

They still had to define what the Prime Meridian was. And Father Caspar admitted that the Isla de Hierro was still the best candidate, as—Roberto had already learned this from Dr. Byrd—there the compass-needle makes no deviation, and the meridian line passes through the point very close to the Pole where the iron mountains are at their highest. Surely a sign of stability.

So then, to sum up, if we agree that Father Caspar had set out from that meridian and moreover found the correct longitude, we still have to admit that while carefully tracing the course as navigator, he had failed as a geographer: the *Daphne* was not at our Solomon Islands but somewhere west of the New Hebrides, and that was that. However, I must reluctantly tell a story that, as we shall see, has to take place on the one-hundred-eightieth meridian, otherwise it loses all its flavor, while I accept that on the contrary it actually takes place God only knows how many degrees away, in one direction or the other.

I will venture, then, a hypothesis that I defy any reader to challenge. Father Caspar had erred to such an extent that he found himself, unwittingly, on *our* hundred-and-eightieth meridian, I mean the one we calculate from Greenwich, the last place on earth he would have thought of, because it lay in the country of schismatic antipapists.

In which case the *Daphne* would be at the Fiji Islands (where the natives are, in fact, very dark-skinned), at the very spot where today our one-hundred-eightieth meridian passes, namely, at the island of Taveuni.

It works, more or less. The outline of Taveuni shows a volcanic chain like the large island Roberto saw to his west. Except that Father Caspar had told Roberto that the fatal meridian passed just in front of the bay of his Island. Now, if we find ourselves with the meridian to the east, we see Taveuni to the east, not to the west; and if to the west we see an island apparently corresponding to Roberto's description, then we surely have to the east some smaller island (my choice would be Qamea), but then the meridian would pass behind anyone looking at the Island of our story.

The truth is that with the data Roberto gives us, it is not possible to determine where the *Daphne* fetched up. Furthermore all those little islands are like the Japanese for the Europeans, and vice versa: they all look the same. But still I wanted to make a try. One day I would like to retrace Roberto's voyage, searching for signs of him. But my geography is one thing, and his history is another.

Our sole consolation is that all these quibbles are absolutely insignificant from the point of view of our tentative romance. What Father Wanderdrossel says to Roberto is that they are on the one-hundred-eightieth meridian, which is the antipode of the Antipodes, and there on the one-hundred-eightieth meridian we find not our Solomon Islands but his Island of Solomon. What does it matter, finally, whether it is there or not? If nothing more, this will be the story of two men who believe they are there, not of two who are there; and if you would listen to stories—this is dogma among the more liberal—you must suspend disbelief.

So: the *Daphne* was facing the one-hundred-eightieth meridian, just at the Solomon Islands, and our Island was— among the Islands of Solomon—the most Solomonic, as my verdict is Solomonic, cutting through the problem once and for all.

"So?" Roberto asked at the end of the explanation. "Do you truly believe you will find on that Island all the riches of which Mendaña spoke?"

"Those are Lügen der spanischen Monarchy! We are facing the greatest prodigium of all human and sacred history, which you still can nicht understand! In Paris you looked at the ladies and followed the ratio studiorum of the Epicureans instead of reflecting on the great miracles of this our Universum, may the Sanctissimum Nomen of our Creator fiat semper praised!"

As it happened, the reasons Father Caspar had set sail bore no resemblance to the larcenous designs of the various navigators of other countries. Everything stemmed from the monumental work that he was writing, a treatise destined to remain more perennial than bronze, on the Great Flood.

A true man of the Church, he intended to prove that the Bible had not lied; but, also a man of science, he wanted to make the Sacred Text agree with the results of the research of his own time. And to this end he had collected fossils, explored the lands of the Orient to discover something on the peak of Mount Ararat, and made very careful calculations of the putative dimensions of the Ark, such as to allow it to contain so many animals (and, mind you, seven pairs of the clean ones), and at the same time to have the correct proportion between the exposed part and the submerged part so the ship would not sink under all that weight or be swamped by waves, which during the Flood cannot have been negligible ripples.

He made a sketch to show Roberto the cross-section of the Ark, like an enormous square building of six storeys, the birds at the top, to receive the sun's light, the mammals in pens that could house not only kittens but also elephants, and the reptiles in a kind of bilge, where the amphibians could also find living space in the water. No room for the Giants, and so that species became extinct. Finally, Noah did not have the problem of fish, the only creatures that had nothing to fear from the Flood.

Still, studying the Flood, Father Caspar had come up against a physicus-hydrodynamicus problem, apparently insoluble. God, the Bible tells us, causes rain to fall on the earth for forty days and forty nights, and the waters rise above the land until they cover even the highest mountains, and indeed they are arrested at fifteen cubits above the highest of the mountains, and the waters cover the earth thus for one hundred and fifty days. All well and good.

"But have you tried ever the rain to collect? It rains all one day, and you cover the little bottom of a barrel. And if it rains one whole week, you scarcely fill the barrel! So imagine then an ungeheuere Regen, so hard you cannot stay from the house in it, and all that rain pours on your poor head, a rain worse than the hurricane of your shipwreck. . . . In forty days ist das unmöglich, not possible, to fill all the earth above the highest mountains!"

"You mean to say the Bible lied?"

"Nein! Certainly not! But I must demonstrate where God all that water found, for it is not possible He made it fall from the sky! That is not enough!"

"So?"

"So, dumm bin ich nicht, not stupid! Vater Caspar has thought what no other human being before now had thought ever. In primis, he read well the Bible, which says, ja, that God opened all the cataracts of Heaven, but also had erupt all the Quellen, the Fontes Abyssy Magnae, all the fountains of the gross abyss. Genesis sieben elf. After the Flood ended was, He has the fountains of the deep closed. Genesis acht zwei! What are these fountains of the deep?"

"What are they?"

"They are the waters that in the deepest depths of the sea are found! God took not only the rain but also the waters of the deepest oceans and poured them on the earth! And He took them here because, if the highest mountains of the earth are around the first meridian, between Jerusalem and Isla de Hierro, certainly the marine abysses the most deep must be here, on the antimeridian, for reasons of symmetry."

"Yes, but the waters of all the seas of the globe are not enough to cover the mountains, otherwise they would always be covered. And if God emptied the waters of the sea onto the earth, He would cover the earth but He would drain the sea, and the sea would become a great empty hole, and Noah fall into it with all of his Ark."

"You say correct. And more: if God take all the water of Terra Incognita and poured that on Terra Cognita, without this water in this hemisphere the earth all change its Zentrum Cravitatis and overturn everything, and perhaps leap into the sky like a ball which you give a kick to it."

"So?"

"So then you try to think what you do if you are God."

Roberto was caught up in the game. "If I am God," he said, forgetting to use the subjunctive mood as the God of the Italians commands, "I create new water."

"You yes, but God no. God can ex nihilo water create, but where to put it *after* the Flood?"

"Then God, from the beginning of time, had put aside a great reserve supply of water beneath the deep, hidden in the center of the earth, and He brought it out on that occasion, just for forty days, as if it were spouting from the volcanoes. Surely this is what the Bible means when we read that He opened the fountains of the deep."

"You think? But from volcanoes comes fire. All the zentrum of the earth, the heart of Mundus Subterraneus, is a gross mass of fire! If in the zentrum is fire, there water cannot also be! If water would be there, volcanoes would be fountains," he concluded.

Roberto refused to give up. "Then, if I am God, I take the water from another world, since worlds are infinite, and I pour it on the earth."

"You have in Paris heard those atheists who of infinite worlds talk. But God has only one world made, and that is enough for His glory. No, think better, if you do not infinite worlds have, and you have not time to make them specially for the Flood and then throw them into the Void again, what do you do?"

"I honestly do not know."

"Because you have mens parva."

"I may, indeed."

"Yes, very parva. Now you think. If God could the water take that was yesterday on all the earth and pour it today, and tomorrow take all that was yesterday and it is already the double, and pour it day after tomorrow, and so on ad infinitum, perhaps comes the day when He all this sphere of ours can fill, to cover all the mountains, nicht?"

"I am poor at sums, but I would say, at a certain point, yes."

"Ja! In forty days he fills the earth with forty times the water found in the seas, and if you make forty times the depth of the seas, you surely cover the mountains: the deep is as much or far more deep than the mountains high are."

"But where did God find yesterday's water, when yesterday was already past?"

"Why, here! Now listen. Think you are on the Prime Meridian. Can you imagine that?"

"Yes, I can."

"Now think that here it is noon, and let us say noon on Holy Thursday. What time is it in Jerusalem?"

"After all that I have learned about the course of the sun and about the meridians, I would say that in Jerusalem the sun would already have passed the meridian some time ago, so it would be late afternoon. I understand where you are leading me. Very well: at the Prime Meridian it is noon, on the one-hundred-eightieth meridian it is midnight, for the sun passed already twelve hours before."

"Gut. Then here is midnight, thus end of Holy Thursday. What happens here immediately after?"

"The first hour of Good Friday begins."

"And not on the Prime Meridian?"

"No, over there it will still be the afternoon of that Thursday."

"Wunderbar. Therefore here it is already Friday and there it is still Thursday, no? But when there it has Friday become, here is already Saturday and the Lord is resurrect here when there still dead, nichtwahr?"

"Yes, all right, but I don't understand—"

"Now you will understand. Where here is midnight and one minute, a minuscule part of one minute, you say that here is already Friday?"

"Yes, of course."

"But think if at the same moment you would not be here on the ship but on that island you see, east of the line of the meridian. Perhaps you say there it already Friday is?"

"No, it is still Thursday. It is midnight less one minute, less one second, but Thursday."

"Gut! At the same moment here is Friday and there, Thursday!"

"Certainly, and—" A thought suddenly arrested Roberto. "And that's not all! You make me realize that if at that same instant I were on the line of the meridian, it would be midnight on the dot, but if I looked to the west, I would see the midnight of Friday and if I looked to the east, I would see the midnight of Thursday. Holy God!"

"You do not say God, bitte."

"Forgive me, Father, but this is something miraculous."

"Und so in the face of a miracle you do not the name of God in vain take! Say Holywood, if you like. But the great miracle is that there is no miracle! All was foreseen *ab initio*. If the sun to circle the earth takes twenty-four hours, to west of the one-hundred-eightieth meridian begins a new day, and east we have still the day before. Midnight of Friday here on the ship is midnight of Thursday on the island. You know what to the sailors of Magellan happened when they finished their voyage around the world, as Peter Martyr tells? They came back and thought it was a day earlier and instead it was a day later, and they believed God had punished them by taking from them a day, because they had not every Friday holy fasting observed. On the contrary, it was very natural: they had traveled from east to west. If from America towards Asia you sail, you lose one day; if in the opposite direction you sail, you gain a day: this is why the *Daphne* followed the route of Asia, and your stupid ship the way of America. You are now a day younger than me. Is that not to laugh?"

"But I would be a day younger only if I went to the Is-land," Roberto said.

"This was my little jocus. But to me is no matter if you are younger or older. To me matters that at this point of the earth there is a line that on this side is the day after and on that side the day before. And not only at midnight but also at seven, at ten, every hour! God then took from this abysso the water of yesterday (that you see there) and emptied it on the world of today, and the next day the same, and so on! Sine miraculo, naturaliter! God had arranged Nature like to a great Horologium! It is as if a Horologium does not show the twelve hours, but the twenty-four. In this Horologium moves the hand or arrow towards the twenty-four, and to the right of the twenty-four it was yesterday, and to the left, today."

"But how could the earth of yesterday remain steady in the sky, if there was no more water in this hemisphere? Did it not lose its Centrum Gravitatis?"

"You think with the humana conceptione of time. For us homines exists yesterday no more, and tomorrow not yet. Tempus Dei, quod dicitur Aevum, is very different."

Roberto reasoned that if God removed the water of yesterday and placed it in today, the earth of yesterday might undergo a succussation thanks to that damned center of gravity, but to human beings this should not matter: in their yesterday the succussation had not taken place; it had happened instead in a yesterday of God, who clearly knew how to handle different times and different stories, as a Narrator who writes several novels, all with the same characters, but making different things befall them from story to story. As if there had been a Chanson de Roland in which Roland died under a pine, and another in which he became king of France at the death of Charles, using Ganelon's hide as a carpet. A thought which, as we shall see, was to accompany Roberto for a long while, convincing him not only that the worlds can be infinite in space but also parallel in time. But he did not want to speak of this with Father Caspar, who already considered profoundly heretical the idea of many worlds, and there was no telling what the good Jesuit would have said of this idea of Roberto's. He therefore confined himself to asking what God did to shift all that water from yesterday to today.

"The eruptione of underwater volcanoes, natürlich! You conceive? They blow hot winds, and what happens when a pan of milk is heated? The milk swells, rises, overflows the pan, spreads over the stove! But at that time it was not milk sed boiling aqua! Gross catastrophe!"

"And how did God take all that water away after the forty days?"

"If it did not rain anymore, there was sun et nunc aqua

evaporated little by little. The Bible says one hundred fifty days it took. If you wash and dry your shirt in one day, you can dry the earth in one hundred fifty. And besides, much water into enormous subterranean lakes flowed, which now lie zwischen the surface and the zentral fire."

"You have almost convinced me," Roberto said, who cared less about how that water had been moved than about the fact of being so close to yesterday. "But by arriving here what have you demonstrated that you could not have demonstrated before through the light of reason?"

"I leave the light of reason to the old theologia. Today scientia wants proof through experientia. And the experientia is that I am here. Then before I arrived here I took many soundings, and I know how deep the sea down here is."

Father Caspar abandoned his geo-astronomical explanation and launched into the description of the Flood. He spoke now his erudite Latin, gesticulating as if to evoke the various phenomena, celestial and infernal, as he paced the deck. While he strode, the sky above the bay was clouding over, announcing a storm of the sort that arrives, all of a sudden, only in the sea of the Tropics. Now, all the fountains of the deep and the cataracts of the sky having opened, what horrendum et formidandum spectaculum was offered to Noah and his family!

People took refuge first on the roofs, but their houses were swept away by the currents that arrived from the Antipodes with the force of the divine wind which had raised and driven them. Men and women climbed into the trees, but these were uprooted like weeds; they could see still the crowns of the most ancient oaks, and they clung to them, but the winds shook them with such rage that none could maintain their grip. Now in the waters that covered valleys and mountains swollen corpses could be seen floating, on which the remaining birds tried to perch, terrified, as if on some ghastly nest, but soon they lost even this last refuge, and they also succumbed, exhausted, to the tempest, their wings limp. "Oh horrenda justitiae divinae spectacula," Father Caspar exulted, and this was nothing—he guaranteed—compared to what it will be given us to see on the day when Christ returns to judge the quick and the dead.

And to the great din of nature responded the animals of the Ark, the howls of the wind were echoed by the wolves, to the roar of thunder the lion made counterpoint, at the shudder of lightning bolts the elephants trumpeted, the dogs barked on hearing the voice of their dying kin, the sheep wept at the crying of the children, the crows cawed at the cawing of the rain on the roof of the Ark, the cows lowed at the lowing of the waves, and all the creatures of earth and air with their calamitous whimpering or mewing took part in the mourning of the planet.

But it was on that occasion, Father Caspar assured Roberto, that Noah and his family rediscovered the language Adam had spoken in Eden, which his sons had forgotten after the Fall, and which the descendants of Noah would almost all lose on the day of the great confusion of Babel, except the heirs of Gomer, who carried it into the forests of the north, where the German people faithfully preserved it. Only the German language—the obsessed Father Caspar now shouted in his native tongue—"redet mit der Zunge, donnert mit dem Himmel, blitzet mit den schnellen Wolken," or, as he inventively continued, mixing the harsh sounds of different idioms, only German speaks the tongue of Nature, "blitzes with the Clouds, brumms with the Stag, gruntzes with the Schweine, zlides with the Eel, miaus with the Katz, schnatters with the Gandern, quackers with the Dux, klukken with the hen, clappers with the Schwan, kraka with the Ravfen, schwirrs with the

Hirundin!" And in the end he was hoarse from his babelizing, and Roberto was convinced that the true language of Adam, rediscovered with the Flood, flourished only in the lands of the Holy Roman Emperor.

Dripping sweat, the priest concluded his evocation. The sky, as if frightened by the consequences of every flood, had held back its storm, like a sneeze that seems almost ready to explode but then is restrained with a grunt.

CHAPTER 22

The Orange Dove

IN THE DAYS that followed it became clear that the Specula Melitensis could not be reached, because Father Wanderdrossel, like Roberto, was unable to swim. The longboat was still over there in the inlet, but it was as if it did not exist.

Now that he had a strong young man at his disposal, Father Caspar could have constructed a raft and made a big oar but, as he had explained, all the tools and materials were on the Island. Without an axe they could not chop down the masts or the yards, without hammers they could not unhinge the doors and nail them together.

But Father Caspar did not seem excessively troubled by his long isolation; indeed, he rejoiced, as he could once again enjoy the use of his cabin, the deck, and some instruments of study and observation.

Roberto still did not understand what Father Caspar Wanderdrossel was. A sage? That, certainly, or at least a scholar, a man curious about both natural and divine science. An eccentric? To be sure. At one moment he let fall that this ship had been fitted out not at the expense of the Society but with his private funds, or, rather, the money of his brother, a rich merchant as mad as he was; on another occasion he confided, complaining, that some of his fellow Jesuits had "stolen many fecondissime ideas" after pretending to reject them as mere scribbling. Which suggested that back in Rome those reverend fathers had not grieved at the departure of this sophistic character. Considering that he was sailing at his own expense and there was a good chance he might be lost along those perilous routes, they may have encouraged him in order to be rid of him.

The company Roberto had kept in Provence and in Paris had been such as to make him skeptical of the assertions of physics and natural philosophy that he heard the old man now make. But as we have seen, Roberto absorbed knowledge to which he was exposed as if he were a sponge, and was not distressed at believing in contradictory truths. Perhaps it was not that he lacked a taste for system; his was a choice.

In Paris the world had appeared to him a stage on which deceptions were depicted, for the spectator wanted to follow and admire a different story every evening, as if the usual things, even if miraculous, no longer enlightened anyone, and only the unusually uncertain or the certainly unusual were able still to stimulate. The ancients had affirmed that for any question a sole answer existed, whereas the great theater of Paris offered him the spectacle of a question to which the most varied replies could be given. Roberto decided to concede only half of his spirit to the things he believed (or believed he believed), keeping the other half open in case the contrary was true.

If such was the disposition of his mind, we can then understand why he was not motivated to deny even the least plausible of Father Caspar's revelations. Of all the tales he had heard, the one told him by the Jesuit was surely the most uncommon. But why consider it false?

I challenge anyone to find himself abandoned on a deserted ship, between sea and sky in a vast space, and not be ready to dream that in his great misfortune he at least has had the good fortune to stumble into the heart of time.

Roberto could also amuse himself by offering many objections to those tales, but often he behaved like the disciples of Socrates, who seemed to implore their own defeat.

Besides, how could he reject the knowledge of a now paternal figure who had suddenly removed him from the condition of stunned castaway to that of a passenger on a ship someone knew and controlled? Whether it was the authority of his cassock or his office as original lord of that marine castle, Father Caspar represented to Roberto's eyes Authority, and Roberto had learned enough of the ideas of his century to know that to authority you must bend, at least in appearance.

If Roberto did begin to have doubts about his host, the latter immediately took him to explore the ship again and showed him instruments that had previously escaped his notice, allowing him to learn so many and such important things, that his trust was won.

For example, the Jesuit showed him some fishing rods and nets. The *Daphne* was anchored in teeming waters, and it was not a good idea to consume the provisions on board when it was possible to have fresh fish. Wearing every day his smoked eyeglasses, Roberto quickly learned to cast the nets and lower the line, and with no great effort he captured creatures of such size that more than once he risked being pulled overboard by the power of their jaws as they snatched the bait.

He laid them on deck, and Father Caspar seemed to know the nature of each and even its name. Whether he then named them according to their nature or christened them at his own whim, Roberto could not say.

While the fish in his hemisphere were gray or at most a

bright silver, these appeared pale blue with cherry-colored fins, they had saffron beards or scarlet snouts. He caught an eel with two heads, one at either end of its body, but Father Caspar showed him that, on the contrary, the second head was actually a tail so decorated by nature that, in flicking it, the animal could frighten its enemies also from behind. Roberto captured a fish with a maculate belly, inky stripes on its back, all the colors of the rainbow circling the eye, a goat-like muzzle, but Father Caspar immediately made him throw it back into the sea, knowing (from other Jesuits' accounts, or his own experience as a voyager, or seamen's tales?) that it was more poisonous than the mortal boletus.

Of another fish—yellow eyes, tumid mouth, teeth like nails—Father Caspar said at once that it was a creature of Beelzebub. It should be left to suffocate on deck until death took it, then away with it, to whence it came. Did he declare this through acquired knowledge or was he judging by the thing's appearance? In any case, all the fish Caspar considered edible proved to be excellent—and, indeed, of one he was able to specify that it was better boiled than baked.

Initiating Roberto into the mysteries of that Solomonic sea, the Jesuit also became more precise in vouchsafing information about the Island, which the *Daphne,* on arriving, had circumnavigated completely. Towards the east the Island had some little beaches, but they were too exposed to the winds. Immediately after the southern promontory, where the crew had landed with the boat, there was a calm bay, but the water there was too shallow to moor the *Daphne.* This point, where the ship now lay, was the most suitable: closer to the Island, they would run aground, and farther away, they would find themselves right in a very strong current that ran through the channel between the two islands from southwest to northeast. It was easy to illustrate this to Roberto: Father Caspar asked him to throw the carcass of Beelzebub's fish with all his strength into the sea to the west, and the corpse of the monster, while it could be seen floating, was violently yanked away by an invisible stream.

Caspar and the seamen had explored the Island, if not entirely, enough to allow them to decide that one hill, chosen as site of the Specula, was the best to command with the eye all that land, vast as the city of Rome.

In the interior there was a waterfall, and splendid vegetation which included not only coconuts and bananas but also some trees with star-shaped trunks, the tips of the star as sharp as blades.

As for the animals—some of which Roberto had seen on the lower deck—the Island was a paradise of birds, and there were even flying foxes. The crew had sighted pigs in the underbrush but had not been able to capture them. There were serpents, but none had proved venomous or fierce, while the varieties of lizards were innumerable.

But the richest fauna were found along the coral barbican. Turtles, crabs, and oysters of every shape, difficult to compare with those found in our seas, big as baskets, as pots, as serving platters, often difficult to open, but once opened, revealing quantities of white flesh, soft and fat; and they were genuine delicacies. Unfortunately they could not be brought on board ship: once out of the water, they immediately spoiled in the sun's heat.

They had seen none of the great ferocious animals in which other Asian countries are so rich, no elephants or tigers or crocodiles. Or, for that matter, anything that resembled an ox, a bull, a horse, or a dog. It appeared that in this land every form of life had been conceived not by an architect or a sculptor but by a jeweller: the birds were colored crystal, the woodland animals were delicate, the fish flat and almost transparent.

It had not seemed to Father Caspar or to the captain or the sailors that in those waters there were Dog Fish, easily recognized even from a distance thanks to that fin keen as an axe. And yet in those seas they are found everywhere. The idea that there were no sharks around the Island was, in my opinion, an illusion of that inspired explorer. But perhaps what he argued was true, namely that, as slightly to the west there was a great current, those animals preferred to dwell there, where they were sure of finding more plentiful sustenance. However it may have been, it is well for the story that follows that neither Caspar nor Roberto feared the presence of sharks, otherwise they would not have had the heart to go down into the water, and I would have no tale to tell.

As Roberto listened, he became more and more captivated by the distant Island; he tried to imagine its shape, its color, the movement of the creatures Father Caspar described. And the corals? What were these corals, which he knew only as jewels that according to poets had the color of a beautiful woman's lips?

Regarding corals Father Caspar remained speechless; he merely raised his eyes to Heaven with an expression of bliss. The corals of which Roberto spoke were dead corals, like the virtue of the courtesans for whom libertines employed that trite simile. On the reef, too, there were dead corals, and it was they that wounded anyone touching them. But they were nothing compared to living corals, which were—how to describe them?—submarine flowers, anemone, hyacinth, ranunculus, gilli-flowers—no, that gave no idea—they were a festival of galls, curls, berries, bowls, burrs, shoots, hearts, twigs—no, no, they were something else: mobile, colorful as Armida's vale, and they imitated all the vegetables of field, garden, wood, from cucumber to mushroom, even the frilled cabbage. . . .

He had seen them elsewhere, thanks to an instrument constructed by a fellow Jesuit (and after some rummaging in his chest, he produced the instrument): it was a kind of leather mask with a great glass eyepiece, the upper orifice edged and reinforced; thanks to a pair of strings it could be bound at the nape, making the mask adhere to the face from brow to chin. In a flat-bottomed boat, which would not run aground on submerged sandbars, he had been able to lower his face until it was in the water, allowing him to see the bottom—whereas if he had immersed his bare head, there would have been only stinging of the eyes and he would have seen nothing.

Caspar thought that the device—which he called a Perspicillum, Eyeglass, or Persona Vitrea (a mask that does not hide but, rather, reveals)—could be worn also by someone who knew how to swim among rocks. Sooner or later, the water did penetrate to the inside, but for a little while, holding your breath, you could continue observing. After which, the swimmer would have to emerge, empty the receptacle, and begin again.

"If you to schwimm would learn, you could these things see down there," Caspar said to Roberto. And Roberto, mocking him, replied, "If I schwumm, my chest would a keg become!" And yet he reproached himself for his inability to go down there.

But at the same time, Father Caspar was adding, "On the Island there was the Flame Dove."

"Flame Dove? What is that?" Roberto asked, and the eagerness in his question seems to us excessive. As if the Island for some time had promised him an obscure emblem, which only now had become radiant.

Father Caspar explained how hard it was to describe the beauty of this bird: you had to see it before you could talk about it. The very day of his arrival, he had glimpsed it through his spyglass. From a distance it was like seeing a fiery sphere of gold, or of gilded fire, which from the top of the tallest tree shot up towards the sky. Once he was on land, he wanted to learn more, and he taught the sailors to identify it.

It was quite a long ambush until they came to understand in which trees the bird lived. It emitted a very special sound, a sort of *tock-tock,* such as we can make by striking the tongue against the palate. Caspar found that if he imitated this call with his mouth or fingers, the bird would respond and, once in a while, let itself be descried as it flew from one bough to another.

Caspar returned several times, to lie in wait, but with a glass, and at least once he saw the bird clearly, almost immobile: the head was a dark olive color—no, perhaps an asparagus green, like the feet—and the beak, the color of lucern, extended like a mask to frame the eye, which was like a kernel of maize, the pupil a glistening black. It had a short bib, gold like its wingtips; but the body from breast to tail, where the feathers were fine as a woman's hair, was—what?—red? No, that was the wrong word. . . .

Ruddy, ruby, rubescent, rubedinous, rubent, rubefacient, Roberto suggested. Nein, nein, Father Caspar became irritated. Roberto went on: like a strawberry, a geranium, a raspberry, a cherry, a radish; like holly berries, the belly of a thrush, the wing of a redwing, the tail of a redstart, the breast of a robin . . . No, no, no, Father Caspar insisted, struggling with his own and other languages to find the proper words. Judging by the synthesis Roberto makes later—and it is hard to tell whether the vehemence is more in the informant or in the informed —it must have been the festive color of a Seville orange, it was a winged sun, in other words; when seen against the white sky it was as if the dawn had flung a pomegranate on the snow. And when it catapulted into the sun, it was more dazzling than a cherub!

That orange-colored bird, Father Caspar said, could live
only on the Island of Solomon, because it was in the Song of
that great king that a dove was spoken of, rising like the dawn,
bright as the sun, terribilis ut castrorum acies ordinata. It had,
as another psalm says, wings covered with silver and feathers
with glints of gold.

Along with this animal, Caspar had seen another almost
its equal, except that its feathers were not orange but greenish,
and from the way the two were normally seen paired on the
same branch, they must have been male and female. That they
were doves was obvious from their shape and frequently heard
cry. Which of the two was the male was hard to say; in any
case Caspar had ordered the sailors not to kill them.

Roberto asked how many doves there could be on the
Island. All Father Caspar knew was that each time he had seen
only one orange ball dart towards the clouds, and only one
couple among the high fronds: so on the Island there might
be just two doves, and just one orange-colored. A supposition
that made Roberto crave that rare beauty—which, if it was
now awaiting him, had always been awaiting him since the
day before.

For that matter, if Roberto chose, Caspar said, he could
remain for hours and hours at the spyglass and see it also
from the ship. Provided he removed those smoked spectacles.
When Roberto replied that his eyes did not allow him to,
Caspar made some scornful remarks about that milksop's ail-
ment, and prescribed the liquids with which he had treated
his bubo (Spiritus, Olea, Flores).

It is not clear whether or not Roberto tried them, or if he
gradually trained himself to look without the glasses, first at
dawn and sunset and then in broad day, and we cannot say if
he was still wearing them when, as we shall see, he tried to
learn to swim; but the fact is that from this moment on his

eyes are no longer mentioned to justify any sort of flight or absence. So we may assume that gradually, perhaps through the therapeutic action of that balmy air or that sea water, Roberto was cured of a complaint that, real or imagined, had turned him into a lycanthrope for more than ten months (unless the reader chooses to insinuate that because from now on I need him on deck full-time, and finding no contradiction among his papers, I am freeing him from all illness, with authorial arrogance).

But perhaps Roberto wanted to be healed, at all costs, in order to see the dove. And he would have flung himself on the bulwarks and spent the day peering at the trees, if he had not been distracted by another unresolved question.

Having ended his description of the Island and its riches, Father Caspar remarked that all these delights could be found nowhere save on the antipodal meridian. Roberto then asked: "Reverend Father, you told me that the Specula Melitensis confirmed that you are on the antipodal meridian, and I believe it. Still, you did not stop and set up the Specula on every island you encountered on your voyage, but only on this one. So somehow, before the Specula told you, you must already have been sure you would find the longitude you were seeking!"

"You think very right. If I here were come without knowing here was here, I could not know I was here. . . . Now I explain you. Since I knew that the Specula was the only correct instrument to arrive where to try out the Specula, I had to use falsch methods. Und so I did."

CHAPTER 23

Divers and
Artificious Machines

As ROBERTO, INCREDULOUS, demanded to know what, and how useless, the various methods to find longitudes had been, Father Caspar replied that while all were erroneous when taken one by one, if taken together the various results could achieve a balance and compensate for the individual defects: "And this est mathematica!"

To be sure, a clock after traveling thousands of miles could no longer tell accurately the time of its place of origin. But how many and various clocks, some of special and careful construction, had Roberto seen on board the *Daphne*? You compare their inexact times, study daily the responses of one against the assertions of the others, and you arrive at a kind of certitude.

What of the loch or the navicella, or whatever you choose to call it? The usual ones do not work, but here is what Father Caspar had constructed: a box with two vertical poles, one that wound as the other unwound a cord of fixed length equivalent to a fixed number of miles; and the winding pole was surmounted by many little blades, which as in a mill turned under the force of the same winds that swelled the sails: their movement accelerated or slowed—and therefore wound or unwound the cord—according to the strength and direction, straight or oblique, of the wind, recording meanwhile also the deviations due to tacking, or sailing against the wind. A method not much more sure than all the others, but excellent if someone compared its results with those of other soundings.

Lunar eclipses? To be sure, observing them during a voyage resulted in endless misunderstandings. But what about those observed on land?

"We must have many observers and in many places of the world, and well disposed to collaborate in the major glory of God, and not exchange insults or spitefulness or scorn. Listen: in 1612, the eighth of November, at Macao, the most reverend pater Iulius de Alessis records an eclipse at eight-thirty that evening until eleven-thirty. He informs the most reverend pater Carolus Spinola, who at Nangasaki, in Iaponia, the same eclipse at nine-thirty of the same evening was observing. And the pater Christophorus Schnaidaa had the same eclipse seen at Ingolstadt at five in the afternoon. The differentia of one hora makes fifteen degrees of meridian, and therefore this is the distance between Macao and Nangasaki, not sixteen degrees and twenty, as says Blaeu. Verstanden? Naturally with these records you must guard against drink and smoke, have correct horologii, not lose the initium totalis immersionis, and maintain correct medium between initium and finis eclipsis, observe the intermediary moments in which the spots are dark, et cetera. If the places are distant, a very little error makes no gross differentia, but if the places are proximi, an error of a few minutes makes gross differentia."

Apart from the fact that in the matter of Macao and Nagasaki it seems to me that Blaeu is closer to the truth than Father Caspar (which proves how complicated longitudes were at that time), this is how the Jesuits, after collecting and collating the observations of their missionary brethren, established a Horologium Catholicum, which—despite the name—was not a clock devoted to the Roman pope but a universal clock. It was in effect a kind of planisphere on which were marked all the headquarters of the Society, from Rome to the borders of the known world, and for each place the local time was marked. Thus, Father Caspar explained, he had not had to bear in mind the hour at the beginning of the voyage but only at the last outpost of the Christian world, whose longitude was beyond debate. Then the margins for error were greatly reduced, and between one station and the next they could also use methods that, in the absolute sense, offered no guarantee, such as the variation of the needle or calculation from lunar spots.

Fortunately he had brethren just about everywhere, from Pernambuco to Goa, from Mindanao to Porto Sancti Thomae, and if winds prevented the *Daphne* from mooring in one port, there would soon be another. For example, at Macao . . . ah, Macao! At the very thought of that adventure, Father Caspar glowered. It was a Portuguese possession; the Chinese called the Europeans men of long noses precisely because the first to land on their shores were the Portuguese, who truly do have long noses, and also the Jesuits, who came with them. So the city was a single garland of blue and white fortresses on the hill, controlled by the fathers of the Society, who had to concern themselves also with military matters, since the city was threatened by the Dutch heretics.

Father Caspar had decided to head for Macao, where he knew a fellow Jesuit very learned in the astronomical sciences, but he had forgotten that he was sailing on a fluyt.

What did the good fathers of Macao do? Sighting a Dutch ship, they manned their cannons and colubrines. In vain

Father Caspar waved his arms at the prow and immediately had the Society's standard run up; those cursed long-noses, his Portuguese brothers in the Society, wrapped in the warrior smoke that invited them to a holy massacre, did not even notice, and they rained balls around the *Daphne*. It was the pure grace of God that the ship was barely able to strike its sails, come about, and escape to sea while the captain in his Lutheran language hurled anathema at those fathers of scant consideration. And this time he was right: sinking the Dutch is all very well, but not when there is a Jesuit on board.

Luckily it was fairly easy to reach other missions not far away, and they turned their bowsprit towards the more hospitable Mindanao. And so, from one port to the next, they kept watch over their longitude (and God help them, I add, considering that, having ended up practically in Australia, they must have lost track of every point of reference).

"Et hora we must novissima experimenta make, ut clarissime et evidenter demonstrate that we are on meridian one hundred eighty. Otherwise the fratres of the Collegium Romanum will think I am a Mamelukke."

"New experiments?" Roberto asked. "Did you not just tell me that the Specula gave you the utmost assurance of being on the one-hundred-eightieth meridian, off the Island of Solomon?"

Yes, the Jesuit replied, he was certain: he had set in competition the various imperfect methods found by others, and the accord of all these weak methods supplied a very strong certitude, as happens in the proof of God's existence by *consensus gentium,* for while it is true that many men inclined to err also believe in God, it is impossible that all should be mistaken, from the forests of Africa to the deserts of China. So it happens that we believe in the movement of the sun and the moon and of the other planets, or in the hidden power of Chelidonium, or that at the center of the earth there is a fire; for thousands and thousands of years men have believed these things, and while believing them, they have been able to live on this planet and achieve many useful results from their reading of the great book of Nature. But an important discovery like this had to be confirmed by further proof, so that even the sceptics would surrender to the evidence.

Besides, science must be pursued not only for the love of learning but in the desire to share it with our brothers. So, since it had cost him such an effort to find the correct longitude, he now had to seek confirmation through other, easier methods, so that this knowledge could become the patrimony of all our brothers, "or at least of the Christian ones, or, rather, the Catholic brothers, because, as for the Dutch or English heretics—or worse, the Moravians—it would be far better if they never came to learn of these secrets."

Now, of all the methods of taking longitude, two seemed sure to him. One, good for terra firma, was that treasure of all methods, namely the Specula Melitensis; the other, appropriate for observation at sea, was the Instrumentum Arcetricum, which lay below but had not yet been set up, because he first had to obtain through the Specula the certitude of their position, then see if the Instrumentum confirmed it, which was the most reliable way to proceed.

Father Caspar would have carried out this experiment long before if what happened had not happened. But the moment now had come, and it would be on that very night: the sky and the ephemerides said that now was the right occasion.

What was the Instrumentum Arcetricum? A device envisioned many years earlier by Galilei—but, mind you, envisioned, narrated, promised, never achieved, until Father Caspar set to work. When Roberto asked him if that Galilei was the same who had advanced a severely condemned hypothesis about the motion of the earth, Father Caspar replied yes, when that Galilei had stuck his nose into metaphysics and the Sacred Scriptures, he had said dreadful things, but as a mechanical he was a man of genius and very great. Asked whether it was not wrong to use the ideas of a man the Church had censured, the Jesuit answered that to the greater glory of God the ideas of a heretic also could contribute, provided they in themselves were not heretical. And we might have known that Father Caspar, who welcomed all existing methods, not swearing by any one of them but exploiting their quarrelsome conference, would exploit also the method of Galilei.

Indeed, it was highly useful both for science and for the faith to develop as soon as possible that idea of Galilei; the Florentine himself had tried to sell it to the Dutch, but fortunately, like the Spaniards a few decades earlier, they did not trust him.

Galilei had drawn some odd conclusions from a premiss that in itself was quite right, namely that of stealing the idea of the spyglass from the Flemings (who used it only to look at ships in port) and training that instrument on the heavens. And there, among the many things that Father Caspar would not dream of doubting, Galilei had discovered that Jupiter, or Jove, as he called it, had four satellites, that is to say four moons, never seen from the beginning of the world until that moment. Four little stars that revolved around it while it revolved around the sun—and we will see that for Father Caspar the idea that Jove revolved around the sun was admissible, provided the earth was left alone.

Now, it is a well-known fact that our moon, when it passes in the shadow of the earth, is eclipsed. Astronomers have long known when lunar eclipses would occur, and the ephemerides were authoritative. It was not surprising, then, that the moons of Jove also had their eclipses. Indeed, for us at least, they had two, one actual eclipse and one occultation.

In fact, the moon disappears from our sight when the earth comes between it and the sun, but the satellites of Jove disappear from our sight twice, when they pass behind it and when they pass in front, becoming united with its light, through a good spyglass you can easily follow their appearances and their disappearances. With the inestimable advantage that while the eclipses of the moon occur only very rarely and take a long time, those of the Jovian satellites occur frequently and are rapid.

Now let us suppose that the hour and the minutes of the eclipses of each satellite (each traveling in an orbit of different breadth) have been precisely established on a known meridian, and the ephemerides bear this out; at which point it is enough to be able to fix the hour and the minute when the eclipse is visible on the (unknown) meridian, and the calculation is quickly made, and the longitude of the point of observation can be deduced.

True, there were minor drawbacks, not worth discussing with a layman, but the enterprise would succeed for a good calculator who had at his disposal a measurer of time, namely a perpendiculum or pendulum, or Horologium Oscillatorium as might be, capable of measuring with absolute precision even to the second. Similarly, he would need two normal clocks that told him faithfully the hour of the beginning and the end of the phenomenon both on the meridian of observation and on that of the Isla de Hierro; and, using the table of sines, he could measure the quantity of the angle made in the eye by the bodies under examination—the angle that, if thought of as the hands of a clock, expressed in minutes and seconds the distance between the two bodies and its progressive variation.

Provided, it is well to repeat, he also had those good ephemerides that Galilei, by then old and infirm, had not been able to complete, but that the brethren of Father Caspar, already so good at calculating eclipses of the moon, had now perfected.

What were the chief flaws, over which Galilei's adversaries had waxed so bitter? That these observations could not be made with the naked eye and the observer needed a strong spyglass, or telescope, as it was now more properly called? And Father Caspar had some of excellent facture such as not even Galilei had dreamed of. That the measuring and the calculating were not within the skill of sailors? Why, all the other methods for determining longitude, except perhaps the log, required the presence of an astronomer! And if captains had learned to use the astrolabe, which itself was not something within the grasp of any layman, they could also learn to use the glass.

But, the pedants said, such exact observations requiring great precision could perhaps be made on land, but not on a ship in motion, where no one could hold a glass fixed on a celestial body invisible to the naked eye. . . . Well, Father Caspar was here to demonstrate that, with a bit of skill, observations could be made also on a moving ship.

Finally, some Spaniards had objected that satellites in eclipse did not appear during the day, nor on stormy nights. "Perhaps these complainers believe that a man claps his hands and there, illico et immediate, lunar eclipses are at his disposal?" Father Caspar was irritated. Who ever said that observations had to be made at every instant? Anyone who has voyaged from one Indies to the other knows that taking the longitude cannot require a greater frequency than what is required for observing the latitude, and this, too, whether with astrolabe or Jacob's cross, cannot be done in moments of great tumult of the sea. To measure it properly, this longitude, even only once every two or three days suffices; then, between one observation and the next it is possible to keep account of the time and the space covered, as was done in the past, using the astrolabe. But until now that was all they could use for months and months. "They seem to me," the good father said, more indignant than ever, "like Huomo that in gross famine you assist with a basket of bread, and instead of saying gratia he is disturbed that also a roasted schweine or a fat rabbit you do not put on the table for him. Oh, Holy Wood! Would you perhaps throw into the sea the cannons of this ship only because, ninety times out of a hundred, the balls fall plop into the aqua?"

So then Father Caspar engaged Roberto in the preparation of an experiment that was to be performed on an evening like the one now ahead of them, astronomically opportune, with clear sky and with the sea in slight motion. If the experiment were done on an evening of calm, Father Caspar explained, it would be like doing it on land, and there—as was already known—it was bound to succeed. The experiment had to provide the observer with the semblance of calm on a hull moving from stern to prow and from side to side.

First of all they had to recover, from among the clocks so maltreated over the past few days, one still in proper working order. Only one, in this fortunate case, and not two: they would set it to the local hour after taking good diurnal bearings (which they did) and, as they were certain of being on the antipodal meridian, there was no reason to have another clock telling the time of the Isla de Hierro. It was enough to know that the difference was exactly twelve hours. Midnight here; noon there.

On sober reflection, however, this decision seems based on a vicious circle. Their position on the antipodal meridian was something the experiment was to prove, not something to take as a given. But Father Caspar was so sure of his previous observations that he desired only to confirm them, and then—

probably—after all the confusion on the ship there was no longer a single clock that still told the time at the other side of the globe, and they had to overcome that obstacle. Actually, Roberto was not so punctilious as to point out the flaw in this argument.

"When I say *go,* you look at the hour and write. And immediately strike the perpendiculum."

The perpendiculum was supported by a little metal armature which acted as a gallows for a copper wand ending in a circular pendulum. At the lowest point of the pendulum's course there was a horizontal wheel in which teeth were set, but shaped so that one side of the tooth was square and jutted above the level of the wheel, and the other oblique. Alternately moving in this direction and that, the pendulum struck with a protruding spike, a bristle, which in turn touched a tooth on its jutted side and moved the wheel; but when the pendulum returned, the little bristle just grazed the oblique side of the tooth, and the wheel remained still. If the teeth were numbered, it was possible, when the pendulum stopped, to count the number of teeth shifted, and thus calculate the number of particles of time that had passed.

"So you are not obliged to count every time one, two, three, et cetera, but in the end when I say *sufficit,* you stop the perpendiculum and count the teeth, verstanden? And write how many teeth. Then you look at the horologium and write this or that hora. And when I again say *go,* you a very strong push give it, and it begins again its oscillatio. Simple, even a parvulus can do."

To be sure, this was not a great perpendiculum, as Father Caspar well knew, but debate on that mechanism was just beginning, and only at some future time would it be possible to construct perfected ones.

"Very difficult, and we must yet much learn, but if God

did not forbid die Wette—how do you say?—the pari . . ."

"Betting."

"Ah. If God did not forbid, I would bet that in the future all will go to seek longitudes and all other phenomena with the perpendiculum. But is very difficult on a ship, and you must make gross attention."

Caspar told Roberto to arrange the devices, together with writing materials, on the quarterdeck, which was the highest observation point on the *Daphne*: there they would set up the Instrumentum Arcetricum. From the soda they had carried up the instruments Roberto had glimpsed while he was still pursuing the Intruder. These were easily transported, except for the metal basin, which the two men hoisted up on the deck with curses and ruinous failures, for it would not pass through the hatches. But Father Caspar, wiry as he was, now that he saw the imminent realization of his plan, revealed a physical energy equal to his will.

Almost alone, with an implement of his that tightened bolts, he mounted the armature of semicircles and little bars of iron, which turned out to be a round frame, and to this a circular canvas was fixed with some rings, so that in the end they had a kind of great basin in the form of half a spherical orb with a diameter of about two meters. It was necessary to tar it so it would retain the malodorous oil with which Roberto filled it, emptying keg after keg, complaining of the stench. Father Caspar reminded him, seraphic as a Capuchin, that they were not using the oil to fry onions.

"What is the use of it, then?"

"On this little sea we try an even more little vessel to put," he said, and made Roberto help him place in the great canvas basin a metallic pan, almost flat, with a diameter only slightly less than that of its container. "You never heard say the sea smooth like oil? There, look, the deck tilts left and oil of the big basin tilts right, and vice versa, or, rather, so to you it seems; truly the oil in equilibrium stays, never up or down, and to the horizon parallel. It would happen also with water, but on oil the pan floats like on a calm sea. And I have already in Rome a little experiment done, with two little bowls, the bigger full of water and the little of sand, and in the sand I stuck a stylus, and I set the little afloat in the big, and I moved the big, and you could see the stylus erect like campanile, not bent like the towers of Bolonia!"

"Wunderbar!" xenoglot Roberto cried approvingly. "And now?"

"Hora we take the pan, where we must in it a whole machine put."

The bottom of the metal pan had some little springs on the outside so that, the Jesuit explained, once it was afloat with its cargo in the larger tub, it would remain separated by at least one finger from the bottom of the container; and if the excessive movement of its guest drove it too far down (What guest? Roberto asked; Now you will see, Caspar replied), those springs should cause it to rise to the surface again without shocks. To the inner pan they affixed a seat with a sloping back, which allowed a man to sit or, rather, recline, looking up, his feet on an iron bar that acted as a counterweight.

Having set up the basin on the deck, and having made it stable with some wedges, Father Caspar sat on the seat and explained to Roberto how to place on his back and fasten to his waist a harness of straps and bandoleers of canvas and leather, to which also a helmet with a vizor should be tied. The vizor had a hole for one eye, while at the level of the nose a rod protruded, surmounted by a small hoop. Through the hoop was inserted the spyglass, from which a little staff hung, ending in a hook. The Hyperbole of the Eyes could be moved freely until a given star was identified; but, once the star was in the center of the lens, the rigid staff was fixed to the pectoral bandoleers, and after that a steady view was assured, fixed against any possible movements of that Cyclops.

"Perfecto!" the Jesuit rejoiced. When the pan was set afloat on the becalmed oil, even the most elusive celestial bodies could be studied and no commotion of the sea in tumult could cause the horoscopant eye to be deflected from the chosen star. "This your Signor Galilei described, and I have made!"

"Very beautiful," Roberto said, "but who will put all this in the tub of oil?"

"Now I untie myself and get down, then we put the empty pan in the oil, then I climb on again."

"I cannot believe that will be easy."

"Much more easier than moving the pan with me in it seated."

Though with some effort, the pan with its chair was hoisted up and set afloat on the oil. Then Father Caspar, in helmet and harness, and the spyglass mounted on the vizor, tried to climb onto the scaffolding while Roberto held him, one hand clutching his hand and the other pushing his bottom. The attempt was repeated several times, but with no success.

It was not that the metal frame supporting the larger tub could not support also an occupant, but it denied him reasonable footholds. And if Father Caspar tried, as he did many times, to set only one foot on the rim, immediately placing the other inside the minor circle, this latter, in the disturbance of the embarkation, tended to glide over the oil towards the opposite side of the basin, making the priest's legs part like a compass as he emitted cries of alarm until Roberto seized him by the waist and drew him closer, that is to say onto the relative terra firma of the *Daphne*—cursing meanwhile the memory of Galilei and extolling his persecutors and killers. At that point Father Caspar sank into the arms of his savior, assuring him with a groan that those persecutors were not killers but most worthy men of the Church, bent only on the preservation of the truth, and that with Galilei they had been paternal and merciful. Then, still cuirassed and immobilized, his gaze towards the sky and the spyglass perpendicular to his face, like a Pulcinella with a mechanical nose, he reminded Roberto that Galilei, at least with this invention, had not erred, and it was just a matter of trying and trying again. "Und so mein lieber Robertus," he then said, "perhaps you have me forgotten and believe me a tortoise, captured with belly oben? Come, push me again, there, help me touch that rim, there now, for man is proper the statura erecta."

Through these several unhappy operations the oil did not remain smooth as oil, and after a while both experimenters found themselves oleate and, what was worse, oleabund—if the context allows the chronicler this coinage without imputation of the source.

When Father Caspar had begun to despair of ever occupying that seat, Roberto observed that perhaps it was necessary first to empty the container of oil, then install the pan, then have the priest climb onto it, and finally pour in the oil again, which, as its level rose, would raise also the pan and, with it, the observer, all floating together.

So it was done, amid praise from the master lavished on his acute pupil, as midnight was approaching. Not that the apparatus gave a great impression of stability, but if Father Caspar took care not to move unduly, they could hope.

At a certain moment Father Caspar triumphed: "I see them!" The cry caused him to move his nose, and the glass, rather heavy, began to slip out of the circle: he moved his arm to arrest it, the movement of the arm jerked his shoulder, and the pan was on the point of capsizing. Roberto abandoned paper and clocks, supported Caspar, re-established the equilibrium of the whole and bade the astronomer remain motionless, allowing only his eyepiece to make very prudent shifts, and above all without expressing emotions.

The next announcement was made in a whisper which, magnified by the great vizor, seemed to resound as hoarse as a Tartar trumpet: "I see them again," and with a measured gesture he fixed the spyglass to the pectoral. "Oh, wunderbar! Three little stars east of Jupiter, one alone west . . . The closest seems smallest and is . . . wait . . . yes, at zero minutes and thirty seconds from Jupiter. Write. Now it is about to touch Jupiter, soon it will disappear. Careful and write exactly the time it disappears. . . ."

Roberto, who had left his place to assist his master, again picked up the tablet on which he was to mark the times, but sitting, he had the clocks behind him. He turned abruptly, knocking over the pendulum. The wand slipped from its notch. Roberto seized it and tried to replace it, but he failed. Father Caspar was already shouting orders to note the time, Roberto turned towards the clock and, in moving, he struck the inkwell with his pen. Not thinking, he set the well upright, to save some of the liquid, but he knocked over the clock. "Did you take the hour? Go! The perpendiculum!" Caspar was shouting, and Roberto replied, "I cannot, I cannot!"

"How can you not, dumbhead?" And hearing no reply, he kept on shouting, "How can you not, foolish? Have you written, have you made note, did you push? It is disappearing. Go!"

"I have lost, no, not lost, I have broken everything," Roberto said.

Father Caspar moved the spyglass away from the vizor, peered sideways, saw the pendulum in pieces, the clock overturned, Roberto's hands stained with ink. Beside himself, he exploded with a "Himmelpotzblitzherrgottsakrament!" that shook his whole body. In that unfortunate movement, he caused the pan to tilt too far, and he slid into the oil of the basin, the spyglass slipping from his hand and his hauberk; then, as the ship pitched, the glass rolled across the quarter-deck, bounced down the ladder, and struck the main deck before it was flung against the breech of a cannon.

Roberto did not know whether to succor first the man or the instrument. The man, flailing in that rancidity, shouted magnanimously to save the spyglass, Roberto rushed down to the elusive Hyperbole, and found it, dented, both lenses broken.

When Roberto finally removed Father Caspar from the oil, the Jesuit, who looked like a piglet ready for the oven, simply said with heroic stubbornness that not all was lost. There was another telescope, equally powerful, mounted on the Specula Melitensis. They had only to go and fetch it from the Island.

"How?" Roberto asked.

"By natation."

"But you told me you cannot swim, nor should you, at your age. . . ."

"I, no. You, yes."

"But I do not know how to swim either!"

"Learn."

CHAPTER 24

Dialogues of the
Maximum Systems

WHAT FOLLOWS IS of uncertain nature: I am not sure if it is a chronicle of dialogues that occurred between Roberto and Father Caspar, or if it is a series of notes that the former took at night to rebut the latter the following day. In any case, it is obvious that for all the time he remained on board with the old man, Roberto wrote no letters to the Lady. And similarly, from his nocturnal existence he was moving, little by little, to a diurnal one.

For example, until now he had looked at the Island early in the morning, and then for only very brief periods, or else at evening, when the outlines and distances lost definition. But now at last he saw that the flux and reflux, the play of the tides, which for a part of the day brought the waters to lap the strip of sand that separated them from the forest and for the rest of the day made them withdraw, revealed a rocky expanse that, as Father Caspar explained, was the last outcrop of the coral reef.

Between the flux, or the afflux, and the reflux, his companion explained, about six hours go by, for such is the rhythm of the sea's respiration under the influence of the moon. Not as some had believed in ancient times, attributing this movement of the waters to the breathing of a monster of the deep, to say nothing of that French gentleman who declared that even if the earth does not move from west to east, it still pitches, so to speak, from north to south and vice versa, and in this periodic pitching it is natural that the sea should rise and fall, as when one shrugs and his cassock moves up and down his neck.

Mysterious, this problem of the tides, because they vary according to the lands and the seas, and the position of the shores varies with respect to the meridians. As a general rule during the new moon, the high water comes at midday and midnight, but then the phenomenon is later each day by four-fifths of an hour, and the man who does not know this, seeing that at such-and-such an hour of such-and-such a day a certain channel is navigable, ventures into it at the same hour the next day and runs aground. Not to mention the currents that the tides provoke, and some of them are such that at the moment of reflux a ship cannot make it to shore.

And further, the old man said, for whatever place you may be in, a different calculation is necessary, and Astronomical Tables are required. He tried, indeed, to explain to Roberto those calculations—that is, how you must observe the delay of the moon, multiplying the days of the moon by four and then dividing by five, or else the reverse. The fact is that Roberto understood none of it, and we shall see later how this slackness of his led to serious trouble. He confined himself merely to being amazed each time the meridian line, which should have run from one end of the Island to the other, sometimes passed through the sea, sometimes through the rocks, and he never knew which was the right moment. Also because, flux or reflux as the case might be, the great mystery of the tides mattered far less to him than the great mystery of that line, beyond which Time went backwards.

We have said that he had no particular inclination not to believe what the Jesuit was telling him. But often he enjoyed provoking him to make him say more, and then Roberto would resort to the whole repertory of argumentation he had picked up in the gatherings of those fine gentlemen that the Jesuits considered if not emissaries of Satan, at least topers and debauchees who had made the tavern their lyceum. Finally, though, it became hard for Roberto to reject the physics of a master who, adhering to the principles of that same physics, was teaching him how to swim.

His first reaction, with his shipwreck still impressed on his mind, was to declare that nothing on earth could induce him to resume contact with the water. Father Caspar pointed out that during that same wreck, it was the water that had supported him—a sign therefore that it was an affectionate and not a hostile element. Roberto replied that the water had supported not him but the plank to which he had been bound, and it was then easy for Father Caspar to point out to him that if the water had borne a piece of wood, an entity without a soul, tending to the Abyss as anyone knows who has thrown a stick from a height, all the more was water suited, then, to bear a living being disposed to enhance the natural tendency of liquids. Roberto should know, if he had ever flung a dog into the water, that the animal, moving its paws, not only remained afloat but quickly returned to shore. And, Caspar added, perhaps Roberto did not know that if infants barely a few months old were put into water, they were able to swim, for nature has made us swimmers like every animal. Unfortunately, of all animals, we are the most inclined to prejudice and error, and therefore, as we grow up, we acquire false notions as to the virtues of liquids, and thus fear and mistrust cause us to lose our inherent gift.

Roberto then asked if he, the reverend father, had learned

to swim, and the reverend father replied that he did not claim to be better than many others who had shunned good things. He had been born in a town very distant from the sea, and he had set foot on a ship only at an advanced age, when—he said—his body was nothing but a withering of the *cutis,* a dimming of the sight, a besnotting of the nose, a whispering of the ears, a yellowing of the teeth, a stiffening of the spine, a wattling of the throat, a gouting of the heels, a spotting of the complection, a whitening of the locks, a creaking of the tibias, a trembling of the fingers, a stumbling of the feet, and his breast was all one purging of catarrhs amid the coughing of phlegm and the spitting of sputum.

But, as he quickly clarified, his mind being keener than his carcass, he knew what the sages of Greece had long since discovered, namely, that if you immerge a body in a liquid, this body receives support and impulse upwards, through all the water it displaces, as water seeks to reoccupy the space from which it has been exiled. And it is not true that this body floats or does not according to its form, and the ancients were mistaken in saying that a flat thing stays up and a pointed thing sinks; if Roberto were to try to thrust something by force into water, say, a bottle (which is not flat), he would perceive the same resistance as if he had tried to thrust a tray.

It was a question therefore of acquiring familiarity with the element, whereupon everything would take its course. And he proposed that Roberto lower himself along the rope ladder hanging from the prow, known also as Jacob's ladder, but for his own serenity he should remain tied to a rope, or hawser, or cord as might be, long and sturdy, bound fast to the bulwarks. Then if he became afraid of drowning, he had only to pull the rope.

It is hardly necessary to say that this master of an art he had never practiced had not taken into consideration an infinity of concomitant accidents, ignored also by the wise men of ancient Greece. For example, to allow Roberto freedom of movement, Caspar supplied him with a rope of notable length, and at the first trial, like every aspirant swimmer, Roberto ended up below the surface of the water, then had difficulty pulling, and before the halyard drew him out, he had already swallowed enough salt water to make him want to renounce, on that first day, any further attempt.

But this was, all the same, an encouraging start. Having descended the ladder and barely touched the water, Roberto realized that the liquid was pleasant. Of the wreck he had a chill and violent memory, and the discovery of a tepid sea invited him to proceed further with the immersion until, never letting go of the ladder, he allowed the water to reach his chin. In the belief that this was swimming, he then wallowed there, abandoning himself to memories of Parisian luxury.

Since his landing on the ship he had performed, as we have seen, some ablutions, like a kitten licking its fur, but dealing only with face and pudenda. For the rest—and as he grew increasingly obsessed with his hunt for the Intruder—his feet became smeared with the dregs of the hold, and sweat glued his clothes to his body. Upon contact with this tepor that washed his body together with his clothing, Roberto remembered the time he discovered, in the Palais Rambouillet, two separate tubs for the use of the marquise, whose concern for the care of her body provided a subject of conversation in a society where washing was not frequent. Indeed, the most refined of her guests believed that cleanliness consisted not in the use of water but in the freshness of one's linen, which it was a sign of elegance to change often. And the many scented essences with which the marquise stunned them were not a luxury but, rather—for her—a necessity, a defense erected between her sensitive nostrils and their greasy odors.

Feeling himself more a gentleman than he had been in

Paris, Roberto, clinging to the ladder with one hand, with the other rubbed shirt and trousers against his dirty body, while scratching the heel of one foot with the toes of the other.

Father Caspar observed him with curiosity but remained silent, wanting Roberto to make friends with the sea. Still, fearing that Roberto's mind might stray in this excessive concern for his body, the Jesuit tried to distract him. He talked to him of the tides and the attractive powers of the moon.

He tried to make Roberto appreciate a proposition that had something incredible about it: if the tides respond to the summons of the moon, they should be present when the moon is present, and absent when the moon is on the other side of our planet. But, quite to the contrary, flux and reflux continue on both parts of the globe, as if pursuing each other every six hours. Roberto lent an ear to this talk, but he was thinking more about the moon—as he had done all those past nights—than about the tides.

He asked how it is that we see always only one face of the moon, and Father Caspar explained that it turns like a ball held on a string by an athlete who makes it revolve, but who can see nothing but the side towards himself.

"But," Roberto rebutted, "this face is seen both by the Indians and the Spaniards; whereas on the moon the same thing is not true with respect to their moon, which some call Volva and which is our earth. The Cisvolvians, who live on the face turned towards us, see the earth always, whereas the Transvolvians, who live in the other hemisphere, are unaware of it. Imagine if they were to move to this side! Think of their shock on seeing at night a shining circle fifteen times bigger than our moon! They would expect it to fall down on them at any moment, as the ancient Gauls always feared the sky would fall on their head! To say nothing of those who live right on the border between the two hemispheres, seeing Volva always on the point of rising at the horizon!"

The Jesuit made some ironic and arrogant remarks about the supposed inhabitants of the moon—an old wives' tale—because all celestial bodies do not share the nature of our earth and are therefore not suited to supporting a living population, so it is best to leave those places to the angelic hosts, who can move spiritually in the crystal of the heavens.

"But how could the heavens be of crystal? If that were so, the comets passing through would shatter them."

"But who ever told you the comets pass in the ethereal regions? The comets pass in the sublunary region, and here we have air, as you can see for yourself."

"Nothing moves that is not body. The heavens move. Hence they are body."

"In order to talk nonsensical, you even become Aristotelian. But I know why you say this. You want air to be also in the heavens, then there is no more differentia between above and below, all turns, and the earth moves its derrière like a strumpet."

"But we see every night the stars in a different position. . . ."

"Richtig. De facto they move."

"Wait. I have not finished. You would have the sun and all the stars, which are enormous bodies, make a revolution around the earth every twenty-four hours, and the fixed stars, or, rather, the great ring in which they are set, should travel more than twenty-seven thousand times two hundred million leagues? For this is what would have to happen if the earth did not make a complete revolution in twenty-four hours. How can the fixed stars move so fast? Their inhabitants would be dizzy!"

"If they have any inhabitants. But this is petitio principii."

And he pointed out that it was easy to invent an argument in favor of the movement of the sun, whereas there were far more arguments against the movement of the earth.

"I know well," Roberto replied, "that Ecclesiastes says 'terra autem in aeternum stat, sol oritur,' and that Joshua stopped the sun and not the earth. But you yourself have taught me that if we take the Bible literally, there would have been light before the creation of the sun. So the Holy Book must be read with a grain of salt, and even Saint Augustine knew that it often speaks more allegorico. . . ."

Father Caspar smiled and reminded him that the Jesuits had long ago given up defeating their adversaries with Scriptural cavils; now they used incontrovertible arguments based on astronomy, on sense, on mathematical and physical reasons.

"What reasons, ad exemplum?" Roberto asked, scraping away a bit of grease from his belly.

"Ad exemplum," Father Caspar replied, irked, with the powerful Argument of the Wheel: "Now you listen me. Think a wheel, all right?"

"I am thinking a wheel."

"Bravo, so you can also think, instead of being Barbary ape and repeating what you heard in Paris. Now think that this wheel is stuck on a pivot, like it is a potter's wheel, and you want to turn this wheel. What do you do?"

"I put my hands on it, perhaps just one finger on the rim of the wheel, I move my finger, and the wheel turns."

"You do not think you had done better to take the pivot, in the center of the wheel, and try to make it turn?"

"No, it would be impossible. . . ."

"So! And your Galileans or Copernicans want to have the sun in the center of the universe fixed and making move all the great circle of the planets around, instead of thinking the movement from the great circle of the heavens comes, while the earth remains still in the center. How could Dominus Deus put the sun in the lowest place and the earth, corruptible and dark, among the luminous and aeternal stars? Understand your error?"

"But the sun has to exist at the center of the universe! The bodies in nature need this radical fire, and it must inhabit the heart of the realm to meet the needs of all the parts. Must not the cause of generation be set in the center of everything? Has nature not placed the seed in the genitals, halfway between the head and the feet? And are the seeds not in the center of the apple? And is the pit not in the middle of the peach? And so the earth, which needs the light and heat of that fire, moves around it, to receive the solar virtue in all its parts. It would be ridiculous to believe the sun turns around a point that is of no use to it, it would be like saying, on seeing a roast lark, that to cook it you made the hearth revolve around it."

"Ah so? Then when the bishop moves around the church to bless it with the thurible, you would have the church revolve around the bishop? The sun can turn because it is of igneous element. And you well know that fire flies and moves and is never still. Have you ever seen the mountains move? Then how does the earth move?"

"The sun's rays, striking it, make it turn, as you can make a ball spin by striking it with your hand, and even by breathing on it if the ball is little. . . . And finally, would you have God make the sun race, when it is four hundred thirty-four times bigger than the earth, only to ripen our cabbages?"

To give the greatest theatrical emphasis to this last objection, Roberto wanted to point his finger at Father Caspar, so he extended his arm and pushed with his foot to make himself good and visible, a bit farther from the side of the ship. In this movement his other hand released its grip, his head moved back, and Roberto finished underwater, unable to make use of the rope, now too slack, to return to the surface, as planned. He then behaved like all threatened with drowning; he made uncoordinated movements and swallowed even more water, until Father Caspar tautened the rope properly, pulling him back to the ladder. Roberto climbed up, vowing he would never go down there again.

"Tomorrow you try again. Salt water is like a medicine, do not think it was gross harm," Caspar consoled him on deck. And as Roberto made peace with the sea, fishing, Caspar explained to him how many and what advantages they would both derive from his arrival on the Island. It was not even worth mentioning the recovery of the boat, with which they would be able to move as free men from ship to shore; they would further have access to the Specula Melitensis.

From Roberto's report, we must infer that this apparatus exceeded his powers of comprehension—or that Father Caspar's account of it, like so many other speeches of his, was made up of ellipses and interjections, as the father spoke now of its form, now of its function, and now of the Idea that governed it.

And the Idea was not even his. He had learned of the Specula leafing through the papers of a deceased brother, who in his turn had learned of it from another brother who during a voyage to the most noble island of Malta, or Melita, had heard praise of this instrument constructed by order of the Most Eminent Prince Johannes Paulus Lascaris, Grand Master of the famous Knights.

What the Specula was like, no one had ever seen: the first brother left only a booklet of sketches and notes, which for that matter had now disappeared. And, on the other hand, Caspar complained, that same opuscule "was brevissimamente scripto, con nullo schemate visualiter patefacto, nulle tabule nec rotule, und nulla specialis instructione."

On the basis of that meager information Father Caspar, in the course of the long voyage on the *Daphne,* setting the ship's carpenters to work, had redesigned or else misconstructed the various elements of the technasma, mounting them then on the Island and measuring, *in situ,* its countless virtues—and the Specula must truly have been an Ars Magna in flesh and blood, or, rather, in wood, iron, canvas, and other substances, a kind of Megahorologium, an Animated Book capable of revealing all the mysteries of the Universe.

It was—Father Caspar said, his eyes glowing like carbuncles—a Unique Syntagma of Novissimi Instrumenti Physici et Mathematici, "in rotas and cycles artfully disposed." Then he drew on the deck or in the air with his finger, and bade Roberto to think of a circular first element, a kind of base or foundation which showed the Immobile Horizon, with the Rhomb of the Thirty-two Winds and all the Ars Navigatoria with forecasts of every storm. "For the Median Section," he then added, "built on this foundation, imagine a Cube with five sides—can you imagine?—nein, not six, the sixth rests on the foundation so you do not see him. In the first side of the Cube (id est the Chronoscopium Universalis) you can see eight wheels arranged in perennial cycles represent the Calendars of Julius and of Gregory, and when recur the Sundays and the Epacts, and the Solar Circle, and the Moveable and Paschal Feasts, and novilunes and plenilunes, quadratures of the sun and moon. In the secundum Cubilatere, id est das Cosmigraphicum Speculum, in primo loco occurs a Horoscopium with which given the hour of Melita present, what hour it is in the rest of our globe can be found. And you see a Wheel with two planispheres: one displays and teaches all the scientia of the Primum Mobile, and the second the doctrine of the Octava Sphaera and the fixed stars, and motion. And the fluxo et refluxo, quid est decrease and increase of the seas, from the movement of the moon stirred in all the Universe. . . ."

This second was the most thrilling side. Thanks to it the

observer could know that Horologium Catholicum mentioned before, with the hour at the Jesuit missions on every meridian; and further, it could also perform the functions of a good astrolabe, in that it revealed as well the quantity of the days and the nights, the height of the sun, the Umbrae Rectae et Versae, the altitude of the stars above the horizon, the quantity of crepuscules, the culmination of the fixed stars by year, month, and day. And it was through repeated experimentation here that Father Caspar had arrived at the certitude finally of being on the antipodal meridian.

There was then a third side that contained in seven united wheels all Astrology, all the future eclipses of the sun and moon, all the Zodiacal figures for the times of agriculture, medicine, and the art of navigation, along with the twelve signs of the Celestial Houses, and the physiognomy of the natural things that depend from each sign, and the corresponding House.

I lack the courage to summarize all of Roberto's summary, so I will only mention the fourth side, which supposedly expounded all the wonders of botanical medicine, spagyrical, chemical, and hermetical, with simple and compound medicines derived from mineral or animal substances, and the "Alexipharmaca, attractive, lenitive, purgative, mollificative, digestive, corrosive, conglutinative, aperitive, calefactive, infrigidative, mundificative, attenuative, incisive, soporative, diuretic, narcotic, caustic, and comfortative."

I cannot explain what was on the fifth side, that is, the roof of the cube parallel to the line of the horizon, which was apparently arranged like a heavenly vault. But there is mention also of a pyramid, whose base could not have coincided with the cube's, otherwise it would have covered the fifth side; more likely, it covered the whole cube like a tent—but then it would have to be of transparent material. It is certain that the pyramid's four faces were meant to represent the four regions of the world, and the alphabets for each of them and the languages of the various peoples, including elements of the primitive Adamic language, the hieroglyphics of the Egyptians, and the characters of the Chinese and the Mexicans. Father Caspar describes it as a "Sphynx Mystagoga, an Oedipus Aegyptiacus, a Monad Ieroglyphica, a Clavis Convenientia Linguarum, a Theatrum Cosmographicum Historicum, a Sylva Sylvarum of every alphabet natural and artificial, an Architectura Curiosa Nova, a Combinatory Lamp, Mensa Isiaca, Metametricon, Synopsis Anthropoglottogonica, Basilica Cryptographica, an Amphitheatrum Sapientiae, Cryptomenesis Patefacta, Catoptron Polygraphicum, a Gazophylacium Verborum, a Mysterium Artis Steganographicae, Arca Arithmologica, Archetypon Polyglotta, an Eisagoge Horapollinea, Congestorium Artificiosae Memoriae, Pantometron de Furtivis Literarum Notis, Mercurius Redivivus, and an Etymologicon Lustgärtlein!"

The fact that all this learning was fated to remain their private appanage, condemned as they were never again to find their way home, did not bother the Jesuit, either because of his faith in Providence or because of his love of knowledge as an end unto itself. But what strikes me at this point is that Roberto, too, could not conceive a single realistic thought, and he was beginning to consider his landing on the Island as the event that would give meaning, forever, to his life.

In the first place, though he cared little about the Specula, he was overcome by the thought that this oracle could tell him where the Lady was and what she was doing at that moment. Proof that to a lover, even one distracted by useful corporal exercises, it is futile to speak of Sidereal Nuncios, for he seeks always and only news of his beautiful suffering and his dear grief.

Further, whatever his swimming master may have said to him, he dreamed of an Island that did not loom before him in the present, where he also was, but instead by divine decree rested in the unreality, or the non-being, of the day before.

What he thought of as he challenged the waves was the hope of reaching an Island that had been yesterday, and of which the symbol seemed to him the Orange Dove, beyond any capture, as if it had fled into the past.

Roberto was still driven by obscure concepts; he sensed he wanted something that was not Father Caspar's goal, but he was not yet sure what it was. And his uncertainty must be understood, because he was the first man in human history to be offered the possibility of swimming twenty-four hours into the past.

In any case he was convinced that he really had to learn to swim, and we all know that a single firm motive helps vanquish many fears. Hence we find him trying again the next day.

In this phase, Father Caspar explained, Roberto should let go of the ladder and move his hands freely, as if following the rhythm of a band of musicians, and impart a lazy motion to his legs. The sea then would support him. The Jesuit induced him to try first with the rope taut, then he slackened the rope without saying anything, or, rather, announced what he had done only when his pupil gained confidence. True, Roberto, at that announcement, immediately felt himself sink, but as he shouted, he kicked his legs instinctively, and found himself again with his head in the air.

These attempts lasted a good half-hour, and Roberto re-alized that he could keep himself afloat. But as soon as he tried to move with greater exuberance, he flung his head back. Father Caspar encouraged him to follow that inclination and let himself go, with his head thrown back as far as possible, the body rigid and slightly arched, arms and legs extended as if he lay on the circumference of a circle; then he would feel himself supported as if by a hammock, and he could remain there for hours and hours, even sleep, kissed by the waves and by the slanting rays of the setting sun. How did Father Caspar know all this, never having swum himself? Through Theoria Physico-Hydrostatica, he said.

It was not easy to find the proper position; Roberto risked strangling himself with the rope, belching and sneezing; but apparently at a certain point he found his equilibrium.

For the first time Roberto felt the sea as a friend. Following Father Caspar's instructions, he also began moving his arms and legs; he slowly raised his head, threw it back, became accustomed to having water in his ears, tolerated its pressure. He could even talk, shouting to be heard up on deck.

"If now you wish, you turn over," at a certain point Caspar told him. "You lower the right arm, as if it hangs under your body, you lift slightly your left shoulder, and ecce you have belly down."

He did not specify that in the course of this maneuver Roberto should hold his breath, since he would find himself with his face in the water, and in a water that wants nothing more than to invade the nostrils of the intruder. So, out of *ignoratio elenchi* on Father Caspar's part, Roberto drank another pitcher's worth of brine.

But by now he had learned how to learn. Two or three times he tried turning over, and he grasped a principle, indispensable to every swimmer, namely, when you have your head in the water, you must not breathe—not even with your nose; indeed you must snort hard, as if to expel from the lungs even the little bit of air that you need so badly. Which seems an intuitive thing, and yet it is not, as this story makes clear.

He had further realized that it was easier for him to lie supine, face in the air, than prone. To me the opposite seems true, but Roberto had learned that way first, and for a day or two he continued in that attitude. Meanwhile he dialogued on the Maximum Systems.

He and the Jesuit had resumed their debate about the movement of the earth, and Father Caspar had engaged him in the Argument of the Eclipses. Removing the earth from the center of the world and putting the sun in its place, you must set the earth either below the moon or above the moon. If you put it below, there can never be an eclipse of the sun, because the moon, being above the sun or above the earth, can never come between them. If you put it above, there can never be an eclipse of the moon, because the earth, being above it, can never be interposed between it and the sun. And further, astronomy could no longer predict eclipses, as it has always done so well, because it bases its calculations on the movements of the sun, and if the sun does not move, the exercise would be in vain.

Roberto should consider also the Argument of the Archer. If the earth were to turn every twenty-four hours, then an arrow, when shot straight up, would fall to the west many miles from the archer. Similar is the Argument of the Tower. If you dropped a weight from the western side of a tower, it would land not at the foot of the edifice but much farther on, for it would fall not vertically but diagonally, because in the meantime the tower (with the earth) would have moved eastwards. But as everyone knows from experience, a weight falls perpendicularly, and so terrestrial motion is proved to be nonsense.

Not to mention the Argument of the Birds, which, if the earth turned in the space of a day, would never be able to keep up with it, however indefatigable they might be. Whereas we can see clearly that if we travel, even on horseback, in the direction of the sun, any bird can overtake and pass us.

"Very well. I do not know the answer to your arguments. But I have heard it said that if the earth turns and all the planets, and the sun stands still, many phenomena are explained, whereas Ptolemy had to invent epicycles and deferents and all sorts of other stupidities that do not exist on earth or in heaven."

"I pardon you, if you wanted to make a Witz. But if you speak serious, then I say you are pagan as Ptolemy and I know well he had many mistakes made. Und so I believe the great Tycho of Uraniborg a very correct idea had: he thought that all the planets we know, namely Jupiter, Mars, Venus, Mercurius, and Saturnus revolve around the sun, but the sun revolves with them around the earth, the moon around the earth revolves, the earth unmoving stands in the center of the circle of the fixed stars. So you explain the mistakes of Ptolemy and say no heresies, whereas Ptolemy made mistakes and Galilei heresies spoke. And you are not obliged to explain how earth, so heavy as it is, goes roaming around the sky."

"And how do the sun and the fixed stars manage?"

"You say they are heavy. I say not. They are celestial bodies, not sublunary. Earth, yes, that is heavy."

"Then how does a ship bearing a hundred cannons sail around on the sea?"

"The sea pulls it, and the wind pushes."

"In that case, if it is a matter of saying new things without irritating the cardinals of Rome, I have heard of a philosopher in Paris who says that the heavens are liquid matter, like a sea, which circulates everywhere, forming something like whirlpools . . . *tourbillons*. . . ."

"What are they?"

"Vortices."

"Ach so. Vortices, ja. But what do these vortices do?"

"This. The vortices pull the planets in their revolution, and a vortex draws the earth around the sun, but it is the vortex that moves. The earth remains immobile in the vortex that pulls it."

"Bravo, Signor Roberto! You would not allow that the heavens are of crystal, because you were afraid the comets would break them, but you like them to be liquid, so the birds inside them drown! Further, this idea of vortices explains that the earth turns around the sun, but does not turn on itself as a child's top spins!"

"Yes, but that philosopher. said also that in this case it is the surface of the seas and the superficial crust of our globe that revolve, while the deep core remains still. I think."

"More stupid than ever. Where did this gentleman write this?"

"I do not know, I think he gave up the idea of writing it, or of publishing it in a book. He did not want to irritate the Jesuits, whom he loves very much."

"Then I prefer Signor Galilei, who had heretical thoughts but confessed them to very loving cardinals, and nobody burned him. I do not like this other gentleman who has thoughts even more heretical and does not confess, not even to Jesuits his friends. Perhaps one day God will Galilei forgive, but not your friend."

"Anyway, it seems to me he revised that first idea. Apparently all the accumulation of matter that goes from the sun to the fixed stars turns in a great circle, borne by this wind. . . ."

"But did you not say the heavens were liquid?"

"Perhaps not. Perhaps they are a great wind. . . ."

"You see? You do not know even—"

"Well, this wind makes all the planets turn around the

sun, and at the same time it makes the sun turn around itself. So there is a minor vortex that makes the moon move around the earth and the earth turn in place. And yet it cannot be said the earth moves, because what moves is the wind. In the same way, if I were sleeping on the *Daphne*, and the *Daphne* went towards that island to the west, I would move from one place to another, and yet no one could say that my body has moved. And as far as daily movement is concerned, it is as if I were seated on a great potter's wheel that moves, and surely you would first see my face, then my back, but it would not be I that moved, it would be the wheel."

"This is the hypothesis of a malicious who wants to be heretic but not seem one. But you tell me now where are the stars. All of Ursa Major, and Perseus—do they turn in the same vortex?"

"Why, all the stars we see are so many suns, and each is at the center of its own vortex, and all the universe is a great circle of vortices with infinite suns and infinite planets, even beyond what our eye sees, and each with its own inhabitants."

"Ach! Now I have got you and your hereticissimi friends! This is what you want: infinite worlds!"

"Surely you will allow me at least more than one. Otherwise where would God have set Hell? Not in the bowels of the earth."

"Why not in the bowels of the earth?"

"Because"—and here Roberto was repeating in a very approximate fashion an argument he had heard in Paris, nor could he guarantee the precision of his calculations—"the diameter of the center of the earth measures two hundred Italian miles, and if we cube that, we have eight million miles. Considering that one Italian mile contains two hundred and forty thousand English feet, and since the Lord must have allowed to each of the damned at least six feet, Hell could contain only forty million damned, which seems few to me, considering all the sinners who have lived in this world of ours from Adam until now."

"That would be true," Caspar replied, not even deigning to go over the calculation, "if the damned were inside their bodies. But this is only after the Resurrection of the Flesh and the Last Judgement! And then there will no longer be either earth or planets, but other heavens and other earths!"

"Agreed, if the damned are only spirits, there will be a thousand million even on the head of a pin. But there are stars we cannot see with the naked eye, and instead are seen with your spyglass. Well, can you not think of a glass a hundred times more powerful which will allow you to see other stars, and then one a thousand times more powerful which will allow you to see stars even more distant, and so on ad infinitum? Would you set a limit to Creation?"

"The Bible does not speak of this."

"The Bible does not speak of Jove, either, and yet you were looking at it the other evening with that damned glass of yours."

But Roberto already knew what the Jesuit's real objection would be. Like that of the abbé on that evening of the duel when Saint-Savin provoked him: If there are infinite worlds, the Redemption can no longer have any meaning, and we are obliged either to imagine infinite Calvaries or to look on our terrestrial flowerbed as a privileged spot of the Cosmos, on which God permitted His Son to descend and free us from sin, while the other worlds were not granted this grace—to the discredit of His infinite goodness. And, in fact, this was the response of Father Caspar, which allowed Roberto to attack.

"When did the sin of Adam take place?"

"My brothers have perfect calculations mathematically made, on the basis of the Scripture: Adam sinned three thousand nine hundred and eighty-four years before the coming of Our Lord."

"Well, perhaps you do not know that travelers who arrived in China, including many brothers of yours, found lists of the monarchs and dynasties of the Chinese, from which it can be determined that the kingdom of China existed more than six thousand years ago, hence before Adam's fall, and if this is true of China, who knows for how many other peoples it may also be true. Therefore the sin of Adam, and the redemption of the Hebrews, and the great truths of our Holy Roman Church deriving from them, affect only one part of humanity, since there is another part of the human race that was not touched by original sin. This does not in any way affect the infinite goodness of God, who behaved towards the Adamites like the father in the parable of the Prodigal Son, sacrificing His only Son for them. But just as the fact that the father of the parable sacrificed the fatted calf for his son the sinner does not mean he loved his good and virtuous children any less, so our Creator loves the Chinese and any others born before Adam, and is happy that they did not incur original sin. If this happened on earth, why should it not have happened also on the stars?"

"Who told you this pack of bull Scheise?" Father Caspar shouted in a fury.

"Many speak of it. And an Arab sage said it could be deduced from a page of the Koran."

"You say me the Koran proved the truth of a thing? Oh, God omnipotens, I implore Thee strike down this vain, windy, bloated, arrogant, turbulent, rebellious beast of a man, the demon, dog, devil, cursed infected hound, let him not set foot on this ship!"

And Father Caspar lifted and snapped the rope like a whip, first striking Roberto on the face, then letting go of the line.

Roberto fell back with his head down, groped and gasped, could not pull the rope hard enough to tauten it, cried for help as he swallowed water, and Father Caspar shouted to him that he wanted to see him give up the Geist and choke to death so he would sink straight to Hell as befitted the ill-born of his race.

Then, since the Jesuit was a Christian soul, when he considered Roberto sufficiently punished, he pulled him up. And for that day both the lesson in swimming and that in astronomy came to an end, and the two went off to sleep, each in his own direction, without exchanging a word.

They made peace the next day. Roberto admitted that he did not believe in this vortex hypothesis, and considered, rather, that the infinite worlds were an effect of an eddying of atoms in the Void, and that this did not in any way exclude the possibility of a provident Divinity commanding these atoms and organizing them in accord with His decrees, as Roberto had learned from the Canon of Digne. Father Caspar, however, rejected this idea also, which required a Void in which atoms could move, and Roberto had no desire to argue further with this generous generalizer who, rather than sever the cord that kept him alive, gave it all too much play.

After receiving a promise there would be no more threats of death, Roberto resumed his swimming experiments. Father Caspar tried to persuade him to move in the water, as this is the fundamental principle of the art of natation, and he suggested slow movements of the hands and the legs, but Roberto preferred to lie idle, floating.

Father Caspar allowed him to linger, and exploited this inaction to rehearse his other arguments against the movement of the earth. *In primis,* the Argument of the Sun. Which, if it remained motionless and we were to look at it precisely at noon from the center of a room through a window, and the earth turned with the supposed velocity—and it would require a great velocity to make a complete revolution in twenty-four hours—then in an instant the sun would vanish from our sight.

The Argument of Hail followed. It falls sometimes for a whole hour but, whether the clouds go to east or west, north or south, it never covers the countryside for more than twenty or thirty miles. But if the earth revolved, and the hail clouds were carried by the wind in its course, hail would necessarily fall over at least three or four hundred miles of countryside.

Then there was the Argument of White Clouds, which drift through the air when the weather is calm, and seem always to proceed with equal slowness; whereas, if the earth revolves, those that go westward should advance at immense speed.

He concluded with the Argument of Terrestrial Animals, which by instinct should always move towards the east, to comply with the movement of the earth that is their master; and they should show great aversion to westward movement, sensing that this movement is against nature.

Roberto accepted all these arguments for a little while, but then he took a dislike to them, and opposed all that learning with his own Argument of Desire.

"But finally," he said to the Jesuit, "do not deprive me of the joy of thinking that I could rise in flight and see in twenty-four hours the earth revolve beneath me, and I would see so many different faces pass by, white, black, yellow, olive, with caps or with turbans, and cities with spires now pointed, now round, with the Cross and with the Crescent, and cities with porcelain towers and lands of bells, and the Iroquois preparing to eat alive a prisoner of war, and the women of the land of Tesso busy painting their lips blue to please the ugliest men of the planet, and those of Camul, whose husbands pass them to the first newcomer, as Messer Milione tells in his book. . . ."

"You see? As I say: when you in the tavern think of your philosophy, it is always thoughts of lust! And if you did not these thoughts have, you could this voyage make if God granted you the gratia to revolve yourself around the earth, which is a gratia as gross as leaving you in the sky suspended."

Roberto was unconvinced, but he could think of no further rebuttal. Then he took a longer way, setting out from arguments he had heard, which similarly did not seem to him in conflict with the idea of a provident God, and he asked Caspar if he agreed in considering Nature a grand theater, where we see only what the Author has put on stage. From our seat we do not see the theater as it really is: the decorations and the machines have been set up to make a fine effect from a distance, whereas the wheels and the counterweights that produce the transformations have been hidden from our view. And yet if in the stalls there was a man practiced in the art, he could guess how a mechanical bird could suddenly be made to fly up. So should the philosopher think when faced by the spectacle of the universe. To be sure, the difficulty for the philosopher is greater, because in Nature the ropes of the machines are hidden so well that for a long time everyone wondered who operated them. And yet, even in this theater of ours, if Phaeton rises towards the sun, it is because a rope pulls him and a counterweight descends.

Ergo (in the end, Roberto was confident, rediscovering the reason why he had initiated this divagation) the stage shows us the sun revolving, but the nature of the machine is quite different, nor can we be aware of it at the outset. We see the spectacle but not the winch that makes Phoebus move, for indeed we live on the wheel of that winch—but here Roberto became lost, because if the metaphor of the winch was accepted, then that of the theater was lost, and all his reasoning became so *pointu*—as Saint-Savin would have said—that it was pointless.

Father Caspar replied that to make a machine sing it was necessary to shape wood or metal and arrange holes, or attach strings and scrape them with bows, or even—as he had done on the *Daphne*—invent a water device; but if we opened the throat of a nightingale, we saw no machine of this sort there, a sign that God followed paths different from ours.

Then he asked if, as Roberto looked with such favor on infinite solar systems revolving in the sky, he could not admit that each of these systems might be part of a larger system that revolved in its turn within a system still larger, and so on—for, proceeding from such premisses, you became like the virgin prey of a seducer: she grants him first a small concession but soon will have to grant him more, and then more, and once embarked on that road, she might arrive at any terrible extremity.

Of course, Roberto said, one can conceive anything. Vortices without planets, vortices that bump into one another, vortices that are not round but hexagonal, so that each face or side fits into another vortex, all of them together forming a kind of hive with its cells, or else they are polygons that, pressed one against the other, create voids that Nature fills with other, lesser vortices, all cogged among themselves like the works of a clock—their entirety moving in the universal sky like a great wheel that turns and propels inside itself other wheels that turn, each with smaller wheels turning within, and all that great circle making in the sky an immense revolution that lasts millennia, perhaps around another vortex or vortices of vortices. . . . At which point Roberto risked drowning, because of the great vertigo that overwhelmed him.

And it was at this moment that Father Caspar had his triumph. Then, he explained, if the earth revolves around the sun, but the sun revolves around something else (and omitting the question of whether this something else revolves around a something else of yet another something else), we have the problem of the *roulette*—of which Roberto must have heard talk in Paris, since from Paris it went into Italy among the Galileans, who would think up anything provided they could disturb the world.

"What is the roulette?" Roberto asked.

"You can call it also trochoid or cycloid, but it is much the same. Imagine a wheel."

"Like before?"

"No. Now imagine you the wheel of a wagon. And imagine on the rim of the wheel a nail. Now imagine the wheel not moving, and the nail just above ground. Now you think that the wagon moves and the wheel turns. What to the nail happens?"

"Well, if the wheel turns, at a certain point the nail will be on top, but when the wheel has made its complete revolution, the nail is again close to the ground."

"So you think this wheel has like a circle moved?"

"Why, yes. Certainly not like a square."

"Now you listen, booby. You say the nail finds itself on the ground where it before was?"

"Wait a moment. . . . No, if the wagon went forward, the nail would be on the same ground, but much farther ahead."

"Therefore it has not made circular movement."

"No, by all the saints in Paradise!"

"You must not say Byallsaintsofparadise."

"Forgive me. But what movement has it made?"

"It has made a trochoid, and for you to understand I say it is like the movement of a ball you throw before you, then it touches ground, then makes another arc of circle, then again   but, while the ball makes smaller and smaller arcs, the nail makes always regular arcs, if the wheel always at the same speed goes."

"And what does this mean?" Roberto asked, anticipating his defeat.

"This means you would have so many vortices and infinite worlds, and that the earth turns, and here your earth turns no more, but goes through the infinite sky like a ball, tumpf tumpf tumpf. . . . Ach! what a fine movement for this most noble planet! And if your vortex theory gut ist, all heavenly bodies would go tumpf tumpf tumpf. . . . Now let me laugh, for this is finally the most gross amusement of mein Leben!"

It was difficult to reply to an argument so subtle and geometrically perfect—and what is more, in perfect bad faith, because Father Caspar should have known that something similar would have happened also if the planets revolved as Tycho posited. Roberto went off to sleep, damp and downcast as a dog. In the night he reflected, wondering if it was not best for him now to abandon all his heretical ideas on the movement of the earth. Let me see, he said to himself, if Father Caspar is right and the earth does not move (otherwise it would move more than it should and be impossible to stop again), does this endanger his discovery of the antipodal meridian, and his theory of the Flood, and also the fact that the Island is there a day before the day it is here? Not at all.

So, he said to himself, perhaps it is best for me not to debate the astronomical opinions of my new teacher, and instead devote myself to swimming, to achieve what really interests me, which is not to prove that Copernicus and Galilei were right, or that other old bloat Tycho of Uraniborg—but to see the Orange Dove, and set foot in the day before—something that not Galilei, not Copernicus, not Tycho, nor any of my masters and teachers in Paris ever dreamed of.

So, then, the next day he presented himself again to Father

Caspar as an obedient pupil in matters both natatory and astronomical.

But Father Caspar, with the excuse of a rough sea and some further calculations that he had to make, postponed that day's lesson. Towards evening he explained that to learn natation, as he said, requires concentration and silence, and you cannot have your head among the clouds. Seeing that Roberto tended to do just that, it was the Jesuit's conclusion that the young man had no aptitude for swimming.

Roberto asked himself why his master, so proud of his mastery, had renounced his plan so abruptly. And I believe the conclusion he came to was the correct one. Father Caspar had got it into his head that lying or even moving in the water, under the sun, had produced in Roberto an effervescence of the cerebrum, which led him to dangerous thoughts. Finding himself in intimacy with his own body, and immersing himself in the liquid, which was also matter, had somehow bestialized him and led him to those thoughts that are peculiar to insane and animal natures.

So Father Wanderdrossel had to find some different means that would allow them to reach the Island but would not endanger the health of Roberto's soul.

CHAPTER 25

Technica Curiosa

WHEN FATHER CASPAR said it was again Sunday, Roberto realized that more than a week had gone by since their first meeting. The Jesuit celebrated Mass, then addressed him with an air of decision. "I cannot wait until you have learned to swim," he said.

Roberto replied that it was not his fault. Father Caspar conceded that it might not be his fault, but meanwhile the weather and the wild animals were ruining the Specula, which required daily care. Hence, *ultima ratio*, only one solution remained: he would go to the Island himself. When asked how he would do this, Caspar said he would try his fortune with the Aquatic Bell.

He explained that for a long time he had been pondering how to travel underwater. He had even thought of constructing a boat made of wood reinforced with iron, double-hulled like a box with a lid. The vessel would be seventy-two feet long, thirty-two feet high, eight feet wide, and heavy enough to descend below the surface. It would be operated by a propeller turned by two men inside, the way donkeys turn a millwheel. And to see where it was going, a tubospicillum would protrude, an eyeglass that through a play of interior mirrors would allow them to observe from within what was happening above, in the open air.

Why had he not built it? Because such is Nature—he said—for the humiliation of our inadequacy: there are ideas that on paper seem perfect, but then, put to the test of experience, they prove imperfect, and no one knows the reason.

Father Caspar had, however, built the Aquatic Bell: "And the plebs ignorans, if one had said them a man can go to the bottom of Rhein and his clothing remain dry, and even swearing and holding his hand in a fire, they would have said it was a madness. But the proof of the experimentum has been made, and almost a century ago in the oppidum of Toleto in Hispania. So I go to the Island now with my Aquatic Bell, walking, as you see me now walk."

He headed for the soda, which was an apparently inexhaustible store: besides the astronomical apparatus there was yet more to be found. Roberto was obliged to carry up on deck other bars and semicircles of metal and a voluminous package wrapped in a skin, which still smelled of its original, horned owner. In vain did he point out that if this was Sunday, the Lord's Day, they should not be working. Father Caspar answered that this was not work, still less was it servile labor, but, rather, the exercise of an art, the noblest of all arts, and their efforts would be crowned by an increase in knowledge of the great Book of Nature. And therefore it was the same as meditating on the Sacred Scriptures, with which the Book of Nature is closely associated.

So Roberto set to work, spurred by Father Caspar, who intervened at the most delicate moments, when the metallic components had to be mounted through previously prepared grooves. Working for the whole morning, they thus assembled a cage shaped like the trunk of a cone, slightly taller than a

man, in which three circles, the highest being of the smallest
diameter, the central and the lowest ones progressively
broader, all three of them held parallel by four inclined bars.

To the middle circle was attached a canvas harness into
which a man could fit. A number of straps fastened around
the shoulders and the chest held his groin steady, to prevent
his sliding down. The same straps secured his shoulder blades
and neck, to prevent his head from striking the upper circle.

While Roberto wondered what the use could be of this
contraption, Father Caspar unwrapped the folded skin, which
was revealed as the perfect case, or glove, or thimble of that
metallic apparatus, over which it easily fit, fixed by some hooks
on the inside so that once assembled, the apparatus could not
be unsheathed. And the finished object was, in effect, a cone
without a tip, open at the top and at the base—or, if you like,
indeed, a kind of bell. On it, between the top and the middle
circles, there was a little glass window. To the roof of the
apparatus a sturdy ring had been attached.

At this point the bell was shifted towards the windlass and
hooked to an arm that through a clever system of pulleys
allowed it to be raised, lowered, lifted over the rail, hoisted
aboard, or unloaded like any bale or case or package of cargo.

The windlass was a bit rusty after many days of disuse, but
finally Roberto managed to operate it and raise the bell to half
its height, so that its interior could be observed.

This bell now awaited only a passenger, who would step
inside, fasten the straps, then dangle in the air like a clapper.

A man of any stature could enter it: he had only to adjust
the harness, loosening or tightening buckles and knots. Now,
once he was well fastened, the inhabitant of the bell could
walk, carrying his little cockpit with him, and the straps kept
the head at the level of the window, while the lower edge
came more or less to his calf.

Now Roberto had only to imagine, the triumphant Father Caspar explained, what would happen when the windlass lowered the bell into the sea.

"What happens is that the passenger drowns," Roberto concluded, as anyone would have. And Father Caspar accused him of knowing very little about the "equilibrium of liquors."

"You may possibly think that the Void exists somewhere, as those ornaments of the Synagogue of Satan may have told you when you in Paris spent all your time with them. But you will perhaps admit that in the bell there is not the Void but air. And when you have a bell full of air lowered into the water, the water does not enter. Either it, or air."

That was true, Roberto admitted. And no matter how deep the sea was, a man could walk without any water entering, at least until the passenger, with his breathing, had not consumed all the air, transformed it into vapor (as you see when you breathe on a mirror) which, being less dense than water, would yield space to it—definitive proof, Father Caspar commented, exultant, that Nature has a horror of the Void. But with a bell of that size, the passenger could count on at least thirty minutes' respiration, he calculated. The shore seemed very far away, if it were to be reached by swimming, but, walking, it would be a stroll, because almost at the halfway point between ship and shore lay the coral barrier—where the boat had not been able to follow a direct course but instead made a wider curve beyond the promontory. And in certain stretches the coral was at the water's surface. If the expedition were begun in a period of reflux, the walking to be done underwater would be further reduced. It would suffice to reach that emergent land, and as soon as the occupant climbed up, even moving only one foot, the bell would again fill with fresh air.

But how could anyone walk on the sea bed, which must

bristle with dangers, and how could he climb up on the barrier, which was composed of sharp stones and corals still sharper? And, further, how would the bell descend without capsizing in the water, or without being thrust up, for the same reasons that a diver returns to the surface?

With a shrewd smile Father Caspar said that Roberto had forgotten the most important objection: that the air-filled bell, pushed into the sea, would displace an amount of water equal to its mass, and this water would weigh far more than the body trying to penetrate it, to which therefore much opposing resistance would be offered. But in the bell there would also be many pounds of man, and, further, there were the metal buskins. And, with the look of someone who has thought of everything, he went and fetched from the inexhaustible soda a pair of boots with iron soles about five fingers thick, fastening at the knee. The iron would serve as ballast, and would also protect the feet of the explorer. They would slow his progress but spare him those concerns for the rough terrain that as a rule enforce a cautious tread.

"But if you have to climb to the shore from the depths here, it will be uphill all the way!"

"You were not here when we dropped anchor! I the first sounding made. No depths! If the *Daphne* went a little more ahead, it would run aground!"

"But how can you support the bell, its weight all on your head?" Roberto asked. And Father Caspar reminded him that in the water he would not feel this weight, and Roberto would know this if he had ever tried to push a boat, or extract from a tub an iron ball with his hand: the effort all came after you had pulled it out, not while it was still immersed.

In the face of the old man's stubbornness, Roberto tried to postpone the moment of his destruction. "But if the bell is lowered with the windlass," he asked, "how do we unhook the cable afterwards? If we do not, the rope will hold you here, unable to move away from the ship."

Caspar answered that once he was on the bottom, Roberto would know, because the rope would slacken; and at that point he was to cut it. Did he perhaps think Caspar would come back by the same means? Once on the Island, he would go and recover the boat, and with that he would come back, God willing.

But as soon as he was on shore, when he had freed himself from the straps, the bell—if another windlass did not keep it aloft—would slump to the ground, imprisoning him. "Do you want to spend the rest of your life on an island, trapped inside a bell?" And the old man replied that once he had freed himself from those underpants, he had only to slash the hide with his knife, and he would emerge like Minerva from Jove's head.

And what if, in the water, he encountered a big fish of some man-eating species? Father Caspar burst out laughing: surely the most ferocious of fish, encountering in its path a self-moving contraption capable of frightening even a human, would rapidly flee in bewilderment.

"In short," Roberto concluded, sincerely concerned for his friend, "you are old and frail. If someone has to make this test, it will be me!" Father Caspar thanked him but explained that he, Roberto, had already given ample evidence of being a scatterbrain, and heaven only knows what a botch he would make of it. He, Caspar, already had some knowledge of that body of water and of the reef, and he had seen similar reefs elsewhere from a flatboat; this bell he had built himself and therefore knew its merits and defects; he had a good notion of hydrostatic physics and would know how to deal with unforeseen circumstances; and, he added, as if presenting the ultimate argument in his favor, "after all, I have the faith, and you not."

And Roberto understood that this was not by any means

the last consideration: it was the first, and surely the most beautiful. Father Caspar Wanderdrossel believed in his Bell as he believed in his Specula, and he believed he had to use the Bell to reach the Specula, and he believed that everything he was doing was for the greater glory of God. And as faith can move mountains, it can surely overcome waters.

So there was nothing to be done but set the bell back on deck and prepare it for immersion. An operation that kept them busy till evening. To treat the hide in such a way that it was both impermeable to water and air-tight, they had to prepare a paste over a slow fire, mixing three pounds of wax, one pound of Venetian turpentine, and four ounces of another varnish used by carpenters. Then the hide had to absorb that substance; so it was left to sit until the next day. Finally, with another paste made of pitch and wax they had to caulk the edges of the window, where the glass had already been fixed with mastic, then tarred.

"Omnibus rimis diligenter repletis," Father Caspar said, and spent the night in prayer. At dawn they examined the bell, the straps, the hooks. The Jesuit waited for the right moment, when the reflux could best be exploited and the sun was high enough to illuminate the sea before him, casting all shadows behind his back. Then the two men embraced.

Father Caspar repeated that it would be an enjoyable enterprise in which he would see amazing things such as not even Adam or Noah had known, and his one fear was of committing the sin of Pride—proud as he was of being the first man to descend into the sea's depths. "However," he added, "this is also a proof of mortification: if Our Lord on the water walked, I will walk under, suitable path for sinners."

Then the bell had to be raised, with Father Caspar fastened inside it, testing the device to guarantee that he was able to move comfortably.

For a few minutes Roberto observed the spectacle of a huge

snail—no, a puffball, an ambulant agaric—advancing with slow and awkward steps, often stopping and half-turning when the Jesuit wanted to look to the left or right. More than a progress, that walking hood appeared to perform a gavotte, a bourrée, which the absence of music made even clumsier.

Finally Father Caspar seemed satisfied with his rehearsal and, in a voice that sounded as if it came from his boots, he said he was ready to set out.

He moved to the windlass; Roberto hooked him up and began turning it, making sure, when the bell was raised, that the feet swayed freely and the old man could not slip down or up. Father Caspar clanked and re-echoed that all was well, but they should hurry: "These buskins are pulling my legs and are about to tear them from my belly. Hurry! Put me in the wasser!"

Roberto shouted a few words of encouragement and slowly lowered the vehicle with its human engine. No easy matter, because he had to perform by himself the task of many sailors. That descent thus seemed eternal to him, as if the sea sank gradually as he multiplied his efforts. But finally he heard a noise from the water, realized the strain was diminishing, and after a few moments (which to him seemed years) he felt the windlass now spinning idly. The bell had touched bottom. He severed the rope, then rushed to the bulwark to look down. And saw nothing.

Of Father Caspar and the bell there was not a sign.

What a brain, that Jesuit, Roberto said to himself with wonder. He has done it! Imagine, down in that water there is a Jesuit walking, and no one would guess. The valleys of all the oceans could be populated with Jesuits, and no one would know!

Then he shifted to more practical thoughts. That Father Caspar was down below was invisibly evident. But that he would come up again was not yet sure.

It seemed to Roberto that the water was stirring. The day had been chosen precisely because it was calm; but, as they were carrying out the final preparations, a wind sprang up which out here merely ruffled the surface a little, but at the shore it created a play of waves that at the submerged reefs could jeopardize Father Caspar's arrival.

Towards the northern point, where an almost perpendicular wall rose, Roberto could glimpse gusts of spume that slapped the rock, scattered in the air like so many little white nuns. It was surely the effect of waves hitting a series of invisible rock formations, but from the ship it seemed as if a serpent from the abyss were exhaling flames of crystal.

The beach, however, was calmer, the swell was only at the halfway point, and for Roberto that was a good sign: it indicated the place where the reef protruded from the water and marked the border beyond which Father Caspar would no longer be in peril.

Where was the old man now? If he had started walking the moment he touched bottom, by now he should be . . . But how much time had elapsed? Roberto had lost all sense of the passing moments, which he had been counting for an eternity, and thus he tended to underestimate the result, and was convinced that the old man had barely descended, was still below the keel, trying to orient himself. But then a sudden fear seized him: that the rope, twisting as it descended, had made the bell execute a half-turn, and that now, unwitting, Father Caspar found himself with the vizor facing west and was heading for the open sea.

Then Roberto told himself that anyone heading for the open sea would realize he was descending rather than climbing, and would change course. But what if at that point there was a little rise westwards, and climbing it, he believed he was going east? Still the sun's reflections would indicate the direction in which the planet was moving. . . . But could the sun be seen in the deep? Did its rays penetrate, as through a stained-glass window, in compact strips, or were they dispersed in a refraction of drops, so that the inhabitants of the abyss saw the light as a directionless gleam?

No, he told himself then: The old man understands clearly where he must go, perhaps he is already halfway between the ship and the reef, or, rather, he is already at the reef, perhaps he is about to climb it with his thick iron shoes, and at any moment I will see him. . . .

Another thought: In reality, before today no one has ever been on the bottom of the sea. How do I know that down there, beyond a few ells' depth, you do not enter an absolute blackness inhabited only by creatures whose eyes emanate a vague glow. . . . And who says that on the bottom of the sea one can still have any sense of direction? Perhaps he is moving in circles and will retrace always the same path, until the air in his chest has been transformed into moisture, which invites its friend, water, into the bell. . . .

Roberto reproached himself for not having brought at least an hourglass up on deck: how much time had gone by? Perhaps already more than a half-hour, too long, alas, and it was he who felt he was suffocating. Then he took a deep breath, was reborn, and he believed this proved that only a very few instants had passed and Father Caspar was still enjoying the purest air.

But if the old man had set off obliquely, it was useless for Roberto to look straight ahead, as if the Jesuit were to emerge along the trajectory of an arquebus ball. He could have made many deviations, seeking the best access to the reef. Had he not said, while they were assembling the Bell, that it was a stroke of luck that the windlass stood precisely where it did? Ten paces to the north the false curtain abruptly formed a steep flank, against which the boat had once struck, while directly in front of the windlass there was a passage through which the boat had passed, running aground a bit farther on, where the rocks of the natural breakwater rose gradually.

Or, erring in direction, perhaps he had found himself facing a wall and was following it southwards, looking for the passage. Or perhaps he was following it to the north. Roberto had to keep his eye on the whole shore, from one extremity to the other; perhaps Caspar would emerge down there, crowned with sea-ivy. . . . Roberto turned his head to the farther end of the bay, then back, fearing that while he was looking to the left, he might miss the Jesuit already emerging on the right. And yet at that distance it was easy to identify a man quickly, let alone a leather bell dripping water in the sun like a copper ladle just washed. . . .

Fish! Perhaps in those waters there was a cannibal fish, not at all frightened by the bell, and it had already devoured the old man whole. No, if there was such a fish, it would live between the ship and the beginning of the coral reef, not beyond, and Roberto would have glimpsed its dark shadow. But perhaps the explorer had already arrived at the reef, and animal or mineral spikes had pierced the bell, releasing what little air it still contained. . . .

Another thought: How do I know that the air in the bell has really sufficed for all this time? Caspar had said it would, but he had already been led astray by his confidence that his basin would work. In the final analysis, dear old Caspar had proved to be a raving eccentric, and perhaps that whole story of the waters of the Flood, and the meridian, and the Island of Solomon was a pack of tall tales. And besides, even if he was right as far as the Island was concerned, he could have been wrong in his calculation of the quantity of air a man needs. And how do I know that all those oils, those essences, really did seal every crevice? Perhaps at this moment the interior of the bell looks like one of those grottoes where water spurts from every corner; perhaps the whole bell sweats like a sponge; is it not true that our own skin is a sieve of pores imperceptible and yet there, since our sweat filters through them? And if this happens with a man's skin, can it not happen also with the hide of an ox? Or do oxen not sweat? And when it rains, does an ox feel wet inside as well?

Roberto wrung his hands and cursed his haste. It was self-evident: here he was, believing hours had passed, and instead only a few pulse-beats had gone by. He told himself he had no reason to fear; the brave old man had many more reasons to do so. Perhaps Roberto should support Caspar's progress with prayer, or at least with fond hope and good cheer.

Besides, he said to himself, I have imagined too many possibilities for tragedy, and it is only proper to melancholics to generate specters that reality is unable to imitate. Father Caspar knows the hydrostatic laws, has already sounded this sea, has studied the Flood also through the fossils found in all seas. I must be calm, I must comprehend that the time passed is slight, and I must wait.

He realized that he had grown to love the man who had been the Intruder, and he was already weeping at the mere thought that harm might have befallen him. Now, old man, he murmured, return, come back to life, be reborn by God, and we will kill the fattest hen. Surely you will not abandon your Specula Melitensis to its fate?

And suddenly he was aware that he could no longer make out the rocks near the shore, a sign that the water had begun to rise; and the sun, which earlier he had seen without having to raise his head, was now truly over him. So from the moment of the bell's disappearance, not minutes but hours had passed.

He had to repeat this truth to himself aloud to make it

credible. He had counted as seconds what had been minutes, he had convinced himself that in his bosom he carried a crazed clock, precipitately ticking, whereas that clock had slowed its pace. For Heaven knows how long, telling himself that Father Caspar had just descended, he had been awaiting a creature who had been without air for some time. For Heaven knows how long he had been awaiting a body lying lifeless somewhere in that expanse.

What could have happened? Everything, everything he had thought—and perhaps everything his misadventured fear had caused to happen, he the bearer of ill fortune. The hydrostatic principles of Father Caspar could be illusory, perhaps the water in a bell does indeed enter from below, especially if the person inside kicks the air outside, and what did Roberto truly know of the equilibrium of liquids? Or perhaps the impact had been too abrupt and the bell had overturned. Or Father Caspar had tripped halfway there. Or had lost his direction. Or his heart, septuagenarian or more, unequal to his enthusiasm, had failed. And finally, who says that at such depth the weight of the water of the sea cannot crush leather as it might squeeze a lemon or hull a pod?

But if he was dead, should his corpse not rise to the surface? No, he was anchored by his iron boots, from which his poor legs would be freed only when the conjoint action of the waters and the host of greedy little fish had reduced him to a skeleton. . . .

Then Roberto had a dazzling thought. What was all this mental jabber about? Why, Father Caspar himself had said it in so many words: the Island Roberto saw before him was not the island of today but that of yesterday. Beyond that meridian it was the day before! Could he expect to see now on that beach, where it was yesterday, a person who had descended into the water today? Surely not. The old man had immersed himself in the early morning of this Monday, but if on the ship it was Monday, on that Island it was still Sunday, and therefore he would not be able to see his friend emerge until the morning of its tomorrow, when on the Island it would be, at last, Monday. . . .

I must wait till tomorrow, he said to himself. Then, however, he added: But Father Caspar cannot wait a day, he has not enough air! And, further, while it is I who must wait a day, he simply re-entered Sunday as soon as he crossed the line of the meridian. My God, then the Island I see is Sunday's, and if he arrived there on Sunday, I should see him already! No, I have it all wrong. The Island I see is today's, it is impossible I should see the past as in a magic crystal. It is there, on the Island—and only there—that it is yesterday. But if I see the Island of today, I should see him, who in the Island's yesterday is already there, and is enjoying a second Sunday . . . And then, whether he arrived yesterday or today, he should have left the disemboweled bell on the beach, and I cannot see it. But he could have also carried it with him into the woods. When? Yesterday. So: let us assume that what I see is the Island of Sunday. I must wait for tomorrow to see him arriving there on Monday. . . .

We could say that Roberto had definitively lost his mind, and with very good reason: no matter how he calculated, the figures would not add up. The paradoxes of time can indeed unhinge us. So it was normal for him not to know what to do; and he ended up doing what anyone, first victim of his own hope, would have done: before succumbing to despair, he prepared to wait for the coming day.

How he did it is hard to reconstruct. Pacing back and forth on deck, not touching food, talking to himself, to Father Caspar, to the stars and perhaps having recourse once more to aqua vitae. The fact is that we find him the next day—as the night fades and the sky takes on color, and then after sunrise—more and more tense while the hours pass, greatly agitated between eleven and noon, beside himself between noon and sunset, until he has to accept reality—and, this time, without any doubt. Yesterday, surely yesterday, Father Caspar lowered himself into the austral ocean and neither yesterday nor today did he subsequently emerge. And since all the wonder of the antipodal meridian is played out between yesterday and tomorrow, and not between yesterday and the day after tomorrow, or tomorrow and the day before yesterday, it was now certain: from that sea Father Caspar would never again come forth.

With mathematical, indeed, cosmographical and astronomical certitude, his poor friend was lost. Nor could anyone have said where the body was. In some unidentified place down below. Perhaps beneath the surface there were violent currents, and the body by now was out in the open sea. Or perhaps not, perhaps beneath the *Daphne* lay a trough, a chasm, the bell had settled there, and from it the old man had been unable to climb up and had expended his scant breath, increasingly watery, in cries for help.

Perhaps, to escape, he had unfastened his bonds, the bell still full of air, and made a leap upwards, but its iron part had arrested that first impulse and held it at half-depth, no knowing where. Father Caspar had tried to free himself from his boots but had failed. Now in this strait, rooted in rock, his lifeless body swayed like seaweed.

And while Roberto was thinking these things, the Tuesday sun was now behind his back, the moment of Father Caspar Wanderdrossel's death growing ever more remote.

The sunset created a jaundiced sky behind the dark green

of the Island, and a Stygian sea. Roberto understood that Nature was mourning with him and, as sometimes happens to one orphaned of someone dear, little by little he no longer wept for the misfortune of that person but for his own renewed solitude.

For a very few days he had escaped that solitude. Father Caspar had become for him friend, father, brother, family, and home. Now he realized that he was again companionless, a hermit. This time forever.

Still, in that disheartenment another illusion was forming. Roberto now was sure that the only escape from his reclusion was to be found not in unbridgeable Space but in Time.

Now he truly had to learn to swim and reach the Island. Not so much to discover some trace of Father Caspar lost in the folds of the past, but to arrest the horrid advance of his own tomorrow.

CHAPTER 26

Delights for the Ingenious:
A Collection of Emblems

FOR THREE DAYS Roberto remained with his eye glued to the ship's spyglass (blaming himself that the other, more powerful one was now useless), staring at the tops of the trees on shore. He was waiting for a glimpse of the Orange Dove.

On the third day he roused himself. He had lost his only friend, he was himself lost on the farthest of meridians, and could feel no consolation unless he saw a bird that perhaps had fluttered only in the head of Father Caspar!

He decided to explore again his refuge to learn how long he could survive on board. The hens continued laying their eggs, and a nest of baby chicks had been hatched. Of the collected vegetables not much was left, they were now too dry, and he would have to use them as feed for the fowl. There were still a few barrels of water, but if he collected rain, he could even do without them. And, finally, there was no shortage of fish.

But then he considered that, eating no fresh vegetables, he would die of scurvy. There were those in the greenhouse, but they would be naturally watered only if rain fell: if a long

drought were to arrive, he would have to water the plants
with his supply of drinking water. And if there was a storm
for days and days, he would have water but would be unable
to fish.

To allay his anxieties he went back to the water organ,
which Father Caspar had taught him how to set in motion:
he heard always and only "Daphne," because he had not
learned how to change the cylinder; but he was not sorry to
listen hour after hour to the same tune. One day he identified
Daphne, the ship, with the body of his beloved Lady. Was not
Daphne after all a creature who had been transformed into a
laurel—an arboreal substance, thus with an affinity to that
with which the ship had been made? The tune hence sang to
him of Lilia. Obviously, the chain of thought was entirely
inconsequent—but this is how Roberto was thinking.

He reproached himself for having allowed himself to be
distracted by the arrival of Father Caspar, for having followed
him in his mechanical frenzies and having forgotten his own
amorous vow. That one song, whose words he did not know,
if it ever had any, was being transformed into the prayer that
he intended to make the machine murmur every day:
"Daphne" played by the water and wind in the recesses of the
Daphne, in memory of the ancient metamorphosis of a divine
Daphne. Every evening, looking at the sky, he hummed that
melody softly, like a litany.

Then he went back to his table and resumed writing to
Lilia.

In doing so he realized that he had passed the previous
days outdoors and in daylight, and that he was again seeking
refuge in the semidarkness that had been his natural ambiance
not only on the *Daphne* before finding Father Caspar, but for
more than ten years, since the days of the wound at Casale.

To tell the truth, I do not believe that during all that time
Roberto lived, as he repeatedly suggests, only at night. That

he avoided the excesses of the blazing noonday sun is probable, but when he followed Lilia, he did so during the day. I believe this infirmity was more an effect of black bile than a genuine impairment of his vision. Roberto realized that the light made him suffer only in his most atrabiliar moments, but when his mind was distracted by merrier thoughts, he paid no attention.

However it was or had been, that evening he found himself reflecting for the first time on the fascinations of shadows. As he wrote, as he raised the pen to dip it into the inkwell, he saw the light either as a gilded halo on the paper or as a waxen fringe, almost translucent, that defined the outline of his dark fingers. As if the light dwelt within his hand and became manifest only at the edges. All around, he was enfolded by the affectionate habit of a Capuchin, that is to say, by a certain hazel-brown glow that, touching the shadows, died there.

He looked at the flame of the lamp, and he saw two fires born from it: a red flame, part of the consumed matter, which, rising, turned a blinding white that shaded into periwinkle. Thus, he said to himself, his love was fed by a body that was dying, and gave life to the celestial spirit of his beloved.

He wanted to celebrate, after some days of infidelity, his reconciliation with the dark, and he climbed onto the deck as the shadows were spreading everywhere, on the ship, on the sea, on the Island, where he could now see only the rapid darkening of the hills. Remembering his own countryside, he sought to glimpse on the shore the presence of fireflies, live winged sparks wandering in the shadows of the hedges. He did not see them, and pondered on the oxymorons of the antipodes, where perhaps nightjars appeared only at noon.

Then he lay down on the quarterdeck and began looking at the moon, letting the deck cradle him while from the Island came the sound of the backwash, mixed with cries of crickets, or their equivalent in this hemisphere.

He reflected that the beauty of day is like a blond beauty,

while the beauty of night is a dark beauty. He savored the contradiction of his love for a blonde goddess which consumed him in the darkness of the night. Remembering the hair like ripe wheat, which annihilated all other light in the salon of Arthénice, he would call the moon beautiful because it diluted, fading, the rays of a latent sun. He proposed to make the reconquered day a new occasion for reading in the glints on the waves the encomium of the gold of that hair and the blue of those eyes.

But he savored also the beauties of night, when all seems at rest, the stars move more silently than the sun, and you come to believe you are the sole person in all nature intent on dreaming.

That night he was on the point of deciding that he would remain on the ship for the rest of his days. But, raising his eyes to Heaven, he saw a group of stars that suddenly seemed to reveal to him the shape of a dove, wings outspread, bearing in its beak an olive twig. Now it is true that at least forty years before, in the austral sky not far from Canis Major, a constellation had been identified and named the Dove. But I am not at all sure that Roberto, from his position then, at that hour and in that season, saw those same stars. In any case, though the observers who had seen in them a dove (like Johannes Bayer in his *Uranometria Nova,* and then much later Coronelli in his *Libro dei Globi*) possessed far more imagination than Roberto, I would still say that any arrangement of stars at that moment would have seemed to him a pigeon, a dove, a turtle, whatever you like. That morning he had doubted its existence, but the Orange Dove was driven into his mind like a nail— or, as we shall see, a golden spike.

We must in fact ask ourselves why, after Father Caspar's first hint of the many marvels the Island could offer him, Roberto chose to take such interest in the Dove.

We shall see, as we continue to follow this story, how in the mind of Roberto (whose solitude day after day made increasingly ardent) that dove barely mentioned at first, becomes all the more vivid the less he manages to see it, becomes an invisible compendium of every passion of his loving soul, his admiration, respect, veneration, hope, jealousy, envy, wonder, and gaiety. It was not clear to him (nor can it be to us) whether the bird had become the Island, or Lilia, or both, or the yesterday to which all three were relegated, for Roberto's exile was in an endless today, whose future lay only in arriving, some tomorrow, at the day before.

We could say Caspar had recalled to him the Song of Solomon, which, as it happens, Roberto's Carmelite had read to him over and over until the boy had almost memorized it; and from his youth he enjoyed mellifluous agonies for a creature with dove eyes, for a dove whose face he could glimpse among the clefts of rock. . . . But this satisfies me only up to a point. I believe it is necessary to engage in an "Explication of the Dove," to draft some notes for a future little monograph that could be entitled *Columba Patefacta*, and the project does not seem to me completely otiose, considering that others have devoted whole chapters to the Meaning of the Whale, that ugly black or gray animal (though if white, it is unique), whereas we are dealing with a *rara avis*, its color even rarer, and a bird on which mankind has reflected far more than on whales.

This in fact is the point. Whether he had spoken with the Carmelite or debated with Padre Emanuele, or had leafed through many books held in high esteem in that time, or whether in Paris he had listened to lectures on what were called Enigmatic Emblems and Devices, Roberto should have known something, however little, about doves.

We must remember that his was a time when people invented or reinvented images of every sort to discover in them recondite and revelatory meanings. It sufficed to see, I will not say a beautiful flower or a crocodile, but merely a basket, a ladder, a sieve, or a column, and one would try to build around it a network of things that at first glance nobody had seen there. This is hardly the place to discuss the difference between a Device and an Emblem, or to describe how in various ways these images were complemented by special verses or mottoes (except to mention that the Emblem, from the description of a particular deed, not necessarily illustrated, derived a universal concept, whereas the Device went from the concrete image of a particular object to a quality or proposition of a single individual, as to say, "I shall be more pure than snow," or, "more clever than the serpent," or again, "I would rather die than betray," arriving at the most celebrated *Frangar non Flectar* and *Spiritus durissima coquit*). The people of that period considered it indispensable to translate the whole world into a forest of Symbols, Hints, Equestrian Games, Masquerades, Paintings, Courtly Arms, Trophies, Blazons, Escutcheons, Ironic Figures, Sculpted Obverses of Coins, Fables, Allegories, Apologias, Epigrams, Riddles, Equivocations, Proverbs, Watchwords, Laconic Epistles, Epitaphs, Parerga, Lapidary Engravings, Shields, Glyphs, Clipei, and if I may, I will stop here—but they did not stop. And every good Device had to be metaphoric, poetic, composed, true, of a soul to be revealed, but even more of a sensitive body that referred to an object of the world. It had to be noble, admirable, new but knowable, evident but effective, singular, proportionate to its space, acute and brief, ambiguous but frank, popularly enigmatic, appropriate, ingenious, unique, and heroic.

In short, a Device was a mysterious notion, the expression of a correspondence: a poetry that did not sing but was made up of a silent figure and a motto that spoke for it to the eyes—precious in that it was imperceptible, its splendor hidden in the pearls and the diamonds it showed only bead by bead. It said more making less noise, and where the Epic Poem required fables and episodes, and History deliberations and harangues, for the Device a few strokes and a syllable sufficed: its perfumes were distilled in impalpable drops, and only then could objects be seen in a surprising garb, as with Foreigners and Maskers. It concealed more than it revealed. It did not charge the spirit with matter but nourished it with essences. It was to be *peregrine* (a term then very much in use), and peregrine meant stranger and stranger meant strange.

What could be more a stranger than an orange dove? Indeed, what could be more peregrine than a dove? Ah, the dove was an image rich in meanings, all the more clever as each conflicted with the others.

The first to speak of the dove were, as is only natural, the Egyptians, as early as the most ancient *Hieroglyphica* of Horapollon, and above its many other qualities, this animal was considered extremely pure, so much so that if there was a pestilence poisoning humans and things, the only ones immune were those who ate nothing but doves. Which ought to have been obvious, seeing that this animal is the only one lacking gall (namely, the poison that all other animals carry, attached to the liver), and Pliny said that if a dove falls ill, it plucks a bay leaf and is healed. And bay is laurel, and the laurel is Daphne. Enough said.

But doves, pure as they are, are also a very sly symbol, because they exhaust themselves in their great lust: they spend the day kissing (redoubling their kisses reciprocally to shut each other up) and locking their tongues, which has inspired many lascivious expressions such as to make the dove with the lips or exchange columbine kisses, to quote the casuists. And columbining, the poets said, means making love as the doves do, and as often. Nor must we forget that Roberto must have known those verses that go, "When in the bed, the ardent try their arts, / to nurture warm and lively yearning / just like a pair of doves, their hearts / lust and collect such kisses, burning." It may be worthy of note, too, that while all other animals have a season for love, there is no time of the year in which the male dove does not mount the female.

To begin at the beginning: doves come from Cyprus, island sacred to Venus. Apuleius, but also others before him, tells us that Venus's chariot is drawn by snow-white doves, called in fact the birds of Venus because of their excessive lust. Others recall that the Greeks called the dove *peristera,* because envious Eros changed into a dove the nymph Peristera, much loved by Venus. Peristera had helped defeat Eros in a contest to see who could gather the most flowers. But what does Apuleius mean when he says that Venus "loved" Peristera?

Aelianus says that doves were consecrated to Venus because on Mount Eryx in Sicily a feast was held when the goddess passed over Libya; on that day, in all of Sicily, no doves were seen, because all had crossed the sea to go and make up the goddess's train. But nine days later, from the Libyan shores there arrived in Trinacria a dove red as fire, as Anacreon says (and I beg you to remember this color); and it was Venus herself, who is also called Purpurea, and behind her came the throng of doves. Aelianus also tells us of a girl named Phytia whom the enamored Jove transformed into a dove.

The Assyrians portrayed Semiramis in the form of a dove, and it was the doves who brought up Semiramis and later changed her into a dove. We all know that she was a woman of less than immaculate behavior, but so beautiful that Scaurobates, King of the Indians, was seized with love for her. Semiramis, concubine of the King of Assyria, did not let a single day pass without committing adultery, and the historian Juba says that she even fell in love with a horse.

But an amorous symbol is forgiven many things, and it never ceases to attract poets: hence (and we can be sure Roberto knew this) Petrarch asked himself: "What grace, what love or what fate—will give me the feathers of a dove!" and Bandello wrote: "This dove whose ardor equals mine / is ardent Love burning in cruel fire / he goes seeking in every place / his mate, and dies of his desire."

Doves, however, are something more and better than any Semiramis, and we fall in love with them because they have this other, most tender characteristic: they weep or moan instead of singing, as if all that sated passion never satisfied them. *Idem cantus gemitusque,* said an Emblem of Camerarius; *Gemitibus Gaudet,* said another even more erotically fascinating. And maddening.

And yet the fact that these birds kiss and are so lewd— and here is a fine contradiction that distinguishes the dove— is also proof that they are totally faithful, and hence they are also the symbol of chastity, in the sense of conjugal fidelity. And this, too, Pliny said: Though most amorous, they have a great sense of modesty and do not know adultery. Their conjugal fidelity is asserted both by the pagan Propertius and by Tertullian. It is said, true, that in the rare instances when they suspect adultery, the males become bullies, their voice is full of lament and the blows of their beak are cruel. But immediately thereafter, in reparation, the male woos the female, and flatters her, circling her frequently. And this idea—that mad jealousy foments love and then a renewed fidelity, and then kissing each other to infinity and in every season—seems very beautiful to me and, as we shall see, it seemed beautiful to Roberto as well.

How can you help but love an image that promises you fidelity? Fidelity even after death, because once its companion is gone, this bird never unites with another. The dove was thus chosen as the symbol for chaste widowhood. Ferro recalls the story of a widow who, profoundly saddened by the death of her husband, kept at her side a white dove, and was reproached for it, to which she replied, *Dolor non color,* it is the sorrow that matters, not the color.

In short, lascivious or not, their devotion to love leads Origen to say that doves are the symbol of charity. And for this reason, according to Saint Cyprian, the Holy Spirit comes to us in the form of a dove, for not only is this animal without bile, but also its claws do not scratch, nor does it bite. It loves human dwellings naturally, recognizes only one home, feeds its young, and spends its life in quiet conversation, living with its mate in the concord—in this case irreproachable—of a kiss. Whence it is seen that kissing can also be the sign of great love of one's neighbor, and the Church has adopted the ritual of the kiss of peace. It was the custom of the Romans to welcome and greet one another with a kiss, also between men and women. Malicious scholiasts say that they did this because women were forbidden to drink wine and kissing them was a way of checking their breath, but the Numidians were considered vulgar because they kissed no one but their children.

Since all people hold air to be the most noble element, they have honored the dove, which flies higher than the other birds and yet always returns faithfully to its nest. Which, to be sure, the swallow also does, but no one has ever managed to make it a friend of our species and domesticate it, as the dove has been. Saint Basil, for example, reports that dove-vendors sprinkled a dove with aromatic balm, and, attracted by that, the other doves followed the first in a great host. *Odore trahit.* I do not know if it has much to do with what I said above, but this scented benevolence touches me, this sweet-smelling purity, this seductive chastity.

The dove is not only chaste and faithful, but also simple (*columbina simplicitas:* Be ye therefore wise as serpents and harmless as doves, says the Bible), and for this reason it is sometimes the symbol of the life of the convent and the cloister. And how does that fit with all these kisses? Never mind.

Another source of fascination is the *trepidius* of the dove: its Greek name, *treron*, derives certainly from *treo*, "I flee, trembling." Homer, Ovid, Virgil all speak of this ("Timorous as pigeons during a black storm"), and we must remember that doves live always in terror of the eagle or, worse, the hawk. In Valerian we read how, for this very reason, they nest in inaccessible places for protection (hence the device *Secura nidificat*); and Jeremiah also recalls this, as Psalm 55 cries out, "Oh that I had wings like a dove! for them would I fly away, and be at rest."

The Jews said that doves and turtledoves are the most persecuted of birds, and therefore worthy of the altar, for it is better to be the persecuted than the persecutor. But according to Aretino, not meek like the Jews, he who makes himself a dove is eaten by the falcon. But Epiphanius says that the dove never protects itself against traps, and Augustine repeated that not only does the dove put up no opposition to large animals, stronger than it, but is submissive even toward the sparrow.

A legend goes that in India there is a verdant leafy tree that in Greek is called *Paradision*. On its right side live the doves, who never move from the shade it spreads; if they were to leave the tree, they would fall prey to a dragon, their enemy. But the dragon's enemy is the tree's shade, and when the shade is to the right, he lies in ambush to the left, and vice versa.

Still, trepid as the dove is, it has something of the serpent's cunning, and if on the Island there was a dragon, the Orange Dove would know what to do. It seems a dove always flies over water, for if a hawk attacks, the dove will see the raptor's reflection. In short, does the bird defend itself or not?

With all these various and even extraordinary qualities, the dove has also been made a mystic symbol, and I need not bore the reader with the story of the Flood and the role played by this bird in announcing peace, calm, and newly emerging land. But for many sacred authors it is also an emblem of the Mater Dolorosa and of her helpless weeping. And of her it it said *Intus et extra,* because she is pure outside and inside. Sometimes the dove is portrayed breaking the rope that keeps her prisoner, *Effracto libera vinculo,* and she becomes the figure of Christ risen from the dead. Further, the dove arrives, it seems certain, at dusk, so as not to be surprised by the night, and therefore not to be arrested by death before having dried the stains of sin. And it is worth mentioning, as we have already indicated, the teaching of John: "I saw the Spirit descending from Heaven like a dove."

As for the other beautiful Columbine Devices, who can say how many Roberto knew? Like *Mollius ut cubant,* because the dove plucks out its feathers to soften the nest of its young; *Luce lucidior,* because it shines when it rises towards the sun; *Quiescit in motu,* because it flies always with one wing folded so as not to tire itself. There was even a soldier who, to crave indulgence for his amorous excesses, chose as his emblem a helmet in which a pair of doves had nested, with the motto *Amica Venus.*

In short, the reader may think that the dove has all too many meanings. But if a symbol or hieroglyph must be chosen as something to die for, its meanings should be multiple, otherwise you might as well call a spade a spade, an atom an atom, a void a void. Something that would please the natural philosophers Roberto met at the Dupuys' but not Padre Emanuele—and we know that our castaway was inclined to be influenced by both. Finally, the wonderful thing about the Dove, at least (I believe) for Roberto, was that it was not only a message, like every Device or Emblem, but a message whose message was the undecipherability of clever messages.

When Aeneas must descend to Avernus—and also find the shadow of his father and therefore somehow the day or days now past—what does the sibyl do? She tells him, true, to go and bury Misenus and to make various sacrifices of bulls and other livestock, but if he really wants to perform a feat that no one has had the courage or the luck to attempt, he must find a leafy, shady tree on which there is a golden bough. The wood hides it and dark valleys encircle it, and yet without that "auricomus" bough no one can penetrate the secrets of the earth. And who is it that enables Aeneas to discover the bough? Two doves, who are also—as we should know by now—maternal birds. The rest is familiar to the bleary aged and to barbers. In short, Virgil had never heard of Noah, but the dove bears a warning, points to something.

It was thought, moreover, that doves acted as oracle in the temple of Jove, where he replied through their mouth. Then one of these doves flew to the temple of Ammon and another to that at Delphi, whence it is clear that both the Egyptians and the Greeks told the same truths, even if darkly veiled. No dove, no revelation.

But today we are still here, asking ourselves what the Golden Bough meant. A sign that doves carry messages, but the messages are in cipher.

I cannot say how much Roberto knew about the kabbalas of the Jews, which were, however, very fashionable in that period, but if he saw much of Monsieur Gaffarel, he must have heard something about these arcana: the fact is that the Jews constructed whole castles based on the dove. We referred to this, or, rather, Father Caspar did: Psalm 68 mentions the wings of a dove covered with silver and her feathers with yellow gold. Why? And why, in Proverbs, does a similar image recur when "a word fitly spoken" is likened to "apples of gold in settings of silver"? And why in the Song of Solomon, addressing the girl "who has doves' eyes," does the speaker say to her, "O my love, we will make thee circlets of gold with studs of silver"?

The Jews commented that the gold here is scripture and the silver refers to the blank spaces between the letters and words. And one commentator, whom perhaps Roberto did not know but who was still an inspiration to many rabbis, said that the golden apples in a silver setting mean that in every sentence of Scripture (and surely in every object or event in the world) there are two faces, the evident face and the hidden face, and the evident one is silver, but the hidden one is more precious because it is of gold. And he who looks at the picture from a distance, with the apples surrounded by its silver, believes that the apples too are of silver, but when he looks closer, he will discover the splendor of gold.

All that the Sacred Scriptures contain *prima facie* shines like silver, but its hidden meaning glows like gold. The inviolable chastity of the word of God, hidden from the eyes of the profane, is as if covered by a veil of modesty and remains in the shadow of mystery. It says that pearls must not be cast before swine. Having the eyes of a dove means not stopping at the literal meaning of words but knowing how to penetrate their mystical sense.

And yet this secret, like the dove, eludes us, and we never know where it is. The dove is there to signify that the world speaks in hieroglyphics, and there is a hieroglyph that itself signifies hieroglyphics. And a hieroglyph does not say and does not conceal; it simply shows.

And other Jews said that the dove is an oracle, and it is no accident that the Hebrew word *tore*, dove, recalls *Torah*, which is their Bible, sacred book, origin of all revelation.

The dove, as it flies in the sun, seems simply to sparkle like silver, but only one who has been able to wait at length to discover its hidden face will see its true gold or, rather, the color of a shining orange.

From the time of the venerable Isidore, Christians have recorded that the dove, reflecting in its flight the rays of the sun illuminating it, appears to us in different colors. It depends on the sun, and its Devices are *Dal Tuo Lume i Miei Fregi* (From Your Light Comes My Ornament) and *Per te m'adorno e splendo* (Through You I Am Adorned and Shine). Its neck is sheathed in the light of varied colors, and yet the dove remains always the same. And thus it is a warning not to trust appearances, but also to find the true appearance beneath the false ones.

How many colors has the dove? As an ancient bestiary says:

> *Uncor m'estuet que vos devis*
> *des columps, qui sunt blans et bis:*
> *li un ont color aierine,*
> *et li autre l'ont stephanine;*
> *li un sont neir, li autre rous,*
> *li un vermel, l'autre cendrous,*
> *et des columps i a plusors*
> *qui ont trestotes les colors.*

What, then, will an Orange Dove be?

To conclude, assuming that Roberto knew something about it, I find in the Talmud that the powerful chiefs of Edom, Israel's enemies, decreed that they would tear out the brain of any man wearing phylacteries. Now Elisha put them on and walked out in the street. A guardian of the law saw him and pursued him when he fled. When Elisha was overtaken, he took off the phylacteries and hid them in his hands.

The enemy said to him: "What do you have in your hands?" And he replied: "The wings of a dove." The other man forced open his hands. And there were the wings of a dove.

I am not sure what this story means, but I find it very beautiful. And so must Roberto have found it.

> *Amabilis columba,*
> *unde, unde ades volando?*
> *Quid est rei, quod altum*
> *coelum cito secando*
> *tam copia benigna*
> *spires liquentem odorem?*
> *Tam copia benigna*
> *unguenta grata stilles?*

What I mean to say is this: the dove is an important sign, and we can understand why a man lost in the Antipodes might decide he had to train his eyes carefully to understand its meaning.

The Island beyond reach, Lilia lost, his every hope beaten, why should the invisible Orange Dove not be transformed into the golden medulla, the philosopher's stone, the end of ends, volatile like everything passionately wanted? To aspire to something you will never have: is this not the acme of the most generous of desires?

It seems so clear to me *(Luce lucidior)* that I have decided to proceed no further with my Explication of the Dove.

Now back to our story.

CHAPTER 27

The Secrets of the Flux and Reflux of the Sea

THE NEXT DAY, at the first light of the sun, Roberto stripped completely. In the presence of Father Caspar, out of modesty, he had lowered himself clothed into the water, but he realized that clothing weighed him down and encumbered him. Now he was naked. He tied the rope around his waist, climbed down the Jacob's ladder, and he was again in the sea.

He remained afloat: that much he had already learned. He now had to learn how to move his arms and legs, as swimming dogs move their paws. He ventured a few strokes, continued for some minutes, and realized he had moved only a few ells away from the ladder. Moreover, he was tired.

He knew how to rest, so he turned supine for a while, letting the water and the sun caress him.

He felt his strength return. Clearly, he should move until he tired, then rest like a dead man for a few minutes, then resume. His progress would be slow, the time very long, but this was the proper way to do it.

After a few trials he came to a courageous decision. The ladder descended on the right-hand side of the bowsprit, towards the Island. Now he would try to reach the western side of the ship. He would rest there, and afterwards he would come back.

The passage below the bowsprit was not long, and the sight of the prow from the other side was a victory. He let himself float, face up, arms and legs wide; on this side, he felt, the waves cradled him more comfortably than on the other.

At a certain moment he felt a tug at his waist. The rope was stretched to its full extent. He returned to the canine position and took stock: the sea had carried him north, many ells beyond the tip of the bowsprit. In other words, a current flowing from south-west to north-west gained in force a little west of the *Daphne*. He had not noticed it when he made his immersions on the right, sheltered by the bulk of the fluyt, but moving to the left, he had been caught in the current, and it would have borne him away if the rope had not held him. He had thought he was lying motionless, but he had moved, like the earth in its vortex. Hence it had been fairly easy for him to round the prow: it was not that his skill had increased; rather, the sea had enhanced it.

Worried, he chose to try returning to the *Daphne* with his own strength, and paddling a little, dog-like, he moved a few inches closer, but realized that the moment he paused to catch his breath, the rope tautened again, a sign that he had been carried back.

He clung to the rope and pulled it towards himself, revolving in order to wind it around his waist, thus in a short time he was back at the ladder. Once on board, he decided that any attempt to reach the shore by swimming would be dangerous. He had to construct a raft. He looked at the supply of wood on board the *Daphne* and found he had no implement with which to shape even the smallest log, unless he spent years hacking at a mast with his knife.

But had he not reached the *Daphne* bound to a plank? So

it was simply a matter of unhinging a door and using it as a raft, propelling it perhaps with his hands. For a hammer there was the hilt of his sword, and inserting the blade as a wedge, finally he managed to rip one of the wardroom doors from its hinges. At the end, the blade snapped. Small harm done; he no longer had to fight against human beings, only against the sea.

But if he lowered himself into the sea on the door, where would the current take him? He dragged the door towards the left side and managed to throw it into the sea.

At first the door floated slothfully, but in less than a minute it was far from the ship, heading to the left, more or less in the direction he himself had floated, then towards northwest.

Now it was proceeding as the *Daphne* would have, had its anchor been weighed. Roberto managed to follow it with his naked eye until it passed the cape, then he had to use his spyglass to see it still moving very fast beyond the promontory. The door sped, as if on the bosom of a broad river that had banks and shores in the midst of a sea that lay calmly on either side of it.

He reflected that if the one-hundred-eightieth meridian extended along an ideal line that linked the two promontories halfway down the bay, and if that stream's course changed immediately after the bay and flowed north, then beyond the promontory it followed precisely the antipodal meridian!

Had he been on that door, he would have navigated along the line separating today from yesterday—or from the yesterday of his tomorrow. . . .

At the moment, however, his thoughts were elsewhere. Had he been on that door, he would have had no way to oppose the current except with the movement of his hands. It took a great effort just to guide his own body, so he could imagine how it would be on a door without prow, poop, or tiller.

On the night of his arrival the plank had brought him beneath the bowsprit thanks only to the effect of some wind or secondary current. To predict a new event of this kind he would have to study carefully the movements of the tides for weeks, perhaps months, flinging into the sea dozens and dozens of planks—and even then, who could say . . .

Impossible, at least with the knowledge he possessed, hydrostatic or hydrodynamic as might be. Better to continue placing his hopes in swimming. To reach shore from the center of a current is easier for a dog that kicks than for a dog in a basket.

So his apprenticeship had to continue. And it would not suffice for him to learn to swim between the *Daphne* and the shore. In the bay, too, at different times of the day, and according to the flux and reflux, minor currents were present: and therefore, at a moment when he was confidently proceeding to the east, a trick of the waters could drag him first to the west and then straight towards the northern point. So he would also have to train himself to swim against the current. With the help of the rope, he should be able to defy the water to the left of the hull as well.

In the days that followed, Roberto, staying on the side with the ladder, remembered how at La Griva he had seen not only dogs swim but also frogs. And since a human body in the water, with arms and legs outspread, recalls more the shape of a frog than that of a dog, he told himself that perhaps he should swim like a frog. He even assisted himself vocally, crying *croax, croax* as he flung out his arms and legs. He stopped croaking when those animal utterances had the effect of giving too much energy to his forward bound, causing him to open his mouth, with consequences that an experienced swimmer might have foreseen.

He transformed himself into an elderly, decorous frog, majestically silent. When he felt his shoulders tiring, through that constant outward movement of the hands, he returned to *more canino*. Once, looking at the white birds that followed his exercises, vociferating, sometimes diving only a few feet from him to snatch a fish (the coup de la mouette!), he tried also to swim as they flew, with a broad wing-like movement of his arms, but learned that it is harder to keep a mouth and nose closed than it is a beak, and he gave up the idea. At this point he no longer knew what animal he was, dog or frog; perhaps a hairy toad, an amphibious quadruped, a centaur of the seas, a male siren.

However, in all these various attempts, he noticed that he was moving, more or less. In fact, having begun his journey at the prow, he found himself beyond the halfway point of the side. But when he decided to reverse his direction and go back to the ladder, he realized that he had no more strength, and he had to allow the rope to tow him.

What he lacked was correct respiration. He could manage to go but not to come back. . . . He had become a swimmer, but in the manner of that gentleman who made the entire pilgrimage from Rome to Jerusalem, half a mile each day, back and forth in his own garden. Roberto had never been an athlete, and the months on the *Amaryllis,* always indoors, then the strain of the wreck and the waiting aboard the *Daphne* (except for the few exercises imposed on him by Father Caspar) had enfeebled him.

Roberto shows no awareness of the fact that through swimming he would gain strength, and he seems instead to think he must strengthen himself in order to swim. Thus we see him swallow two, three, even four egg yolks at a time, or devour a whole chicken before attempting another dip. Luckily there was the rope. Once he was seized by such convulsions in the water that he could hardly climb back on deck.

Here he is at evening, meditating on this new contradiction. Before, when he could not even hope to reach it, the Island seemed always within reach. Now, as he was learning the art that would take him there, the Island was receding.

Indeed, as he sees it distant not only in space but also (backwards) in time, from this moment on, whenever he mentions that distance, Roberto seems to confuse space and time, and he writes, "The bay, alas, is too yesterday," and, "How hard it is to arrive over there which is so early," or else, "How much sea separates me from the day barely ended," and even, "Threatening rainclouds are coming from the Island, whereas today it is already clear. . . ."

But if the Island moves ever farther away, is it still worth the effort to learn to reach it? Over the next few days Roberto abandons all attempts at swimming, while he renews his search with the spyglass for the Orange Dove.

He sees parrots among the leaves, he distinguishes fruits, from dawn to sunset he follows the quickening and the extinction of different colors in the foliage, but he does not see the Dove. Once more he is tempted to think that Father Caspar lied to him, or that he was a victim of a Jesuitical joke. At times he is convinced that even Father Caspar never existed—since he finds no trace of his presence on the ship. He no longer believes in the Dove, but neither does he believe now that on the Island there is the Specula. He finds this a source of consolation, because, he tells himself, it would have been irreverent to corrupt the purity of that place with a machine. And he thinks once more of an Island made to his measure, or, rather, to the measure of his dreams.

———

If the island rose in the past, it was the place he had to reach at all costs. In that unhinged time he was not to find but to invent the condition of the First Man. Not the site of a fountain of eternal youth but itself a fountain, the Island could be the place where every human creature, forgetting his own melancholy learning, would find, like a child abandoned in a forest, that a new language could be born from a new contact with creation. And with it would rise a new and the only genuine science, from the direct experience of Nature, with no adulteration by philosophy (as if the Island were not father transmitting to son the words of the Law, but, rather, mother teaching him to stammer his first names).

Only thus could a reborn castaway discover the rules that govern the course of celestial bodies and the meaning of the acrostics they trace in the sky: not flailing among Almagests and Quadripartites but directly reading the approach of eclipses, the passage of the argyrocomate meteors, and the phases of the stars. Only a nose bleeding because struck by a falling fruit would really allow him to understand, at one blow, both the laws that draw the grave to gravity and *de motu cordis et sanguinis in animalibus*. Only after observing the surface of a pond and poking it with a twig, reed, or one of those long and rigid metallic leaves, would the new Narcissus—without any dioptric or sciatherical computing grasp the alternating skirmish of light and shadow. And perhaps he would be able to understand why the earth is an opaque mirror that swabs with ink what it reflects, and water a wall that makes diaphanous the shadows imprinted on it, whereas images in the air never find a surface from which to rebound, and so penetrate it, fleeing to the farthest limits of the aether, only to return sometimes in the form of mirages and other ostents.

But was possession of the Island not possession of Lilia? And then what? Roberto's logic was not that of those recreant, caitiff philosophers, intruders into the atrium of the lyceum, who affirm always that a thing, if it is seen in one form, cannot also be of the opposite form. By an error of the errant imagination characteristic of lovers, Roberto already knew that the possession of Lilia would be, at once, the source of every revelation. To discover the laws of the universe through a spyglass seemed to him only the longest way to arrive at a truth that would be revealed to him in the deafening light of pleasure, if it were granted him to lay his head on the lap of his beloved, in a Garden in which every shrub was the Tree of Good.

But since—as even we should know—to desire something that is distant summons the spirit of someone who will steal it from us, Roberto had to fear that into the delights of that Eden a serpent had also crept. He was then gripped by the idea that on the Island the quicker one, the usurper, Ferrante, was awaiting him.

CHAPTER 28

Of the Origin of Novels

LOVERS LOVE THEIR misfortunes more than their blessings. Roberto could think of himself only as separated forever from the one he loved, but the more he felt separated from her, the more he was obsessed by the thought that some other man might not be.

We have seen how, accused by Mazarin of having been somewhere he was not, Roberto got it into his head that Ferrante was present in Paris and had on some occasions taken his place. If this was true, then while Roberto was arrested by the Cardinal and conducted on board the *Amaryllis*, Ferrante remained in Paris, and for everyone (including Her!) he was Roberto. Now Roberto had only to think of Her at the side of Ferrante, and lo, his marine Purgatory was transformed into a Hell.

He knew that jealousy is generated outside of any reference to what is, is not, or perhaps will never be; that it is a transport that from an imagined sickness derives real pain; that the jealous man is like a hypochondriac who sickens for fear of being sick. Beware, then, of allowing yourself to be caught by this tormenting gossip that obliges you to picture Her with a Him,

and remember: Nothing more than solitude encourages suspicion, nothing more than daydreaming transforms suspicion
into certainty. However, he added, as I am unable to avoid
loving, I cannot avoid jealousy, and unable to avoid jealousy,
I cannot avoid daydreaming.

In fact jealousy, among all fears, is the least generous: if
you fear death, you can take comfort in the thought that you
may nevertheless enjoy a long life or that in the course of a
voyage you may find the fountain of eternal youth; or if you
are penniless, you may take comfort in the thought of discovering a treasure. For every feared thing there is an opposing
hope that encourages us. Not so when you love in the absence
of the beloved. Absence is to love as wind to fire: it extinguishes
the little flame, it fans the big.

If jealousy is born from intense love, he who does not feel
jealousy of the beloved is not a lover, or he loves lightheart-
edly, for we know of lovers who, fearing their love will fade,
nourish it by finding reasons for jealousy at all costs.

The jealous man (who still wants his beloved to be chaste
and faithful) can only think of her as worthy of jealousy, and
therefore capable of betrayal, and thus he rekindles in present
suffering the pleasure of absent love. Also because your imagining yourself in possession of the distant beloved—well aware
it is not true—cannot render the thought of her, her warmth,
her blushes, her scent, as vivid as the thought of those same
gifts being enjoyed by an Other. Of your absence you are sure,
but of the presence of the enemy you are if not sure then at
least unsure. The amorous contact imagined by the jealous
man is the only way he can picture with verisimilitude the
beloved's connubiality, which, if doubtful, is at least possible,
whereas his own is impossible.

Hence the jealous man is not able, nor does he have the
will, to imagine the opposite of what he fears, indeed he cannot feel joy except in the magnification of his own sorrow,

and by suffering through the magnified enjoyment from which he knows he is banned. The pleasures of love are pains that become desirable, where sweetness and torment blend, and so love is voluntary insanity, infernal paradise, and celestial hell —in short, harmony of opposite yearnings, sorrowful laughter, soft diamond.

Thus Roberto, suffering but remembering that infinity of worlds which he had discussed in previous days, had an idea or, rather, an Idea, a great and anamorphic stroke of genius.

He thought, namely, that he might construct a story, of which he was surely not the protagonist, inasmuch as it would not take place in this world but in a Land of Romances, and this story's events would unfold parallel to those of the world in which he was, the two sets of adventures never meeting and overlapping.

What would Roberto gain by this? Much. By inventing the story of another world, which existed only in his mind, he would become that world's master, able to ensure that the things that happened there would not exceed his capacity of endurance. On the other hand, as reader of the story whose author he was, he could share in the heartbreak of its characters: for does it not happen that readers of romances may without jealousy love Thisbe, using Pyramus as their vicar, and suffer for Astrée through Celadon?

To love in the Land of Romances does not mean experiencing any jealousy at all: there, that which is not ours is still somehow ours, and that which in this world was ours and was stolen from us, there does not exist—even if what does exist there resembles what in existence we lost or did not lose.

So, then, Roberto would write (or conceive) the story of Ferrante and of his loves with Lilia, and only by constructing that fictional world would Roberto forget the gnawing of his jealousy in the real world.

Further, he reasoned, to understand what happened to me

and how I fell into the trap set by Mazarin, I must reconstruct the History of those events, finding the causes, the secret motives. But is there anything more uncertain than the Histories we read, wherein if two authors tell of the same battle, such are the incongruities revealed that we are inclined to think they write of two different conflicts? On the other hand, is there anything more certain than a work of fiction, where at the end every Enigma finds its explanation according to the laws of the Realistic? The Romance perhaps tells of things that did not really happen, but they could very well have happened. To explain my misadventures in the form of a Novel means assuring myself that in all the muddle there exists at least one way of untangling the knot, and therefore I am not the victim of a nightmare. An Idea insidiously antithetical to the first, for in this way the invented story will be superimposed on the true story.

And finally, Roberto continued to argue, mine is the tale of love for a woman: now, only stories, and surely not History, deal with questions of Love, and only stories (never History) are concerned with explaining the thoughts and feelings of those daughters of Eve who from the days of the Earthly Paradise to the Inferno of the Courts of our time have always so influenced the events of our species.

All reasonable arguments when considered individually, but not when taken together. In fact, there is a difference between a man who writes a story and one who suffers jealousy. A jealous man enjoys picturing what he wishes would not happen—but at the same time he refuses to believe that it can happen—whereas a storyteller resorts to every artifice to see not only that the reader enjoys imagining what has not happened but also that at a certain point he forgets that he is reading and believes it really did happen. It is a source of the most intense suffering for a jealous man to read a story written

by another, because whatever is said seems to refer to his per
sonal story. So imagine a jealous man who pretends to invent
the story that is his own. Is it not said of the jealous that they
give body to shadows? So, however shadowy the creatures of
a romance may be, as the Romance is a full brother to History,
those shadows appear too corporeal to the jealous man, and
even more so if they are his own.

On the other hand, for all their virtues, romances have
their defects, which Roberto should have known. As medicine
teaches also about poisons, metaphysics disturbs with inoppor-
tune subtleties the dogmata of religion, ethics recommends
magnificence (which is not of help to everyone), astrology
fosters superstition, optics deceives, music rouses lust, geometry encourages unjust dominion, and mathematics avarice—
so the Art of the Romance, though warning us that it is pro-
viding fictions, opens a door into the Palace of Absurdity, and
when we have lightly stepped inside, slams it shut behind us.

But it is not in our power to keep Roberto from taking
this step, since we know for sure that he took it.

CHAPTER 29

The Soul of Ferrante

AT WHAT POINT should he take up the story of Ferrante? Roberto considered it best to begin from that day when Ferrante, having betrayed the French, on whose side he was pretending to fight at Casale, passing himself off as Captain Gambero, sought refuge in the Spanish camp.

Perhaps he was received with enthusiasm there by some great gentleman who had promised to take him, at the war's end, to Madrid. And in that city Ferrante's rise began, at the outer edge of the Spanish court, where he learned that the virtue of sovereigns is their caprice, and Power is an insatiable monster, to be served with slavish devotion in order to snatch every crumb falling from that table. Ferrante was able to make a slow and rough ascent—first as henchman, assassin, and confidant, then as a bogus gentleman.

He could not help but be of lively intelligence, even when constrained to villainy, and in that environment he immediately learned how to behave. He therefore heard (or guessed) those principles of courtesan education in which Señor de Salazar had tried to catechize Roberto.

Ferrante cultivated his own mediocrity (the baseness of his

bastard origins), not fearing to be eminent in mediocre things, so as to avoid one day being mediocre in eminent things.

He understood that when you cannot wear the skin of the lion, you wear that of the fox, for after the Flood more foxes were saved than lions. Every creature has its own wisdom, and from the fox he learned that playing openly achieves neither the useful nor the pleasurable.

If he was invited to spread a slander among the domestics so that gradually it would reach the ears of their master, and he enjoyed the favors of a chambermaid, he would promptly say that he would plant the lie at the tavern with the coachman; or, if the coachman was his companion in debauchery at the tavern, he would affirm with a smile of complicity that he knew how to win the ear of a certain chambermaid. Ignorant of how he acted or how he would act, his master lost a point to him, for Ferrante knew that the man who does not show his cards leaves his adversary in suspense, and that such mystery inspires respect in others.

In eliminating his enemies, who at the beginning were pages and grooms, then gentlemen who believed him their peer, he understood that he had to aim obliquely, never directly: wisdom fights with carefully studied subterfuges and never acts in the predictable fashion. If he hinted at a movement, it was only to deceive; if he dextrously sketched a gesture in the air, he then behaved in a manner that contradicted the displayed intention. He never attacked when his adversary was at the peak of his strength (he made a show, instead, of friendship and respect for him), but only at the moment when the man appeared helpless. Ferrante then led him to the precipice with the air of one rushing to his aid.

He lied often but never pointlessly. He knew that to be believed he had to make everyone see that sometimes he told the truth to his own disadvantage, and kept silent when the truth might win him praise. On the other hand, he tried to gain the reputation of a man sincere with his inferiors, so that their words would reach the ears of the powerful. He became convinced that to simulate with one's equals is a fault, but not to simulate with one's superiors is foolhardiness.

Still he did not act too frankly, and in any case not always frankly, fearing that others would become aware of his patterns and one day anticipate him. Nor did he exaggerate in his duplicity, lest it be discovered a second time.

To become wise he trained himself to tolerate the foolish, and he surrounded himself with them. He was not so imprudent as to attribute to them all his errors, but when the stakes were high, he made sure that beside him there was always a straw man (impelled by vain ambition to be seen always in front, while Ferrante remained in the background), whom not Ferrante but others would then hold responsible for any misdeed. In short, he appeared to do everything that could redound to his credit, but arranged for another hand to do whatever might earn him a grudge.

In displaying his own virtues (which we would better call diabolical talents) he knew that a half displayed and a half barely glimpsed are worth more than a whole openly asserted. At times he made ostentation consist of mute eloquence, in a heedless show of his own excellences, and he had the ability never to reveal all of himself at once.

As his position gradually rose and he had to measure himself against those of superior station, he became very able in mimicking their gestures and their language, but he did so only before persons of inferior condition whom he had to charm for some illicit end; with his betters he took care to make his ignorance evident, while seeming to admire in them what he already knew.

He carried out every unsavory mission that his patrons

entrusted to him, but only if the evil he did was not of such dimensions as to inspire their revulsion; if they asked of him crimes too great, he refused, first to prevent their thinking he might one day be capable of doing as much to them, and secondly (if the sin cried to Heaven for vengeance) so as not to become the undesired witness of their remorse.

In public he openly manifested piety, but valued only betrayed loyalty, tarnished virtue, self-love, ingratitude, contempt of the sacred; he cursed God in his heart and believed the world to be the offspring of chance, while he trusted in a fate prepared to shift its own course to favor those who knew how to bend it to their own account.

To cheer his rare moments of repose, he had commerce only with married prostitutes, incontinent widows, shameless maids. But this always in great moderation, as in his machinations, Ferrante sometimes forewent an immediate reward if he felt attracted by another machination, for his villainy never gave him respite.

He lived, in short, day by day, like a murderer in motionless ambush behind an arras, where daggers' blades do not glint. He knew that the first rule of success was to await opportunity, but he suffered because opportunity seemed still far off.

This grim, stubborn ambition deprived him of all inner peace. As he believed Roberto had usurped the place which was his by right, no success could appease him, and the only form that happiness and well-being could assume in the eyes of his spirit was his brother's misfortune, and the day when he could be its author. Hazy, embattled giants swarmed in his head, for him there was no sea or land or sky that could afford him relief and calm. Everything that had offended him, everything he desired was a source of torment.

He never laughed if not in the tavern to urge drink on

some unwitting accomplice. But in the secret of his room he examined himself every day in the glass, to see if the way he moved revealed his impatience, if his eye looked too insolent, if his head was inclined more than was proper, if it did not betray hesitation, or if the wrinkles, too deep on his brow, did not make him seem envenomed.

When he interrupted these exercises and, weary, laid aside his masks late in the night, he saw himself as he really was— ah, and then Roberto could not refrain from murmuring some verses he had read a few years earlier:

> In those eyes where sadness dwells and death
> Flaming light flares murky and bold scarlet,
> Sidelong glances and averted eyes are comets;
> The lashes, lamps, wrathful, proud and desperate
> While thunder are the moans; and lightning, breath.

Inasmuch as no one is perfect, not even in evil, and Ferrante was not totally able to control the excess of his own villainy, he could not avoid making a misstep. Charged by his master to organize the abduction of a chaste maiden of high degree who was betrothed to a noble gentleman, Ferrante began by writing her love letters signed with the name of his employer. Then, when she drew back, he penetrated to her bedchamber, and made her the prey of a violent seduction and ravishment. In a single blow he had deceived her, her betrothed, and the man who had ordered the abduction.

After the crime was reported, Ferrante's master was found guilty, then killed in a duel with the betrothed; but by this time Ferrante was on his way to France.

In a moment of good humor, Roberto caused Ferrante to attempt, on a January night, the crossing of the Pyrenees astride a stolen mule, which must have taken the vows of some order of reformist tertiaries, considering the monkish qualities it evinced, being so wise, sober, abstinent, and of upright life, that to emphasize the mortification of the flesh, clearly visible in the boniness of its ribs, it knelt down at every step and kissed the earth.

The steep mountainsides seemed laden with clotted milk, or plastered over with whitewash. The few trees not completely buried under the snow looked so white that they seemed to have stripped off their bark and were shaking more because of the cold than because of the wind. The sun was locked inside its palace and dared not even peer out on the balcony. And if it did show its face for an instant, it hid its nose in a cowl of clouds.

The few wayfarers encountered on that path seemed so many Monteoliveto friars in procession singing Lavabis me et super nivem dealbabor. . . . And Ferrante, seeing himself so white, felt transformed into one dusted by the Divine Baker with the flour of virtue.

One night, tufts of cotton fell from Heaven, so thick and big that, as someone else once became a pillar of salt, Ferrante suspected he had become a pillar of snow. The owls, bats, grasshoppers, and moths made arabesques around him as if they wanted to catch him. In the end he struck his head against the feet of a hanged man who, swaying from a tree, made of himself a grisaille grotesque.

But Ferrante—though a Romance must be decked out with pleasant descriptions—could not be a figure in a comedy. He had to head for his goal, imagining to his own measure the Paris he was approaching.

Whence he yearned: "O Paris, boundless gulf in which whales shrink to dolphins, land of sirens, emporium of vanities, garden of satisfactions, maze of intrigues, Nile of courtiers, and ocean of deception!"

Here, wishing to invent a passage that no author of novels had yet conceived, to portray the feelings of that greedy youth preparing to conquer the city that was a compendium of Europe's civility, Asia's profusion, Africa's extravagance, and America's riches, where novelty had its realm, deceit its palace, luxury its center, courage its arena, beauty its hemicycle, fashion its cradle, and virtue its grave, Roberto put into Ferrante's mouth an arrogant cry: "Paris, à nous deux!"

From Gascony to Poitou, beyond the Ile de France, Ferrante had occasion to carry out a few bold strokes that allowed him to transfer a modest capital from the pockets of some gulls into his own, and thus he arrived at the capital in the garb of a young gentleman, reserved and pleasant, Signor del Pozzo. Since no news had reached there of his knaveries in Madrid, he presented himself to some Spaniards close to the Queen, who immediately appreciated his ability to render discreet services for a sovereign who, while faithful to her husband and apparently respectful of the Cardinal, maintained relations with the enemy court.

His reputation as a reliable executant reached the ears of Richelieu, who, a profound scholar of the human spirit, decided that a man without scruples who served the Queen and was notoriously short of money, if offered a richer reward, would serve him, and he began employing Ferrante, so secretly that not even the Cardinal's intimates were aware of that young agent's existence.

Apart from his long practice in Madrid, Ferrante had the rare gift of learning languages easily and imitating accents. It was not his habit to boast of his talents, but one day when Richelieu received, in his presence, an English spy, Ferrante demonstrated that he could converse with the traitor. Whereupon Richelieu, in one of the most difficult moments in the relations between France and England, sent the youth to London, where he was to pretend he was a Maltese merchant while gathering information about the movement of ships in the ports

Now Ferrante had made a part of his dream come true: he was a spy, no longer in the pay of just any gentleman but of a Biblical Leviathan whose arms extended everywhere.

Espionage (Roberto was shocked and terrified), the most contagious plague of courts, harpy that swoops down on the royal table with rouged face and hooked claws, flying on batwings and listening with ears endowed with great tympana, an owl that sees only in the dark, a viper among roses, cockroach on flowers converting into venom the juice it sips at its sweetest, spider of antechambers weaving the strands of its subtle talk to catch every passing fly, parrot with curved beak reporting everything it hears, transforming truth into falsehood and falsehood into truth, chameleon that receives every color and dresses in all save the one that is its true garb. All qualities of which anyone would be ashamed, save the one who by divine (or infernal) decree is born to the service of evil.

But Ferrante was not content simply to be a spy and have in his power those whose thoughts he reported, he wanted to be, as they said at that time, a double spy, who like the monster of legend could walk in two opposing directions. If the arena where the Powers contend can be a maze of intrigues, who in that maze is the Minotaur who represents the union of both combatant natures? The double spy. If the field on which the battle between Courts is played out can be called an Inferno where in the bed of Ingratitude flows with rapid flood the Phlegethon of oblivion, and where the murky water of Passion boils, who is the three-throated Cerberus who barks after discovering and sniffing those who enter there to be torn apart? The double spy . . .

Once arrived in England, while spying for Richelieu, Ferrante decided to enrich himself by also doing the English some service. Wresting information from hirelings and petty functionaries over great mugs of beer in rooms smoky with mutton grease, he introduced himself into ecclesiastical circles as a Spanish priest determined to abandon the Roman Church, whose foul deeds he could bear no longer.

Music to the ears of the antipapists eager for any opportunity to document the turpitude of the Catholic clergy. And there was no need even for Ferrante to confess what he did not know. The English already had in their hands the anonymous confession, presumed or real, of another priest. Ferrante then confirmed that document, signing it with the name of a coadjutor to the bishop of Madrid, who had once treated him with scorn, for which he swore vengeance.

When he received from the English the assignment to return to Spain to gather further declarations from priests prepared to slander the Holy See, Ferrante encountered in a tavern of the port a Genoese traveler. Gaining his confidence, he soon discovered that the man was actually one Mahmut, a renegade who in the East had embraced the faith of the Mohammedans, but, disguised as a Portuguese merchant, was collecting information about the English navy, while other spies in the hire of the Sublime Porte were doing the same in France.

Ferrante avowed that he had worked for Turkish agents in Italy and had embraced the same religion, assuming the name of Dgennet Oglou. He immediately sold his new acquaintance his news of movements in the English ports, and was given a sum to take a message to Mahmut's brothers in France. The English ecclesiastics believed he had already set out for Spain, but he was unwilling to reject a chance to earn more from his stay in England. So, getting in touch with men of the Admiralty, he described himself as a Venetian, Messer Scampi (a name he invented, recalling Captain Gambero), who had performed secret duties for the Council of that Republic, with particular reference to the plans of the French merchant marine. Now, banished as a consequence of a duel, he had to seek refuge in a friendly country. To show his good faith, he was able to inform his new masters that France had obtained information on the English ports through Mahmut, a Turkish spy now living in London disguised as a Portuguese.

In the possession of Mahmut, promptly arrested, notes on the English ports were duly discovered, and thus Ferrante or, rather, Scampi, was judged reliable. Promised a situation in England and blessed with a good initial sum, he was sent to France to join other English agents there.

On arriving in Paris, he immediately passed on to Richelieu some of the information the English had taken from Mahmut. Then he found the friends whose addresses the Genoese renegade had given him, and he presented himself as Charles de la Bresche, a former monk who had gone over to the service of the crescent and had just arranged in London a plot to cast discredit on the whole breed of Christians. Those agents gave him credence, because they had already learned of a pamphlet in which the Anglican Church had published the malefactions of a Spanish priest—and in Madrid, when the news reached there, they arrested the prelate to whom Ferrante had attributed his treason, and now the man was awaiting death in the dungeons of the Inquisition.

Ferrante persuaded the Turkish agents to confide in him the information they had gathered about France, and he sent it straightaway to the English Admiralty, receiving further payment. Then he returned to Richelieu and revealed to him the existence in Paris of a Turkish plot. Once again Richelieu admired Ferrante's skill and loyalty. And he invited him to undertake a task still more arduous.

For some time the Cardinal had been concerned about activities in the salon of the marquise de Rambouillet, and he had been seized by the suspicion that among those free spirits there was murmuring against him. He first made the mistake of sending to La Rambouillet a faithful courtier of his, who foolishly made enquiries about possible sedition. Arthénice replied that her guests were so familiar with her regard for His Eminence that even if they had misgivings about him, they would never dare speak anything but the greatest good of him in her presence.

Richelieu now planned to have a foreigner appear in Paris, one who could gain admittance to those consistories. Now Roberto had no desire to invent all the cabals by which Ferrante achieved an introduction to that salon, but he found it proper to have him arrive there forearmed with some recommendation, and in disguise: a wig and a white beard, a face aged with pomades and tinctures, a black patch over the left eye—and voilà, the Abbé de Morfi.

Roberto could not think that Ferrante, in every way similar to him, had been at his side on those now distant evenings, but he remembered seeing an elderly abbé with a black patch on his eye, and he decided that the old man must have been Ferrante.

So in that world—and after ten or more years—he had found Roberto again! It is impossible to express the joyous rancor with which the deceiver rediscovered his hated brother. With a face that would have seemed transfigured and overwhelmed by malevolence had it not been hidden beneath his

disguise, Ferrante told himself that at last he had the opportunity to annihilate Roberto, and to take possession of his
name and his wealth.

First, he spied on him, for weeks and weeks in the course
of those evenings, studying that face to catch in it the trace
of every thought. Accustomed as he was to concealing, he was
also very skilled at discovering. For that matter, love cannot
be hidden: like any fire, it is revealed by smoke. Following
Roberto's glances, Ferrante immediately understood that he
loved the Lady. He then told himself that his first step would
be to take from Roberto what he held most dear.

Ferrante noticed that Roberto, after attracting the attention of the Lady with his talk, lacked the courage to approach
her. His brother's shyness served the spy's purposes: the Lady
could easily interpret it as indifference, and to scorn affection
is the most effective way to extinguish it. Roberto was clearing
the path for Ferrante. Ferrante allowed the Lady to suffer in
uncertain expectation, then—calculating the right moment—
he set himself to flatter her.

But could Roberto allow Ferrante a love equal to his own?
Certainly not. Ferrante considered woman the portrait of inconstancy, minister of fraud, fickle in speech, belated in action,
and quick in caprice. Educated by would-be ascetics who never
ceased reminding him that El hombre es el fuego, la mujer la
estopa, viene el diablo y sopla, he was accustomed to considering every daughter of Eve an imperfect animal, an error of
Nature, a torture for the eyes if ugly, a suffering of the heart
if beautiful, tyrant of any who loved her, enemy of any who
scorned her, disordered in her desires, implacable in her dis-
likes, capable of enchanting with the mouth and enchaining
with the eyes.

But it was this very disdain that impelled him to entrap;

from his lips came words of adulation, but in his heart he was celebrating the degradation of his victim.

Ferrante was thus preparing to lay his hands on that body that Roberto had not dared graze with his thoughts. Was he, despiser of everything that for Roberto was object of devotion, ready—now—to steal Lilia and make her the insipid ingénue of his comedy? What torture. And what painful duty, to follow the insane logic of Romances, which imposes participation in the most odious affects, for you must conceive as the children of your own imagination the most odious of protagonists.

But there was nothing to be done. Ferrante would have Lilia—otherwise why create a fiction, if not to die of it?

What happened and how, Roberto could not picture (nor was he ever tempted to try). Perhaps Ferrante late one night stole into Lilia's chamber, clinging to some ivy (whose tenacious embrace is a nocturnal invitation to every loving heart) that climbed up to her window.

There is Lilia, showing signs of outraged virtue, to such a degree that anyone would be convinced of her indignation, anyone except a man like Ferrante, ready to believe the readiness of all human beings to betray. And here is Ferrante, sinking to his knees before her and speaking. What does he say? He says, in a false voice, everything that Roberto would not only have liked to say to her but has said, without her knowing that he said it.

How can the villain have managed—Roberto asked himself—to learn the tenor of the letters I sent her? And further, of the letters Saint-Savin dictated to me at Casale, which I later destroyed. And even the letters I am writing now, on this ship. And yet there is no doubt, Ferrante is declaiming in sincere tones sentences Roberto knew very well:

"My Lady, in the wondrous architecture of the Universe it has been written since the first day of Creation that I would encounter you and love you. . . . Forgive the raving of a desperate man, or, better, pay no heed to it; it was never said that sovereigns had to justify the death of their slaves. . . . Have you not made of my eyes two alembics, the better to distill my life and convert it into limpid water? I beseech you, do not turn your lovely head away: bereft of your gaze, I am blind, for you do not see me, deprived of your word, I am mute, for you do not speak to me, and I shall be without memory if you do not remember me. . . . Oh, let love at least make of me an insensible shard, a mandrake, a fountain of stone that weeps away every anguish!"

The Lady now surely trembled, in her eyes burned all the love she had formerly concealed, burned with the strength of a prisoner whose bars of Reserve someone has broken, offering the silken ladder of Opportunity. Ferrante had only to press on, and he did not confine himself to saying what Roberto had written; he knew other words that he now poured into the ears of the bewitched Lady, bewitching also Roberto, who could not recall having written them.

"O my pale sun, at your sweet pallor the vermilion dawn loses all its fire! O sweet eyes, of you I ask only to be ill. And in vain do I flee through fields or woods to forget you. No forest covers the earth, no tree rises in a forest, no bough grows on a tree, no frond sprouts from a bough, no flower laughs in the frond, no fruit is born from the flower, in which I do not see your smile. . . ."

And, at her first blush: "Oh, Lilia, if you knew! . . . I have loved you without knowing your face or your name. I sought you, and I did not know where you were. But one day you appeared to me like an angel. . . . Oh, I know, you are wondering why this love of mine does not remain pure in silence, chaste in distance. . . . But I am dying, O my heart, now you see my soul is already escaping me, do not allow it to dissolve in the air, grant that it may dwell on your lips!"

Ferrante's accents were so sincere that Roberto himself

now wanted her to fall into that sweet lime. Only thus could he have the certainty that she loved him, Roberto.

So Lilia bent to kiss him, then did not dare. Willing and unwilling, three times she held her lips to the desired breath, three times she drew back, then cried: "Oh yes, yes, if you do not ensnare me, I shall never be free, I will not be chaste if you do not violate me!"

And, taking his hand, and kissing it, she raised it to her bosom; then she drew him to her, tenderly stealing the breath from his lips. Ferrante leaned over that urn of happiness (to which Roberto had entrusted the ashes of his heart), and the two bodies melted into a single soul, the two souls into a single body. Roberto no longer knew who was in those arms, since she believed she was in his, and he, in yielding her mouth to Ferrante, tried to withdraw his own, so as not to concede that kiss to the Other.

Thus, while Ferrante kissed, and she kissed in return, the kiss now dissolved into nothing, and Roberto was left only with the knowledge of having been robbed of everything. But he could not avoid thinking of what he refused to imagine: for he knew that it is in the nature of love to exceed.

At that outraged excess, forgetting that she was giving to Ferrante, believing him Roberto, the proof that Roberto had so desired, he hated Lilia, and running about the ship, he howled: "Oh, wretch! I would offend all your sex if I called you woman! What you have done is more proper to a fury than to a female, and even the title of beast would be too great an honor for such an animal of Hell! You are worse than the asp that poisoned Cleopatra, worse than the horned viper whose deceits delight the birds then sacrificed to its hunger, worse than the amphisbaena that, on anyone it grasps, scatters such venom that in an instant he dies, worse than the dread leps that, armed with four venomous teeth, corrupts the flesh it bites, worse than the jacule that darts from trees and strangles its victim, worse than the colubra that vomits its poison into fountains, worse than the basilisk that kills with his gaze! Infernal termagant, who knows neither Heaven nor earth, neither sex nor faith, monster begot of a stone, an alp, an oak!"

Then he stopped, realized again that she had yielded to Ferrante believing him Roberto, and that therefore she was not to be damned but forgiven for that subterfuge. "Careful, my beloved, he presents himself to you with my face, knowing that you could love no one who was not I! What am I to do now, except hate myself to be able to hate him? Can I allow you to be betrayed, enjoying his embrace believing it mine? I have already accepted life in this prison to pass all my days and my nights devoted to the thought of you; can I now permit you to believe you are bewitching me while in fact succumbing to his spell? Oh, Love, Love, Love, have you not punished me enough already, is this not a death undying?"

CHAPTER 30

Anatomy of Erotic Melancholy

FOR TWO DAYS Roberto again fled the light of day. In his sleep he saw only the dead. His mouth and gums were irritated. From his viscera the pain spread to his chest, then to his back, and he vomited acid substances, though he had taken no food. The black bile, gnawing and undermining his whole body, fermented and erupted in bubbles such as those water expels when subjected to intense heat.

He had surely fallen victim (and it is inconceivable that he realized this only then) to what is generally called Erotic Melancholy. Had he not been led to explain, that evening at Arthénice's, how the image of the beloved awakes love, insinuating itself as simulacrum through the meatus of the eyes, those doorkeepers and spies of the soul? But afterwards the amorous impression allows itself to glide slowly through the veins until it reaches the liver, stimulating concupiscence, which moves the whole body to sedition, leads straight to the conquest of the citadel of the heart, whence it attacks the more noble powers of the brain and enslaves them.

Which is to say that its victims virtually lose their reason, the senses stray, the intellect is beclouded, the imagination is depraved, and the poor lover grows thin, wan, his eyes become hollow, he sighs, and is steeped in jealousy.

How is it to be cured? Roberto thought he knew the remedy above all remedies, which, however, was denied him: to possess the beloved person. He did not know that this is not enough, for melancholics do not become such through love; rather, they fall in love to express their melancholy—preferring desolate places for spiritual converse with the absent beloved, thinking only of how to arrive in her presence; although, arriving there, they become all the more afflicted, and would like still to attain some other goal.

Roberto tried to recall what he had heard from men of science who had studied Erotic Melancholy. Apparently it was caused by idleness, by sleeping supine, and by an excessive retention of seed. For too many days he had lived in enforced idleness, but as far as retention of seed was concerned, he shunned any enquiry into its causes or any thought of remedy.

He had heard talk about hunting parties as a stimulus of oblivion, and decided he would intensify his natatory endeavors, and would not sleep on his back; but among the substances that excite the senses is salt, and in swimming one swallows a fair amount of salt. . . . Further, he remembered having heard that the Africans, exposed to the sun, were more addicted to vice than the Hyperboreans.

Was it perhaps food that had unleashed his saturnalian propensities? Doctors forbade game, goose liver, pistachios, truffles, and ginger, but they did not say which fish were not advisable. They warned against overly comfortable clothing, such as sable and velvet, and also against music, amber, nutmeg, and Cyprus Powder. But what could he know of the unknown power of the hundred perfumes released from the greenhouse below, or of those borne by the winds from the Island?

He could have warded off many of these unfortunate influences with camphor, borage, wood sorrel; with enemas, with a vomitory of salt of vitriol dissolved in broth, and finally with leeching of the median vein of the arm or that of the brow; and then by eating only chicory, endive, lettuce, and melons, grapes, cherries, plums, and pears and, above all, fresh mint. . . . But none of these were at hand on the *Daphne*.

He resumed moving among the waves, trying not to swallow too much salt, and resting as seldom as possible.

Certainly he did not cease thinking about the story he had summoned up, but his irritation with Ferrante was now translated into fits of arrogance, and he measured himself against the sea as if, subjecting it to his will, he were making his enemy his subject.

After a few days, one afternoon he remarked for the first time the amber color of the hair on his chest and—as he notes with various rhetorical contortions—his groin. He realized that his whole body had become tanned, also strengthened, for on his arms he saw a rippling of muscles he had never noticed before. He considered himself a Hercules at this point, and he lost all sense of prudence. The next day he descended into the water without the rope.

He would abandon the ladder, moving along the hull to the right as far as the rudder, then he would round the stern, and swim back along the other side, passing beneath the bowsprit. And he put his arms and legs to work.

The sea was not calm, and wavelets flung him against the ship's side, forcing him to redouble his efforts, whether to stay close to the ship or to move away from it. He was breathing heavily, but he advanced without fear. Until he reached his halfway point, the stern.

He realized that he had expended all his strength. He was now too weak to swim the length of the ship, but he could not turn back either. He tried clinging to the rudder, which offered him only a dubious hold, covered as it was with mucilage, while it slowly creaked under the alternating slaps of the waves.

Above his head he could see the gallery, imagining beyond its windows the safe haven of his quarters. He told himself that if by misadventure the ladder at the prow had come loose, he might spend hours and hours before his death yearning for that deck he had so often wished to leave.

The sun was covered by a patch of clouds, and he was already growing numb. He stretched his head back, as if to sleep. After a moment he opened his eyes, turned, and realized that what he had feared was happening: the waves were pulling him away from the ship.

He made an effort and swam back to the side, touching it as if to derive strength. Above his head he glimpsed a cannon that protruded from a gun-port. If he had his rope, he thought, he could make a noose, throw it up, and catch by the throat that mouth of fire, then hoist himself, holding the rope with his arms and pressing his feet against the hull. . . . But the rope was absent, and worse still, he lacked the spirit and the strength to scale such a height. . . . It made no sense to die like this, beside his refuge.

He came to a decision. Now, doubling the stern, whether he turned back along the right side or continued along the left, the distance between him and the ladder was the same. As if casting lots, he resolved to swim to the left, taking care that the current did not separate him from the *Daphne*.

He swam, clenching his teeth, his muscles strained, not daring to let himself relax, fiercely determined to survive, even—he said—if he died in the attempt.

With a jubilant cry he reached the bowsprit, clung to the prow, then came to the Jacob's ladder—praise Jacob, and may all the holy patriarchs of the Sacred Scriptures be blessed by the Lord God of Hosts.

His strength was gone. He remained clinging to the ladder for perhaps half an hour. But in the end he managed to pull himself up to the deck, where he tried to add up the sum of his experience.

First, he could swim, enough to go from one end of the ship to the other and back; second, an exploit of this kind took him to the extreme limit of his physical possibilities; third, since the distance between ship and shore, even at low tide, was many, many times greater than the entire perimeter of the *Daphne*, he could not hope to swim long enough to be able finally to grasp something solid; fourth, the low tide did indeed bring terra firma closer, but with its reflux it made his progress more difficult; fifth, if by chance he reached the halfway point and lacked the strength to go forward, he would not be able to return either.

Therefore he had to continue with the rope, and for a much longer time. He would go east as far as his strength allowed, and then he would tow himself back. Only exercising like this, day after day, would he be able to venture farther on his own.

He chose a calm afternoon, when the sun was behind him. He fitted himself out with a very long rope, one end fixed tightly to the mainmast; it lay on the deck in many coils, ready to play out gradually. He swam calmly, not tiring himself too much, resting often. He looked at the beach and the two promontories. Only now, from below, did he realize how far he was from that ideal line which extended from one cape to the other, from south to north, beyond which he would enter the day before.

Having failed to understand Father Caspar properly, he was convinced that the coral barrier began only at the point where little white waves marked the first reefs. Whereas obviously the coral began earlier. Otherwise the *Daphne* would have anchored closer to land.

So his bare legs scraped against something below the surface. Almost at the same time his eye caught an underwater movement of colored forms, and he felt an unbearable stinging at his thigh and shin. It was as if he had been bitten or clawed. To get away from that reef he pushed with a heel, wounding a foot also in this act.

He seized the rope, tugging on it so hard that when he was back on board, he saw his hands were excoriated; but he was more concerned about the condition of his leg and foot. There were clusters of painful pustules. He bathed them with fresh water, which soothed the stinging a bit. But towards evening, and through the night, the burning was accompanied by an acute itching, and in his sleep he probably scratched himself, so the next morning the pustules oozed blood and white matter.

He then had recourse to Father Caspar's preparations (Spiritus, Olea, Flores) which calmed the infection to some degree, but for a whole day he still felt the instinctive impulse to claw at those buboes.

Once again he calculated the sum of his experience, and came to four conclusions: the reef was closer than the reflux suggested, which encouraged him to try the venture again; some creatures living on it, crabs, fish, perhaps the corals, or some sharp stones, had the power to infect him with some kind of pestilence; if he wanted to return to those stones, he had to be shod and clothed, which would make his movements more awkward. In any case, since he could not shield his whole body, he had to be able to see underwater.

This last conclusion made him recall that Persona Vitrea or mask for seeing underwater that Father Caspar had shown him. He tried fastening it at his nape, and discovered that it enclosed his face, allowing him to look out as if through a window. He tried breathing, and realized that a bit of air came in. If air entered, then water would enter as well. So while using it, he would have to hold his breath—the more air remained in it, the less water would enter—and he would return to the surface as soon as the mask had filled.

It would not be an easy operation, and Roberto spent three days testing all its phases in the water, but close to the *Daphne*. Near the sailors' paillasses he found a pair of canvas hose that protected his feet without weighting him too much, and a pair of trousers to be tied at the calf. It took him half a day to relearn those movements that had now become so easy for him when he was naked.

Then he swam with the mask. In deep water he could not see much, though he did glimpse a school of gilded fish passing many ells below him, as if they were navigating in a tub.

Three days, we said. In the course of those days Roberto first learned to look below him while holding his breath, then to move as he looked, then to remove the mask while he was in the water. In this enterprise, instinctively, he also learned a new position, which consisted of filling and swelling his chest, kicking as if he were walking in haste, while he thrust his chin upwards. But it was more difficult, maintaining the same equilibrium, to put the mask back on and fasten it at his nape. He promptly reminded himself, further, that once at the reef, if he assumed that vertical position, he would strike the rocks; if on the other hand he kept his face out of the water, he would not see what he was kicking. Hence he considered it would be better not to fasten the mask but instead press it with both hands and hold it over his face. Which, however, obliged him to proceed moving only his legs, while keeping them outstretched horizontally to avoid striking anything below: an action he had never tried, and which required long practice before he could execute it confidently.

In the course of these experiments he transformed every fit of rage into a new chapter of his Romance of Ferrante.

And he caused his story to take a more spiteful turn, as Ferrante was duly punished.

CHAPTER 31

A Breviary for Politicals

IN ANY CASE he could not delay resuming his story. It is true
that Poets, after having spoken of a memorable event, neglect
it for a while in order to keep the reader in suspense—and in
this skill we recognize also the well-planned novel. But the
theme must not be abandoned for too long, so the reader
should not become lost among too many other, parallel actions. So it was time to return to Ferrante.

Stealing Lilia from Roberto was only one of the goals Ferrante had set for himself. The other was to cause Roberto to
fall into disfavor with the Cardinal. Not easy to achieve: the
Cardinal did not even know of Roberto's existence.

But Ferrante knew how to make the most of opportunities.
One day Richelieu was reading a letter in his presence, and
said to him: "Cardinal Mazarin tells me a story about the
English and a certain Powder of Sympathy they have. Did you
hear any talk of it in London?"

"What is it, Your Eminence?"

"Signor Pozzo, or whatever your name is, learn that you
must never answer a question with another question, especially if it is asked by someone of a station higher than your

394

own. If I knew what it was, I would not ask you about it. In any event, if you know nothing of this powder, have you heard any mention of a new secret method for determining longitudes?"

"I confess I know nothing on this subject. If Your Eminence would enlighten me, perhaps I—"

"Signor Pozzo, you would be amusing if you were not insolent. I would not be the master of this country if I were to enlighten others about things they do not know—unless those others were the king of France, which does not seem to be your case. So do only what you know how to do: keep your ears open and learn things of which before you knew nothing. Then you will come and report them to me, and afterwards you will take care to forget them."

"That is what I have always done, Your Eminence. Or at least I think so, for I have forgotten doing it."

"Now that is to my liking. You may go."

Some time later came that memorable evening when Ferrante heard Roberto expound the theory of the powder. He could hardly believe his luck, able to draw to Richelieu's attention an Italian gentleman who consorted with the Englishman d'Igby (notoriously connected, some time ago, with the Duc de Bouquinquant) and who seemed to know a great deal about the powder.

At the moment when he began casting discredit on Roberto, Ferrante still had to arrange how to take his place. So he revealed to the Cardinal that he, Ferrante, passed himself off as Signor del Pozzo because his job as informer obliged him to remain incognito, but in reality he was the true Roberto de la Grive, a valorous fighter with the French during the siege of Casale. The other man, who so slyly talked about the English powder, was a rascal adventurer. Exploiting a vague physical resemblance, under the name of Mahmut the Arab, he had recently served as a spy in London taking orders from the Turks.

Thus Ferrante prepared for the moment when, having ruined his brother, he could assume his identity, becoming the one and true Roberto not only to the relatives still left at La Griva but in the eyes of all Paris—as if the other had never existed.

In the meantime, as he masked himself with Roberto's face to conquer Lilia, Ferrante learned, like everyone else, of the misfortune of Cinq-Mars; and risking a great deal surely, but ready to give his life to consummate his revenge, again in the guise of Roberto he made a show of belonging to the company of that conspirator's friends.

Then he whispered to the Cardinal that the false Roberto de la Grive, who knew so much about a secret dear to the English, was clearly conspiring, and Ferrante promptly produced witnesses who could declare they had seen Roberto with this or that man.

As is clear, a castle of lies and travesties lay behind the trap into which Roberto had fallen. But Roberto had fallen for reasons and in ways unknown to Ferrante himself, whose plans were then upset by the death of Richelieu.

What, in fact, had happened? Richelieu, highly suspicious, was using Ferrante without mentioning him to anyone, not even to Mazarin, whom he obviously distrusted, seeing him by now poised like a vulture over an ailing body. Still, as his disease progressed, Richelieu did pass some information to Mazarin, without revealing its source: "By the way, my good Jules. . . ."

"Yes, Eminence and my beloved father . . ."

"Keep an eye on one Roberto de la Grive. He goes in the

evening to Madame de Rambouillet. It seems he knows a great deal about your Powder of Sympathy. . . . And, further, according to an informer of mine, the young man also frequents a circle of conspirators. . . ."

"You must not tire yourself, Eminence. I will deal with everything."

And so Mazarin initiated, on his own, an enquiry into Roberto, until he had learned the little he made a great show of knowing on the night of the arrest. But in all of this he knew nothing of Ferrante.

Meanwhile Richelieu was dying. What would happen to Ferrante?

Richelieu dead, Ferrante was without protection. He had to establish some contact with Mazarin, for a scoundrel is an evil heliotrope turning always in the direction of the most powerful. But he cannot go to the new minister without bringing some evidence of his worth. He finds no further trace of Roberto. Can Roberto be ill? Has he set off on a journey? Ferrante thinks of everything save the possibility that his slanders have had their effect and Roberto has been arrested.

Ferrante does not dare show himself publicly in the guise of Roberto, for fear of arousing the suspicions of those who know that La Grive is far away. Whatever may have happened between him and Lilia, Ferrante ceases all communication with her, impassive as a man aware that every victory costs much time. He knows, also, he should make use of distance; the finest qualities lose their glow if displayed too often, and fancy travels farther than sight; even the phoenix resorts to distant habitats to keep its legend alive.

But time is pressing. On Roberto's return, Mazarin must already suspect him and want him dead. Ferrante consults his peers at court, and discovers that Mazarin can be approached through the young Colbert, to whom he sends a letter hinting at an English threat and the matter of longitudes (knowing nothing about them, and having heard them mentioned only once, by Richelieu). In exchange for his revelations he asks for a considerable sum, and is granted a meeting, at which he appears dressed as an elderly abbé, with a black eye-patch.

Colbert is not ingenuous. This abbé's voice sounds familiar, the few things he says have a dubious ring. Colbert summons two guards, goes to the visitor, tears off the patch and the beard, and whom does he find before him? The same Roberto de la Grive he himself consigned to his agents, charging them to put this Italian on board Dr. Byrd's ship.

In telling himself this story, Roberto exults. Ferrante has walked straight into the trap, all on his own. "You? San Patrizio?" Colbert promptly cried. Then, seeing Ferrante start and remain silent, he ordered the man flung into a dungeon.

It was a great joke for Roberto to imagine the colloquy between Mazarin and Colbert, who immediately informed the Cardinal.

"The man must be mad, Your Eminence. To dare evade his mission, I can understand, but to try to come here to sell us what we had already given him can only be evidence of madness."

"Colbert, no one could be so mad as to take me for a fool. So our man is playing a game, convinced that he holds winning cards."

"In what sense?"

"For example, suppose he boarded that ship and immediately discovered what he was to have learned, so he no longer needed to stay there."

"But if he had wanted to betray us, he would have gone to the Spanish or to the Dutch. He would not have come here to challenge us. And to ask what of us, after all? Money? He knew quite well that if he acted loyally, he could have had even a place at court."

"Obviously he is convinced he has discovered a secret worth more than a place at court. Believe me, he knows much. We can only lead him on. I will see him this evening."

Mazarin received Ferrante while with his own hands he was putting the final touches to a table he had laid for his guests, a triumph of things that seemed to be other things. On the board, wicks glowed, protruding from goblets of ice, and bottles in which the wine was of unexpected colors stood among baskets of lettuces garlanded with artificial flowers and fruits artificially aromatic.

Mazarin, who believed that Roberto, that is to say Ferrante, was in possession of a secret from which he wanted to derive great profit, had determined to make a show of knowing everything (everything, in short, that he did not know) to induce the rogue to let some hint escape him.

On the other hand, Ferrante—when he found himself in the Cardinal's presence—had already guessed that Roberto was in possession of a secret from which great profit could be derived, and he had determined to make a show of knowing everything (everything, in short, that he did not know) to induce the Cardinal to let some hint escape him.

Thus we have on stage two men, each of whom knows nothing of what he believes the other knows, and to deceive each other reciprocally both speak in allusions, each of the two hoping (in vain) that the other holds the key to this puzzle. What a beautiful story, Roberto said to himself as he sought the thread of the skein that he had twisted.

"Signor di San Patrizio," Mazarin said as he moved a dish of live crayfish that seemed cooked closer to another dish of cooked crayfish that seemed alive, "a week ago we put you on board the *Amaryllis* in Amsterdam. You cannot have abandoned your mission: you were well aware you would pay for that with your life. Therefore you must have already discovered what you were sent to discover."

Ferrante, confronted with this dilemma, saw that it was not in his interest to confess having abandoned the mission. So there was only one course open to him. "If it please Your Eminence," he said, "in a sense I have learned what Your Eminence wanted me to learn," and he added to himself: "And meanwhile I have learned that the secret is on board a ship named the *Amaryllis,* and that it sailed from Amsterdam a week ago. . . ."

"Come, sir, do not be modest. I know very well that you now know more than I was expecting. After your departure I received other information, for you surely do not imagine you are the only agent I have. Thus I know that what you have found is of great value, and I am not here to haggle. I cannot help wondering, however, why you chose to come back to me in such a tortuous way." And at the same time he indicated to the servants where they should set some meats in wooden forms shaped like fish, on which he had them pour not broth but julep.

Ferrante was more and more convinced that the secret was priceless, but he told himself it is easy to kill a bird in flight if it flies in a straight line, but not if it constantly changes direction. Therefore he took his time, sounding out the adversary: "Your Eminence knows the prize at stake required tortuous means."

"Ah, you rascal," Mazarin said to himself, "you are not sure what your discovery is worth and you are waiting for me to set the price. But you must be the one to speak first." To the center of the table he shifted some sorbets so confected that they seemed peaches still clinging to their bough, then he spoke: "I know what you have. You know that you can bring it only to me. Do you think it a good idea to pass white off as black and black as white?"

"Ah, you damned fox," Ferrante muttered under his breath, "you do not in the least know what I should know, and the trouble is that I do not know it either." Then he also spoke: "Your Eminence knows well that sometimes the truth can have the essence of bitterness."

"Knowledge never harms."

"But sometimes it hurts."

"Hurt me, then. I will not be more hurt than when I learned you had stained your honor with treason. I should have left you in the hands of the executioner."

Ferrante finally realized that in playing the part of Roberto, he risked ending on the gallows. Better to reveal himself for what he was, and risk at most a beating from a lackey.

"Your Eminence," he said, "I have made the mistake of not telling you the truth at once. Monsieur Colbert took me for Roberto de la Grive, and his error has perhaps also misled even a gaze as acute as that of Your Eminence. But I am not Roberto, I am only his natural brother, Ferrante. I presented myself to offer some information I thought would interest Your Eminence, since Your Eminence was the first to mention to the late and never to be forgotten Cardinal the plot of the English, as Your Eminence knows . . . the Powder of Sympathy and the problem of longitude. . . ."

At these words Mazarin made a gesture of pique, almost knocking over a tureen of fake gold decorated with jewels exquisitely simulated in glass. He blamed a servant, then murmured to Colbert: "Put this man back where he was."

It is quite true that the gods blind those they wish to destroy. Ferrante thought to arouse interest by revealing that he knew the most private secrets of the late Cardinal, and exaggerating in his sycophantic pride, he tried to show himself better informed than his deceased master. But no one had yet told Mazarin (and it would have been difficult to prove it to him) that there had been commerce between Ferrante and Richelieu. Mazarin found himself facing someone, whether Roberto or another, who not only knew what he had said to Roberto but also what he had written to Richelieu. From whom had he learned this?

When Ferrante was led away, Colbert said, "Does Your Eminence believe what that man said? If he were a twin, all would be explained. Roberto would still be at sea, and—"

"No, if this man is Roberto's brother, the case is even more inexplicable. How has he come to know what was known first only to me, you, and our English informer, and then to Roberto de la Grive?"

"His brother must have told him."

"No, his brother learned everything from us only that evening, and afterwards he was never out of someone's sight, until the ship set sail. No, no, this man knows too many things he should not know."

"What shall we do with him?"

"Interesting question, Colbert. If he is Roberto, he knows what he has seen on that ship and he must speak. If he is not, we must absolutely discover where he obtained his information. In either case, excluding the very thought of haling him before a judge, where he would say too much and in the presence of too many people, we cannot simply make him disappear with a few inches of steel in his back: he still has much to tell us. If he is not Roberto but, as he says, Ferrand or Fernand . . ."

"Ferrante, I believe."

"No matter. If he is not Roberto, who is behind him? Not even the Bastille is a secure place. People are known to have sent messages from there and received them. We must wait till he speaks, and find the way to open his mouth, but in the meantime we should shut him up somewhere unknown to all, and make sure no one finds out who he is."

And it was at this point that Colbert had a darkly luminous idea.

A few days before, a French vessel had captured a pirate ship off the coast of Brittany. It was, by strange coincidence, a Dutch fluyt with the name, naturally unpronounceable, of *Tweede Daphne*, that is to say, *Daphne the Second*, a sign—Mazarin remarked—that somewhere there must be a *Daphne the First*, which showed how those Protestants lacked not only faith but also imagination. The crew was made up of people of every race. The only thing to do was hang them all, but it was worth investigating whether or not they were in the hire of England and from whom they had seized the ship, which might then be advantageously bartered with its legitimate owners.

So it was decided to moor the ship not far from the Seine estuary, in a little half-hidden bay that escaped the notice even of the pilgrims for Santiago who, coming from Flanders, passed a short distance away. On a tongue of land that enclosed the bay there was an old fortress which had once served as a prison but was now more or less abandoned. And there the pirates were cast into dungeons, guarded by only three men.

"Enough," Mazarin said. "Take ten of my guards, put them under the command of a good captain not without prudence. . . ."

"Biscarat. He has always done things well, from the days when he duelled with the musketeers over the Cardinal's honor. . . ."

"Perfect. Have the prisoner taken to the fort and put him in the guard room. Biscarat will eat his meals with the prisoner in that room and accompany him if he is taken out for air. A guard at the door of the room also, at night. Time in

confinement weakens even the most stubborn spirit; our obstinate spy will have only Biscarat to speak to, and he may let
some confidence slip. And, above all, no one must recognize
him, either during the trip or at the fort. . . ."

"If he goes out for air . . ."

"Come, Colbert . . . where's your inventive spirit? Cover
his face."

"Might I suggest . . . an iron mask closed with a lock, the
key thrown into the sea?"

"Come now, Colbert, are we in the Land of Romances?
Last night we saw those Italian players wearing leather masks
with long noses that alter their features yet leave the mouth
free. Find one of those, put it on him in such a way that he
cannot remove it, and give him a mirror in his cell, so he can
die of shame day by day. He chose to mask himself as his
brother, did he not? Then let him be masked as Polichinelle!
And remember: from here to the fort, a closed carriage, stopping only at night and in open country, no showing himself
at the post-stations. If anyone asks questions, a lady high degree is being escorted to the frontier, a conspirator against the
Cardinal."

Ferrante, embarrassed by his burlesque disguise, now had
been staring for days (through a grating that allowed scant
light into his room) at a gray amphitheater surrounded
by bleak dunes, with the *Tweede Daphne* riding at anchor in the
bay.

He controlled himself when he was in Biscarat's presence,
letting the captain believe sometimes he was Roberto, sometimes Ferrante, so that the reports sent to Mazarin were always
puzzling. He managed to overhear, in passing, some conversation among the guards, and had learned that in the dungeons of the fort a band of pirates lay in chains.

Wanting to take revenge on Roberto for a wrong he had not inflicted, Ferrante racked his brain for a way to encourage a revolt, to free those rogues, seize the ship, and set out on Roberto's trail. He knew where to begin: in Amsterdam he would find spies who could tell him something of the destination of the *Amaryllis*. He would overtake it, would discover Roberto's secret, rid himself of that tedious double in the sea, and then he would be able to sell something to the Cardinal at a high price.

Or perhaps not. Once he discovered the secret, he might decide to sell it to others. But why sell it, indeed? For all he knew, Roberto's secret could involve the map of a treasure island, or else the secret of the Alumbrados and the Rosy-Cross, of which people had been talking for twenty years. He would exploit the revelation to his own advantage, would no longer have to spy for a master, would have spies in his own service. Wealth and power gained, not only would he possess the ancient name of his family, but the Lady would be his as well.

To be sure, Ferrante, steeped in rancor, was not capable of true love, but—Roberto told himself—there are people who would never have fallen in love if they had not heard love talked about. Perhaps, in his cell, Ferrante finds a love story, reads it, and convinces himself he is in love as a way of feeling himself elsewhere.

Perhaps She, in the course of that first encounter, gave Ferrante her comb as a pledge of love. Now Ferrante is kissing it, and as he kisses it, he is wrecked, oblivious, in the gulf whose waves the ivory prow had fended.

Perhaps—who knows?—even such a scoundrel could succumb to the memory of that face. . . . Roberto now saw Ferrante seated in the darkness at the mirror that reflected only the candle set before it. Contemplating two little flames, one aping the other, the eye stares, the mind is infatuated, visions rise. Shifting his head slightly, Ferrante sees Lilia, her face of virgin wax, so bathed in light that it absorbs every other ray and causes her blond hair to flow like a dark mass wound in a spindle behind her back, her bosom just visible beneath a delicate dress, its neck cut low. . . .

Then Ferrante (at last! Roberto exulted) sought to gain too much from the vanity of a dream, and set himself, insatiable, before the mirror, and saw behind the reflected candle only the disfiguring black snout.

An animal unable to bear the loss of an undeserved gift, he resumed touching her comb; but now, in the smoking of the candle-end, that object (which for Roberto would have been the most adorable of relics) seemed to Ferrante a toothy mouth ready to bite his dejection.

CHAPTER 32

A Garden of Delights

AT THE IDEA of Ferrante shut up on that island looking at a *Tweede Daphne* he would never reach, separated from the Lady, Roberto felt, and we must allow it, a reprehensible but comprehensible satisfaction, not unconnected with a certain satisfaction as narrator, since—with fine antimetabole—he had managed to seal up also his adversary in a siege spectacularly dissimilar to his own.

You from that island of yours, with your leather mask, will never reach the ship. I, on the contrary, from my ship, with my mask of glass, am now on the verge of reaching my Island. Thus he spoke (to him, to himself) as he prepared to attempt once more his journey by water.

He remembered the distance from the ship to the point where he had been wounded, and therefore he swam calmly at first, the mask at his belt. When he believed he was drawing close to the reef, he slipped on the mask and sank to explore the sea bed.

For a while he saw only patches; then, like a seaman on a ship in a foggy night, approaching a cliff, which suddenly looms, sheer, before his eyes, he saw the rim of the chasm over which he was swimming.

He took off the mask, emptied it, replaced it, holding it with his hand, and with a slow kicking motion he headed for the spectacle he had just glimpsed.

So this was coral. His first impression, to judge by his later notes, was confused, dazed. It was an impression of being in the shop of a merchant of stuffs who draped before his eyes sendals and taffetas, brocades, satins, damasks, velvets, and bows, fringes and furbelows, and then stoles, pluvials, chasubles, dalmatics. But the stuffs moved with a life of their own, sensual as Oriental dancing-maids.

In that landscape—which Roberto does not describe because, seeing it for the first time, he cannot find in his memory images capable of translating it into words—now suddenly a host of creatures erupted and these, indeed, he recognized, or at least could compare to others previously seen. They were fish, intersecting like shooting stars in an August sky, but in composing and distributing the hues and patterns of their scales, Nature must have wanted to demonstrate the variety of accents that exists in the Universe and how many can be placed together on a single surface.

Some were striped in several colors, lengthwise or breadthwise, some had slanting lines and others had curving lines. Some seemed worked like intarsia with crumbs of spots brilliantly deployed, some were speckled or dotted, others patched, spattered, or minutely stippled, or veined like marble.

Still others had a serpentine design, or a pattern like several interwoven chains. Some were spotted with enamels, sown with shields and rosettes. And one, beautiful above the rest, seemed circled with cordons forming two rows of grapes and milk; and it was miraculous that not once did the row that enfolded the belly fail to continue on the flank, as if it were the work of an artist's hand.

Only at that moment, seeing against the background of fish the coralline forms he had not been able to recognize at first, could Roberto make out bunches of bananas, baskets of bread rolls, corbeilles of bronze loquats over which canaries and geckos and hummingbirds were hovering.

He was above a garden, no, he was mistaken, now it seemed a petrified forest, and at the next moment there were mounds, folds, shores, gaps and grottoes, a single slope of living stones on which a vegetation not of this earth was composed in squat forms, or round, or scaly, that seemed to wear a granulated coat of mail, or else gnarled, or else coiled. But, different as they were, they were all stupendous in their grace and loveliness, to such a degree that even those worked with feigned negligence, roughly shaped, displayed their roughness with majesty: they were monsters, true, but monsters of beauty.

Or else (Roberto crosses out and revises, and is unable to report, like someone who must describe for the first time a squared circle, a coastal plain, a noisy silence, a nocturnal rainbow) what he was seeing were shrubs of cinnabar.

Perhaps, holding his breath so long, he had grown befuddled, and the water entering his mask blurred shapes and hues. He thrust his head up to let air into his lungs, and resumed floating along the edge of the barrier, following its rifts and anfracts, past corridors of chalk in which vinous harlequins were stuck, while on a promontory he saw reposing, stirred by slow respiration and a waving of claws, a lobster crested with whey over a coral net (this coral looked like the coral he knew, but was spread out like the legendary cheese of Fra Stefano, which never ends).

What he saw now was not a fish, nor was it a leaf; certainly it was a living thing, like two broad slices of whitish matter edged in crimson and with a feather fan; and where you would have expected eyes there were two horns of whipped sealing-wax.

Cypress-polyps, which in their vermicular writhing revealed the rosy color of a great central lip, stroked plantations of albino phalli with amaranth glandes; pink minnows dotted with olive grazed ashen cauliflowers sprayed with scarlet, striped tubers of blackening copper . . . And then he could see the porous, saffron liver of a great animal, or else an artificial fire of mercury arabesques, wisps of thorns dripping sanguine and finally a kind of chalice of flaccid mother-of-pearl . . .

That chalice then looked to him like an urn, and he thought that among those rocks was inhumed Father Caspar's corpse. No longer visible, if the action of the water had covered it with coralline cartilage; but the corals, absorbing the terrestrial humors of that body, had assumed shapes of flowers and garden fruits. Perhaps in a little while he would recognize the poor old man transformed into an alien creature down here: the globe of the head made from a hairy coconut, two withered apples for the cheeks, eyes and eyelids turned into two unripe apricots, the nose of sow thistle knotty like an animal's dung; below, in place of lips, dried figs, a beet with its apiculate stalk for the chin, and a wrinkled cardoon functioning as the throat; and at both temples, two chestnut burrs to act as sidecurls, and for ears the halves of a split walnut; for fingers, carrots; a watermelon as belly; quinces, the knees.

How could Roberto dress such funereal thoughts in such a grotesque form? No, in quite different form the remains of his poor friend would have proclaimed in this place their fateful *Et in Arcadia ego.* . . .

There, perhaps in the form of that gravelly coral skull . . .
that double of a stone that seemed already uprooted from its
bed. Whether out of piety, in memory of his lost master, or
to rob from the sea at least one of its treasures, he grasped it
and, having seen too much for that day, clutched this booty
to his bosom and returned to the ship.

CHAPTER 33

Mundus Subterraneus

THE CORAL HAD challenged Roberto. After discovering the extent of Nature's capacity for invention, he felt bidden to a contest. Could he leave Ferrante in that prison, leave his own story only half-finished? Assuage his bitterness towards his rival and mortify his storyteller's pride? No. But what could he make happen to Ferrante?

The idea came to Roberto one morning when, as usual, he had placed himself in ambush, at dawn, to catch the Orange Dove unawares. Early in the morning the sun struck his eyes, and Roberto had even tried to construct around the larger lens of his spyglass a kind of shield, using a page from the ship's log, but at certain moments he was reduced to seeing only glints. When the sun finally did appear on the horizon, the sea mirrored it, doubling its every ray.

But that morning, Roberto was convinced he had seen something rise from the trees towards the sun, then melt into its luminous sphere. Probably it was an illusion. Any bird in that light would have seemed to glitter. . . . Roberto was convinced he had seen the Dove, and yet was disappointed at

having lied to himself. In this contradictory mood he felt once
again defrauded.

For a creature like Roberto, who by now had reached the
point where he jealously enjoyed only what was stolen from
him, it took little to dream that Ferrante had been given what
to him was denied. But since Roberto was the author of this
story and unwilling to grant Ferrante too much, he decided
that the wretch would deal only with the other dove, the blue-
green one. And this was because Roberto had decided, though
without any certitude, that of the couple the orange must be
the female, as if to say She. Since in the story of Ferrante the
dove was not to represent the conclusion but, rather, the agent
of possession, for the present the male fell to him.

Could a blue-green dove, which flies only over the South
Seas, go and light on the sill of that window where Ferrante
was pining for his freedom? Yes, in the Land of Romances.
And anyway, could not the *Tweede Daphne* have returned only
recently from these seas, more fortunate than her older sister,
bearing in the hold this bird, now set free?

In any case, Ferrante, ignorant of the Antipodes, could not
ask himself such questions. He saw the dove, first fed it a few
bread crumbs merely to pass the time, then he wondered if it
could not be used to further his own purposes. He knew that
doves sometimes served to carry messages: of course, entrusting a message to that animal did not mean it would necessarily
reach its destination, but in this total ennui the effort was
worth making.

To whom could he appeal for help, he who out of enmity
towards all, himself included, had made only enemies, and the
few people who had served him were shameless, prepared to
follow him only in good fortune and surely not in disaster?
He said to himself: I will ask help of the Lady, who loves me

(But how can he be so sure? the envious Roberto wondered, after he invented that self-confidence).

Biscarat had left him writing materials, in the possibility that the night would bring counsel and persuade him to send a confession to the Cardinal. So on one side of the paper Ferrante wrote the address of the Lady, adding that whoever delivered the message would receive a reward. On the other side he wrote where he lay (he had heard a name spoken by his warders), victim of an infamous plot of the Cardinal, and he begged to be rescued. Then he rolled up the paper and tied it to the leg of the bird, urging it to fly off.

To tell the truth, he then forgot, or almost forgot, this action. How could he think that the azure dove would actually fly to Lilia? Such things happened only in fairy tales, and Ferrante was not a man to trust in tales. Probably the dove was shot by a hunter, to plunge among a tree's boughs, losing the message. . . .

Ferrante did not know that the bird instead was caught in the snare of a peasant, who thought to profit from what, judging by appearances, was a signal sent to someone, perhaps to the commander of an army.

Now this peasant took the message to be examined by the one person in his village who knew how to read, namely, the curate, who then organized everything properly. Having identified the Lady, he sent a friend to her to negotiate the delivery, deriving from it a generous offering for his church and a reward for the peasant. Lilia read, wept, sought out trusted friends for advice. Try to touch the Cardinal's heart? Nothing easier for a beautiful woman of the court, but this woman frequented the salon of Arthénice, whom Mazarin distrusted. Satirical verses about the new minister were already circulating, and some said they came from those rooms. A précieuse who went to the Cardinal to implore mercy for a friend would be sentencing that friend to sterner punishment.

No, a band of brave men had to be assembled, who could be persuaded to mount a surprise attack. But to whom could she turn?

Now Roberto was at a loss. If he had been, say, a musketeer of the king or a cadet of Gascony, Lilia could have appealed to those men, brave, renowned for their ésprit de corps. But who would risk the wrath of a minister, perhaps of the king himself, for a foreigner who spent his time among librarians and astronomers? And as for librarians and astronomers, it was best to forget them: though bent on continuing his novel, Roberto could not imagine the Canon of Digne or Monsieur Gaffarel galloping full tilt towards his prison—or, rather, the prison of Ferrante, who at this point everyone thought to be Roberto.

A few days later Roberto had an inspiration. He had set aside the story of Ferrante to continue his exploration of the coral reef. That day he was following a school of fish whose snouts bore a yellow vizor, like swirling warriors; they were about to enter a cleft between two towers of stone where the corals were the crumbling palaces of a sunken city.

Roberto imagined those fish were wandering amid the ruins of that city of Ys he had heard of, which presumably still existed not many miles off the coast of Brittany, where the waves had engulfed it. There, the largest fish was the ancient king of the city, followed by his dignitaries, and all were riding out in search of their treasure swallowed up by the sea. . . .

But why recur to an ancient legend? Why not consider these fish the inhabitants of a world that has its forests, its peaks, its trees, and its valleys, and knows nothing of the world above the surface? Similarly, we live with no knowledge that the curved sky conceals other worlds, where people do not walk or swim but fly and navigate through the air. If what we call planets are the keels of their vessels, of which we see only the shining bottom, then these children of Neptune must see above them the shadow of our galleons and consider them heavenly bodies moving through their aqueous firmament.

And if it is possible that creatures live underwater, could not creatures also live under the earth, nations of salamanders capable of arriving, through their tunnels, at the central fire that animates the planet?

Reflecting in this way, Roberto remembered an argument of Saint-Savin's: We think it is difficult to live on the surface of the moon, believing there is no water there, but perhaps water up there exists in subterranean hollows, and Nature has dug wells on the moon, which are the spots we see. How do we know that the inhabitants of the moon do not find refuge in those niches, to escape the intolerable proximity of the sun? Did not the first Christians live underground? And so the moon-folk live always in catacombs, which to them seem homely.

Nor is there any reason that they must live in the dark. Perhaps there are many holes in the crust of the satellite, and the interior is illuminated through thousands of slits; theirs is a night traversed by brilliant shafts, not very different from the interior of a church or the lower deck of the *Daphne*. Or perhaps, instead, on the surface there are phosphorescent stones that during the day soak up the sunlight, then release it at night, and the lunarians collect those stones at every sunset so that their tunnels are always more brilliant than any royal palace.

Paris, Roberto thought. Is it not a known fact that, like Rome, the whole city is underlaid with catacombs, where it is said that at night malefactors and beggars take refuge?

Beggars! Here was the idea for rescuing Ferrante! The Beggars, who, as the story goes, are governed by their own king and by a code of iron laws; the Beggars, a society of grim rabble living off thievery and misery, assassinations and extravagances, filth, villainy, and treachery, while they pretend to subsist on Christian charity!

An idea that only a woman in love could conceive, Roberto told himself. For her confidences Lilia did not approach courtiers or gentlemen of the robe, but, rather, the least of her maidservants, a woman engaged in unscrupulous traffickings with a waggoner who knew all the taverns around Notre-Dame, where at sundown the Beggars congregated after spending their day whining in doorways. . . . This was the path to take.

Now her guide conducts her, in the heart of the night, to the church of Saint-Martin-des-Champs, lifts a stone of the floor in the choir, and leads her down into the catacombs of Paris, advancing by torchlight in search of the King of the Beggars.

And this is when Lilia, disguised as a gentleman, a supple androgyne who passes through tunnels, down steps, and along low passages, where in the darkness she can discern here and there, huddled amid rags and tatters, legless bodies and faces marked with warts, pimples, erysipelas, scabs, impetigoes, boils, and cankers, all gaggling, with hand extended whether to ask for alms or to mime an invitation—with a chamberlain's mien—"Proceed, forward, our master is expecting you."

And there the master was, in the center of a hall a thousand leagues under the surface of the city, seated on a cask, surrounded by cutpurses, barrators, counterfeiters, and saltimbanques, a scum laureate in every abuse and corruption.

What could the King of the Beggars be like? Wrapped in a tattered cloak, his brow covered with tubercules, his nose gnawed by a tabes, his eyes of marble, one green and one black, a weasel's gaze, brows sloping downwards, a harelip revealing wolf's teeth sharp and protruding, kinky hair, sandy skin, hands with stubby fingers and curving nails. . . .

Having heard out the Lady, he replied that he had at his service an army compared to which the army of the French King was a provincial garrison. And far less costly: if these people were recompensed in an acceptable manner, say, twice the amount they could collect begging in the same period of time, they would have themselves killed for so generous an employer.

Lilia slipped a ruby ring from her finger (as is usual in such situations), asking with regal manner, "Is this enough?"

"Enough," the King of the Beggars said, fondling the jewel with his vulpine gaze. "Tell us where." And having learned where, he added: "My people do not use horses or carriages, but that place can be reached on barges, following the Seine."

Roberto imagined Ferrante at sunset on the tower of the little fort conversing with Captain Biscarat, who suddenly saw them coming. They appeared first on the dunes, then spread out over the open field.

"Pilgrims for Santiago," Biscarat remarked with contempt, "and of the worst sort, or the most unhappy. They go seeking health when they have one foot in the grave."

In fact, the pilgrims, in a very long file, were advancing closer and closer to the shore, and Ferrante and Biscarat could discern a mass of blind men with extended hands, the maimed on their crutches, lepers bleared, abscessed, and scrofulous, a jumble of cripples mutilated, clad in rags.

"I would not want them to come too close, or to ask for shelter for the night," Biscarat said. "They would bring only filth inside the walls." And he ordered a few musket shots fired in the air, to make it clear that this little castle was not a place of hospitality.

But those shots seemed to act like a summons. As more rabble appeared in the distance, the leaders came nearer and nearer to the fortress, and already their animal mumbling could be heard.

"Keep them off, by God!" Biscarat shouted, and he had some bread thrown down at the foot of the wall, as if to say to them that such was the charity of the place's master and they could expect nothing more. But the foul band, its ranks swelling visibly, drove its vanguard to the very walls, trampling that gift underfoot and staring upwards, as if seeking something better.

Now they could be seen one by one, and they bore no resemblance to pilgrims, or to unhappy wretches asking relief for their ailments. Beyond doubt—Biscarat said, worried— they were ragtag adventurers. Or so it seemed at least for a while, as it was now dusk, and the field and the dunes had become only a gray teeming of giant rats.

"To arms, to arms!" Biscarat cried, finally realizing that this was no pilgrimage, no alms-begging, but an assault. And he ordered shots fired at those who had already reached the wall. But, as if it was indeed a pack of rodents, more came, shoving the first, the fallen were trampled and used as a step for others pressing from behind, and now the first could be seen clinging with their nails to the clefts of that ancient fabric, digging their fingers into the cracks, setting their feet in the gaps, clutching the bars of the lowest windows, thrusting their sciatical limbs into the slits. Meanwhile another part of that crowd was swaying on the ground, heaving their shoulders against the portal.

Biscarat ordered it barricaded on the inside, but the sturdiest planks of those doors were beginning to creak under the pressure of that bastard force.

The guards continued firing, but the few attackers who fell

were immediately trodden on by others of the horde; now only a seething mass was visible, from which eels of rope rose, flung into the air, and it was clear that they were iron grapples, and already some of them were hooked to the battlements. And no sooner did a guard lean out a bit to unfasten those hooked irons than the first attackers, who had hoisted themselves up, struck him with spikes and clubs, or caught him in nooses and pulled him below, where he vanished into the press of those diabolical fiends, his death-rattle drowned in their roar.

In no time, anyone following events from the dunes would have been unable to see the fort, only a teeming of flies over a corpse, a swarm of bees on a stalk, a confraternity of hornets.

Meanwhile, from below, the crash of the great door was heard as it gave way, then a tumult in the yard. Biscarat and his men rushed to the other end of the platform—no longer concerned with Ferrante, who flattened in the arch of the door that gave onto the stairs, not very frightened, for he had a presentiment that these attackers were somehow friends.

Which friends, at this point, had reached and passed the battlements. Prodigal with their lives, falling at the last rounds of musket fire, heedless of their exposed breasts, they passed the barrier of drawn swords and horrified the guards with their villainous eyes, their frenzied faces. Thus the Cardinal's guards, otherwise men of iron, dropped their weapons, imploring mercy from Heaven against what they now believed a band from Hell, and the hellions first felled them with blows of their clubs, then flung themselves on the survivors, laying about, slapping, cuffing, smiting, thwacking, and they tore open throats with their bare teeth, quartered with their claws, they overwhelmed by spitting bile, they committed atrocities on the dead, and Ferrante saw one cut open a man's chest, grab the heart, and devour it amid shrill cries.

The last survivor was Biscarat, who had fought like a lion. Seeing himself finally defeated, he stood with his back to a parapet, drew a line on the ground with his bloody sword, and cried. "Icy mourra Biscarat, seul de ceux qui sont avec luy!"

But at that instant a one-eyed man with a peg leg, brandishing an axe, emerged from the stairs, gave a signal, and put an end to the butchery, ordering Biscarat to be tied up. Then he saw Ferrante, recognized him by the very mask that was to have made him unrecognizable, greeted him with a broad gesture of his armed hand, as if to sweep the ground with the plume of a hat, and said, "Sir, you are free."

He drew a message from his jerkin, with a seal Ferrante knew at once, and handed it to him.

It was she who advised him to make free use of that army, horrid but trustworthy, and to await her there, as she would arrive at dawn.

To begin with, Ferrante, once freed from his mask, released the pirates and signed a pact with them. They would regain the ship and sail under his orders, asking no questions. Their recompense: a share of a treasure as vast as a dozen Eldorados. True to his character, Ferrante had no thought of keeping his word. Once he found Roberto again, it would be enough to denounce his own crew at the first port of call, and he would have them all hanged, remaining master of the vessel.

He no longer needed the beggars, and their leader, an honorable man, told him they had received payment for this undertaking. He wished to leave the area as soon as possible. They scattered inland and returned to Paris, begging from village to village.

It was easy to board a shallop kept in the basin of the fort, reach the ship, and fling into the sea the two men who guarded it. Biscarat was chained in the hold, since he was a hostage who could be bartered advantageously. Ferrante granted himself a brief rest, returned ashore before dawn, in time to welcome a carriage from which Lilia stepped, more beautiful than ever in her male garb.

Roberto felt that he would suffer greater torment at the thought of the two greeting each other with reserve, not giving themselves away before the pirates, who believed their passenger to be a young gentleman.

They boarded ship. Ferrante made sure everything was ready to sail and, as the anchor was weighed, he went down to the chamber he had ordered to be made ready for his guest.

Here she awaited him with eyes that asked for nothing save to be loved; in the fluent exultation of her hair, now released over her shoulders, she was ready for the most joyous of sacrifices. O errant locks, locks gilded and beloved, locks unlocked that fly and play and, in playing, err—Roberto rhapsodized on Ferrante's behalf.

Their faces were close, to reap a harvest of kisses from a past sown with sighs, and at that moment Roberto drank, in thought, at that lip of fleshy pink. Ferrante kissed Lilia, and Roberto imagined himself in that act and in the thrill of biting that true coral. But then he felt she was eluding him like a gust of wind, he lost the warmth he thought he had felt for an instant, and he saw her, icy, in a mirror, in other arms, on a distant bridal bed on another ship.

To protect the lovers he lowered a curtain of jealous transparence, for those bodies, now bared, were books of solar necromancy, whose holy accents were revealed only to the two elect, who uttered them in turn from mouth to mouth.

The ship sailed away swiftly, Ferrante its master. In him she loved Roberto, into whose heart these images fell like sparks on a bundle of dry twigs.

CHAPTER 34

Monologue on the Plurality of Worlds

WE WILL REMEMBER, I hope—for Roberto has borrowed from the novelists of his century the habit of narrating so many stories at once that at a certain point it becomes difficult to pick up the thread—that from his first visit to the world of coral our hero brought back the stone double, which seemed to him a skull, perhaps Father Caspar's.

Now, to forget the loves of Lilia and Ferrante, he was seated on deck at sunset, contemplating that object, examining its form.

It did not seem a skull. It was, rather, a mineral hive composed of irregular polygons, but the polygon was not the elementary unit of that object: each polygon revealed in its center a spoked symmetry of very fine threads, among which appeared—if you sharpened your eyes—cavities that perhaps formed other polygons and, if the eye could penetrate still further, it would perhaps see that the faces of those tiny polygons were made of other, still tinier, polygons, until—dividing the parts into parts of parts—the point came when they would end, having arrived at those parts not further divisible, which are the atoms. But since Roberto did not know to what degree matter could be divided, it was not clear to him how far his eyes—alas, not lynx-like, since he did not possess that lens through which Caspar had been able to identify even the animalcules of the plague—could descend into the abyss, finding new forms within the forms he perceived.

Even the head of the abbé, as Saint-Savin had shouted that night during the duel, could be a whole world for his lice—and, ah! Roberto, hearing the words again, thought of the world inhabited by those happiest of insects, the lice of Anna Maria (or Francesca) Novarese! But since lice are not atoms either but vast universes for the atoms that compose them, perhaps inside the body of the louse there are other animals still tinier who live there as in a spacious world. And perhaps my very flesh—Roberto thought—and my blood are no more than wefts of minuscule animals, that, in moving, lend me movement, allowing themselves to be conducted by my will, which serves them as coachman. And my animals are surely wondering where I am taking them now, subjecting them to an alternation of marine coolness and solar ardor, and, confounded by this turmoil of unstable climes, they are as uncertain of their destiny as I am of mine.

And what if even more minuscule animals found themselves in an equally unlimited space?

What stops me from thinking this? Only the fact that I have never learned anything about it? As my friends in Paris used to say to me, someone on the tower of Notre-Dame, looking down from that height at the Faubourg Saint-Denis, could never think that ill-defined spot was inhabited by beings similar to us. We see the planet Jove, which is very big, but from Jove they do not see us, and they cannot even conceive of our existence. And even yesterday, would I have suspected that beneath the sea—not on a remote planet or in a drop of water, but in a part of our own world—Another World existed?

And for that matter, until a few months ago, what did I know of the Austral Land? I would have said it was the fancy of heretic geographers; and perhaps—who knows?—in these islands, in times past, they burned some of their own philos ophers for asserting in guttural grunts the existence of Monferrato and of France. And yet now I am here, and I must perforce believe that the Antipodes exist—and that, contrary to the opinion once held by very wise men, I am not walking with my feet up and my head down. Simply, the inhabitants of this world occupy the stern of the vessel, and we occupy the prow, and, each knowing nothing of the other, we are both sailing.

The art of flying is still unknown and yet—if we can believe one Mr. Goodwin, of whom M. d'Igby told me—one day we will go to the moon as we have gone to America, even if before Columbus no one suspected that the continent existed, nor that one day it would be given that name.

Sunset gave way to evening, and evening to night. The moon was now full, and Roberto, seeing it in the sky, could make out its spots, which children and ignoramuses consider the eyes and mouth of a benevolent face.

To provoke Father Caspar (in what world, on what planet of the righteous was the dear old man now?), Roberto had once spoken to him about the inhabitants of the moon. But can the moon really be inhabited? Why not? It was as Saint-Denis said: What do the humans of this world know of what is up there?

Roberto reasoned: If, standing on the moon, I fling a stone high, will it perhaps fall on the earth? No, it will fall on the moon. So the moon, like any other planet or star, as may be, is a world that has a center of its own, and a circumference, and this center attracts all the bodies that live within the sphere of that world's dominion. As on the earth. Then why can all the other things that happen on earth not happen also on the moon?

There is an atmosphere that enfolds the moon. On the Palm Sunday of forty years ago did not someone see, as I have been told, clouds on the moon? On that planet, in the imminence of an eclipse, is it not possible to see a great trepidation? And what is this if not proof that there is air? The planets evaporate, and so do the stars: what else are the spots that are said to be on the sun, which generate the shooting stars?

And on the moon there is surely water. How explain otherwise her spots than that they are the image of lakes (in fact, someone has suggested that these lakes are artificial, like human works, so neatly defined are they and arranged at regular distances)? Moreover, if the moon had been conceived as a great mirror serving to reflect the sun's light onto the earth, why would the Creator have blemished that mirror with spots? Therefore the spots are not imperfections but perfections, and hence ponds, or lakes, or seas. And up there, if water exists, and air, then so does life.

A life perhaps different from ours. Perhaps that water has the flavor of (let us say) glycyrrhizin, or cardamon, or even of pepper. If there are infinite worlds, this proves the infinite ingenuity of the Engineer of our Universe, but then there is no limit to this Poet. He can have created inhabited worlds everywhere, but inhabited by ever-different creatures. Perhaps the inhabitants of the sun are sunnier, brighter, and more illuminated than are the inhabitants of the earth, who are heavy with matter, and the inhabitants of the moon lie somewhere in between. On the sun live beings who are all Form, or all Act, if you prefer, while on the earth beings are made of mere Potentials that evolve, and on the moon they are *in medio fluctuantes,* lunatics, so to speak. . . .

Could we live in the moon's air? Perhaps not, it might make us dizzy; for that matter, fish cannot live in ours, nor can birds in the air of fish. The air of the moon must be purer than ours, but like ours, thanks to its density, it serves as a natural lens that filters the sun's rays, though the Selenites see the sun quite differently. Dawn and twilight, which illuminate us when the sun has not yet come or has just left, are a gift of our air which, rich in impurities, captures and transmits its light; this is light lavished on us to excess. Yet those rays prepare us for the acquisition and the loss of the sun little by little. Perhaps on the moon, since the air is finer, their days and nights arrive all of a sudden. The sun rises abruptly on the horizon like the parting of a curtain. Then, from the most dazzling light, all plunges at once into the most bituminous darkness. And the moon would lack the rainbow, an effect of vapors mixed with air. But perhaps for the same reason they have neither rain nor thunder and lightning.

And the inhabitants of the planets closer to the sun, what can they be like? Fiery as Moors, but much more spiritual than we. How big will the sun be for them? How do they tolerate its light? Up there, do metals melt in nature and flow like rivers?

But are there really infinite worlds? A question of this sort provoked a duel in Paris. The Canon of Digne said he did not know the answer. Or, rather, the study of physics would lead him to say yes, in accord with the great Epicurus. The world can only be infinite. Atoms crowd into the Void. That bodies exist is borne out by sensation. That the Void exists is borne out by reason. How and where could the atoms move otherwise? If there were no Void, there would be no motion, unless bodies penetrate one another. It would be ridiculous to think that when a fly presses a particle of air with its wing, that particle shifts another below it, and that yet another, so that the scratching of a flea's leg, from movement to movement, would finally produce a lump at the far end of the world!

On the other hand, if the Void were infinite and the number of atoms finite, they would never cease moving on all sides, they would never jostle one another (as two people would never meet, if not through inconceivable coincidence, wandering through an endless desert), and so they would not produce their composites. And if the Void were finite and bodies infinite, there would not be room to contain them.

Naturally, it would suffice to imagine a Void inhabited by atoms in a finite number. The Canon told me this is the more prudent opinion. Why obligate God like some theatrical manager to produce infinite performances? He manifests His freedom eternally through the creation and maintenence of a single world. There are no arguments against the plurality of worlds, but there are also none in its favor. God, who was before the world, has created a sufficient number of atoms, in a space sufficiently wide, to compose His masterpiece. A part of His infinite perfection is also the Genius of Limitation.

To see if and how many worlds there were in a dead thing, Roberto went into the little museum on the *Daphne,* and he lined up on the bridge, as if he had before him so many astragals, all the dead objects he found there: fossils, pebbles, fish bones; he shifted his eyes from one to the other, continuing to reflect on Chance and chances.

But how do I know (he asked himself) that God tends to limitation, when my experience constantly reveals to me other, new worlds, whether up above or down below? It could then be that not God but the world is eternal and infinite and has always been so and ever shall be, in an infinite recomposition of its infinite atoms in an infinite void, according to laws I do not know yet, through unpredictable but regulated shifts of the atoms, which otherwise would move wildly. And then the world would be God. God would be born of eternity as Universe without shores, and I would be subject to its law, without knowing what that law was.

Fool, some say, you can speak of the infinity of God because you are not called upon to conceive it with your mind, but only to believe in it as one believes in a Mystery. But if you want to speak of natural philosophy, you must also conceive this infinite world, and you cannot.

Perhaps. But let us think, then, that the world is both full and finite. And let us try to conceive the Nothingness that comes after the world has ended. When we think of that Nothingness, can we perhaps picture it as a wind? No, because it would have to be truly nothing, not even wind. In terms of natural philosophy—not of faith—is an interminable nothing conceivable? It is much easier to imagine horned men or two-tailed fish through composition of parts already known: we can only add to the world, where we believe it ends, more parts similar to those we already know (an expanse made again and always of water and land, stars and skies). Without limit.

But if the world were finite, Nothingness, inasmuch as it is nothing, could not be, and what then would lie beyond the confines of the world? The Void. And so, to deny the infinite we affirm the Void, which can only be infinite, otherwise at its end we would have to think again of a new and inconceivable expanse of nothing. Thus it is better to think at once and freely of the Void and people it with atoms, reserving the right to think of it as empty, emptier than any emptiness.

Roberto discovered he was enjoying a great privilege, which gave a meaning to his defeat. Here he was holding the clear proof of the existence of other skies, but at the same time without having to ascend beyond the celestial spheres, for he intuited many worlds in a piece of coral. Was there any need to calculate the number of forms which the atoms of the

Universe could create—burning at the stake all those who said their number was not finite—when it sufficed to meditate for years on one of these marine objects to realize how the deviation of a single atom, whether willed by God or prompted by Chance, could generate inconceivable Milky Ways?

The Redemption? A false argument, indeed—Roberto protested, to avoid trouble with the next Jesuit he might meet—the argument of those who cannot conceive the Lord's omnipotence. Who can deny the possibility that in the great plan of Creation, Original Sin was realized at the same time on all worlds, in different and unheard-of ways yet all equally, so that Christ died on the Cross for all, including the Selenites and the Syrians and the Coralines who lived on the molecules of this tunneled rock when it was still living?

To tell the truth, Roberto was not entirely convinced by his own arguments; he was composing a dish that had too many ingredients, or, rather, he was cramming into a single argument things heard in various places—and he was not so ingenuous that he did not realize as much. So, having defeated one possible adversary, he restored speech to him and identified himself with the opponent's rebuttal.

Once, in speaking of the Void, Father Caspar had silenced him with a syllogism which Roberto could not answer: the Void is not being, but not being cannot be, ergo the Void cannot be. The reasoning was sound, because it denied the Void while granting that it could be conceived. In fact, we can quite easily conceive things that do not exist. Can a chimera, buzzing in the Void, devour second intentions? No, because chimeras do not exist, in the Void no buzzing can be heard, and intentions are mental things—an intended pear does not nourish us. And yet I can think of a chimera even if it is chimerical, namely, if it is not. And the same with the Void.

Roberto recalled the reply of a nineteen-year-old youth who one day in Paris had been invited to a gathering of his philosopher friends because he was said to be designing a machine capable of arithmetical calculations. Roberto had not clearly understood how the machine was supposed to work, and he had considered the boy (perhaps out of acrimony) too wan, too sad, and too pedantic for his age, whereas Roberto's libertine friends were teaching him that you could be learned in a playful fashion. And Roberto had tolerated it still less when, as they were discussing the Void, the boy insisted on speaking, even with a certain impudence: "There has been too much talk of the Void. Now it must be demonstrated through experiment." And he said this as if that task would one day fall to him.

Roberto asked what experiment he had in mind, and the boy replied that he did not yet know. To embarrass him, Roberto listed all the philosophical objections he could think of: If the Void existed, it would not be matter (which is full), nor would it be spirit, for we cannot conceive a spirit that is void, nor would it be God, because it would lack even its self, it would be neither substance nor accident, it would shed its light without being hyaline. . . . What, then, would it be?

The boy replied with humble boldness, his eyes lowered: "Perhaps it would be something halfway between matter and nothingness, and would partake of neither. It would differ from nothingness because of its dimension, and from matter because of its immobility. It would be almost a not-being. Not supposition, not abstraction. It would be. It would be—how shall I say it?—a fact. Pure and simple."

"What is a fact pure and simple, lacking any determination?" Roberto asked with scholastic arrogance. Though he had no opinions on the subject, he, too, wanted to talk pedantically.

"I am unable to define what is pure and simple," the youth answered. "For that matter, sir, how can you define being? To define it, it would be necessary to say that it is something. Thus to define being you would first have to say *is* and therefore use in the definition the term being defined. I believe there are terms impossible to define, and perhaps the Void is one of them. But I may be mistaken."

"You are not mistaken. The Void is like time," one of Roberto's libertine friends commented. "Time is not the quantity of movement, because movement depends on time and not vice versa; it is infinite, increate, continuous, it is not an accident of space. . . . Time is, and that is that. And the Void is. And that is also that."

Some protested, saying a thing that is *and that is that,* without having a definable essence, might just as well not be. "Gentlemen," the Canon of Digne then said, "it is true, space and time are neither body nor spirit, they are immaterial, if you like, but this does not mean they are not real. They are not accident and they are not substance, and yet they came before Creation, before any substance and any accident, and they will exist also after the destruction of every substance. They are immutable and invariable, whatever you may put inside them."

"But," Roberto objected, "space also extends, and extension is a property of bodies. . . ."

"No," the libertine friend rebutted, "the fact that all bodies extend does not mean that everything extended is a body— as a certain gentleman would have it, who moreover would not deign to reply to me, because it seems he no longer wants to return from Holland. Extension is the disposition of all that is. Space is absolute extension, eternal, infinite, increate, illimitable, uncircumscribed. Like time, it has no end, is inaccessible, impossible to disperse, it is an Arabian phoenix, a serpent biting its tail. . . ."

"Sir," the Canon said, "let us not put space in God's stead. . . ."

"Sir," the libertine replied, "you cannot present to us ideas that all of us consider true, then demand that we not draw from them the ultimate consequences. I suspect that at this point we no longer need God or His infinity, because we already have enough infinities on all sides reducing us to a shadow that lasts only an instant without return. So, then, I propose banishing all fear, and going—in a body—to the tavern."

Shaking his head, the Canon took his leave. And so did the youth, who seemed quite troubled by this talk; head bowed, he excused himself and said he had to return to his house.

"Poor boy," the libertine then said, "he builds machines to count the finite, and we have terrified him with the eternal silence of too many infinities. Voilà, the end of a fine vocation."

"He will not recover from the blow," another of the Pyrrhonians said. "He will try to make peace with the world, and he will end up among the Jesuits."

Roberto thought now of that dialogue. The Void and space were like time, or time was like the Void and space. Sidereal spaces exist where our earth appears like an ant, and so do spaces such as the world of corals, the ants of our Universe—and all these spaces are one inside the other. . . . Was it therefore unthinkable that there could be worlds subject to different times? Has it not been said that on Jove one day lasts a year? Therefore worlds must exist that live and die in the space of an instant, or survive beyond our ability to calculate both the Chinese dynasties and the date of the Flood. Worlds where all movements and the response to those movements do not occupy the time of hours and minutes but of millennia.

Did there not exist—and close at hand—a place where the time was yesterday?

Perhaps he had already entered one of those worlds where, once an atom of water had begun corroding the shell of a dead coral, now crumbled and scattered by the many years that had passed, as many as those from the birth of Adam to the Redemption. And was he not living his own love in this time, where Lilia, like the Orange Dove, had become something for whose conquest he now had at his disposal the tedium of centuries? Was he not preparing to live in an infinite future?

Towards many similar reflections a young gentleman who had only recently discovered those corals felt himself driven. . . . And there is no knowing where he would have arrived if he had had the spirit of a true philosopher. But Roberto was not a philosopher; instead he was an unhappy lover barely emerging from a venture, all things considered, not crowned with success: towards an Island that eluded him in the icy brumes of the day before.

He was, however, a lover who though educated in Paris had not forgotten his country life. Therefore he came to conclude that the time he was thinking about could be stretched in a thousand ways like dough made with egg yolks, as he had seen the women at La Griva knead it. I do not know why Roberto hit upon this simile—perhaps too much thinking had whetted his appetite, or perhaps, terrified by the eternal silence of all those infinities, he would have liked to be home again in the maternal kitchen. He soon went on to recall other rustic delicacies.

There were the pies stuffed with little birds, hares, and pheasants, as if to affirm that there can be many worlds, one next to the other or a world within a world. But his mother also made those cakes known as "German-style," with seven layers or stripes of fruit partitioned with butter, sugar, and cinnamon. And from that idea he went on to envision a salted cake, where amid various strata of pastry he put first one of ham, then one of sliced hard-boiled egg, then one of green vegetable. And this led Roberto to think that the Universe could be a pan in which different stories were cooking at the same time, each at its own rate but perhaps all with the same characters. And as the eggs that are below in a pie have no notion of what is happening, beyond their layer of pastry, to their fellow eggs or to the ham above them, so in one stratum of the Universe one Roberto could not know what the other was doing.

Granted, this is not a refined way of reasoning, and with the belly, moreover. But it is obvious he already had in mind the point at which he wanted to arrive: In a single moment many different Robertos could be doing different things, perhaps under different names.

Perhaps under the name of Ferrante? In that case, could the story he believed he was inventing about an enemy brother not be the obscure perception of a world where to him, Roberto, other vicissitudes were occurring, different from those he was experiencing in this world and at this time?

Come now, he said to himself, of course you would have liked to be the one experiencing what Ferrante experienced when the *Tweede Daphne* unfurled her sails to the wind. But this we know because, as Saint-Savin said, there exist thoughts we do not think about at all, though they make an impression on the heart without the heart (still less the mind) becoming aware; and it is inevitable that some of these thoughts—which at times are nothing but obscure desires, and not even all that obscure—should be introduced into the universe of the Romance that you think you are conceiving for the pleasure of portraying the thoughts of others. . . . But I am I, and Ferrante is Ferrante, and now I will prove it, having him experience adventures of which I could not be the protagonist—and which, if they take place in any universe, it is that of Imagination, parallel to none other.

And he took pleasure, all that night long, heedless of the corals, in conceiving an adventure that, however, would lead him once again to the most lacerated delight, the most exquisite suffering.

CHAPTER 35

Joyfull Newes out of the Newfound Worlde

FERRANTE HAD TOLD Lilia, now ready to believe any falsehoods that might come from those beloved lips, a story almost true, except that in it he played the part of Roberto, and Roberto that of Ferrante; and he convinced her to sacrifice all the jewels in the casket she had brought with her to find the usurper and tear from him a document of capital importance to the fate of the Nation, which the other had torn from him, and with which, returning it, he could obtain the Cardinal's pardon.

After fleeing the French shores, the *Tweede Daphne's* first port of call was Amsterdam. There Ferrante, double spy that he was, could find someone able to give him information of a ship named the *Amaryllis*. Whatever that information was, a few days later he was in London looking for someone else. And the man to whom he addressed himself could only have been a villain of his own stamp, ready to betray those for whom he was betraying others.

So Ferrante, having received from Lilia a diamond of great purity, was seen entering at night a pothouse where he was welcomed by a creature of dubious sex, perhaps a former eunuch of the Turks, with a glabrous face and a mouth so small you would have said he smiled only by moving his nose.

The room Ferrante stole into was frightful thanks to the smuts from a pile of bones burning in a smoldering fire. In one corner a naked corpse was hanging by its feet, secreting a nettle-colored liquid from its mouth into a copper basin.

The eunuch recognized Ferrante as a brother in crime. He heard the question, saw the diamond, and betrayed his masters. He led him into another room that looked like an apothecary's shop, filled with jars of clay, glass, tin, copper. All contained substances that served to alter the aspect of their users: crones who wanted to appear young and beautiful, miscreants who sought to disguise their features. There were rouges, emollients, asphodel roots, tarragon bark, and a substance made with stag marrow and water of honeysuckle that refined the skin. He had pastes to turn the hair blond, a mixture of green ilex, rye, white horehound, soda niter, alum, and yarrow; or to change the complexion there were compounds of stallion, bear, camel, snake, rabbit, whale, mare, bittern, doe, wildcat, and otter. Also an oil for the face made of styrax, lemon, pine-nut, elm, lupin, vetch, and chickpea, and a shelf of bladders with which strumpets could seem virgins. For those who would ensnare a lover he had viper tongues, quail heads, asses' brains, pilewort, badgers' paws, stones from eagles' nest, hearts shaped in tallow thick with broken needles, and other objects made of mud and lead most repugnant to the sight.

In the center of the room stood a table, and on it was a basin covered with a bloodied cloth, to which the eunuch pointed with a look of complicity. Ferrante did not understand, and his host assured him he had come to the right man. In fact, the eunuch was none other than he who had wounded Dr. Byrd's dog and who, every day at the agreed time, dipping into vitriol water the cloth steeped in the animal's blood, or holding the same cloth to the fire, had been transmitting to the *Amaryllis* the signals Byrd awaited.

The eunuch related everything about Byrd's voyage and about the ports where he would surely have called. Ferrante, who truly knew little or nothing of the matter of longitudes, could not imagine that Mazarin had sent Roberto on that ship only to learn something that to him now seemed obvious, so he concluded that what Roberto was really meant to reveal to the Cardinal was the location of the Islands of Solomon.

He believed the *Tweede Daphne* swifter than the *Amaryllis,* he trusted his luck, he thought he would easily overtake Byrd's ship, and, since it would have landed on the Islands, he could more easily surprise the crew ashore, exterminate them (Roberto included), and then dispose of that territory at his pleasure, as he would be its sole discoverer.

It was the eunuch who suggested to him the method of proceeding without mistaking his course: it would suffice to wound another dog, and every day act upon a sample of its blood, as the eunuch did for the *Amaryllis* dog, and Ferrante would receive the same daily messages that Byrd received.

"I will sail at once," Ferrante said, and when the other reminded him that first a dog would have to be found, "I have a far better dog on board," he exclaimed. He took the eunuch onto the ship, made sure that among the crew there was a barber expert in phlebotomy and other similar chores. "I, Captain," declared one who had eluded a hundred nooses and a thousand fetters, "when we ran the seas, I cut off more arms and legs of comrades than I wounded enemies!"

Descending into the hold, Ferrante chained Biscarat to two stakes crossed obliquely and, grasping a knife, deeply cut the captain's hip. As Biscarat moaned, the eunuch collected the dripping blood with a cloth he had put in a bucket. Then he explained to the barber how he should keep the wound open for all the duration of the voyage, not allowing the wounded man to die but also not allowing the wound to heal.

After this latest crime, Ferrante ordered the men to set sail for the Islands of Solomon.

Having written this chapter, Roberto felt disgust and weariness, himself crushed by the labor of so many evil deeds.

He no longer wanted to imagine the sequel, and instead he wrote an invocation to Nature, praying that—as a mother, wishing to make her baby sleep in his cradle, draws a cloth over it and covers him in his own little night—she draws deep night over the planet. He prayed that Night, stealing everything from his view, bid his eyes close; that, together with darkness, silence come; and that—as at the rise of the sun, lions, bears, and wolves (to whom, as to thieves and assassins, daylight is hateful) run to hide in caves where they find refuge and safety—as the sun withdrew beyond the west, all the din and the tumult of his thoughts retire. That, once the light was dead, the spirits that the light revived in him would be stunned, and mute repose would reign.

When he blew out the lamp, his hands were illuminated only by a lunar ray entering from outside. A fog rose from his stomach to his brain and, falling on his eyelids, closed them so that his spirit could no longer peer out and see any distracting object. And not only did his eyes and ears sleep, but also his hands and feet—everything save the heart, which never rests.

Does the soul also sleep during such repose? Alas, no. It remains wakeful, only it withdraws behind a curtain and becomes theater: then phantom zanies come on stage and perform a comedy, but such as a company of drunken or mad actors might play, so travestied seem the characters, so strange

the dress and lewd the attitudes, so inappropriate the situations, so outrageous the speech.

As when you cut a centipede into several parts, and the
separated sections run off blindly, because except for the first,
which comprises the head, the others cannot see; and each,
like a healthy roach, goes off on the five or six legs left him,
carrying away that piece of soul that is his. Similarly, in
dreams, from the stem of a flower you see a crane's neck
sprout, ending in a baboon's head with four snail's horns that
spit fire, or you see blossoming from an old man's chin a
peacock's tail as beard; another man's arms look like twisted
vines, and his eyes are lights glowing in a conch shell, and his
nose is a reed-pipe.

Roberto, who was sleeping, thus dreamed Ferrante's voyage
as it continued; only he was dreaming it as a dream.

A revelatory dream, I would say. It almost seems that Roberto, after his meditations on infinite worlds, no longer
wanted to imagine a plot unfolding in the Land of Romances
but, rather, a real story in a real land, a land he also inhabited,
except that—as the Island lay in the simple past—his story
could take place in a not distant future, which could satisfy
his desire for a space less confined than that to which his
shipwreck had sentenced him.

If he had begun the story by presenting a generic Ferrante,
an Iago, his rancor conceived for an offense never suffered, a
Ferrante who now, unable to bear the sight of the Other at
Lilia's side, was taking his place, then—daring to recognize his
darkest thoughts—Roberto would have admitted openly that
Ferrante was himself.

Now Roberto was persuaded that the world could be experienced from infinite parallaxes; before, he had set himself
up as an indiscreet eye to study Ferrante's actions in the Land
of Romances, or in a past that had also been his own. (That

past had barely touched him, touched him without his realizing it, as it was determining his present.) Roberto was now
becoming the eye of Ferrante, for in the company of his adversary he wanted to enjoy the events that fate held in store.

So now the vessel proceeded across the liquid meadows,
and the pirates were docile. Watching over the voyage of the
two lovers, the buccaneers confined themselves to discovering
marine monsters and, before arriving on the American shores,
they sighted a Triton. As for the part visible out of the water,
the creature had a human form, except that the arms were
short in proportion to the body: the hands were big, the hair
gray and thick, and it had a beard down to its stomach. Its
eyes were large, its skin rough. As they approached it, it
seemed submissive and moved towards the net. But as soon as
it felt the men drawing it to the boat, and even before it could
reveal itself below the navel, showing whether or not it had a
fish's tail, it ripped the net with one blow and vanished. Later
it was seen taking the sun on a rock, but still hiding the lower
part of its body. Looking at the ship, it waved its arms as if
applauding.

After entering the Pacific Ocean, they arrived at an island
where the lions were black and the hens clad in wool, where
the trees flowered only at night, the fish had wings and the
birds scales, stones floated and wood sank, butterflies shone in
the dark, and water was intoxicating like wine.

On a second island they saw a palace built of rotting wood,
painted with colors that offended the eye. They entered and
found themselves in a hall lined with raven's feathers. In every
wall there were niches where instead of stone busts they saw
homunculi with emaciated faces, who by an accident of Nature
had been born without legs.

On a filthy throne sat the King, who with a wave of his

hand initiated a concert of hammers, drills that screeched against stone slabs, and knives that squeaked on porcelain plates. At the noise six men appeared, all skin and bones, abominable in their distorted gaze.

Opposite them appeared some women, the fattest imaginable: bowing to their companions, they began a dance that underlined their deformity and awkwardness. Then six brutes burst in, looking as if all had been born of one womb, their noses and mouths so big, and backs so gibbous, that they seemed not so much creatures as lies of Nature.

After the dance our travelers, having heard not one word uttered and assuming that on this island a language was spoken different from their own, tried asking questions with gestures, that universal language in which one can communicate also with Savages. But the man replied in a language that resembled, rather, the Lost Language of Birds, made of trills and whistles, and they understood it as if it were their native tongue. They learned that whereas in every other place beauty was prized, in this palace only the hideous was appreciated. And this was what they should expect if they continued their voyage to lands where what is normally above lies below.

Resuming the journey, they reached a third island, which seemed deserted, and Ferrante, alone with Lilia, ventured into the interior. As they advanced, they heard a voice that counseled them to flee: this was the Island of Invisible Men. At that very instant there were many natives around the couple, pointing at the two visitors who shamelessly exposed themselves to the gaze of others. For these people, in fact, being looked upon, one became the victim of another's gaze and lost his own nature, transformed into the opposite of himself.

On a fourth island they found a man with hollow eyes, a thin voice, his face all a single wrinkle, but with fresh colors. His beard and hair were like cotton wool, his body so palsied that when he turned, he had to make a complete revolution. He said he was three hundred and forty years old, and in that time he had renewed his youth three times, having drunk the water from the Fount of Youth, which rose in that very land, prolonging life but not beyond three hundred forty years— hence in a short while he would die. The old man warned the travelers not to seek the fountain: living there, becoming first the double then the triple of oneself was a source of great afflictions, and in the end one no longer knew who one was. And worse: living the same sorrows three times was a suffering, but it was a suffering to relive even the same joys. The joy of life is born from feeling, whether it be joy or grief, always of short duration, and woe to those who know they will enjoy eternal bliss.

But the Antipodal World was beautiful in its variety, and, sailing another thousand miles, they reached a fifth island, which was only a pullulation of ponds. Each inhabitant spent his life on his knees at a pond, contemplating himself, believing that one who is not seen is as if nonexistent, and if they were to look away, ceasing to see themselves in the water, they would die.

They landed then at a sixth island, still farther to the west, where all the natives talked among themselves incessantly, one telling another what he would like the other to be and do, and vice versa. Those islanders, in fact, could live only if they were narrated; if a transgressor told unpleasant stories about others, forcing them to enact the events, the others would cease telling anything about him, and he would die.

But their concern was to invent for each individual a different story: if they all had the same story, they would not be able to tell one another apart, because each is what his experiences have created. That is why they had constructed a great wheel which they called Cynosura Lucensis. Erected in the village square, it was made up of six concentric circles that revolved separately. The first was divided into twenty-four slots or windows, the second into thirty-six, the third into forty-eight, the fifth into seventy two, the sixth into eighty four. In the various slots, according to a system that Lilia and Ferrante could not grasp in so short a time, were written actions (such as come, go, die), passions (such as hate, love, indifference), then manners (good or ill), sorrow or happiness, and places and times (at home or next month).

Spinning the wheels created stories like "He went yesterday to his home and met his enemy who was suffering, and helped him," or else "He saw an animal with seven heads and killed it." The inhabitants declared that with this machine they could write or think seven hundred twenty-two million different stories, and there were enough to give meaning to the lives of each of them for centuries to come. This pleased Roberto, because he would be able to build a wheel of this sort and go on thinking up stories even if he were to remain on the *Daphne* for ten thousand years.

Many and bizarre were the discoveries of lands that Roberto himself would have liked to discover. But at a certain point in his dreaming he wanted a less populous place for the two lovers, so that they could bask in their love.

Thus he had them arrive at a seventh and most lovely beach, enhanced by a little wood standing at the shore of the sea. They crossed it and found themselves in a royal garden where, along a shady allée among lawns decorated with beds of flowers, many fountains played.

But Roberto, as if the pair were seeking a more private refuge and he new sufferings, caused them to reach a flowering arch, beyond which they stepped into a little vale where reeds of some marshy cane rustled in a breeze that scattered in the air a mixture of perfumes. And from a little pool, down glistening steps, a line of water bubbled as pure as a string of pearls.

He wanted—and I feel his staging followed all the rules—the thick shade of an oak to encourage the lovers at their feast, and he further added gay plane trees, humble arbutus, prickly junipers, fragile tamarisks, and supple limes garlanding a lawn illuminated like an Oriental tapestry. With what would Nature, the painter of the world, have adorned it? Violets and narcissus.

He left the two to their abandon, while a limp poppy raised from heavy oblivion its drowsy head to drink in those dewy sighs. But then he preferred that, humiliated by such beauty, it flush with shame and self-contempt. As he, Roberto, did; and we can only say it served him right.

To avoid seeing further what he would so have liked himself to be seen doing, Roberto then rose with his morphetic omniscience to overlook the entire island, where now the fountains commented on the amorous miracle of which they wished to be patrons.

There were little columns, ampoules, phials from which a single jet spurted—or many, from many little spouts—and others had at their summit a kind of ark from whose windows a flow descended, forming as it fell a doubly weeping willow. One, a single cylindrical stem, generated at its head many smaller, similar cylinders facing in various directions, as if it were a casemate or fortress or ship of the line armed with cannon—an artillery of water.

Some were plumed, or maned, or bearded, in as many varieties as the stars of the Magi in Nativities, whose tails their jets imitated. On one stood the statue of a boy holding an umbrella in his left hand, its ribs ending in as many jets; while in his right the child held his tiny member and mingled in a stoup his urine with the waters coming from the dome above him.

In another, on a capital lay a tailed fish that seemed to have just swallowed Jonah, and it expelled water from its mouth as well as from two holes opening above its eyes. And astride it was a cupid armed with a trident. A fountain in the form of a flower supported, with its central jet, a ball; while another was a tree, whose many blooms, each one, made a sphere spin, and it seemed so many planets were moving one around the other in the globe of the water. There were fountains where the very petals of the flower were of water, pouring from a continuous slit bordering a wheel set on a column.

Replacing air with water, organ pipes emitted not sounds but liquefied breaths, and others were like candelabra, water enacting fire, where flames burning in the center of the column cast lights on the foam rising on all sides.

Another seemed a peacock, crested, with a broad tail opened, for which the sky supplied the colors. Not to mention fountains that looked like stands to support a wig and were adorned with flowing locks. In one, a sunflower opened in a single dew. Another had the face of the sun itself, finely sculpted, with a series of nozzles around its circumference, so that the celestial body emitted not rays but coolness.

On one a cylinder rotated, ejaculating water from a series of spiral furrows. There were fountains with the mouths of lions or tigers, with gryphon's maw and serpent's tongue, and one was a female weeping from her eyes and her teats. And for the rest it was all a vomiting of fauns, a purling of winged creatures, a whispering of swans, a showering from Nile elephants' trunks, a spilling of alabaster vessels, an emptying of cornucopias.

Visions that for Roberto—on closer study—were a fall from the frying-pan into the fire.

Meanwhile in the vale the now-sated lovers had only to

reach out and accept from a leafy vine the gift of its treasures, and a fig, as if wishing to weep tenderly over the spied-on union, distilled tears of honey, while on an almond tree bejewelled with blossoms lamented the Orange Dove. . . .

Then Roberto woke, soaked with sweat.

"What?" he said to himself reproachfully. "I succumbed to the temptation to live through Ferrante, and now I realize that it is Ferrante who has lived through me, that as I was moping, he was truly experiencing what I permitted him to experience!"

To cool his anger, and to have visions that—these, at least—were denied Ferrante, he again set out early in the morning, rope around his loins and Persona Vitrea on his face, towards his world of coral.

CHAPTER 36

The Rule and Exercises of Holy Dying

REACHING THE EDGE of the reef, Roberto swam with his face submerged among those endless loggias, but he was unable to admire the animated rocks serenely because a Medusa had transformed him into inanimate stone. In his dream he had seen the looks Lilia bestowed on the usurper; and if in the dream those looks had enflamed him, now in waking memory they froze him.

Roberto wanted to regain possession of his Lilia; he swam, thrusting his face down as far as possible, as if that embrace with the sea could award him the prize that in his dream he had awarded Ferrante. It did not require a great effort, on the part of his spirit trained to form concepts, to imagine Lilia in every undulant cadence of that submerged park, to see her lips in every flower, where he would lose himself like a greedy bee. In transparent greenery he found again the veil that had covered her face on the first nights, and he stretched out his hand to raise that screen.

In this intoxication of his reason, he regretted that his eyes could not rove as freely as his heart wished, and among the corals he sought his beloved's bracelet, her snood, the bangle

449

that beguiled the lobe of her ear, the sumptuous necklaces that adorned her swan-like neck.

Lost in his search, he allowed himself at one point to be attracted by a jewel that appeared to him in a crevass; he removed his mask, arched his back, raised his legs vigorously, and forced himself towards the sea bed. The thrust was excessive, he tried to grasp the edge of a shelf; just before closing his fingers around a crusted rock, he seemed to see a fat and sleepy eye open. At that same instant he remembered Dr. Byrd had spoken to him of a Stone Fish that lurks among the coral caverns to surprise any living creature with the venom of its scales.

Too late. His hand had rested on the Thing and an intense pain shot through his arm to his shoulder. With a twist of his trunk he managed miraculously not to end up with his face and chest on top of the Monster, but to arrest his momentum he had to strike it with the mask. In the impact the mask shattered, but he had to let go of it anyway. Pressing his feet against the rock below, he pushed himself up to the surface while in the space of a few seconds he saw the Persona Vitrea sink out of sight.

His right hand and his entire forearm were swollen, his shoulder numb; he was afraid he might faint; he found the rope and with great effort gradually succeeded in pulling it, a little at a time, with one hand. He climbed the ladder, much as he had on the night of his arrival, not knowing how, and, as on that night, he slumped to the deck.

But now the sun was already high. His teeth chattering, Roberto recalled Dr. Byrd telling him that after an encounter with the Stone Fish most humans were doomed; a few did survive, but no one knew an antidote against that suffering. Though his eyes were clouded, he tried to examine the wound—it was no more than a scratch, but it must have been enough to allow the mortal substance to penetrate his veins. He lost consciousness.

When he woke, his fever was raging and he felt an intense thirst. He realized that on this edge of the ship, exposed to the elements, far from food and drink, he would not last long. He crawled below and reached the partition between the stores and the chicken pen. He drank greedily from a keg of water, but he felt his stomach contract. He fainted again, his face in his own vomit.

During a night racked by fierce dreams, he attributed his sufferings to Ferrante, whom he now confused with the Stone Fish. Why did Ferrante want to block his way to the Island and to the Dove? Was this why he had set out in pursuit of Roberto?

He could see himself lying there and looking at another self seated opposite him, beside a stove, dressed in a house robe, trying to decide if the hands he touched and the body he felt were his. He, who saw the other, felt his clothes on fire. Then, while the other was clothed, he was naked—but he no longer knew which of the two was awake and which asleep, and he thought that both were surely figures produced by his mind. No, not he, because he thought, and therefore he was.

The other (but which?) at a certain point stood up, but he had to be the Evil Genius who was transforming Roberto's world into dream, for already he was no longer himself but Father Caspar. "You've come back!" Roberto murmured, holding out his arms. But the priest did not answer or move. He looked at him. It was surely Father Caspar, but as if the sea —giving him up—had cleansed and rejuvenated him. His beard was trimmed, his face plump and roseate like Padre Emanuele's, his habit unwrinkled and neat. Then, still motionless, like an actor declaiming, and in impeccable language, a skilled orator, he said with a grim smile: "It is useless for you to defend yourself. Now the whole world has a single destination, and it is Hell."

He went on in a loud voice, as if speaking from the pulpit of a church: "Yes, Hell, of which you know little, you and all those who along with you are proceeding with light foot and mad spirit! Did you believe that in Hell you would find swords, daggers, wheels, razors, streams of sulphur, potions of molten lead, frozen waters, cauldrons and grates, saws and clubs, awls to gouge out eyes, pincers to pull teeth, combs to rip open flanks, chains to pound the bones, animals that gnaw, hooks that pull, thongs that choke, racks, crosses, goads, and axes? No! Those are merciless torments, true, but such as the human mind can still conceive, as we have also conceived bronze bulls, seats of iron, and sharpened reeds to push under fingernails. . . . You hoped Hell was a reef made up of Stone Fish. No, the torments of Hell are something different, because they are born not from our finite mind but from the infinite mind of a wrathful and vindictive God, forced to display His fury and show that as His mercy was great in absolution, no less great is His justice in punishment! They must be such torments that in them we can see the gulf between our impotence and His omnipotence!"

"In this world," that messenger of penance continued, "you are used to seeing that for every ill a remedy is found, that there is no wound without its balm, no venom without its theriac. But you must not think it is the same in Hell. Burns there, it is true, are highly troublesome, but there is no liniment that soothes them; thirst sears, but there is no water to slake it; hunger is rabid, but no food allays it; unendurable is the shame, but no cover can cover it. If there were at least death to put an end to such woe, death, death . . . But this is the worst, for there you can never hope for a deliverance, even one as grievous as your own extermination! You will seek death in all its forms, you will seek death and never be fortunate enough to find it. Death! Death, where art thou, you will shout constantly, but what demon would be merciful and offer it to you? And you will understand that down there the suffering never ends!"

The old man paused, extended his arms, his hands turned towards Heaven, as he muttered in a whisper, as if to confide a tremendous secret that should never go beyond that nave. "Suffering that never ends? Does that mean we shall suffer until a little goldfinch, drinking one drop every year, succeeds in draining all the world's seas? No, longer. *In saecula.* Shall we suffer until a plant louse, taking one bite every year, has devoured every forest? No, longer. *In saecula.* Will we suffer, then, until an ant, taking one step every year, has circled the entire earth? No, longer. *In saecula.* And if all this Universe were desert and once every century a single grain were taken from it, would we perhaps end our suffering when the Universe was empty? Not even then. *In saecula.* Assume that a damned soul, after millions of centuries, can shed only two tears, will we then continue suffering until his weeping has sufficed to form a flood greater than that which in ancient times destroyed the human race? Come now, enough of this, we are not children! If you want me to say it, then: *In saecula, in saecula* must the damned suffer, *in saecula,* which means centuries without number, without end, without measure."

Now Father Caspar's face seemed that of the Carmelite at La Griva. He raised his eyes as if to find in Heaven a sole hope of mercy. "But what of God," he said with the voice of a penitent worthy of compassion, "yes, what of God? Does He not suffer at the sight of our sufferings? Will He not feel a pang of concern, in the end will He not reveal Himself, so we can be consoled at least by His weeping? Alas, ye innocent!

God, unfortunately, will show Himself, but you still cannot imagine how! When we raise our eyes, we will see that He (must I say it?) . . . we will see that He, having become for us a Nero, not in injustice but in severity, will not console us or succor us or sympathize with us, but, rather, He will laugh with inconceivable delight! Imagine what ravings must then seize us! We burn—we will say—and God laughs? We burn, and God laughs? Oh, most cruel God! Why do You not torture us with Your thunderbolts, rather than insult us with Your laughter? Redouble, merciless One, our flames, but do not rejoice in them! Ah, Your laughter for us is more bitter than our tears! Ah, Your joy to us is more grievous than our woes! Why does our Hell not have chasms where we can flee the countenance of a God that laughs? Too long have we been deceived by those who told us that our punishment would be the sight of the face of a scornful God. A laughing God, we should have been told, a laughing God. . . . Rather than see and hear that laughter we would have the mountains collapse on our heads, or the earth disappear beneath our feet; but no, in our misfortune we shall see what pains us, and be blind and deaf to everything except to what we wish to be blind and deaf!"

Roberto smelled the sour odor of the chicken feed in the gaps of the planks, and from outside came the mewing of the sea birds, which he had mistaken for the laughter of God.

"But why Hell for me?" he asked. "And why for all? Was it not to keep it only for a few that Christ redeemed us?"

Father Caspar laughed like the God of the damned. "Why, when did He redeem you? On what planet, in what universe do you think you are living now?"

He took Roberto's hand, raising him violently from where he lay, and dragged him through the maze of the *Daphne* as the sick man felt a gnawing at his intestine, and it was as if his head housed only foliot clocks. Clocks, he thought: time, death. . . .

Caspar dragged him into a room he had never discovered, its walls white; there Roberto saw a closed catafalque with a circular eye on one side. Before the eye, on a grooved runner, was inserted a little wooden strip fitted with several eyes, all the same size, framing pieces of opaque glass. As the strip was moved along the groove, the eyes could be aligned serially with the eye of the box. Roberto recalled having once seen in Provence a smaller version of this machine that, it was said, could bring light to life thanks to shadows.

Father Caspar opened the side of the box, allowing a glimpse of a great lamp on a tripod; on the side opposite the spout the lamp had, not a handle, but a round, specially curved mirror. When the lamp's wick was lit, the mirror projected the luminous rays into a pipe, a short spyglass whose terminal lens was that external eye. From here (as soon as Caspar had closed the box again) the rays passed through the glass of the strip, broadening in a cone and casting on the wall some colored images, which to Roberto seemed truly alive, so vivid and precise were they.

The first figure represented a man with a demon's face chained to a rock in the midst of the sea, lashed by the waves. Roberto could not tear his eyes from that apparition, he blended it with those that followed (as Father Caspar caused them to appear, sliding the strip of wood) and composed them all—dream within dream—without distinguishing what was being said to him from what he was seeing.

A ship was approaching the rock, and he recognized it as the *Tweede Daphne;* from it Ferrante descended, now freeing the chained man. All was clear. In the course of his voyaging, Ferrante had found Judas—as the legend assures us he was to be found—imprisoned upon the open sea, to expiate his betrayal.

"Thank you," Judas said to Ferrante—but to Roberto the voice surely came from the lips of Caspar. "From the time I was bound here until the ninth hour today I have hoped to be able yet to atone for my sin. . . . I thank you, brother. . . ."

"You have been here only a day, or even less?" Ferrante said. "But your sin was committed in the thirty-third year after the birth of Our Lord, and therefore one thousand six hundred and ten years ago. . . ."

"Ah, simple mind," Judas replied, "it is surely one thousand six hundred and ten of your years since I was set on this rock, but it is not yet and never will be one day for me. You do not know that, entering the sea that surrounds this island of mine, you penetrated another world that flows alongside and within yours, and here the sun moves around the earth like a tortoise whose every step is slower than the one before. So in this my world, at the beginning my day lasted two of yours, and then three, and so on, more and more, until now, after one thousand six hundred and ten of your years, I am still and always at the ninth hour. And soon time will be even slower, and then slower still, and I will live always at the ninth hour of the year thirty-three after that night in Bethlehem. . . ."

"But why?" Ferrante asked.

"Why, because God has willed that my punishment consist in living always on Good Friday, to celebrate always and every day the Passion of the man I betrayed. The first day of my suffering, when for other human beings sunset approached, and then night, and then the dawn of Saturday, for me only an atom of an atom of a minute of the ninth hour of that Friday had gone by. As the course of my sun began to move even more slowly, for the rest of you Christ was rising from the dead, but I was still barely a step from that hour. And now, when centuries and centuries have passed for you, I am still only a crumb of time from that instant. . . ."

"But still this sun of yours moves, and the day will come, even if after ten thousand years and more, when you will enter your Saturday."

"Yes, and then it will be worse. I will have left my Purgatory to enter my Hell. My grief at the death I caused will not cease, but I will have lost the possibility, which still remains to me, of making what happened not happen."

"But how?"

"You do not know that not far from here runs the antipodal meridian. Beyond that line, both in your world and in mine, lies the day before. If I, now freed, could cross that line, I would be in my Holy Thursday, for this scapular that you see on my back is the bond that requires my sun to accompany me like my shadow, and guarantee that wherever I go, all time has the duration of mine. I could then reach Jerusalem, traveling through a very long Thursday, and I could arrive there before the completion of my wickedness. And I would save my Master from His fate."

"But," Ferrante objected, "if you prevent the Passion, then there will never be the Redemption, and the world will still be stained by original sin."

"Aii!" Judas shouted, crying. "I was thinking only of myself! But what must I do then? If I continue to let myself act as I acted, I remain damned. If I amend my error, I confound the plan of God and will be punished by damnation. Was it then written from the beginning that I was damned to be damned?"

The procession of images went dark at the weeping of Judas, as the oil of the lamp was consumed. Father Caspar was speaking again, in a voice Roberto no longer recognized as his.

The scant light now came from a fissure in the wall and illuminated only half of the priest's face, distorting the line of his nose and making the color of his beard uncertain, very white on one side and very dark on the other. The eyes were both hollows, because the one exposed to the light seemed also in shadow. Roberto realized only then that it was covered by a black patch.

"And it is at that point," he said now, this man who was surely the Abbé de Morfi, "it is at that moment that your brother conceives the masterstroke of his Genius. If he makes the journey Judas has suggested, he can prevent the Passion from taking place, and thus prevent Redemption from being granted us. No Redemption, all men victims of the same original sin, all doomed to Hell, your brother a sinner—but a sinner like all humankind, and therefore justified."

"But how could he, how can he, how did he?" Roberto asked.

"Oh"—the abbé smiled with horrid glee—"it required very little. It sufficed only to deceive the Almighty as well, who is incapable of conceiving every travesty of the truth. It sufficed to kill Judas, as I promptly did on that rock, put on his scapular, send my ship ahead to the opposite shore of the Island, arrive here in disguise to prevent your learning the correct rules of swimming so you could never precede me over there, then force you to construct with me the aquatic bell to enable me to reach the Island." And as he spoke, he slowly removed his habit, appearing in pirate garb, then equally slowly he removed the beard, rid himself of the wig, and Roberto thought he was seeing himself in a mirror.

"Ferrante!" he cried.

"In person, my dear brother. I, who—as you were struggling like a dog or a frog—found my ship again on the far side of the Island, and sailed through my long Thursday to-

wards Jerusalem, found the other Judas on the verge of betraying, hanged him from a fig tree, preventing him from
handing over the Son of Man to the Sons of Darkness, entered
the Garden of Olives with my men and abducted Our Lord,
stealing Him from Calvary! And now you, I, all of us are living
in a world that has never been redeemed!"

"But Christ? Where is Christ now?"

"Do you then not know that the ancient texts already said
there are doves the color of flame because the Lord, before
being crucified, wore a scarlet tunic? Have you not yet understood? For one thousand six hundred and ten years Christ has
been prisoner on the Island, whence He tries to escape in the
form of an Orange Dove, but is unable to abandon that place,
where next to the Specula Melitensis I have left Judas's scapular, and where it is therefore forever the same day. Now all
I have to do is kill you, and live free in a world where remorse
is banned, Hell is certain for all, and where one day I shall be
crowned the new Lucifer!" And he drew a dirk, took a step
towards Roberto to commit his final crime.

"No!" Roberto shouted. "I will not allow it! I will kill you
and free Christ. I can still wield my sword, and it was to me,
not to you, that my father taught his secrets!"

"I have had only one father, one mother: your festered
mind," Ferrante said with a sad smile. "You taught me only
to hate. Do you think you have given me a great gift, giving
me life so that in your Land of Romances I could embody
Suspicion? As long as you are alive, thinking for me what I
must think, I will never cease to despise myself. So whether
you kill me or I kill you, the end is the same. En garde!"

"Forgive me, my brother," Roberto cried. "Yes, let us fight.
It is fitting that one of us die."

What did Roberto want? To die, to set Ferrante free
by making him die? Prevent Ferrante from preventing the

Redemption? We will never know, for he did not know the answer himself. But this is the way of dreams.

They climbed up on deck. Roberto hunted for his weapon and found it reduced (as we will recall) to a stump; but he shouted that God would give him strength, and a good swordsman can fight even with a broken blade.

The two brothers confronted each other for the first time, to begin their last conflict.

The heavens were ready to abet the fratricide. A reddish cloud suddenly cast between ship and sky a bloody shadow as if, up above, they had slaughtered the Horses of the Sun. A great concert of thunder and lightning erupted, followed by a downpour, and sky and sea deafened the duellers, dazzling their vision, striking their hands with icy water.

But the two darted here and there among the thunderbolts that rained around them, attacking each other with blows and side cuts, suddenly falling back, clutching a hawser, almost flying to avoid a thrust, hurling abuse, cadencing every attack with a cry, among the equal cries of the wind howling around them.

On that slippery deck Roberto was fighting so that Christ could be nailed to the Cross, and he invoked divine aid; Ferrante, to prevent Christ's suffering, invoked the names of all the devils.

Called to assist him was Astaroth, as the Intruder (now intruding also into the plans of Providence) offered himself involuntarily to the coup de la mouette. Or perhaps this is what he wished, to conclude that dream that had neither beginning nor end.

Roberto pretended to fall, the other rushed to finish him off; Roberto, leaning on his right hand, thrust the broken sword at his opponent's chest. He did not spring up with the agility of Saint-Savin, but Ferrante at this point had accumulated too much impetus and could not avoid being stuck, or, rather, impaling himself at his sternum on the stump of the blade. Roberto choked on the blood that poured from the mouth of his enemy, in death.

He tasted blood in his mouth, and probably in his delirium he had bitten his tongue. Now he was swimming in that blood, which spread from the ship to the Island; he did not want to advance for fear of the Stone Fish, but he had completed only the first part of his mission, Christ was waiting on the Island to shed His blood, and Roberto was now His sole Messiah.

What was he doing now in his dream? With Ferrante's dirk he had begun tearing a sail into long strips, which he then knotted together with the help of ropes. On the lower deck he had captured, using thongs, the hardiest of the cranes or storks or whatever they might be, and he was now binding them by their legs, as coursers, to that flying carpet of his.

With his aerial ship he rose in flight towards the now attainable land. Under the Specula Melitensis he found the scapular and destroyed it. Having restored space to time, he saw descending upon him the Dove, which finally, ecstatic, he saw in all its glory. But it was natural—or, rather, supernatural— that the bird now should appear to him not orange but white. Yet it could not be a dove, for the dove is not suited to represent the Second Person of the Trinity; it was perhaps a Pious Pelican, as the Son must be. Roberto could not clearly see what bird was offered him as sweet topsail for that winged vessel.

He only knew that he was flying upwards, and images followed one another as the mad phantoms would have it. They were now navigating in the direction of all the innumerable and infinite worlds, to every planet, to every star, so that on each, as if in a single moment, the Redemption would be achieved.

The first planet they reached was the pure moon, on a

night illuminated by the earth's midday. And the earth hung on the line of the horizon, an enormous looming boundless polenta of cornmeal still cooking in the sky and almost falling upon him, gurgling with fevered and feverish fevery ferocity in boiling boils on the boil, plop ploppity plop. The fact is that when you have the fever, you become polenta, and the lights you see all come from the boiling of your head.

And there on the moon, with the Dove . . .

We will not have looked for coherence and verisimilitude, I trust, in all I have narrated thus far, because we have been describing the nightmare of a man poisoned by a Stone Fish. But what I am preparing to narrate surpasses all our expectations. The mind or the heart of Roberto, or in any case his *vis imaginativa,* was ordering a sacrilegious metamorphosis: on the moon he now saw himself not with the Lord but with the Lady, Lilia finally recovered from Ferrante. Roberto, by the lakes of Selene, was receiving what his brother had stolen from him among the ponds of the island of fountains. He kissed her face with his eyes, contemplated her with his mouth, sucked, bit again and again, and the enamoured tongues jested, jousting.

Only then did Roberto, whose fever was perhaps abating, come to, but remaining fond of what he had experienced, as happens after a dream departs, leaving not only the spirit affected but also the body.

He did not know whether to weep with happiness at his regained love, or to weep with remorse for having turned— thanks to the fever, which ignores the Laws of Genre—his Sacred Epic into a Libertine Comedy.

That moment, he told himself, will truly gain me Hell, for I am surely no better than Judas or Ferrante—indeed, I am

only Ferrante and till now I have simply exploited his wickedness in order to dream of doing what my cowardice has
always kept me from doing.

Perhaps I shall not be called to answer for my sin, because
it is not I who sinned, but the Stone Fish that made me dream
in its own way. However, if I have arrived at such mindlessness,
it must be a sign that I am truly about to die. I had to wait
for the Stone Fish to make me think of death, whereas this
thought should be the first duty of every good Christian.

Why have I never thought of death, and of the wrath of
a laughing God? Because I was following the teachings of my
philosophers, for whom death is a natural necessity and God
is He who into the disorder of atoms introduced the Law that
composes them in the harmony of the Cosmos. Could such a
God, master of geometry, produce the disorder of Hell, even
if out of justice, and could He laugh at the subverting of every
subversion?

No, God does not laugh, Roberto said to himself. He bows
to the Law that He Himself willed, the Law that wills the body
to decay, as mine is surely decaying in this decadence. And
Roberto saw the worms near his mouth, but they were not
an effect of his delirium; amid the filth of the hens, they had
formed through spontaneous generation, descendants of that
excrement.

He then gave welcome to those heralds of decomposition,
for he understood that this confounding of himself with viscid
matter was to be experienced as the end of all suffering, in
harmony with the will of Nature and of Heaven that administers it.

I have only a little while to wait, he murmured, as in a
prayer. In the space of not many days my body, now still well
composed, will change color and become wan as a bean, then

blacken from head to foot and be sheathed in a dark heat. Then tumefaction will begin, and on that bloat a fetid mold will generate. Nor will it be long before the belly begins exploding here and splitting there, releasing rottenness, and here a wormy half-eye will be seen swaying, there a shred of lip. In this mud then a quantity of little flies will be born and other tiny animals that cluster in my blood, and they will consume me bit by bit. One part of these creatures will rise from my bosom, another will drip like mucus from the nostrils; others, drawn by my putrescence, will enter and leave the mouth, and the most sated will gurgle in the throat. . . . And all this while the *Daphne* little by little becomes the realm of the birds, and germs arriving from the Island cause animalesque vegetables to grow here, whose roots, now digging into the bilge, will be nourished by my secretions. Finally, when my whole corporeal fabric has been reduced to pure skeleton, in the course of the months and the years—or perhaps the millennia—that armature will also slowly become a powder of atoms on which the living will walk, not understanding that the whole globe of the earth, its seas, its deserts, its forests, and its valleys, is nothing but a living cemetery.

There is nothing more conducive to healing than an Exercise in Happy Death, the rehearsal of which reassures us. So the Carmelite had once said to him, and so it was, for now Roberto felt hunger and thirst. Weaker than when he dreamed of the fighting on the deck, but less so than when he lay by the hens, he found the strength to suck an egg. The liquid that trickled down his throat was good. And even better was the milk of a nut that he opened in the larder. After all that meditating over his dead body, now, to heal it, he incorporated into his body the healthy bodies to which Nature gives life every day.

This is why, except for some admonitions from the Car melite, at La Griva no one had taught him to think of death. During family conversation, almost always at dinner and at supper (after Roberto had returned from one of his explorations of the ancient house, and had perhaps lingered in a great shadowy room redolent of apples set on the floor to ripen), the talk was only of the goodness of the melons, the reaping of the wheat, and the expectations for the vintage.

Roberto remembered how his mother taught him he could live happily and peacefully if he would employ to advantage all the good things that La Griva gave him: "And it would be well for you not to forget to provide yourself with salted meat of the ox, the sheep, or the ram, and of calf and pig, for they keep for some time and are of great use. Cut the pieces of meat not very big, put them in a pot with much salt over them, leave them for one week, then hang them from the beams in the kitchen so they can dry in the smoke, and do this in crisp, cold weather, with the westerly winds, after Martinmas, for the meat will then last as long as you wish. In September come the little birds, and lambs for the whole winter, not to mention the capons, the old hens, the ducks, and such like. Do not scorn even the ass if it breaks a leg, for they produce little round sausages that you afterwards score with a knife and set to fry, and they are a dish for a lord. And in Lent, let there always be mushrooms, soups, nuts, grapes, apples, and all God's bounty. And also for Lent turnips must be kept ready, and herbs that, floured and cooked in oil, are better than a lamprey; and you will make sweet Lenten dumplings, with a paste of oil, flour, rose-water, saffron, and sugar, with a drop of Malmsey, cut in rounds like old window panes, filled with grated bread, apples, cloves, and crushed walnuts, which, with a pinch of salt you will set in the oven and cook, and you will eat better than any prior. After Easter come the kids, asparagus, pigeons. . . . Later the ricotta arrives and the fresh cheese. But you must also know how to make use of peas and boiled beans floured and fried, which are excellent ornaments for the table. . . . This, my son, if you live as our elders lived, will be a life of bliss, far from all travail. . . ."

No, at La Griva there was no talk of death, judgement, Hell, or Paradise. Death, for Roberto, had appeared at Casale, and it had been in Provence and in Paris that he had been led to ponder it, amid virtuous discourse and carefree discourse.

I shall surely die, he said to himself, if not now thanks to the Stone Fish, in any case later, since it is clear that from this ship I shall never wander, now that I have lost—with the Persona Vitrea—also the means of approaching the barrier safely. What illusion was I harboring? I would die, perhaps later, even if I had not arrived on this wreck. I entered life knowing that the Law requires us to leave it. As Saint-Savin said, we play our role, some long, some not so long, and then we leave the stage. I have seen others go before me, others will see me go, and they will give the same performance for their successors.

For that matter, how long was the time when I did not exist, and for how long in the future will I not be? I occupy a very small space in the abyss of the years. This little interval does not succeed in distinguishing me from the nothingness into which I shall go. I came into the world only to swell the ranks. My part was so small that even if I had remained in the wings, everyone would still have declared the play perfect. It is like a storm at sea: some drown immediately, others are dashed against the rocks, still others are cast up on an abandoned ship, but not for long, not even they. Life goes out, on its own, like a candle that has consumed its substance. And we should be accustomed to it, because, like a candle, we have been shedding atoms since the moment we were lit.

It is no great wisdom to know these things, Roberto told himself. We should know them from the moment we are born. But usually we reflect always and only on the death of others. Ah yes, we all have strength enough to bear others' ills. Then the moment comes when we think of death because the illness is our own, and we realize it is impossible to stare directly at the sun and at death. Unless we have had good teachers.

I did. Someone said to me that truly few know death. As a rule it is tolerated through stupidity or habit, not through resolve. We die because we cannot do otherwise. Only the philosopher can think of death as a duty, to be performed willingly and without fear. As long as we are here, death is not here, and when death comes, we have gone. Why would I have spent so much time conversing about philosophy if now I were not capable of making my death the masterwork of my life?

His strength was returning. He thanked his mother, whose memory had led him to abandon thoughts of the end. She could not do otherwise, she who had given him the beginning.

He set to thinking about his birth, of which he knew far less than of his death. He told himself that thinking of origins is proper to the philosopher. It is easy for the philosopher to justify death: that we must plunge into obscurity is one of the clearest things in the world. What obsesses the philosopher is not the naturalness of the end, it is the mystery of the beginning. We can lack interest in the eternity that will follow us, but we cannot elude the anguished question of which eternity preceded us: the eternity of matter or the eternity of God?

This was why he had been cast up on the *Daphne*, Roberto concluded. Because only in that restful hermitage would he have had the leisure to reflect on the one question that frees us from every apprehension about not being and consigns us to the wonder of being.

CHAPTER 37

Paradoxical Exercises Regarding the Thinking of Stones

BUT HOW LONG had he been sick? Days? Weeks? Or had a storm in the meantime struck the ship? Or, even before encountering the Stone Fish, concentrated as he was on the sea and on his Romance, had he not noticed what was happening around him? For how long had he so lost his sense of reality?

The *Daphne* had become a different ship. The deck was dirty and the casks leaked, were coming apart; some sails had unfurled and were torn, hanging from the arms like masks, winking and grinning among their rents.

The birds complained, and Roberto hurried to feed them. Some were dead. Luckily the plants, nourished by rain and air, had grown and some had forced their way into the cages, offering pasture to many; for others, the insects had multiplied. The surviving animals had even procreated, and the few dead had been replaced by many living.

The Island remained unchanged; except that for Roberto, who had lost his mask, it had moved farther away, drawn by the currents. The reef, now that he knew it was defended by the Stone Fish, had become insuperable. Roberto could swim again, but only for the love of swimming, while keeping well away from the rocks.

"Oh, human machinations, how chimerical you are," he murmured. "If man is nothing but a shadow, you are smoke. If nothing but a dream, you are phantoms. If nothing but a dot, you are zeroes."

So many deeds, Roberto said to himself, only to learn that I am a zero. Indeed, more of a zero than I was at my arrival as derelict. The shipwreck shook me and led me to fight for life, but now I have nothing to fight for or to fight against. I am condemned to a long repose. I am here to contemplate not the Void of spaces, but my own: and from it only ennui will come, sadness, and despair.

Soon not only I but the *Daphne* itself will be no more, I and it reduced to fossil, like this coral.

For the coral skull was still there on the deck, immune to universal wear; and so, immune to death, it was the only living thing.

This alien form gave new vigor to the thoughts of the castaway, who had been educated to discover new lands only through the telescope of the word. If the coral was a living thing, he said to himself, it was the only truly thinking being amid the general disorder of thought. It could think only of its own ordered complexity, about which it knew everything, and thus would have no expectation of unforeseen disruptions of its own architecture.

Do objects live and think? The Canon had said to him one day that to justify life and its development it is necessary that in every thing there be some burgeoning of matter, some *spora,* some seeds. Molecules are determined arrangements of determined atoms under a determined form, and if God has imposed laws on the chaos of atoms, their composites can tend only to generate analogous composites. Is it possible that the stones we know are still those that survived the Flood, that they, too, have not developed, and that from them other stones have not been generated?

If the Universe is nothing but a collection of simple atoms that clash to generate their composites, it is not possible that the atoms, once composed into their composites, should cease moving. In every object a continuous movement must be maintained: a whirling movement in winds, a fluid and regulated movement in animal bodies, a slow but inexorable movement in vegetables, and surely much slower but not absent in minerals. Even this coral, dead to coraline life, enjoys its own subterranean stirring, proper to a stone.

Roberto reflected. Let us assume that every body is composed of atoms, even those bodies purely and solely extended, flat, with which Geometricians deal; and let us assume, further, that these atoms are indivisible. It is certain that every straight line can be divided into two equal parts, whatever its length may be. But if its length is minimal, it is possible that we may be dividing into two parts a straight line composed of an odd number of indivisibles. This would mean that if we do not want the two parts to be unequal, the indivisible median has been divided in two. But this, since it is in its turn extended and therefore also a straight line, though of imperceptible brevity, should be in its turn divisible into two parts. And so on *ad infinitum*.

The Canon said that the atom is still always made up of parts, only it is so compact that we could never divide it within its confines. We. But what about others?

No solid body exists as compact as gold, and yet we take an ounce of this metal, and from that ounce a goldsmith can make a thousand gold leaves, and one half of those leaves suffices to gild the entire surface of an ingot of silver. And taking that same ounce of gold, those who prepare the gold and silver filaments for decorating lace can reduce it with their die to the breadth of a hair, and that thread will be as long as a quarter-league or perhaps more. The artisan stops at a certain point because he does not possess adequate instruments, nor can he with the naked eye still discern the thread he might obtain. But some insects—so minuscule that we cannot see them, and so industrious and wise that their skill outstrips that of all the artisans of our species—could refine that thread still further, until it stretched from Turin to Paris. And if there existed insects of those insects, to what refinement could they not draw that same thread?

If with the eye of Argus I could penetrate the polygons of this coral and the filaments that spread inside it, and inside each filament that which makes up the filament, I could go seeking the atom unto infinity. But an atom divisible to infinity, producing parts ever smaller and ever more divisible, would lead me to a moment where matter would be nothing but infinite divisibility, and all its hardness and its fullness would be sustained by this simple balancing among voids. Matter, rather than feeling a horror of the Void, would then worship it, and would be composed of it, would be void-in-itself, absolute vacuity. Absolute vacuity would be at the very heart of the unthinkable geometrical point, and this point would be only the island of Utopia we dream of, in an ocean made always and only of water.

Hypothesizing a material extension made of atoms, then, we arrive at having no atoms. What remains? Vortices. Except that the vortices would not pull the suns and planets, true matter that feels the influence of their wind, because the suns and planets would themselves be vortices, drawing minor vortices into their spiral. Then the maximum vortex, which makes the galaxies spin, would have in its center other vortices, and these would be vortices of vortices, whirlpools made of other whirlpools, and the abyss of the great whirlpool of whirlpools would sink into the infinite, supported by Nothingness.

And we, inhabitants of the great coral of the Cosmos, believe the atom (which still we cannot see) to be full matter, whereas, it too, like everything else, is but an embroidery of voids in the Void, and we give the name of being, dense and even eternal, to that dance of inconsistencies, that infinite extension that is identified with absolute Nothingness and that spins from its own non-being the illusion of everything.

So here I am illuding myself with the illusion of an illusion—I, an illusion myself? I, who was to lose everything, happened on this vessel lost in the Antipodes only to realize that there was nothing to lose? But, understanding this, do I not perhaps gain everything, because I become the one thinking point at which the Universe recognizes its own illusion?

And yet, if I think about it, does this not mean I have a soul? Oh, what a tangle. The all is made of nothing, and yet to understand it we must have a soul, which, little as it may be, is not nothing.

What am I? If I say *I* in the sense of Roberto della Griva, I say so inasmuch as I am the memory of all my past moments, the sum of everything I remember. If I say *I* in the sense of that something that is here at this moment and is not the mainmast or the coral, then I am the sum of what I feel now. But what is what I feel now? It is the sum of those relations between presumed indivisibles that have been arranged in that system of relations in that special order that is my body.

And so my soul is not, as Epicurus would have it, a matter composed of corpuscles finer than the others, a breath mixed with heat; it is the way in which these relations are felt as such.

What tenuous condensation, what condensed tenuousness! I am only a relation among my parts that are perceived while they are in relation to each other. But these parts are in turn divisible into other relations (and so on), therefore every system of relations, being aware of itself, being indeed the awareness of self, is a thinking nucleus. I think me, my blood, my nerves; but every drop of my blood thinks itself.

Does it think itself as I think me? Surely not, in Nature man perceives himself in quite a complex way, the animal a bit less (it is capable of appetite, for example, but not of remorse), and a plant feels itself growing, and surely it feels when it is cut, and perhaps even says *I*, but in a far more cloudy way than I do. Every thing thinks, but according to its complexity.

If this is so, then stones also think. This stone, too, which actually is not stone but was a vegetable (or animal?). How does it think? Like a stone. If God, who is the great relation of all relations in all the universes, thinks Himself thinking, as the Philosopher would have it, this stone thinks only itself stoning. God thinks entire reality and the infinite worlds He creates and maintains with His thought; I think of my unhappy love, of my solitude on this ship, of my deceased parents, of my sins and of my death; and this stone thinks only I stone, I stone, I stone. But perhaps it cannot even say *I*. It thinks: Stone, stone, stone.

That must be boring. Or am only I the one who feels bored? I who can think more, while it (or he or she) is entirely content with being stone, as happy as God—because God enjoys being All, as this stone enjoys being almost nothing, but since it knows no other way of being, it is pleased with its own way, eternally satisfied with itself. . . .

But is it true, then, that the stone feels nothing but its stoniness? The Canon used to say to me that even stones are bodies that on some occasions burn and become other. In fact, a stone falls into a volcano and through the intense heat of that unguent of fire, which the ancients called Magma, it melts and fuses with other stones, becomes one incandescent mass, and a short (or long) time later it finds itself part of a larger stone. Is it possible that in ceasing to be that first stone, and at the moment of becoming another, it does not feel its own calefaction, and with it the imminence of its own death?

The sun was striking the bridge, a light breeze tempered its heat, Roberto's sweat dried on his skin. After all this time spent picturing himself as stone petrified by the sweet Medusa who had ensnared him in her gaze, he resolved to try to think as stones think, perhaps to prepare himself for the day when he would be a simple pile of white bones exposed to that same sun, that same wind.

He stripped, lay down, with his eyes closed and his fingers in his ears so as not to be disturbed by any sound, as is surely the case of a stone, which has no sensory organs. He tried to erase every personal memory, every demand of his own human body. If it had been possible, he would have erased his own skin; unable to, he tried to make it as insensitive as he could.

I am a stone, I am a stone, he said to himself. And then, to avoid even mentioning himself: Stone, stone, stone.

What would I feel if I were truly a stone? First of all, the movements of the atoms that compose me, that is, the stable vibration of the positions that the parts of my parts of my parts maintain among themselves. I would feel the hum of my stoning. But I could not say I, because to say I there must be others, something else against which to oppose myself. In principle the stone cannot know if there is anything outside itself. It hums. Its stoning is a stoning of stoning. Of the rest it knows nothing. It is a world. A world that worlds along on its own.

Still, if I touch this coral, I feel that the surface has retained the sun's warmth on the exposed part, whereas the part that rested on the deck is colder; and if I were to split it in half, I could perhaps feel how the heat decreases from the top to the bottom. Now, in a warm body the atoms move more furiously, and therefore this rock, if it feels movement, cannot help but feel in its interior a differentiation of movements. If it were to remain eternally exposed to the sun in the same position, perhaps it would begin to distinguish something like an above and a below, if merely as two different types of motion. Unaware that the cause of this difference is an external agent, it would conceive itself in that way, as if that motion were its nature. But if there was an avalanche and the stone rolled downhill and ended in another position, it would feel that other parts of itself were moving, parts formerly slow, whereas those formerly fast would be moving at a slower pace. And as the terrain slid (and it could be a very slow process), the stone would feel that the heat, or, rather, the motion consequent to it, was passing gradually from one part of it to another.

Thinking like this, Roberto slowly exposed different sides of his body to the sun's rays, rolling across the deck until he came to a patch of shadow, darkening slightly in it, as would have happened to the stone.

Who knows? he asked himself. Perhaps in these motions the stone begins to have, if not the concept of place, at least the notion of part: certainly, of change. Not of passion, however, because the stone does not know its opposite, which is action. Or perhaps it does. For the fact of being stone, so composed, is something it feels constantly, whereas its being hot here or cold there is felt alternately. So in some way it is capable of distinguishing itself, as substance, from its own accidents. Or not. Because it feels itself as relation, it would feel itself as relation among different accidents. It would feel itself as substance in evolution. What does that mean? Do I feel myself in a different way? Who knows if stones think like Aristotle or like the Canon? All this in any case would take it millennia, but that is not the problem: it is whether the stone can store up successive perceptions of itself. Because if it feels itself now hot above and cold below, and now vice versa, but in the second condition it does not remember the first, then it will believe always that its interior movement is the same.

But why, if it perceives itself, should it not have memory? Memory is a power of the soul, and however small the soul of the stone, it will have a proportionate memory.

To have memory means to have a notion of before and after, otherwise I would also believe always that the suffering or the joy I remember are present at the moment I remember them. Instead I know they are past perceptions, because they are fainter than the present ones. The problem therefore is having a sense of time. Which perhaps not even I could have if time were something that is learned. But did I not say to myself days or months ago, before my sickness, that time is the condition of movement and not the result? If the parts of the stone are in motion, this motion will have a rhythm that even if inaudible will be like the sound of a clock. The stone is the clock of itself. Feeling oneself in motion means feeling one's own time beating. The earth, great stone in the sky, feels the time of its motion, the time of the respiration of its tides, and what it feels I see drawn on the starry vault: the earth feels the same time that I see.

So the stone knows time, indeed it knows it before perceiving its own changes of temperature as movement in space. As far as I know, it does not even need to sense that the change of temperature depends on its position in space: it could understand this as a phenomenon of change in time, like the passage from sleep to waking, from vigor to weariness, just as I realize now that, lying still, my left foot is growing numb.

No, the stone must also feel space, if it senses motion where formerly there was stillness and stillness where formerly there was motion. It knows, then, how to think *here* and *there*.

But let us now imagine that someone picks up this stone and sets it among other stones to build a wall. If, before, it sensed the play of its own internal positions, it was because it felt its own atoms bent in the effort to compose themselves like the cells in a beehive, crammed one against the other and one among others, as the stones in the dome of a church should feel, where one presses the other and all press towards the central keystone, and the stones near the keystone press the others downwards and outwards.

But accustomed to that play of thrusts and counterthrusts, the whole dome must feel itself as such, in the invisible movement its bricks make, thrusting one another reciprocally; similarly, it should feel the effort that someone makes to demolish it, and should understand that it ceases to be dome at the moment the wall below and its buttresses collapse.

The stone, then, pressed among other stones to such a degree that it is on the verge of breaking (and if the pressure were greater, it would crack), must feel this constriction, a constriction it did not feel before, a pressure that somehow must influence its own inner movement. Will not this be the moment when the stone senses the presence of something external to itself? The stone would then have perception of the World. Or perhaps it would think that the force oppressing it is something stronger than itself, and it would identify the World with God.

But on the day the wall collapses, ending the constriction, would the stone feel a sense of Freedom—as I would feel if I decided to emerge from the constriction I have imposed on myself? But I can wish to stop being in my condition; the stone cannot. Therefore freedom is a passion, whereas the will to be free is an action, and this is the difference between me and the stone. I can will. The stone at most (and why not?) can only tend to return as it was before the wall, and feel pleasure when it becomes again free, but it cannot decide to act in order to achieve what gives it pleasure.

But can I really will anything? At this moment I feel the pleasure of being stone, the sun warms me, the wind makes acceptable this adjustment of my body, I have no intention of ceasing to be a stone. Why? Because I like it. So then I too am slave to a passion, which advises me against wanting freely its opposite. However, willing, I could will. And yet I do not. How much freer am I than a stone?

There is no thought more terrible, especially for a philosopher, than that of free will. Out of philosophical pusillanimity, Roberto dismissed it as a thought too grave—for him, surely, and all the more for a stone to which he had given passions but had deprived of any possibility of action. In any case the stone, even without being able to ask itself questions about the possibility or impossibility of damning oneself wilfully, had already acquired many and very noble faculties, more than human beings had ever attributed to it.

Roberto now asked himself if, at the moment when it fell into the volcano, the stone was aware of its own death. Surely not, because it had never known what dying meant. But when it disappeared completely into the magma, could it have had a notion of its death as a thing that happened? No, because that composed, individual stone no longer existed. On the other hand, have we ever known of a man aware of having died? If something was thinking itself, it would now be the magma: I magma, I magma, I magma, shlup shlup shlup, I flow, fluid, plop plop splupp, I bubble bub bub, I sizzle, spittle, spatter, patter, platter. Plap. And Roberto, imagining himself magma, spat like a hydrophobe dog and tried to make his viscera grumble. He almost had a bowel movement. He was not made to be magma, better return to thinking like a stone.

But what did it matter to the ex-stone that the magma was magmizing its magmating self? For stones there is no life after death. There is none for anyone to whom it has been promised and granted, after death, to become a plant or animal. What would happen if I died and all my atoms were recomposed, after my flesh was well distributed in the earth and filtered through roots, into the lovely shape of a palm tree? Would I say *I palm*? The palm would say it, no less thinking than a stone. But when the palm says *I*, will it mean *I Roberto*? It would be wrong to deprive it of the right to say *I palm*. For what sort of palm would it be if it said *I Roberto am palm*? That composite able to say *I Roberto*, because it perceived itself as that composite, is no longer. And if it is no longer, having lost that perception, it has lost also the memory of itself. It cannot even say *I palm was Roberto*. For if such memory were possible, I should now know that I Roberto was at one time . . . what? Something. But I have absolutely no such memory. What I was before, I no longer know, just as I am incapable of remembering that foetus I was in my mother's womb. I know I was a foetus because others have told me so, but as far as I am concerned, I might never have been it.

My God, I could enjoy the soul, and even the stones could enjoy it, and precisely from the soul of stones I learn that my soul will not survive my body. Why am I thinking and playing at being a stone, when afterwards I will know nothing further of myself?

But in the final analysis, what is this *I* that I believe thinks me? Have I not said that it is only the awareness that the Void, identical to extension, has of itself in this particular composite?

Therefore I am not I who thinks, but I am the Void, or ex
tension, that thinks me. And so this composite is an accident,
in which Void and extension linger for the blink of an eye, to
be able afterwards to return to thinking otherwise. In this great
Void of the Void, the one thing that truly is, is the history of
this evolution in numberless transitory compositions. . . .
Compositions of what? Of the one great Nothingness, which
is the Substance of the whole.

Substance governed by a majestic necessity, which leads it
to create and destroy worlds, to weave our pale lives. I must
accept this, succeed in loving this Necessity, return to it, and
bow to its future will, for this is the condition of Happiness.
Only by accepting its law will I find my freedom. To flow back
into It will be Salvation, fleeing from passions into the sole
passion, the Intellectual Love of God.

If I truly succeeded in understanding this, I would be the
one man who has found the True Philosophy, and I would
know everything about the God that is hidden. But who would
have the heart to go about the world and proclaim such a
philosophy? This is the secret I will carry with me to my grave,
in the Antipodes.

As I have said before, Roberto did not have the makings
of a philosopher. Having achieved this Epiphany, which he
polished with the severity of an optician grinding a lens, he
experienced—once more—an amorous apostasy. Since stones
do not love, he sat up, again a loving man.

But then, he said to himself, if to the great sea of the great
and sole Substance we must all return, down below or up
above, or wherever it is, I will be united, identical, with my
Lady! We will both be part and all of the same macrocosm
. . . I will be she, she will be I. Is this not the deepest meaning

of the myth of the Hermaphrodite? Lilia and I, one body and one thought . . .

But have I not foretold this event? For days (weeks, months?) I have been making her live in a world that is all mine, even if through Ferrante. She is already thought of my thought.

Perhaps conceiving Romances means living through our own characters, making them live in our world, and delivering ourselves and our creatures to the minds of those to come, even when we will no longer be able to say I. . . .

But if this is so, it is up to me alone to banish Ferrante from my own world, forever, to have his banishment governed by divine justice, and to create the conditions whereby I can be united with Lilia.

Filled with renewed enthusiasm, Roberto decided to conceive the last chapter of his story.

He did not know that, especially when their authors are now determined to die, stories often write themselves, and go where they want to go.

CHAPTER 38

An Enquiry into the Nature and Place of Hell

ROBERTO TOLD HIMSELF how Ferrante, wandering from island to island and seeking more his pleasure than the correct course, refused to be instructed by the warnings evident in the signals the eunuch sent to Biscarat's wound, and finally he lost all notion of where he was.

The ship meanwhile sailed on, the inadequate provisions spoiled, the water began to stink. To keep the crew in ignorance, Ferrante decreed that each man go below only once a day to the hold and in the darkness take the minimum supplies required for survival, and no one was to look around there.

Lilia realized nothing, for she bore every torment with serenity and seemed to thrive on a drop of water and a crumb of biscuit, anxious for her beloved to succeed in his enterprise. As for Ferrante, insensitive to that love except for the pleasure he drew from it, he went on inciting his mariners, flashing images of wealth before the eyes of their greed. And so a blind man blinded by rancor led other blind men blinded by avidity, holding prisoner in his fetters a blind beauty.

Still, many of the crew, in their great thirst, felt their gums begin to swell and cover their teeth; their legs became spotted with abscesses, and their pestilential secretion rose even to their vital parts.

So it was that, sailing below the twenty-fifth degree of latitude south, Ferrante had to face a mutiny. He quelled it, relying on a group of five corsairs, the most faithful (Andrapod, Boride, Ordogne, Safar, and Asprando), and the mutineers were set adrift in the sloop with a few victuals. But in so doing, the *Tweede Daphne* had deprived itself of a means of rescue. What does that matter, Ferrante said, soon we will be in the place to which we are lured by our cursed hunger for gold. But the men remaining were too few to sail the ship.

Nor did they wish to; having lent a hand to their chief, they now considered themselves his equals. One of the five had spied on that mysterious young gentleman who came up on deck so rarely, and discovered he was a woman. Then those cut-throats confronted Ferrante, demanding the passenger. Ferrante, Adonis of aspect but Vulcan at heart, set more store by Pluto than by Venus, and it was fortunate Lilia did not hear him when in a murmur he assured the mutinous five that he would reach an agreement with them.

Roberto could not permit Ferrante to carry out this final villainy. He then chose to have Neptune become enraged that mortals had traversed his domain without fear of his wrath. Or else, rather than put the story in such pagan as well as fanciful terms, he imagined it was impossible (if a Romance must also convey a moral lesson) that Heaven would not punish that vessel of perfidies. And he rejoiced imagining that the Austral Winds, with Boreas and Eurus, staunch enemies of the calm of the sea—even if till now they had left to the placid Zephyrs the responsibility of following the path along which the *Tweede Daphne* continued her voyage—were beginning to show signs of impatience in the confinement of their subterranean chambers.

He made them burst forth all at once. The groan of the timbers covered the ground bass of the sailors' lamentations, the sea vomited upon them and they vomited into the sea, and sometimes a wave so enfolded them that from the shore one might have mistaken that deck for a coffin of ice, around which the thunderbolts flared like wax tapers.

At first the storm set clouds against clouds, waters against waters, winds against winds. But soon the sea abandoned its prescribed limits and grew, swelling, towards the sky, and rain came pouring down, the water mixed with the air, the birds learning to swim and the fish to fly. It was no longer a struggle of Nature against the seamen but a battle of the elements among themselves. Not one atom of air swirled but that it was not transformed into a pellet of hail, and Neptune rose to extinguish the fire in Jove's hands, to rob him of the pleasure of burning those humans whom Neptune wanted instead to drown. The sea dug a grave in its own bosom to rob the earth of them and Neptune, seeing the vessel heading uncontrolled towards a rock, with a sudden slap sent it off in another direction.

The ship was immersed, stern and prow, and every time it dipped, it seemed to fly from the top of a tower; the poop sank until the gallery was swamped, and at the prow the waves were bent on engulfing the bowsprit.

Andrapod, who was trying to secure a sail, was torn from the yardarm and, plunging into the sea, struck Boride as he was pulling a hawser, and broke his neck.

The hull refused to obey Ordogne the helmsman, while another gust abruptly tore away the mizzen topsail. Safar tried hard to furl the sails, urged on by Ferrante's curses, but he could not finish lashing the crow's nest before the ship swung around and its flank received three waves of such dimensions that Safar was washed overboard. The mainmast shattered and plunged into the sea, not without having first devastated the deck and crushed Asprando's skull. And finally the tiller broke to pieces as with a wild blow it took the life of Ordogne. Now this wooden relic was without a crew, and the last rats poured overboard, falling into the water they wanted to escape.

It seems impossible that Ferrante, in such a witches' Sabbath, should think of Lilia, for we would expect him to be concerned only with his own safety. I cannot say whether Roberto considered he was violating the laws of verisimilitude, but to make sure that she to whom he had given his heart did not perish, he had to grant a heart also to Ferrante—if only for an instant.

So Ferrante drags Lilia up on deck, and what does he do? Experience has taught Roberto to have Ferrante bind her fast to a plank, allowing her to slip into the sea, trusting that not even the wild beasts of the Deep will deny mercy to such beauty.

After which, Ferrante seizes another piece of wood, preparing to tie it to himself. But at that moment, onto the deck, freed in some unknown fashion from his torment by the upheaval of the hold, his hands still chained together, more like a corpse than a living man but with eyes alive with hate— steps Biscarat.

Biscarat, who throughout the voyage has remained, like the dog on the *Amaryllis,* suffering in bonds as every day they reopen that wound which is then briefly treated—Biscarat, who has passed these months with a single thought: to avenge himself upon Ferrante.

Deus ex machina. Biscarat appears suddenly behind Ferrante, who already has one foot on the bulwarks; the officer raises his arms and brings them down before Ferrante's face, his chain making a noose at Ferrante's throat. And shouting, "With me, to Hell at last!" Biscarat is seen—almost felt— giving such a tug at Ferrante's neck that it breaks as the tongue protrudes between those blasphemous lips and accompanies their final rage. Then the lifeless body of the executed man, falling, drags after it like a cloak the still-living body of his executioner, who, victorious, meets the warring waves with peace finally in his heart.

Roberto could not imagine Lilia's feelings at that sight, and he hoped she had seen nothing. Since he could not remember what had happened to him after he was caught in the maelstrom, he could not imagine what now happened to Her.

The truth is, he was so fully occupied by the duty to send Ferrante to his proper punishment, resolving to follow his fate into the next world, that he left Lilia in the vast upheaval.

The lifeless body of Ferrante had meanwhile been cast up on a desert island. The sea was calm, like the water in a cup, and on the shore there was no surf. All was enveloped in a light haze, as happens when the sun has just disappeared and the night has not yet taken possession of the sky.

Immediately beyond the beach, with no trees or bushes to mark its end, a plain could be seen, totally mineral, where even what from the distance seemed cypresses proved to be leaden obelisks. On the horizon to the west rose a mountainous area, now dark to the view except for some flickering along the slopes, which gave the place the aspect of a cemetery. But above that height lay long black clouds, their bellies like dying coals, solid and compact in form, or like those cuttlefish bones seen in certain paintings or drawings, which if you look at them sideways freeze into the shape of skulls. Between the clouds and the mountain, the sky still had some tinges of yellow—and you would have thought it was the last aerial space touched by the dying sun if it were not for the impression that this last burst of sunset had never had a beginning and would never have an end.

Where the plain began to rise, Ferrante could make out a little band of men, and he moved towards them.

Men—or, in any case, human beings—they seemed from the distance, but as Ferrante reached them, he saw that if they had once been human, now they had become, or were on the way to becoming, exhibits for an anatomy theater. Which is how Roberto wanted them, because he recalled having visited one day one of those places where a group of physicians in dark clothes—with rubicund faces, little veins glowing on nostrils and cheeks, in pose like so many executioners—stood around a cadaver to expound from the outside what there was inside, and to reveal in the dead the secrets of the living. They removed the skin, incised the flesh, bared the bones, separated the bundles of nerves, untangled the knotted muscles, opened the organs of the senses, isolated all the membranes, undid all the cartilages, detached all the entrails. Having distinguished every fiber, opened every artery, probed every marrow, they displayed to their audience the vital workshop: Here, they said, is where the food is digested, here the blood cleansed, alimentation distributed here, here humors formed, here spirits tempered. . . . And someone next to Roberto observed in a whisper that after our terrestrial death, Nature would do much the same to us.

An anatomist-God had, in a different way, touched those inhabitants of the island, whom Ferrante was now seeing closer and closer.

The first was a body without skin, the ropes of muscle taut, the arms in a gesture of abandonment, the suffering face turned heavenwards, all skull and cheekbones. The hands of the second had flayed skin hanging from its fingertips, barely attached, like a glove, and the skin of the legs was rolled up to the knee like a supple boot.

On the next, first the skin, then the muscles had been so splayed that the whole body, especially the face, seemed an open book. As if to show skin, flesh, and bones at the same time, thrice human and thrice mortal. It seemed an insect, of which those tatters would have been the wings if there had been on that island a wind to stir them. But these wings did not move by any impulse of the air, stagnant in that twilight; they barely shifted at the movements of the body, akimbo.

Nearby, a skeleton was leaning on a spade, perhaps to dig its grave, its eyesockets peering at the sky, a grimace on the crooked arc of the teeth, the left hand held out as if to beg for compassion and a hearing. Another skeleton, bent forward, proferred the curved back of its spine, walking in jerks, bony hands over a lowered face.

One, whom Ferrante also saw only from behind, still had some cropped hair on its fleshless skull, like a cap pulled forcibly over it. The felt lining, pale and pink as a seashell, which sustained the fur, was formed by the cutis slit at the nape and turned inside out.

There were bodies from which almost everything had been removed, and they seemed sculptures of nerves alone; on the stumps of necks, now acephalous, they waved what once had clung to brains. The legs seemed a plait of withes.

There were others with abdomens opened, where saffron intestines throbbed, sad gluttons stuffed with ill-digested tripes. Where once penises had been, now peeled and reduced to pegs, only dried-up testicles swayed.

Ferrante saw some who were now only veins and arteries, the mobile laboratory of an alchemist, pipes and tubes in perpetual motion distilling the bloodless blood, wan fireflies in the light of an absent sun.

The bodies stood in great and painful silence. In some the

signs could be seen of a very slow transformation that from statues of flesh was reducing them to statues of fibers.

The last of them, excoriated like a Saint Bartholomew, held up in his right hand his still-bleeding skin limp as an unused cape. It was possible yet to recognize a face there, with the holes of the eyes and nostrils and the cavern of the mouth, which seemed the ultimate melting of a wax mask, dripping, exposed to sudden heat.

And that man (or, rather, the toothless and deformed mouth of his skin) spoke to Ferrante.

"Ill-come," he said to him, "to the Land of the Dead, which we call Insula Vesalia. Soon you, too, will follow our fate, but you must not believe that we all pass with the rapidity granted by the grave. According to our punishment, each of us is led to a stage of disintegration all his own, as if to allow us to savor extinction, which for each of us would be the greatest joy. Oh what bliss, to imagine ourselves as brains that would turn to pulp at a bare touch, fats liquefying! But no. As you see us, we have come, each, to his present state without being aware of it, through imperceptible mutation during which every fiber of our being has been worn away in the course of thousands of thousands of thousands of years. And no one knows the extreme point to which it is decreed he must decay, so that those you see over there, reduced to mere bones, still hope to be able to die a little, and perhaps they have spent millennia in that expectation; others, like me, have been in this form since we no longer know when—because in this always imminent night we have lost all sense of time's passage—and yet I hope that I have been granted a very slow annihilation. Thus each of us yearns for a decomposition that—as well we know—will never be total; we wish that for us Eternity has not yet begun, yet we fear that we have been in it ever since our remote arrival on this shore. Living, we believed Hell was the place of eternal despair, because so they told us. Alas, no, for it is the place of undying hope, which makes each day worse than the one before, as this thirst, which is kept alive in us, is never slaked. Having always a glimmer of body, and every body tending to growth or to death, we never cease hoping—and thus did our Judge condemn us to suffer *in saecula*."

Ferrante asked: "But what is it that you hope for?"

"You might as well ask what you will hope for yourself. . . . You will hope that a wisp of wind, a slightest swell of the tide, the arrival of a single hungry leech, can return us, atom by atom, to the great Void of the Universe, where we would again somehow participate in the cycle of life. But here the air does not stir, the sea remains motionless, we feel neither heat nor cold, we know neither dawn nor sunset, and this earth, more dead than we, generates no animal life. O worms that death once promised us! O beloved little worms, mothers of our spirit that could still be reborn! Sucking our bile, you would spatter us mercifully with the milk of innocence! Biting us, you would heal the bites of our sins; cradling us with your spells of death, you would give us new life, because for us the grave is as good as the maternal womb. . . . But none of this will happen. We know it, and yet our body forgets it at every instant."

"And God—?" Ferrante asked. "Does God laugh?"

"No, alas," the excoriated man replied, "because even humiliation would exalt us. How beautiful it would be if we could see at least a laughing God come to taunt us! What distraction, the spectacle of the Lord who from His throne, among His saints, makes sport of us. We would have the sight of another's joy, as cheering as the sight of another's frown. No, here no one is outraged, no one laughs, no one shows himself. God is not here. Here there is only hope without goal."

"My God, a curse on all saints," Ferrante wanted to shout,

in his villainy. "If I am damned, I must have the right to enact the spectacle of my fury." But his body was spent, and the voice that came from his bosom faint. He could not even curse.

"You see," the skinned man said to him, his mouth unable to smile, "your punishment has already begun. Not even hatred is permitted anymore. This island is the one place in the Universe where pain is not allowed, where a listless hope cannot be distinguished from a bottomless boredom."

Roberto went on constructing Ferrante's end as he lay on the deck naked, for he had stripped himself for his imitation of a stone; and in the meanwhile the sun burned his face, chest, and legs, restoring to him the feverish warmth that had only recently left him. Now prepared to confuse not only his fiction with reality but also the heat of his spirit with that of his body, he felt once more ablaze with love. And Lilia? What had happened to Lilia while Ferrante's cadaver sought out the isle of the dead?

With a device not uncommon among Poets when they are incapable of restraining their impatience and no longer observe the unities of time and place, Roberto leaped over some events to find Lilia again some days later, clinging to that plank as it drifted over a now-calm sea glittering in the sun—and she approached (and this, Dear Reader, you never would have dared predict) the eastern shore of the Island of Solomon, that is to say, the side opposite the one off which the *Daphne* rode at anchor.

There, as Roberto had learned from Father Caspar, the beaches were less friendly than those to the west. The plank, by now too fragile to withstand an impact, shattered against a rock. Lilia woke and clung to that rock as the fragments of her raft were lost among the currents.

Now she was there, on a rock that could barely house her,

as a stretch of water—but for her it was an ocean—separated her from the shore. Shaken by the typhoon, wasted by hunger, tormented even more by thirst, she could not drag herself from the rock to the sand, beyond which, her vision blurred, she discerned the colors of vegetable forms.

But the rock was searing beneath her tender thigh and, hardly breathing, instead of cooling her inner blaze, she drew the burning air into herself.

She hoped that not far away darting little streams would spring from shady cliffs, yet these dreams did not appease but, rather, exacerbated her thirst. She wanted to ask help of Heaven, but as her dry tongue cleaved to her palate, her voice could utter only abbreviated sighs.

As time passed, the scourge of the wind scratched her with a raptor's claws, and she feared not so much dying as living until the work of the elements had disfigured her, making her an object of revulsion, no longer one of love.

If she could have reached a brook, a trickle of living water, and put her lips to it, she would have seen her eyes, once two bright stars that promised life, now two frightful eclipses, and that countenance, where jesting cupids once made their home, now the horrid dwelling-place of abhorrence. If she could have actually reached a pond, her eyes would have poured out, in pity for her own state, more drops than her lips would have taken from it.

This at least is what Roberto made Lilia think. But it irritated him. He was irritated that, close to death, she should be in anguish over her own beauty, as Romances often would have it, but his irritation was more with himself, who could not look squarely, without mental hyperboles, at the face of his dying love.

How would Lilia be, really, in that extremity? How would

she appear if stripped of that dress of death woven from words?

After the sufferings of her long voyage and the wreck, her hair would be straw streaked with white; her bosom would surely have lost its lilies, her face would be furrowed by time. Wrinkled, now, her throat and breast.

No, to celebrate her fading was another way of entrusting himself to the poetic machine of Padre Emanuele. . . . Roberto wanted to see Lilia as she truly was. Her head thrown back, her eyes staring and, narrowed by suffering, appearing to be too distant from the bridge of her nose, now sharpened; and those same eyes were weighed down with bags, the corners marked by a fan of little wrinkles, prints left by a sparrow on the sand. Nostrils slightly dilated, one more fleshy than the other. The mouth chapped, of amethyst color, two arcs at the sides, and the upper lip, a bit protruding, raised to display two little teeth no longer of ivory. The skin of the face gently sagging, two limp folds under the chin, detracting from the line of the neck . . .

And yet this withered fruit was a prize he would not have bartered for all the angels of Heaven. He loved her also like this, nor could he know if she had been different when he first loved her, wanting her as she was then, behind the curtain of her black veil, that distant evening.

He had allowed himself to be misled during his time as a castaway, wanting her to be harmonious, like the system of the spheres; but now they had also told him (and he had not dared confess this, too, to Father Caspar) that perhaps the planets did not pursue their journey along the perfect line of a circle but instead in a strabismic turn around the sun.

If beauty is clear, love is mysterious: he discovered that he loved not only the spring but all the seasons of his beloved; she was even more desirable in her autumnal decline. He had always loved her for what she was and could have been, and

only in this sense is love a giving of the self, without anticipation of return.

He had allowed himself to be dazed by his wave-pounding
exile, seeking always another self—dreadful in Ferrante, ex
cellent in Lilia, through whose glory he had wanted to make
himself glorious. But, to love Lilia meant to want her as he
himself was, both of them sentenced to the travail of time.
Until now he had used her beauty to foster the soiling of his
mind. He had made her speak, putting into her mouth the
words he wanted, words with which he was nevertheless discontent. Now he wanted her near, to love her suffering beauty,
her wan voluptuousness, her bruised grace, her thin naked-
ness, to caress all eagerly, listening to her words, her own, not
the ones he had lent her.

He had to have her, dispossessing himself of himself.

But it was too late to pay proper homage to his sick idol.

On the other side of the Island, in Lilia's veins, liquefied,
flowed Death.

CHAPTER 39

Itinerarium Extaticum Coeleste

WAS THIS ANY way to end a romance? Not only do romances arouse hatred so that we may finally relish the defeat of those we hate, but also they invite compassion in order to lead us then to discover, when the danger is over, those we love. Roberto had never read a Romance that ended so badly.

Unless this romance was not yet finished, and there was a secret Hero in store, capable of a feat conceivable only in the Land of Romances.

Out of love, Roberto decided to perform that feat, entering the story himself.

If I had arrived at the Island by now, he said to himself, I could save her. It is only my indolence that has kept me here. Now we are both anchored in the sea, desiring the opposite shores of a single body of land.

And yet not all is lost. I see her dying at this moment, but if at this same moment I were to reach the Island, I would be there a day before she arrives, waiting for her, ready to rescue her.

It is of little matter that I draw her from the sea when she is on the point of breathing her last. It is a known fact that when the body reaches that stage, a strong emotion can restore it to new vigor, and there have been cases of the dying who, on learning that the cause of their misfortune has been removed, suddenly reanimate.

And what greater emotion, for that dying woman, than to rediscover, alive, the beloved person? In fact, I would not even have to reveal to her that I am different from the one she loved, because it was to me and not to him that she gave herself; I would simply be taking the place that has been my due from the beginning. And what is more, Lilia, without realizing it, would sense a different love in my gaze, free of all lust, trembling with devotion.

Is it possible—as anyone would ask himself—that Roberto had not reflected on the fact that this rescue would be granted him only if he were to reach the Island within that day, or at most by the early hours of the following morning: an exploit that his most recent experiments hardly made probable? Is it possible he did not realize that he was planning to land in reality on the Island to rescue a woman who was arriving there only through his narrative?

But Roberto, as we have seen, having begun with the idea that the Land of Romances was completely separate from his own world, had finally come to make the two universes flow effortlessly one into the other, and he had mingled their laws. He thought that he could arrive at the Island because he was imagining his arrival, and that he could imagine hers at the moment when he was already there, because this was what he wished. On the other hand, he was transferring to his own world that freedom to will events and to see them achieved which makes Romances unpredictable. Finally, he would reach the Island for the simple reason that if he did not reach it, he would no longer know what story to tell.

Around this idea, which anyone who has not followed us thus far would judge mad or madness, as you also may, he now reflected in a mathematical fashion, not hiding from himself any of the eventualities that intelligence and prudence suggested.

As a general defines, the night before the battle, the movements his troops will execute on the coming day, and not only pictures the difficulties that could arise and the accidents that could disturb his plan, but also plumbs the mind of the opposing general, to foresee his actions and counteractions, and to arrange his future by acting in consequence of what the other might arrange in consequence of those consequences, so Roberto weighed means and ends, causes and effects, pros and cons.

He had to abandon the idea of swimming to the reef and passing it. He could no longer see the submerged passages, and he could not reach the part that emerged except by facing invisible traps, surely mortal. And finally, even assuming he could reach it—whether underwater or on the surface—there was no certainty he could walk on it with his makeshift boots, or that it did not conceal pits into which he would fall, never to reappear.

He could therefore reach the Island only by repeating the course of the boat, that is, by swimming southwards, following the shore at a distance, more or less at the *Daphne*'s distance, then turning east once he had rounded the southern promontory, until he gained the inlet of which Father Caspar had spoken.

This plan was not reasonable, and for two reasons. First, until now he had barely managed to swim as far as the reef, and at that point his strength was already exhausted; so it was not sensible to think he could cover a distance at least four or five times that—and without rope, not so much because he did not have a rope that long but because this time, if he went, it was to go, for if he did not arrive, it would make no sense to turn back. The second reason was that swimming southwards meant moving against the current; and knowing by now that his strength sufficed to fight it for only a few strokes, he would be inexorably pulled to the north, beyond the other cape, farther and farther from the Island.

After sternly calculating these possibilities (admitting that life was short, art long, opportunity instantaneous and experiment uncertain), he told himself that it was unworthy of a gentleman to be daunted by such petty calculations, like a bourgeois computing the odds he had in staking at dice his greedily hoarded wealth.

To be sure, he then said, a calculation must be made, but it must be sublime, if the stakes are sublime. What was he gambling in this wager? His life. But his life, if he never succeeded in leaving the ship, was worth little, especially now, if his solitude was accompanied by the knowledge that he had lost Her forever. What would he win if he came through the test? Everything, the joy of seeing her again and saving her, or at worst, of dying on her dead body, covering it with a shroud of kisses.

True, the wager was not fair. There were more possibilities of perishing in the attempt than of reaching land. But even so the *alea* was advantageous: as if they had told him he had a thousand chances of losing a pitiful sum against one single chance of winning an immense treasure. Who would not accept?

Finally he was seized by another idea, which immeasurably reduced for him the risk of this bet, indeed, saw him victor in either eventuality. Assume, then, that the current did carry him in the wrong direction. Well, but once he passed the other promontory (he knew this because of his experiment with the plank), the current would bear him along the meridian. . . .

If he were to let himself float, his eyes staring at the sky, he would never again see the sun move: he would drift along that border that separates today from the day before, outside time, in an eternal noon. Stopping time for himself, he would arrest it also on the Island, infinitely delay her death, because by now everything that happened to Lilia depended on his narrative decision. If he was suspended, the story of the Island would be suspended.

A highly acute chiasmus, above all. She would find herself in the same position he had occupied now for an incalculable time, a few yards from the Island, and his losing himself in the ocean would make her a gift of what had been his hope, would keep her suspended on the edge of an interminable desire—both of them without a future and hence without a future death.

Then he lingered to picture what his journey would be, and because of the conflation of universes which by now he had sanctioned, he felt as if this was the voyage of Lilia. It was the extraordinary vicissitude of Roberto that would guarantee also for her an immortality that the warp of longitudes would not otherwise have granted her.

He would move northwards at a gentle and uniform speed: on his right and on his left the days and nights would follow one another, the seasons, eclipses, tides; brand-new stars would cross the heavens bearing pestilences and upheavals of empires, monarchs and pontiffs would grow old and vanish in puffs of dust, all the vortices of the Universe would perform their windy revolutions, more stars would be formed from the holocaust of older ones. . . . Around him the sea would be unleashed and then subdued, the Trades would perform their girandoles, and he in his calm furrow would not change at all.

Would he stop one day? From what he remembered of the maps, no other land save the Island of Solomon lay on that longitude, at least not until that meridian connected with all the others at the Pole. But if a ship, with a following wind and a forest of sails, took months and months to travel a course like the one he was undertaking, how long would he last? Perhaps years before arriving at the place where he no longer knew what would become of day and night, or of the passing of centuries.

But in the meantime he would repose in a love so much refined that it would be careless of losing eyes, lips, and hands. The body would be drained of all lymph, blood, bile, and phlegm, water would enter every pore; penetrating the ears, it would varnish his brain with salt, would replace the vitreous humor of his eyes, would invade his nostrils, dissolving every trace of the terrestrial element. At the same time the sun's rays would nourish him with igneous particles, and this would dilute the liquid in a single dew of air and fire that by sympathetic force would be recalled upwards. And he, by now light and volatile, would rise and be united first with the spirits of the air, then with those of the sun.

And the same would happen to her, in the steady light of that rock. She would expand like gold to airy thinness beat.

Thus in the course of days they would be united in that understanding, instant after instant they would be to each other like the stiff twin compasses, each moving with the motion of its companion, one leaning when the other goes farther, to follow or to return together to the center.

Then both would continue their journey in the present, straight towards the star awaiting them, their dust of atoms among the other corpuscles of the Cosmos, a vortex among

vortices, now eternal as the world because embroidered with
Void. Reconciled to their fate, because the motion of the earth
carries evils and fears, but the trepidation of the spheres is
innocent.

So in either case the wager will bring him a victory. He
should not hesitate. Neither should he prepare for that tri-
umphal sacrifice without observing the correct rites. Roberto
entrusts to his papers the last actions he intends to make, and
for the rest he leaves us to guess deeds, times, cadences.

As a first liberating lavacrum, he spent almost an hour
removing a part of the grating that separated the upper deck
from the lower. Then he went below and set about opening
every cage. As he gradually pulled away the withes, he was
struck by a general flapping of wings, and he had to defend
himself, raising his arms before his face, but at the same time
crying "Shoo shoo!" He had to push some clucking hens unable to find an egress on their own.

When he climbed back up on deck, he saw the populous
flight rise through the rigging, and it seemed to him that for
a few seconds the sun was covered by all the colors of the
rainbow, striped across their breadth by marine birds who had
hastened, curious, to join in this festival.

The birds freed, he flung into the sea all the clocks, not
thinking for a moment that he was wasting valuable time: he
was erasing time to favor a journey against time.

Finally, to avert any cowardice in himself, he collected on
deck, under the mainmast, logs, planks, empty casks, sprinkled
them with the oil of all the lamps, and set fire to them.

A first flame blazed up, which immediately licked at the
sails and the rigging. When he was certain the fire was being
fed by its own strength, he prepared for his farewell.

He was still naked, as he had been since he began dying by turning himself to stone. Stripped even of the rope, which would no longer limit his voyage, he descended into the sea.

He planted his feet against the wood, thrusting himself forward to move away from the *Daphne,* and after following the side to the stern, he left it forever, towards one of the two happinesses that were surely awaiting him.

Before destiny, and the waters, decide for him, I hope that—pausing for breath every so often—he allows his eyes to move from the *Daphne,* as he bids it farewell, to the Island.

There, above the line traced by the treetops, his eyes now very sharp, he should see rising in flight—like an arrow eager to strike the sun—the Orange Dove.

Colophon

THERE. AND WHAT later happened to Roberto I do not know or think it will ever be known.

How to draw a novel from a story, so novelistic, when the end—or, for that matter, the true beginning—is missing?

Unless the story to be told is not that of Roberto but of his papers—though here, too, all must be based on conjecture.

If the papers (fragmentary, in any case, from which I have devised a story, or a series of intersecting or skewed stories) have come down to us, it is because the *Daphne* did not burn entirely. That much is obvious. Who knows, perhaps the fire barely singed the masts, then died out on that windless day. Or else—there is nothing to prevent us from believing this— a few hours later a torrential rain fell and extinguished the blaze. . . .

How long was the *Daphne* there before someone found it and discovered Roberto's writings? I can venture two hypotheses, both fruit of the imagination.

As I have already mentioned, a few months before these events, in February 1643 to be exact, Abel Tasman—having set out from Batavia in August of 1642, then after reaching Van Diemen's Land, later to become Tasmania, seeing New Zealand only from a distance and heading for the Tongas (already reached in 1615 by Schouten and Le Maire and named the Coconut Islands and the Traitors Islands), then proceeding north—discovered a series of little sand-girt islands, recording them at 17.19 degrees latitude south and 201.35 degrees longitude. We will not go into the matter of longitude here, but those islands, which he named Prins Willelms Eijlanden, if my hypotheses are correct, should not have been far from the Island of our story.

Tasman ends his voyage, he says, in June, and hence before the *Daphne* could have arrived in those parts. But we cannot be sure that Tasman's diaries are reliable (and, indeed, the original no longer exists).[1]

Let us try to imagine, then, that through one of those fortuitous detours in which his voyage is so rich, he returned to the area, say in September of that year, and discovered there the *Daphne*. No hope of repairing it, without sails and rigging as it was by then. He inspected it, to learn its origin, and came upon Roberto's papers.

Though his knowledge of Italian was poor, he realized that the papers included some discussion of the problem of longi-

---

1. The reader can easily verify the truth of what I have written by consulting P. A. Leupe, "De handschriften der ontdekkingreis van A. J. Tasman en Franchoys Jacobsen Vissche 1642–3," in *Bijdragen voor vaderlandsche geschiedenis en oudheidkunde,* N. R. 7, 1872, pp. 254–93. No objection can be made, surely, to the documents collected as *Generale Missiven,* including an extract from the "Daghregister van het Casteel Batavia" dated 10 June 1643, in which Tasman's return is reported. But my hypothesis is still plausible, for it would be easy to suppose that in order to maintain a secret like that of longitude, even a document of this sort would be manipulated. With communications that from Batavia had to reach Holland (and there is no telling when they arrived there) a gap of two months would pass unnoticed. Moreover, I am not at all sure Roberto arrived in the area in August and not earlier.

tudes, so they had to be considered highly secret, to be delivered only to the Dutch East India Company. Therefore in his own diary he says nothing about the matter and perhaps falsifies the dates to eliminate traces of his adventure. Thus Roberto's papers end up in some secret archive. Tasman made another voyage the next year, and God only knows where he went.[2]

Let us imagine the Dutch geographers leafing through those papers. As we know, there was nothing of interest to be found in them, except perhaps Dr. Byrd's canine method, which—I am willing to bet—several spies must have ferreted out already from various sources. There is mention of the Specula Melitensis, but we must remember that, after Tasman, one hundred thirty-eight years had to go by before Cook rediscovered those islands, which would never have been rediscovered by following Tasman's directions.

Then, finally, and a century after our story, Harrison's invention of the marine chronometer puts an end to the frantic search for the *Punto Fijo*. The problem of longitude is no longer a problem, and some archivist of the Company, eager to clear his cupboards, discards, gives away, sells—who knows? —Roberto's papers, now a mere curiosity for some maniacal collector of manuscripts.

The second hypothesis is more like a novel, enthralling. In May 1789 a fascinating character passes through those parts. He is Captain Bligh, whom the mutineers of the *Bounty* had loaded into a sloop with eighteen loyal men, entrusting them to the mercy of the waves.

That exceptional man, whatever his defects of character may have been, manages to sail more than six thousand

---

2. Absolutely no log or documentation of this voyage exists. Why?

kilometers and land finally at Timor. In carrying out this enterprise, he skirts the Fiji archipelago, almost arrives at Vanua Levu, and crosses the Yasawa group. This means that if he had deviated only slightly to the east, he could easily have landed somewhere around Taveuni, where I like to think our Island can be found. And if evidence is to be enlisted in the question of believing or not believing, well, I am assured that an Orange Dove or Flame Dove or, better, a Ptilinopus Victor exists only there—but at the risk of spoiling the whole story, I must add that the orange bird is the male of the species.

Now a man like Bligh, if he had found the *Daphne* in barely reasonable condition, arriving there in a mere sloop, would have done everything possible to put the vessel in shape. But by now almost a century and a half had passed. Some storms had further racked the hull, disanchored it, the ship had keeled over on the coral reef—or no, it had been caught by the current, drawn north, and flung on other shoals or on the rocks of a nearby island, where it lay exposed to the work of time.

Probably Bligh boarded a phantom vessel, its bulwarks encrusted with shells, green with seaweed, water stagnating in its riven hold, a refuge of mollusks and poisonous fish.

Perhaps, rickety, the quarterdeck survived, and in the captain's cabin, dry and dusty—or no, damp and rotting but still legible—Bligh found Roberto's papers.

These were no longer times of great anguish over longitudes, but perhaps he was attracted by the references, in an unknown language, to the Islands of Solomon. Almost ten years earlier, a certain Monsieur Buache, Geographer to the King and of the French navy, had presented a paper to the Academy of Sciences on the subject of the Existence and Position of the Islands of Solomon, asserting that they were none other than that Bay of Choiseul that Bougainville found in

1768 (and whose description seemed to conform to the ancient one of Mendaña) and the Terres des Arsacides found in 1769 by Surville. So while Bligh was still at sea, an anonymous writer, probably Monsieur de Fleurieu, was about to publish a book entitled *Decouvertes des François en 1768 & 1769 dans le Sud-Est de la Nouvelle Guinée.*

I do not know whether Bligh had read Monsieur Buache, but surely in the English navy there was irritated talk of that piece of arrogance on the part of their French cousins, who boasted of having found the unfindable. The French were right, but Bligh might not have known that, or wished it. He could therefore have conceived the hope of having got his hands on a document which not only gave the lie to the French but would proclaim him discoverer of the Islands of Solomon.

I would imagine that, first, he mentally thanked Fletcher Christian and the other mutineers for having set him brutally on the road to glory; then he decided, good patriot that he was, to keep quiet with everyone about his little detour eastwards and his discovery, and to deliver the papers to the Admiralty in strictest confidence.

But in this case, too, someone must have considered them of little interest, of no value as evidence, and—again—exiled the papers among bundles of erudite rubbish for littérateurs. Bligh gives up the Islands of Solomon, is content with being named admiral for his other undeniable virtues as a navigator, and will die equally content, unaware that Hollywood will make him odious to all posterity.

And so, if the narrative continued according to either one of my hypotheses, such an end would not be worthy of narration, it would leave every reader discontent and frustrated. In this way Roberto's story would not inspire any moral lesson—and we would still be wondering why what happened to him happened to him—concluding that in life things happen because they happen, and it is only in the Land of Romances that they seem to happen for some purpose or providence.

For if I had to draw a conclusion from it, I would go and rummage again among Roberto's papers to find a note, dating surely from those nights when he still worried about a possible Intruder. That evening Roberto was looking yet again at the sky. He was remembering how at La Griva, when the family chapel had collapsed with age, that Carmelite tutor of his, who had had experience in the East, advised rebuilding the little chapel in Byzantine style, a round form with a central dome, which had nothing at all to do with the style to which they were accustomed in the Monferrato. And old Pozzo, refusing to stick his nose into matters of art and religion, heeded the advice of the holy man.

Seeing the antipodal sky, Roberto realized that at La Griva, in a landscape surrounded on every side by hills, the heavenly vault appeared to him like the dome of the chapel, clearly defined by the brief circle of the horizon, with one or two constellations that he could identify; so while he knew that the spectacle changed from one week to the next, he never realized, since he went to sleep early, that it changed even in the course of the same night. And therefore that dome had always seemed to him stable and round, and consequently he conceived the Universe as stable and round.

At Casale, in the center of a plain, he saw that the sky was more vast that he had believed, but Padre Emanuele convinced him to imagine the stars as described by concepts rather than to look at those above his head.

Now, antipodal spectator of the infinite expanse of an ocean, he saw a boundless horizon rise. And above his head he observed constellations never seen before. Those of his hemisphere he had read according to patterns others had established—here the polygonal symmetry of the Wain, there the alphabetic exactitude of Cassiopeia. But on the *Daphne* he had no pre-established patterns, he could join any point to any other, derive the outlines of a serpent, a giant, locks of hair, or the tail of a poisonous insect, and then dismantle them and essay other forms.

In France and Italy he observed even in the sky a landscape defined by the hand of a monarch who had fixed the lines of the postal services and the roads, leaving between them stands of forest. Here, on the contrary, Roberto was a pioneer in an unknown land, and he had to decide by which paths he would connect a peak to a lake, without any criterion of choice, because there were not yet cities and villages on the slopes of the one or on the shores of the other. Roberto did not simply gaze at the constellations: he was obliged to define them. He was alarmed that the whole was disposed as a spiral, a snail shell, a vortex.

It is at this point that he recalls a church, quite new, seen in Rome—and this is the only time he allows us to imagine that he has visited that city, perhaps before his journey to Provence. The church seemed to him very different both from the dome at La Griva and from the naves, geometrically arranged in ogives and cross vaults, of the churches at Casale. Now he understood why: it was as if the vault of that church were an austral sky, which lured the eyes to essay ever new lines of flight, never resting on a central point. Wherever you stood under that cupola, when you looked up, you felt always at the edge.

He realized now that in a less specific, less obviously theatrical fashion, experienced through little surprises day after day, this sensation of Repose Denied was something he had known first in Provence, then in Paris, where everyone he encountered somehow destroyed a certitude of his, each proposing a different map of the world, but the various proposals never cohered into a finite design.

He heard of machines that could alter the order of natural phenomena, so what was heavy rose and what was light sank, so that fire would moisten and water burn, as if the very Creator of the Universe were capable of revising Himself and could finally compel plants and flowers to disobey the seasons, and the seasons to engage in a struggle with time.

If the Creator consented to change His mind, did an order that He had imposed on the Universe still exist? Perhaps He had imposed many, from the beginning; perhaps He was prepared to change them day by day; perhaps a secret order existed, presiding over the constant change of orders and perspectives, but we were destined never to discover it, to follow instead the shifting play of those appearances of order that were reordered at every new experience.

Then the story of Roberto della Griva would be merely the tale of an unhappy lover, condemned to live beneath an exaggerated sky, a man unable to reconcile himself to the idea that the earth wandered along an ellipse of which the sun was only one of the fires.

Which, as many will agree, is too little to make a story with a proper beginning and a proper end.

Finally, if from this story I wanted to produce a novel, I would demonstrate once again that it is impossible to write except by making a palimpsest of a rediscovered manuscript —without ever succeeding in eluding the Anxiety of Influence. Nor could I elude the childish curiosity of the reader, who would want to know if Roberto really wrote the pages on which I have dwelt far too long. In all honesty, I would have to reply that it is not impossible that someone else wrote them, someone who wanted only to pretend to tell the truth. And thus I would lose all the effect of the novel: where, yes, you pretend to tell true things, but you must not admit seriously that you are pretending.

I would not even know how to come up with a final event whereby these letters fell into the hands of him who presumably gave them to me, extracting them from a miscellany of other defaced and faded manuscripts.

"The author is unknown," I would, however, expect him to say. "The writing is graceful, but as you see, it is discolored, and the pages are covered with water-stains. As for the contents, from the little I have seen, they are mannered exercises. You know how they wrote in that century. . . . People with no soul."

Translator's Postscript

MANY PEOPLE—THE author, first of all—have been of inestimable help in the preparation of this English text. I would like in particular to thank Nicholas Adams of Vassar College and Silvio Bedini of the Smithsonian Institution. I am indebted to my colleagues at Bard College, Elizabeth Frank, Daniel Freedman, Frederick Hammond, William Mullen, and Hope Konechny; to Pietro Corsi of the *Nuova Rivista dei Libri,* Florence; Antonio Clericuzio of the Università di Cassino; Mara Miniati of the Museo di Storia della Scienza, Florence; and Valentina Pisanty and Alasdair McEwan, Milan.

This translation is dedicated to the cherished memory of Francis Steegmuller.

W. W.